A journalist a[...]delson is a New Yorker who [...] the author of four novels featuring the detective Artie [...] detective every woman would like to find in her bed' *Guardian*): *Hot Poppies, Red Mercury Blues, Sex Dolls* and *Bloody London*. Her non-fiction book *Comrade Rockstar*, the story of the American émigré who became the biggest rock star in the history of the Soviet Union, is to be made into a film starring Tom Hanks.

'A hundred years from now seekers after truth will be reading this book to learn what it was like to live in New York in the anguished months that followed the events of 9/11. It's also a thriller – and a very good one . . . [Nadelson's] story is suffused with a bitter tang of the here and now that gives weight and poignancy to the narrative . . . Nadelson winds up her book brilliantly, logically and unexpectedly . . . Someone should put a copy of Nadelson's splendid novel in a time capsule so that we remember what it was like.' *Literary Review*

'A thoughtful and interesting crime novel that remains with the reader long after it is finished.' *Independent on Sunday*

'*Disturbed Earth* winds its way to a genuinely surprising and chilling ending.' *Evening Standard*

'A brilliant, unexpected final twist resolves the suspense . . . The denouement is stunning.' *Daily Telegraph*

'The best crime novels are a barometer of contemporary life, incorporating real events which other types of fiction struggle to respond to. This is particularly true of the Twin Towers terrorist attacks that are a brooding presence in Reggie Nadelson's latest Artie Cohen mystery . . . Her writing is strikingly confident, with barely a word out of place.' Joan Smith in the *Sunday Times*

ALSO BY REGGIE NADELSON

Bloody London
Sex Dolls
Red Mercury Blues
Hot Poppies

Somebody Else
Comrade Rockstar

Disturbed Earth

Reggie Nadelson

arrow books

Published in the United Kingdom in 2005 by Arrow Books

1 3 5 7 9 10 8 6 4 2

Copyright © Reggie Nadelson 2004

Reggie Nadelson has asserted her right under the Copyright, Designs
and Patents Act, 1988 to be identified as the author of this work

First published in the United Kingdom in 2004 by William Heinemann

Arrow Books
The Random House Group Limited
20 Vauxhall Bridge Road, London, SW1V 2SA

Random House Australia (Pty) Limited
20 Alfred Street, Milsons Point, Sydney
New South Wales 2061, Australia

Random House New Zealand Limited
18 Poland Road, Glenfield
Auckland 10, New Zealand

Random House (Pty) Limited
Endulini, 5a Jubilee Road, Parktown 2193, South Africa

The Random House Group Limited Reg. No. 954009

www.randomhouse.co.uk

A CIP catalogue record for this book
is available from the British Library

Papers used by Random House
are natural, recyclable products made from wood grown in
sustainable forests. The manufacturing processes conform to
the environmental regulations of the country of origin

ISBN 0 099 46548 5

Typeset by SX Composing DTP, Rayleigh, Essex
Printed and bound in Great Britain by
Cox & Wyman Ltd, Reading, Berkshire

For Steven Zwerling,
from Brooklyn

"Chapter One: He adored New York . . ."
Woody Allen, *Manhattan*

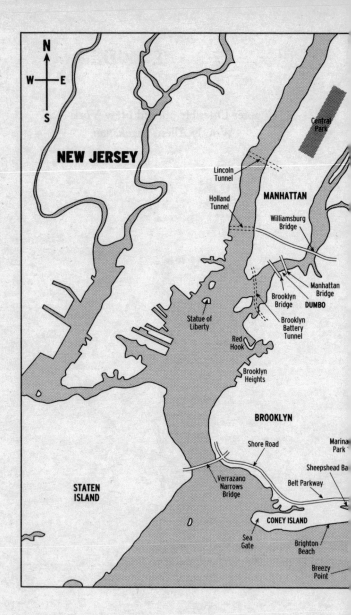

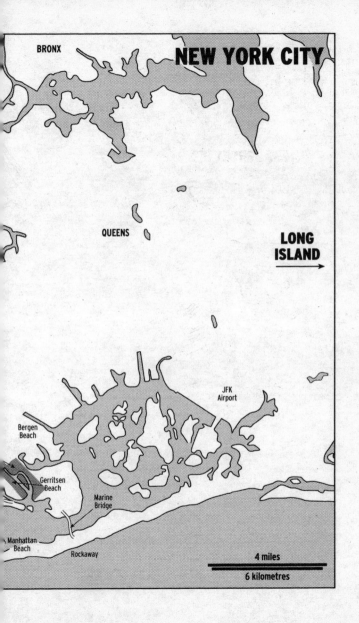

If it hadn't been for the The Queen of the Bay *being full, maybe it would never have happened. As Billy watched the Queen slip out into the water of Sheepshead Bay, he felt the faint breeze off the water, hot, humid and salty, on his face, and listened to the voice of a fisherman selling his catch, and the noise of customers bargaining, and the music from a radio set down near the bucket of fish. Billy could smell the catch. Often he went home and his mother said he smelled of fish, and made him wash with soap and lemons. He shut his eyes tight and stayed calm. This was important when things went wrong, like missing the boat. He had learned it, at school, at home: you sealed yourself up from the inside out and then they stopped bugging you and asking how you felt and let you be, figuring you were OK.*

He held tight to his half of the bag, feeling the rough canvas strap, and the weight of the bag that he and Artie carried together. There was bait in it they'd bought at the old bait and tackle shop overlooking the inlet; there were sandwiches and sodas and the sweater his mother made him bring though it was August and hot.

1

For weeks Billy had begged her to let him go out fishing at night. He was almost twelve, he said. It would be OK. He made a list of reasons he could and should go and he argued them so fiercely, she finally said, OK, just this once, go on. It was because of the sheepshead. He had heard rumors that you could catch sheepshead best at night. All summer he was crazy to see the fish that had given the place its name and then disappeared decades ago, a fish, he had read, whose mouth and teeth made it look like a sheep.

Up to now he had seen porgies, weakfish, blues, fluke, blacks, sea bass, all the fish you could catch out here off the Brooklyn coast. Sometimes he rode his bike from home to the docks and watched as men cleaned fish from a fresh catch. Sometimes they let him help.

He was interested in the boats, too, intent on learning their names. Party boats, they called them in Brooklyn, and they went from seven in the morning until three in the afternoon, or seven at night until three in the morning, and though Artie had taken him on a morning boat four times already that summer, this time they were going late. Billy wanted to fish by moonlight. There was a picture of a fishing boat in a book he had with the full moon making silver steps across the ocean; it would be like that when they fished at night. When the Queen went without them, he tried to stay calm, but he was having trouble, and a kind of panicky feeling came up inside. Then he felt a tug on the canvas bag.

He looked up at Artie, who said, come on, come on, let's run for it, he said, gesturing at the boat in the next slip, and they ran and there was just time and there was space on board. The boat was called Just a Fluke, and Artie explained it was a pun, a sort of joke, fluke being both a common fish and a fluke also

2

meaning a chance happening. Like them being on this boat instead of the Queen. A fluke, Billy liked the word.

A heavyset man with a smile Billy could see was fake, a smile just plastered on his face that didn't mean anything, took their money. He wore a battered old Brooklyn Dodgers baseball cap and told them it was his boat, brand new, space for over a hundred people, but only half full. His name was Stanley. Mr. Stanley, Billy thought. Mr. Stanley.

They fished all night, though you were only supposed to take two fish and even the fluke had to be 17 inches, but the fat man in the Dodgers hat let them keep extra, and they fished and ate salami sandwiches and Billy thought nothing had ever tasted as good.

Around midnight, the storm boiled up out of nowhere. The humidity rose even higher the way it sometimes did at night like steam in a bathroom with the door closed. The sky got dark. The moon disappeared. Out over the ocean lightning crackled up, and zigzagged across the sky like a zipper yanked open. Rain poured on them.

They laughed, him and Artie, laughed and laughed, soaked to the skin. The boat returned early and they got back to the pier still laughing as rain came down in huge horizontal sheets, the wind pushing it sideways.

Between them, each one with a hand on it and the other on his fishing rod, the bag was heavy. It was full of empty soda cans and sandwich bags and fish. They skidded over the wet planks of the dock, and the bag fell. Fish spilled out. Artie tried to capture them, but they slithered on the wet wood.

It's OK, Billy said, and pulled a net out of the bag, he always kept a net, and tossed it over the fish and trapped them and laughed gleefully. I've got them, he said. A man struggling

3

with his own catch saw them, and said to Artie, is this your boy? Is this your son?

Artie said, no, he's my godson. Afterwards, when they were safe in the car, Billy tugged his hand and said, very seriously, how come you lied, and Artie said, what? You know you're my real father, he said, and smiled. Come on, Artie, you know you're my real dad, and he could see how happy Artie looked. Suddenly Billy knew he was in on the game, too, pretending they were father and son.

Part One

1

A woman in a red fox coat walked down the boardwalk that was bleached white from snow and salt, a pair of large black poodles at the end of the leash in her hand. The wind whipped her backwards so the dogs seemed to pull her along as if on a sled. Above her the Parachute Drop, broken down, shut up, loomed against the winter sky, the Coney Island amusement park haunted by relics of its old dreamscape.

Inside Nathan's, as I passed, a trio of workers on the early shift, in their red Nathan's jackets, huddled together watching the cops outside. In the fluorescent light of the restaurant, I could see the faces of the three workers clearly; they had flat brown Indian faces, as if they'd come direct from some Andean village to the coast of America to serve up hot dogs dripping with yellow mustard. Like everyone in Brooklyn, they clung to their tribe; no matter how fragile or tiny it was, there was some kind of protection in it, or that's what I still thought that morning. One of them laughed suddenly. He flashed white teeth.

I'd been eating breakfast, key lime pie and coffee, in the city twenty minutes earlier when my phone rang and it was my boss, Sonny Lippert, at the other end.

"I need you."

"Tell me."

"It's a little girl," he said. "A child. They found some stuff a few hours ago."

Coney Island, he mumbled. You could see the old Parachute Drop from where they dumped it, you could see Nathan's, he said. Some slob probably eating hot dogs could have stopped it, but no one admitted seeing anything. They were all fucking blind, he yelled into the phone, they never see, they never tell, fucking monkeys, he added. They're piling on the sauerkraut and mustard and they don't fucking look out the window, you know, man? There's an empty stretch of ground out by the Keyspan Park where they play baseball now. Some jogger stumbled on it this morning. You with me? The stream of fury had poured into my ear, and I said, "OK, I'm coming, I'm there. OK?"

"Art?"

"Yeah, Sonny."

His voice cracked like, I was going to say cracked like a cold sore, but it didn't. It was never like that. In real life there were no metaphors; just dead people. His voice broke up; he was crying.

"I know she's dead. I can feel it."

"Feel what? Where's the body?"

But the line was bad and all I heard him say after that was, "Her shoes." Then the line broke.

All the time, while I drove from Manhattan out to

Brooklyn, what lay just ahead, what Lippert had found out at Coney Island, was in my mind. I knew it was a child; I figured the kid was dead. Abused. Mutilated. It was everywhere, this thing with kids, the porn rings, the child abuse; babies were used, too, and you thought, who does this kind of thing? I thought of the killer in Boston who dug an underground tunnel and kept little girls in a row of cages. His sex slaves, he said. Some of them he kept for years. They clawed at the bars while they had energy then, broken, just sat and waited for him.

You never got used to it, you got drunk, you got ulcers, you smoke yourself into a fog, you went crazy from stuff you saw. Any cop who gets used to it should quit.

I parked the car just beyond Nathan's and climbed up on the boardwalk and looked at the beach that stretched for miles along the Brooklyn coast. Beyond it was the ocean, the color of steel and out on the horizon was a ship that looked like a toy. Wind blew off the water.

I walked a couple of hundred yards. Away from the ocean and the beach, on the other side of the boardwalk, was a stretch of waste ground; a couple of blue and whites, their lights flashing, were parked nearby. I ran down the steps from the boardwalk. The half-frozen ground was littered with junk, soda cans, used condoms, cigarette butts, syringes—the detritus of a Friday night. As I got closer I could see there was a hole in the ground, like an empty grave, cordoned off by yellow tape. Dead weeds were scattered on the mounds of earth beside it. While I watched, a black body bag was loaded onto a waiting EMS truck.

Near the hole in the ground stood two cops, like gravediggers, one male, one female, holding shovels, seeming to wait for an order. Move on. Dig some other place. Keep at it. But no one said it. It was like a play, no one moving, people looking down with the expressions frozen on their faces. Somewhere a siren wailed.

Suddenly, Sonny Lippert materialized from behind the EMS van.

"Art? Artie?"

As soon as he saw me, he started in my direction at about a hundred miles a minute, a human cannonball, compact, fast on his feet, pulling his little camel's hair coat close to him. Fast and tightly wrapped, Sonny was a small man.

"It's a serial," he said. "I knew it would happen, sooner or fucking later, I so goddamn knew."

"Who is she?"

He shook his head.

"I don't know. No one's claimed her. No one's reported a child missing anywhere in the area. What kind of people don't know their kid is missing, man?"

Lippert was probably sixty; he looked ten years younger. He used "man" every second word; when I first knew him, he thought of himself as a fifties hipster; he gave it up a while back, the clothes, the walk, except for the verbal tic. It made him sound weirdly young, now that "man" and "cool" fell out of the mouths of every wannabe hipster kid in every bar on the Lower East Side and Williamsburg.

"How old is she?" I said.

"They don't know."

10

"So make a guess."

Sonny said, "Ever since I started running this unit, I feel like I stepped in a sewer that has no bottom, just dropped down and all there is, is shit."

Lippert was at the head of a special unit that prosecuted cases involving kids: kidnapping; pedophiles; kiddie porn; priests—the country was littered with lousy priests. The whole miserable business had exploded in the last few years.

Kids were big business; they were cheap. You could get a kid for less than an adult, and it was global. And not just in Asia or some remote part of Africa where they stole children for soldiers or slaves. In Eastern Europe you could buy a kid for sex for less than you could rent a car. You went to Teplice and other border towns—in the Czech Republic, not India, not Africa, in Europe—and people stood at the side of the highway and handed their own children down to men in cars. Little kids. Their own parents luring them with candy. Take the candy, darling, go with the nice man. I'd been there. I'd seen it.

In California last summer, two little girls were killed so brutally they never told the public the details. Couldn't. I heard from some friends over there. I didn't think about it if I could help it. There had been so many kids abducted the last couple of years, so many high profile cases. Thousands of kids just disappeared. Tens of thousands. You saw the flyers on lamp-posts, you saw the milk cartons. Like dust scattering; like garbage; like insects. Just gone. Where did they go?

Lippert took on as much as he could and it was a lousy

11

job. He had to keep everyone happy, the families, the local precincts, the local kidnap detectives, and some from homicide squads and the people at Police Plaza who also worked on child cases. He had been a cop and a federal prosecutor; he was a born politician and I didn't completely trust him, but I owed him and I'd made my peace with it.

He got me my first job as a cop after I graduated the academy. Said he talent spotted me, that's what he said when we were out together and a little bit drunk. I spoke a few languages; he said it was handy to have someone around who knew Russian, Hebrew, a little French, a little Arabic. Since his divorce he sometimes invited me to eat with him, at Peter Luger in Brooklyn because he loved the steak and hash browns, or at Rao's in Harlem; I went because he was the only person I knew who could get a table at Rao's, and because he liked me.

A beefy detective, a local who looked like he ate steroids with his Wheaties, glanced at me and I knew he was pissed off that Lippert was here and had called me out from the city. They were territorial in this part of Brooklyn and I already had a reputation for interfering in cases involving Russians in Brighton Beach, a mile or so west along the coast. Lippert ignored him and pulled me towards the boardwalk, then leaned against the railing and for a second pressed his hand against his temple as if he had a migraine that nothing could fix.

"Christ," he said, and the horror he seemed to feel transmitted itself like disease; it wrapped itself around me and I hoped Lippert didn't ask me to look at the body.

Don't ask, I thought. Please don't ask. I can't do it.

This got to me in a way few things did; this thing with kids. I thought about Billy Farone, my cousin's boy.

"I want you to look," Sonny said. "I want you to see."

Like a tugboat at my side, he ferried me to the van. He signaled to the EMS guy to remove the black rubber bag and place it on the ground. I waited, listening to the bang of the door, the snap of the latex gloves as the EMS guy pulled them on, the zipper. For me the sound of death wasn't a gun or the hot howl of fire at a crematorium or the thud of a coffin lowered into the earth; it was the sound of the zipper on a body bag.

"Look." He tossed me a pair of latex gloves and I put them on and bent over the clothes.

Inside the bag was a pair of green sneakers. So soaked in blood were the All Star high tops that only a scrap of green canvas showed. There was a kid's T-shirt that had been white and was smeared with blood. I picked it up by its edge and saw there were cuts across the front and back, as if it had been sliced from the kid's body with a razor. There were faded jeans. A blue baseball jacket, Yankees logo, also bloody. Saturated with blood, the blue of both garments looked dark, almost black. The left sleeve of the jacket was ripped.

"That's all?"

"It's enough," he said.

"What about the body?"

"There's no body, man," he said. "Habeas corpus. Not. You understand me?"

"What do you mean there's no body?"

He got agitated and kept repeating there was no body and it didn't matter.

13

"Calm down," I said. I had only seen Lippert like this a few times, but it happened. He got overloaded, he felt personally involved, he lost it.

"You don't even know she's dead," I said. "You don't even know who she is. You don't even know it's a girl. You're getting crazy, and about what?"

"Fuck you, man," he said. "Don't patronize me with that 'calm down' shit." He pushed me away from the others, pushed me with the flat of his hand against my chest. "I know is how I know I know. Twice before already this kind of thing happened, once about five years back when they found a kid's clothes first and then the body on Long Island, then around eighteen months ago, twenty, yeah, it was the summer before last, July maybe, I got a call, middle of the night, there were clothes, you understand me, there were kids' clothes and they were drenched in blood, just like this, in a hole in the ground out by Rockaway," he said and gestured towards the beach as it stretched west. "Then we found the body, a piece at a time. They had cut off her feet. They took off her sneakers and then her feet, and the feet floated up in the canal over by Sheepshead Bay. Somebody went fishing off a party boat and caught one. Enough? OK? You want more?" He stopped and caught his breath. "She was eight, and some piece of shit cut off her feet. Other parts. You want me to draw you a picture? It was, what, a couple miles from here? We found her eventually. I remember, there were sneakers then, the same kind of sneakers. Green high tops."

"I don't remember."

"You were in Bosnia or some other fucking place.

14

Working private," he said and I knew he blamed me for leaving the job. When Lippert felt vindictive, he made it a moral thing; you worked just for money, you were a lousy human being. You had failed.

"You ever see parents ID their child, Art? You want to do that? You want to say to the mother, is this your kid with her feet missing? Her hands? Her face?"

The blood vessels in his face constricted; he turned a strange dark red, the color of pastrami.

"I knew it wasn't over. I knew he'd surface. They always do. They can't stop and I said, don't let it go cold, not this one, but they did and nobody worked cold cases over 9/11. The son of a bitch has started up again. I knew he was a serial."

"Or it's a copycat."

"The other cases have been out of the papers for too long for a copycat. Both cases. The one on Long Island, the one I worked out in Rockaway. But I know it's the same fucking bastard, and I'm going to get him fried this time. Fried and fried. If they let me stick the needle in myself, I'll do it and then I'll celebrate."

"Sonny?"

"Yeah?"

"Never mind."

"You were going to ask if they cut off her feet before or after?"

I didn't answer.

He said, "I don't know. I don't know when they did it." I could feel his breath.

"When they called me with this earlier," he said gesturing to the scene, "I figured we'd hear a little girl

15

was missing, you know? Give me a cigarette, Art, OK?"

I fumbled in my jacket pocket and got a squashed pack of Marlboros and handed it to him. Sonny, who doesn't smoke, stuck one in his mouth and I lit it for him. The wind from the ocean blew out the match and I lit another one.

"I can't stand the smell," he said.

All I could smell was the fresh bright air and a faint taste of salt.

"What smell?"

"I don't know. I got something in my mind that stinks and I can't get it out and ever since I got here I keep smelling it. Never mind." He pulled on the cigarette then tossed it as far as he could.

A camera van from a local station rolled into view and Sonny yelled, "Get those fuckers out of there." He turned back to me, and then looked down at the blood-soaked clothes on the black rubber bag.

"Nobody called, you know, man? Nobody cares enough to make a call." He gestured to the van with the body bag. "Who does this, Artie? Who does this shit to a child? I stay up all night reading big books so I can find out who's evil enough to do things like this, man, and I still don't know anything. I thought it gave you wisdom. It doesn't give you shit."

"What about the age?" I said. "You made a guess by the size of the clothes?"

"Yeah, maybe eleven. But we're guessing."

"By her jacket?"

"Yeah."

"What else?"

"The T-shirt, it was a girl's T-shirt for an eleven-year-old, we checked with the store already. Also, the feet," he said. "The size of the sneakers."

It hung there. We stood, two helpless guys, looking at the way the words seemed to hang frozen on the late morning air, and neither of us wanting to touch them.

"What else?" I said.

"Skin," he said. "Skin in the bottoms of the sneakers. Skin and blood, like somebody ripped them off her."

"What about socks?"

"No socks."

"Isn't that weird? It's freezing. What kid goes out without socks in this weather?"

"Yeah, I don't know, there were no fucking socks, anyhow. Or maybe the socks are some other place. That's why they're digging all those holes." His voice was flat, affectless.

I threw my half smoked cigarette on the ground and looked down at the black bag again, at the zipper that threw silver sparks in the bright sunlight. Sonny held onto my arm like a dog caught in my sleeve and I followed him away from the van and back towards the site.

A construction guy—someone must have called him in—was using a jackhammer to dig into a piece of still frozen ground. People milled around. Somewhere I heard a flag flap in the wind, that eerie sound a flag makes when it's battered by the wind, and the metal pulleys clank against the pole. I couldn't see it and it bothered me, no flag in sight, only the noise, the whipping of the fabric like wet laundry.

17

"Art?" Sonny was moving again, back to the ambulance.

I was distracted. I put on my sunglasses.

"Why the bags?" I asked finally.

He shrugged. "I didn't know where to put the clothing," he said. "I didn't want it out in plain sight."

I lit a fresh cigarette for myself.

"What do you need?" I said.

"I need help. I need to follow this. How are you fixed this weekend?"

"Nothing special," I said. "It's a holiday Monday so I took the three days, but I'm OK for whatever you need. Just tell me. You want me to go into the office, whatever; just say."

"I wanted you here because the jogger who found the baseball jacket is a Russki, you know, and her English isn't great. She's over there." He gestured to one of the police cars. A woman in sweatpants leaned against the hood of Lippert's car, head down, her hands over her face.

"You want me to talk to her?"

"Yeah, talk to the jogger, man, and go home and wait. I want you by the phone where I can get you."

"I have my cell."

"I want you by your regular phone. I don't want people listening in, the cell's like a megaphone, any fucker can clone it, you know? I don't want some rookie dickhead at the station house out here either fucking it up. They're obsessed now, make a collar, get a case. I want you by the phone, twenty-four seven, you understand? So talk to the Russian. I'll put it around I want you on the case because of your language skills. I'll make that the deal."

I was surprised. "But it's not?"

He shrugged.

"You'll have a dozen people working this," I said. "Including a detective I saw from the local house who probably speaks some Russian. So why am I really here?"

"I trust you."

"I don't understand, you mean there's cops involved, you think there's other guys in this?"

"I just want someone I trust in a clean space. It's just a feeling," he added. "I'll say it's because of you speaking Russian, OK?" He repeated himself for the second time: "Like the old days, man? I'll say I need you because you speak Russian, that you know the community, OK, man? Which is true, right? More or less."

I nodded.

"Evidence like this, a little girl dead someplace, no one knows anything, no one even knows who the fuck she is, when the body turns up, we'll get blamed. They'll say we didn't work fast enough. We didn't care about it because it was out here, out in Brooklyn, by the water, in certain communities where there's only immigrants, you know? The shit will rain down on us, you know that. Media shit. Everyone just waiting to stoke the fear," he said. "And there's nothing you can do about it, you say, remember the snipers, you say, remember the other kidnappings, you remember, and you beg them, we beg the fuckers give us a little space to deal with this and their lawyers scream First Amendment. Christ, I'm sick of the fucking Constitution."

19

He reached out again as if to take my hand, a gesture I'd never seen him make; all he did was grab the sleeve of my jacket.

He said, "I'm scared, man. I'm scared about what's coming down. There's this little girl and there been others around the state, around the country, not to mention the cold cases. I can't even get this on the Amber alert unless I have more evidence. There were other cases I never told you about, I couldn't. We don't know who the hell she is or why someone would do it, but I'm scared. I'm scared about copycats. I'm scared. I'm scared of all of it, the crazies, the terror junkies. I think about it and in my mind I see paper dolls, you know, like I used to make for the kids, a row of paper dolls holding hands and then someone sets fire to them."

"You think this is terrorists?"

"Why not? You want to scare people, how about taking their kids?"

"Come on!"

"You think it couldn't happen? I don't think anymore. I just try to cover my ass." He hesitated. "I can't get rid of the stink."

We had pretended we were OK, like everyone else; we pretended the recovery was complete, but the city was still on the edge of a nervous breakdown even after all this time, and Sonny Lippert had been in the World Trade Center that day.

He had been on his way to a meeting at Two World Trade when it happened and I knew he was going, I'd talked to him ten minutes earlier. I thought he was dead.

I spent half the day thinking Sonny was dead, that a bunch of other people I knew were dead. Later I found him. He was digging at the site, still in his good gray suit, covered in dust, digging and looking for the living and there was no one. For a week we stayed there together. I couldn't leave him. I couldn't leave the hole. Maybe I should have gone home to Lily instead. Maybe if I'd gone home she would have stayed with me. She didn't. She left me and married somebody else.

Sonny said, "If you really have to go out, keep with your cell phone, at least, and call me back on a landline, OK? I mean stay with it all the time, when you take a piss, when you're sleeping. You get a message, you get a beep, anything. OK? And you don't do anything else. You don't do anything else without telling me. Just the phone. OK?"

Lippert could be crazy and lucid at the same time and I wasn't going up against him on this one.

I said, low-key as I could manage, "Maybe she's still alive, Sonny. Maybe this is about something else, the blood, the clothes. She could be alive, you know that?"

"Listen to me. She's not alive, but we'll pretend we're hopeful, like you say. I don't want any of this leaked. I don't want anything on TV. I know you know people around here, but you'll keep your mouth shut, won't you?"

"I hear you."

"I don't want anyone knowing we think this is a repeat of the others, that there's a serial killer involved, OK? We'll take it a step at a time. Because if news about this gets out, we'll have every family on our back,

21

everyone whose kid has been out of the house for half an hour. You hear me? Keep it zipped, man, OK?"

He was over-reacting, he was blowing it out of all proportion, he was way out of the ballpark on this, I was sure of it. What made me go along finally, what made me believe him, was that Sonny Lippert said something I'd almost never heard him say in more than twenty years.

"It was my fault," he said. "The other girl. I didn't act fast enough. It was my fault," he said and walked away.

I kept my mouth shut.

2

The jogger's name was Ivana Galitzine. She was tall and thin with long arms, and she wore gray sweatpants and a thick hooded sweatshirt and pink All Star high tops, same as the blood-drenched sneakers in the black rubber bag; only pink. The laces on the left shoe were untied and trailed on the ground. I couldn't help looking at the shoes; she saw me looking, then put her hands back over her face and leaned against Lippert's dark green Jaguar that he got on a lease cheap. Like a child's, the girl—Galitzine—her fingernails were bitten and the bright pink polish was chipped. I tapped her on the arm and said softly in Russian, "Are you alright? Do you want to see a doctor?"

She put her hands down and looked at me. She was great looking in spite of the frightened brown eyes that darted towards the gang of cops, the mound of earth, then down to her sneakers. Her dark hair was soaked with sweat from her run and she'd scraped it back off her high round forehead. When she finally looked at me, she stared hard, but her light gray eyes were uncomprehending. Nodding, she wiped the back of her hand across her forehead.

"I'm OK now," she said in Russian. She gestured at the mounds of dirt. "I tripped." She was shivering now. "I tripped and I saw it."

"What did you see?"

"The bloody sneakers. The green sneakers." She looked down at her feet. "Like mine, only green and for a child, a little girl."

"We don't know that it's anything more than sneakers," I said.

"I hate people that does this to children." She was on the verge of hysteria.

"Come on, we'll get some hot coffee and maybe you can tell me exactly what happened. Alright?"

"Yes."

I took her by the arm and we walked silently across to the other side of Surf Avenue and a coffee shop. We sat at a table near the front window and I ordered coffee and asked if she wanted food. She shook her head and, when the lone waitress brought the coffee, picked up a cup and drank the scalding liquid down without flinching. There was no one else in the place except us and the waitress in a pink nylon uniform.

When Ivana had finished, she put the empty cup on the table and asked for a cigarette.

I got the pack out and gave her one and lit it.

"Can you tell me what happened?" I said.

"Sure," she said in English. "OK."

"In Russian if you want," I said.

Through the window I saw Sonny Lippert and the

24

others, the cops, the cars, the TV van, all in a dumb show. No voices came through the glass.

Galitzine was confused about how she found the sneakers. First she said she stumbled over them and dug a hole in the ground, and when I asked how she dug in when the ground was frozen, she said the shoes weren't buried, only covered with newspaper, dead leaves, debris. I let it go for the time being and listened. She talked to me in Russian, in a low voice. I took a few notes. For the first time it occurred to me how much power you had as an interpreter. Languages were just something I did; I'd moved around, I picked them up; it was something that ran in my family. But now, suddenly, I realized you could translate the words anyway you wanted. You controlled the scene. Weird, I'd never thought about it before.

Every Saturday morning, Ivana Galitzine said, she ran on the beach early, especially in the winter when it was deserted; she loved this time, she said. She loved the winter, the snow on the sand, the ice cold water, and when she felt brave enough, she went for a dip. She had been a swimmer in high school and she was tall and lean with long arms and broad shoulders, though now she was curled up, hunched over the coffee. But always, every Saturday, she ran, for miles, ran from Brighton Beach to Coney Island and back again and in between she stopped for breakfast.

She had arrived in New York a year earlier and she lived with her aunt and her cousins in a noisy, over-crowded house on one of the back lanes off Brighton Beach Avenue. Galitzine worked in the city at a medical lab and supply company on Lexington Avenue between a Tasti-Delite store and a cell phone outlet and where she could take the 6 train. Her science training mattered more than her English at this job, she said. At night she studied. She went to English class, she watched TV, she read the newspapers; slowly she read the papers, one page at a time, spelling out the words, looking in her dog-eared dictionary. She liked math best, she said; and physics. Reading was harder, but math! When she said it, it lit her up and you could see in her face the studious girl who had once been top of her class at her Moscow high school.

"I wake up late today, but still I am going for run," she switched to English. "I run and run, is beautiful morning today, sky blue, very cold and no one around. I run hard and then after I run down from boardwalk going for breakfast, then I fall on this thing. It is still partly buried."

Habitually she ran until she reached Coney Island, where she got breakfast. It was her Saturday treat, she explained; she'd get coffee and the Russian newspapers—on Saturday she allowed herself to read in Russian—and sit for hours and read and drink coffee and eat, one apple pastry shaped like a triangle with powdery sugar, one jelly donut.

That morning she had taken a short cut across the waste ground, where she fell, she said, flat on her face. She wasn't hurt; she was curious. She was a curious girl. She noticed something sticking up and she pulled at it. It was a sneaker. Blood on it. She pawed some of the debris out of the way and found the jacket. A cop was up on the boardwalk and she ran to him and told him about the clothes. If she'd thought about it, she would have ignored the whole thing. Around here, she said, people did not talk to cops much. The police, she added, we don't trust. But he had asked her to wait and she waited.

He ran back with her and she showed him the spot.

"Why?" I said. "What bothered you so much if it was only a kid's sneaker? Was it the blood?"

After a second cup of coffee, she unzipped her sweat-shirt. She wore a tight T-shirt underneath; her midriff was bare. She smoked and told me that, at first, she thought it was a foot that she'd found. She freaked out, she went into some kind of trance, she said, she sat on the ground and stared at the thing, unsure what it was; a small animal, she thought. She thought it was the flesh of a dead animal. Then a foot. Then she re-focused and saw it was a sneaker.

"With blood," she said.

"Did you see anyone at all around?" I said.

She shook her head. "Nobody," she said. "Only these mounds of sand and earth."

I didn't believe her. It was impossible to imagine a time when the area was deserted, even in the early morning. There must have been a kid on his way to basketball practice or someone on the handball courts or a crazy Russian swimming in the middle of the winter or a junkie or drunk still sleeping off Friday night under the boardwalk. She must have seen someone; she said no, she had not seen anyone. Definitely.

Ivana Galitzine worked on her third coffee and answered my questions politely. But she'd seen nothing at all, nothing except the unfrozen grave. It was her phrase; she used it melodramatically in Russian. Unfrozen grave, she said again with the serious expression of a schoolgirl, and her voice was very young and shrill.

I put some money on the table and got up to leave. I gave her the number of my cell phone and she put the scrap of paper in her pocket, straightened her sweatshirt, pulled the hood up over her damp hair and looked at me.

"Will you invite me for coffee again?" She wrote her number on the back of the check. "Please." For the first time, she smiled. Her teeth were crooked.

"How old are you?" I said.

"Twenty-two," she said. "I am twenty-two today. This is my birthday." She looked out the window to the desolate scene. "It's my birthday and they stole it from me."

3

"Someone is stealing my stuff," Johnny Farone said to me. "Somebody is walking out of here with stuff, you know, I mean money, white truffles, some of my Super Tuscans, which pisses me off, Art, you know? You know how many dogs they have to use to snuffle around, dig up those white truffles? Jesus. I spent a fucking fortune. And the wine. I had to beg for them, you know, some *Guido*, worse, he was a *gavone*, in a vineyard in Italy thinks he's a prince, a duke, whatever, so I schlep to Italy to get the stuff and now some little pisser walks out with them under his coat, other stuff, not to mention cash, and I'm mad."

Johnny Farone sat in my car in the parking lot of his restaurant. He pummeled his chubby thigh with his fist and looked at me helplessly. He had fattened up over the years; his Armani jacket fit snugly over his hips. He glanced at the cream leather interior of my red Cadillac.

"Nice, very nice. New?"

"Yeah, I wish. Pre-owned, like they say. Pre-loved. Listen, how's Billy?"

"He's good, yeah, Artie, he's great." He beamed at me. "You really love the kid, don't you?"

I had stopped in to see Johnny at his restaurant that overlooked Sheepshead Bay and the fishing boats which were docked there; it was only a mile, maybe two, from Coney Island and more or less on my way home. Johnny had been leaving messages for a week. My head was ready to split: Lippert's recitation; the girl, Galitzine; the blood-soaked sneakers—I didn't tell Johnny any of it; it would scare him; Johnny was a sweet guy.

He'd been waiting for me. As soon as I pulled into the empty lot he emerged from the back door of his restaurant. He wasn't wearing a coat. His thighs rubbed together. Between his plump hands he held a tray with a pot of espresso, a pitcher of steamed milk and a plate loaded with biscotti. He got into the car. He balanced the tray carefully between us on the CD box.

"I made you coffee," he said. "Do you mind if we talk out here, Artie? I don't want the guys inside to hear this, and a few are setting up for dinner."

"At one in the afternoon?"

"Yeah, we don't do lunch on Saturday because Saturday night is huge, you know? You want some lunch? I could get you something fixed up."

"No thanks." I picked up the pot and poured myself some coffee and drank it.

I said, "The coffee's great. So tell me some stuff about how Billy's doing in school." I was shy about it; sometimes I felt I'd stolen Billy's affection from his real father.

But Johnny was OK with it, he had no malice, no jealousy, and he grinned and said, "Yeah, not bad. He's doing pretty good, Artie. It's good the way you and him are, you know? He needs to know some regular guys like you. He told me you even showed him how to drive a little. You put him on a telephone book or something, like my pop did for me?"

"Something like that. Is that alright, Johnny? I mean we only practice in parking lots."

"It's good, man, honest. I like that. I don't want a mama's boy. Biscotti?" he added. "Homemade. Pistachio. Go on. Please."

I'd been on a case in Brighton Beach when I first met Johnny Farone. Back then, he was a skinny guy in a short-sleeved nylon shirt and a cheap striped tie who owned an auto parts company off Brighton Beach Avenue. He was Italian but he did OK because he had learned some Russian and the locals trusted him. He was friendly to their kids. He didn't ask any questions. He paid cash for spare parts. When he opened his restaurant, he had plenty of local backers.

In the nineties, Brighton Beach was swimming in cash. People were always looking for cash deals. Older Russians, poor people, people who would always be immigrants, stuffed their money under the bed or stuck it into safety deposit boxes; the younger generation trawled for deals where you could turn a quick buck and the IRS didn't notice. In the beginning, when he was setting up, a business like Farone's served as a local laundry for dirty money. He was established now and I didn't think Johnny ever really knew, anyhow; he thought people put up the dough because they liked his food.

I met Johnny and because of it he met my cousin, Evgenia. Johnny opened the restaurant, he proposed to her, they got married. They had Billy, he bought her a big house and a car. The American dream.

Good natured, Johnny didn't have much education, but he was accommodating and he was making good money and Gen—Johnny called her Gen and it stuck and became her American name—she couldn't believe her luck: Johnny was an American; he had a business; he was crazy about her. Sometimes Genia's delight seemed a little robotic. There wasn't much passion. She learned to make great pasta, though.

Next to me in the car, Johnny picked up the coffee pot, then put it down. He was nervous.

"What's the matter?"

"You won't tell Gen, will you, you won't say I asked you to help me, you won't, will you, Artie?" He talked so fast the words seemed to fall out of his mouth like the letters in alphabet soup.

"Why, she'll beat you up with a piece of wet spaghetti?"

"She says don't stick our neck out, she says we don't want to get involved, we don't talk to cops out here, you know? She says, if someone is taking a little here and there, don't make a fuss. She's fucking paranoid, Artie."

"She's Russian. She worries. It's normal."

"Yeah, I hear you, but I want whoever is doing this. I don't want money walking out. I don't even mind the cash, but they take my best white truffles, they take wines I had to beg for at some vineyard, stuff no one else has, I'm upset. Did I tell you I got a 26 in Zagat?" He

32

laughed. "Can you believe it, me, they call up and beg for tables. They come out here from the city! They pay cash for the privilege." Farone chuckled. "I charge them whatever. They like it if I charge a lot."

I'd eaten at Farone's a few times, but he always comped it.

"You only take cash?" I said.

He laughed. "It's an old Italian custom," he said. "If you can get away with it, why not?"

He pushed the plate of biscotti at me and I ate one and licked the crumbs off my lips. It was crammed with pistachios. I could still remember the taste of the risotto with the white truffles I'd had the last time I was at Johnny's place.

"You'll help me, Artie?"

"I can't do anything official, I mean I'm not on the job in this area, you know? But give me your receipts, a disk, your books, whatever you got. You put it on a computer? I'll take a look if you want."

Farone said, "I keep handwritten records, too. I already made copies for you. Gen goes through the books three, four times a year. She's studying to be a CPA, you know. She likes doing the books, she says it's good practice. She said we could fire the fucking accountant and save the money."

"And she didn't notice?"

"I don't know. But I didn't tell her I looked at the books. She'd tell me, lay off the books. You're making yourself nuts."

"Johnny?"

"What's that?"

"You have any ideas who's doing this? I'm sitting here and I'm thinking you have some ideas but you don't want to say the names, could that be right?"

He was silent. I tried to focus, but my mind was on the bloodied clothing and the Russian jogger and the missing girl.

"Johnny?"

"Yeah," he mumbled. "I think it might be a couple of guys that work for someone."

"I can't hear you."

"Whatever."

"Come on."

"I'm thinking it's Elem Zeitsev," he said. "Maybe. Maybe Zeitsev."

If Johnny was trying to pin it on Zeitsev he was out of his mind.

"Come on! Zeitsev doesn't need your white truffles. He's loaded. Also, he's straight now his old man is dead. He gave up all the crooked shit they did. It's over."

Johnny looked up.

"I'm not that dumb, man," he said. "I didn't mean Zeitsev himself, I meant some of his guys, some of the crooks he left behind, you know? I mean they're hungry now he dropped them all."

"I'll ask around."

"Thanks, dude, really, thanks."

"Sure." I looked at my watch. "I better get back to the city. Tell Billy I'll call him over the weekend, OK?"

"Wait a sec," he said. "Let me get you a good bottle for later. I have this fantastic Barolo. Please, let me. And I'll get the books, if you're serious, if you'll take a look."

I hesitated.

"We're family, Art. OK? Lily liked my Barolo. Remember?"

I remembered. I changed the subject.

"So tell Billy, right? I'll call. I'll try to come over."

"You're a good godfather, Artie, even if you don't believe in no religion shit. I saw how you held Billy when he was baptized. I remember. Hey, I found some old film I got developed, pictures of the kid, you want to see?"

"Sure."

Farone pulled them out of his pocket and passed them over, then opened the car door, got out and leaned down to pick up the tray of coffee and biscotti. He waddled away like a fat waiter and disappeared through the heavy bronze doors of the restaurant in search of Barolo.

The pictures were 4 by 6, and while I waited, I looked through them, fanning them out idly, like playing cards: Billy on the deck of a fishing boat; Billy sitting on the edge of a pier with a fishing pole; Billy holding a huge plastic fish between his hands; Billy outside a church in a navy blue blazer and a tie. Farone was Catholic; Gen didn't care. Like me, she was raised nothing. She was happy for Johnny to take the boy to his own church. For him, she converted. They had named him William John, but everyone called him Billy.

I lit a cigarette and looked at the last picture. Billy, not looking at me or the camera, his face seeming distracted, aloof, and in his hands a dark blue Yankees jacket. He was holding it out to show the logo, as if someone on the

35

other side of the camera had said, "Show us the jacket, Billy. Come on. Hold it up." My heart banged in my chest; my throat dried; the hair on my arms stood up.

The radio was still on and I turned it off. The sun streamed in and dappled the cream leather upholstery. The heat was on, but my skin felt so cold that I started shivering. I reached in the back seat and got my jacket. Then I started to sweat.

I picked up the photograph. It was the jacket I'd bought for Billy the day I took him to the World Series at Yankee Stadium the year before last. They gave out tickets to cops and firemen, and I got two and I wanted him there with me; I wanted him to experience New York that way, so I got Gen to let me take him, though she was scared of Billy being in crowds right after 9/11. I said, I'll take care of him, and we went and we cheered for the Yanks and the crowd swayed together in some kind of communal mourning ritual; no one was scared, no one worried, just the game and the songs, and me and Billy. I could feel his weight beside me; he was warm against my side. But he was distracted all day. He spent the day looking at a book about fish.

I had assumed the blood-soaked clothes belonged to a girl. Sonny Lippert assumed it. Missing kids, the ones you heard about, were mostly little girls. I looked at the baseball jacket again and at Billy. There were a million Yankees jackets. A million kids wore them. I couldn't see his shoes in the picture. I looked at the jacket hard. There was a tear on the sleeve. I remembered Billy caught the sleeve on a nail as we'd left the stadium.

Johnny reappeared with a bottle under one arm and

two plastic shopping bags in his other hand. He got into the car and put the bags on the floor, then held out the bottle to me.

"The last one," he said. "Let me know what you think, Art." He picked up the first plastic bag. "The account books, OK, man?" he said, and noticed, finally, I was looking at the photograph of Billy with the Yankees jacket.

"You remember?" he said.

I didn't answer.

"Yo, Artie."

"What?"

"You took him to that game and I took that picture when he got home. I kept asking him about the game, the players, but it was like he wasn't there, Art. All he could think about was his fishing stuff. I don't get it. He's a bright kid, you know? The teachers say he's really smart. His IQ is really up there. He was talking whole sentences way before he was three. And street smart, right? I mean he goes over to his grandmother alone and helps her sometimes, you know? He's very OK, like that. He's OK. You think he's OK, don't you?"

"Sure, Johnny," I said. "He's a great kid."

"I worry, man. I mean they fight, him and his mom, and then I go to him and he won't talk to me, I can see in his face he thinks I'm a dumb-ass. He just shuts the door to the garage and fools around with that fish tank I got him, and stays in there. Sometimes I think he likes the fish more than me."

"It's a stage," I said because I'd heard people say it.

"All parents go through that stuff with their kids," I added and saw Johnny's sweet dumb face light up.

"You think?"

What I knew and Johnny couldn't was that Billy was a special kid; he was really smart; he had been talking like a grown-up since he was seven or eight; he made me show him how to drive and he picked it up fast.

Billy invented worlds of his own with characters and languages; it was the kind of stuff you read about in the papers when some kid suddenly produces a whole book and people go nuts about it. If it was your kid and you were Johnny, though, you could think he was weird, or sullen, or strange. I understood Billy and Billy knew it, and we had a thing together, but I didn't want to hold it over his father, I didn't want to play tug of war over his boy; I'd seen that happen.

So I kept my distance, I called once a week, and every month or two I picked him up and took him fishing which was all he cared about, sometimes out of Sheepshead Bay, sometimes on the island, sometimes just off Battery Park with the old Chinese guys. When the weather was lousy, we went to the Aquarium or we browsed shops for tackle. With Johnny, or Genia if she asked me, which she almost never did, either I kept my mouth shut or parroted stuff I heard on self-help shows. "It's a stage, man, All kids go through it."

I lit a cigarette. I wanted to ask about the jacket, about Billy.

"You already got one burning, man," Johnny said and stubbed it out for me in the ashtray. "What's the matter with you? You want some more coffee? You want to come inside?"

My pulse was racing, sweat broke out again on my forehead as I said, "Johnny?"

"Yeah, Art?"

"I don't know, I thought maybe I'd stop by and see Gen and Billy at home. They're around? They're at home?"

"I'm not sure."

"What do you mean?"

"Sometimes, when it goes really late, if I have one too many, I stay here, you know, Friday nights. Get the last drunks out, have a couple with the waiters, the bussers. Good relations with the help. I keep a sofa bed in the office, an old Castro Convertible from when I lived alone in that dump over by Marine Park before I met Gen. Wait a sec, you know what, Billy was going someplace with this kid, the dad was taking them someplace, they have a country house upstate, I think that was it. Stevie. The kid's name is Stevie Gervasi. Gen says it's good for him to be with other kids. I didn't pay that much attention, honest to God, I had a Friday night from hell coming up. You want me to call Gen?"

I nodded.

He dialed and listened a while, then hung up. "No one home," he said. "Billy's with the other kid, I'm sure. Genia probably went to her class."

"What kind of class?"

"She's doing her CPA degree, like I said."

"Call her on her cell," I said. "Just do it, Johnny, OK. Just call her."

He dialed the number and waited. There was a brief exchange. I could tell Genia was busy, maybe at her class, and irritated by the interruption.

Johnny finished the call and turned to me. "Like I said, Billy went with this other kid, Stevie Gervasi. Lives across the street from us. You want me to call him on his cell? You want to try?"

"Sure," I said, casual as I could manage.

Johnny dialed again and passed the phone to me. There was no service in the area, the robot on the other end said. No service.

I said to Johnny, "You stayed here last night?"

"Yeah. Hey, Art, dude, you look terrible. Listen, I got a good joke for you."

Johnny's idea of cheering you up was a joke, so I grinned and said, "Go on."

"So, did you hear the one about the dyslexic rabbi who stubbed his toe and yelled YO!"

I tried smiling and gave him back his phone.

I didn't want to make Johnny crazy; I had no evidence the clothes by the beach were Billy's. I knew I worried too much about Billy, but I liked him and I liked that he liked me. It made me less lonely, especially with Lily gone and Beth with her. I still talked to Beth, the little girl I'd helped Lily adopt, but with the two of them in London, it was never the same. After they left, I began seeing more of Billy; I tried to replace Beth with Billy. Sometimes I felt like a middle-aged adolescent, unmarried, no kids, still looking for escape routes. Billy gave me a sense I could care for a child, that I was a grown-up, a man like—I was going to say a man like my father—but he was never really a grown-up either.

I examined the photograph and the dark blue baseball jacket in it.

"You OK, Artie?"

"I'm fine, Johnny. I'm OK. Can I have this picture of Billy? I'd like to keep it."

"Sure. I'll make myself a copy. He's a good kid, isn't he, Artie? You think he's a good kid?"

"Sure. Sure I do."

"It's just like Gen sometimes goes nuts because he's off in his own world, and I tell her, listen, he's a kid, this fishing thing matters, and just because he doesn't like it when she slobbers all over him, I say, come on, Gen, he wants to be a big boy, like macho, like the boys on the street. Right? Let him be. I mean she has to let go."

"Sure."

"So give Gen a call later if you want. Come out and eat with us at home tomorrow. Bring a nice girl. You have someone? You always got some good-looking girl, right?" he stuttered. "I mean no one's as nice as Lily, but, you know."

"Yeah, I know."

"You want to do me one more little favor?" he said, "I mean, only if you have time. I mean I'm like so overwhelmed with it being Saturday, and three guys away for the weekend and one more says he has the fucking flu."

"What?"

He picked up the second plastic bag from the floor.

"What is it?"

"Listen, you're going home to the city from here? So it would be like only five minutes out of your way to

41

drop this at my mother's house. You remember, right? You met her at Billy's christening, right? At his communion, no, you weren't there, were you, but you'll like her, Artie, swear to God and you only have to drop the bag. She's part Polack, anyhow, I mean that's like Russian, right? Her name is Tina. You can call her Tina, it's OK, you don't have to say Mrs. Farone, OK?"

He held out a piece of paper with an address.

I wasn't crazy about the idea, but Johnny begged and I took the bag and the address and Johnny got out of the car, and before he closed the door said, "Get back to the city safe, Artie."

I pulled away from the lot and turned the car around, and in the rear view I saw Johnny watching me go, waving and smiling.

The city. It still surprised me the way people in the other boroughs, Queens, the Bronx, Staten Island, here in Brooklyn, the vast colonies that surrounded Manhattan and with it made up New York City, still referred to it as "the city." "I'm going into the city," they'd say, meaning Manhattan. It was a foreign country. I knew people in Brooklyn who never ventured over the bridge, immigrants who clung to the coast, terrified of the noise, the crowds, the sheer power. I met one old guy over in Red Hook who, last time he'd been to Manhattan, it was VE Day and he had been a GI in Europe and he went to Times Square. And that was it. He lived a whole life in Brooklyn looking at the Manhattan skyline and never got closer and said to me, what for? What should I go there for?

All the concrete and money and people packed onto a thirteen-mile slice of land, it scared people. Connected to the outside world only by tunnels and bridges, Manhattan was vulnerable to terrorists and traffic jams and self-importance. It was the center of the world; this was what we believed, even that winter when things were pretty grim. Once, on our way to New Jersey for some fishing, as we drove through the Holland Tunnel, Billy Farone had asked me, "What if the tunnel breaks? What if the river comes through? Artie? What?" But he had seen too many disaster movies.

Checking the map on the seat next to me, I drove towards Johnny's mother's place. Coming into Brooklyn was like entering a foreign country, it was that big and unknowable, the way it sprawled south-east from the tip of Manhattan down to the Atlantic Ocean. Across the bridges, through the tunnel, were two and a half million people, most in low lying buildings, the sublime old brownstones, the chic lofts, the cheap tenements, the classic two-family houses.

The sections of Brooklyn nearest Manhattan, Brooklyn Heights, Williamsburg, and DUMBO, where the artists had gone and people ate a hundred bucks' worth of sushi for dinner, was where the money went. The endless interior, classic Brooklyn—Flatbush, Bensonhurst, Sunset Park—was jammed with immigrants and their descendants, Italian, Irish, Jewish, Asian, South American, Russian, black. It went on forever, people vying for space, for religion, a foothold on the ladder up.

The boroughs, but especially Brooklyn, always spread

towards water, from the Hudson River, the East River, down to the Atlantic Ocean. The seacoast of New York. Ten miles from Manhattan. Easy to remember here on the coast that the city was an archipelago, a series of islands and inlets, beaches and marshes, rivers, basins, derelict shipyards, wetlands where birds congregated, Jamaica Bay where the planes came in low like big water birds.

I drove through Sheepshead Bay and looked at the fishing boats and thought about Billy. He was upstate with his pal. Johnny might be stupid about his kid but he loved him and he said he was upstate, so it was OK.

Out on the dock a solitary fisherman sold fish from a bucket and the customers were lined up, some waiting, some stuffing fish in waxed paper into their bags or carts and lugging it away.

The neighborhood had changed. For years, except for the fishing, it had been run down, with shabby houses in yards overgrown with weeds. Some Russians had moved in from Brighton Beach. Chinese had come out from Sunset Park. Real estate prices went up, pushed by the boom that spread from Manhattan.

Along the inlet were the restaurants: Farone's, El Greco, the Sahara. Lundy's, the huge fish place, had reopened, and there was Baku, a new Russian joint in pale fake stone with silver doors. You could get eel salad with teriyaki sauce and listen to Russian rock.

I passed a couple of old age homes—a lot of old people got warehoused out here in Brooklyn—and a motel without any sign; it was the original hot sheet motel, someone told me, where you could still get rooms by the hour. A massive sewage treatment plant loomed ahead of me, a cathedral of shit with a sign that read "Building a Better Brooklyn."

The further I drove, the quieter it got; the villages here that seemed to turn in on themselves were set apart, insular and mostly white. There were no subways and only a few bus lines; most people drove their own cars. Much of the area had been made of landfill.

A lot of the area had been marshland until the fifties and sixties. When new buildings went up in Manhattan, the land was dumped on the Brooklyn coast and new villages were made. Dirt roads were paved. I made the trip warily to Gerritsen Beach. I loved the ocean and the smell of the air, but I had never liked it here. There was too much fear.

4

American flags hung from every door in Gerritsen Beach where Johnny Farone's mother lived. It was ten minutes along the coast from Sheepshead Bay, a backwater that ended abruptly at Marine Park where Indians played cricket in the summer.

From the small cramped houses that were crowded together, flags hung, sometimes two or three of them, from every door. Ira, Hazel, Frank, Noel, Lester, Hyman, Ivan, the streets had first names; maybe the narrow streets had been named for people who had settled when there were only dirt roads.

At some houses, little flags on sticks were also stuck in cement planters, the plants dead and crusted with dirty snow. At others a large black flag with the initials POW MIA flapped beside the stars and stripes. The houses were layered over as if every new owner had aspired to something a little better; aluminum siding, plastic tile, fake fieldstone, fake brick, real brick, they had been fixed and altered and remade so the small houses of Brooklyn's coastal communities looked ripe for an archaeological dig. In one yard, dead petunias covered in dirty snow were crammed in a decorative cement donkey cart. On a fence a piece of cardboard, battered by the weather, proclaimed "It's a Boy!" with the baby's name and weight and two blue balloons shriveled like used condoms.

It was desolate on the winter afternoon and silent. A man in an orange down vest spreading salt on his front walk watched me wordlessly as I drove by. There were not a lot of red Caddys here; there were never any strangers. The houses looked eyeless, shut up, shut in.

Mrs. Farone's house had a red brick façade in front and white aluminum siding around the back, and there were two plaster cherubs near the three steps that led up to her porch, where there was a wrought iron bench and a potted plastic dahlia. I leaned on the bell. I heard the footsteps and the door opened.

The minute I saw Johnny Farone's mother, I disliked her. It was worse than that. One look and I wanted to turn and leave. I'd been a cop for more than twenty years. I've met a lot of creeps, sat with people who should have been locked up and never would be, and some who should have had a needle stuck in their arm, but I'd never met anyone I disliked so much and I didn't know why. The smell, maybe, or the large eyes that shifted away from my face and into the middle distance, looking for something, or someone. She wore black leggings and a blue sweatshirt with NYFD across the front, probably one of those 9/11 fire department souvenirs; around her neck was a diamond cross.

An aura of malice, like a silky scarf, fluttered around

47

her. It wasn't just her brusque manner or the way she talked. I figured she wasn't expecting me, she wanted Johnny to come and see her and she was pissed off it was me and I was OK with that, but it was something else. I couldn't pin it down.

I had been expecting an old Italian woman, feet in backless scuffs, pictures of bleedings saints on the wall and tomato sauce in a pot on the stove. Mrs. Farone—I couldn't think of her as Tina—was a good-looking woman. She'd had some work done, face lift, something like that, so she looked more like Johnny's sister than his mother. The eye-lids were very large and smooth and heavily made-up, the purple shadow thick as chalk. There wasn't much expression in her face; the lines were gone; the smile, when it appeared which wasn't often, was rigid.

Grudgingly, she let me into the house, which was low and dark and smelled of vanilla, probably cheap candles. I only went in because it was freezing out, and I wanted to ask her about Billy and how he was. Rationally I knew he was fine, but it was still on my mind.

"What is it?" Mrs. Farone's voice could have shattered Coke bottles as she looked at me impatiently. We were in the living room—she called it a parlor—and I held out the bag Johnny had given me. She glanced inside then put it on the wrought iron coffee table.

"You've seen Billy recently?" I asked as casually as I could.

"What's it your business?" she said.

"I like Billy," I said. "I'm his godfather. I think you know that."

"So ask his mother." She crossed her legs and closed her face.

"I'm asking you."

"You're the cop, aren't you? You're the relative who's a cop. You're related to the mother."

"Genia's my cousin," I said.

Mrs. Farone delivered the party line, what a good boy he was, how he went to church and visited his grandmother regularly and how except for Genia, she hinted, it would have been fine. She showed me a picture of Billy dressed as an angel for a Christmas pageant. I reached for the picture and saw she wanted to stop me but didn't.

"You made the costume for him? It's nice. It looks good," I said.

"Yeah, I did." She smoothed her hair, fixed her collar; she preened. She was a woman who needed attention.

"That's a nice sweater."

"Thank you," she said coldly.

"I take Billy fishing sometimes," I said.

"I know. He talks about fishing. He talks about you. All the time it's fishing. I tell Johnny, he needs friends his own age."

Before she could say anything else, the phone rang from the kitchen and she broke off to answer it, trailing that smell of vanilla behind her, so I realized it was her skin not the candles. I waited, listening to her on the phone, hearing her voice but not the words.

After a few minutes, she reappeared,

"Go on with what you were saying," I said.

"I forgot." She was sullen. "Yeah, so thanks for bringing me the cookies." She gestured at the bag Johnny had sent. "I have to go out." She held open the door impatiently.

I got up and zipped my jacket, went out, got into the car and looked at the map. A few minutes later, Mrs. Farone's door opened and she came out, carrying a wire shopping cart down her front steps. She had fixed herself up for the expedition and she was wearing tight jeans and a short, padded pink ski jacket and big earrings and high-heeled boots. She was smoking and she saw me. She saw me watching her, but she didn't wave or smile or call out. She just turned her head in the other direction and walked away.

The smell of her vanilla skin stayed in my nostrils as I turned the car around and headed to Brighton Beach. Sonny Lippert wanted me near the phone but I had my cell with me and I still thought he was crazy, obsessed with the blood-soaked clothes. There was no body, no one had called in a missing kid.

Saturday afternoon. I drove down Brighton Beach Avenue. An old woman in a headscarf lugged a suitcase across the street; an elderly man watched her, suspicious, food in his beard as he gnawed a knish; two women, draped in cheesy furs that looked like rat pelts, linked arms and crossed the street, both yapping into their cell phones at the same time.

Up and down the avenue, people jammed together under the overhead platform where the elevated train ran, shopped and yakked and hung out in front of stores and restaurants, smoking and talking; the insistent voices carried through the afternoon.

I figured I'd get some sturgeon at one of the food stores. The Russian behind the counter looked at me with hostility and I asked again for a half pound of sturgeon and half of Nova. I smiled at her, but anger was the air she breathed. It was all she knew. For her, anger was more useful than despair, and both better than the paranoia she had probably learned in Russia. Like my cousin Genia's. Gen guarded herself and her husband and child and her business even from me.

The bag of smoked fish in my hand, I left the stove and walked a little, past the Odessa, where a bouncer in thick black leathers eyed me briefly; past more food stores crammed with food: black breads the shape of footballs; chubs with glistening gold skins and fish eyes; blue cans of caviar. The food, the supermarkets, the banks, the clothing stores, all Russian.

I crossed the street and went up on the boardwalk. I leaned on the railing. On the ocean at the edge of the flat, slate colored surface of the water, lights from a ship blinked. Immigrants had once come on those ships; they had made a break, willing to leave everything they knew for a foreign place, for a better life, or for streets lined with gold. Now people came in airplanes and called home on their cell phones. The break was never sharp; they clung to the place they'd come from.

From the Olympia Café a few yards down the board-walk, I could hear Russian music. A crooner with a baritone that oozed sentimentally into the cold afternoon was warming up. Already people were drinking. They were laughing and singing and drinking, and none of them had anything to do with the blood-soaked clothes a mile away down the beach. I thought about getting a drink at one of the cafés but it wasn't a good idea, me hanging out in Brighton Beach.

Nothing much had changed since I'd been here a few years earlier except a complex of fancy apartment buildings with water views had gone up. As far as I knew the big time hoods had moved up and out. Long Island. The city. New Jersey. St Tropez. They left their parents, the older generation, tucked up in gated communities by the beach.

It was as Russian as ever, as much a weird slice out of the former Soviet Union as it had been when I first came here. More. It had become a kind of theme park with stuff in the shops—dresses with glitter, big furs, fancy china—you probably couldn't even find in Moscow anymore. A lot of the people were old. Their kids have moved on, out into America.

I was OK now, being here. For years, I'd kept my distance. I never went to Brighton Beach unless I had to on a case and then I hated it. And I kept the hate active, I fired it up, I laughed secretly at the provincial manners, at the women with their bleached blonde big hair, at their stonewashed jeans, at how they resembled hookers. I could stoke up a line in sarcasm about them, and about their men and about their lousy neighborhood. Worse, I nursed it.

At first, when I got to New York, I worked on my English; I got rid of my accent and learned to talk like a New Yorker. Hating the Russians ate me up for years and then, after a while, I tried to let it go. I met Tolya

Sverdloff. I went to Moscow on a case and fell in love with Svetlana, Tolya's cousin. Then Svetlana was blown up by a car bomb.

But the past finally faded. There was no one left in Russia I cared about. As soon as I let it go, I felt better; I even spoke the language with pleasure. I loved its sounds that insinuated themselves back into my being. Sometimes I read Russian to keep it fresh; sometimes, though I could only admit it to Tolya, I enjoyed it. They could write, those bastards; they could write novels like nobody else, poetry, too; I mean Pushkin wasn't chopped liver.

I turned onto Coney Island Avenue and pulled up at Batumi Books next door to the Hello, Gorgeous Beauty Salon. As soon as he saw me, my friend Dubi Petrovsky ran from behind the counter waving a book.

Dubi had come from Russia via Israel, like me, but he clung to his Russianness; he was a scholarly man, about seventy, tall like an immense bird with a haunted hollow face and sunken pale blue eyes and a huge laugh. He knew everyone around Brighton Beach and he relished it. He could come and go to Manhattan for his book groups or the opera or to prowl the secondhand bookstores, and he had treasures no one else could get.

From the back of the shop, *Sergeant Pepper* played softly. Above all, Dubi was a crazed Beatles fan. It was said of him, in the old days, he told me, that he was the first to decipher a picture of the Beatles torn from some Western newspaper. It was Dubi, he said, referring to himself in the third person, who first looked at the picture, maybe 1969, and said, here is John, this is

George, Paul is here. He had written, he told me, but never published a history of the Beatles in the USSR. Currently he was five years into a tome on the fall of empires.

A piece about Dubi and the shop from the *New York Times* hung, behind glass, on the wall. The shop smelled of old books, of old leather bindings and used paperbacks.

"Hello, Artemy," he said softly and we shook hands and hugged. "I have this for you." He held out the brown paper package tied neatly with twine, my name and address written out by hand.

"How much do I owe you?" I said.

"I should charge you three hundred because this is something special, but it's you, so give me one fifty? That's OK? You're not too broke? I know you, you're always broke and you drive that big Caddy which is why you're broke."

"I'm not too broke," I lied and wrote a check.

"You've seen the piece from the *New York Times*?" he asked for the millionth time.

I read it again.

"So how are things out here? You're OK? Business?"

Dubi made a face and rolled a cigarette. "Lousy. After 9/11, it was lousy. People here didn't buy books, they sat in front of the TV. They were scared. They had come here because it was safe and it wasn't safe anymore, and after that the shit started in Russia. More shit, I mean. The Chechens take over a theater and kill people in Moscow. I have a lady, a customer, her niece was in that theater. They look around, they see the empire is still breaking up, still spewing shit."

"What empire?"

"Russian. American."

"You mean like your book? How's the book going?"

"I don't know. I'm not sure an analysis of the break-up of the Soviet and American empires as a kind of chain reaction is going to make it to the bestseller list, you know? Maybe I'll put some sex in, what do you think? I meet them, though, Artemy, I meet people who look at America and see the arrests, no charge, people interned they think America looks like Soviet Union. They get scared shitless."

"Yeah?"

"Come on, Artemy. They got some smart people out here. Not all Russians on Brighton Beach are creeps and hookers and idiots. They think, they read, they travel. OK, a lot of the kids leave, they don't like it, they think it's old fashioned, but there's still smart people. They understand that the old empires are all gone, nothing holds together, it's all in pieces, nothing safe. Some of them think about going back home where they won't be immigrants. Some melting pot, they say; they just melt you down until you turn into American. No culture. No nothing. Just this crazy religion where they believe in the Bible as fact like it's the telephone book."

Dubi made me laugh.

I said, "I have to go. Good luck with the book. You writing in Russian?"

"Both," he said. "I do my own translation. But you're OK, Artie? You're doing OK?"

"I'm OK."

"You know what I can't get used to? I can't get used

to the feeling war is coming. I remember this when I was a tiny boy in Leningrad, you know, and war was coming, and again in Israel later. I stare at the ceiling at night and think, not again. What the fuck are we going into Iraq for? So listen, come out one day and have a tea with me, OK, or some food. Come home one time."

"I will, Dube. Yeah I will. Thanks."

"You want to stay for lunch? I could order in?"

"That's OK," I said. "I have a date."

5

At Totonno's, I got a pizza, then I picked up Cropsey
Avenue on my way to Shore Drive. Maxine's phone was
busy, so I put my cell on redial.

It used to surprise me that even when a case loomed,
even when there was the possibility of murder, you
could think about pizza. Pizza, the dentist, calling my
mother, buying a birthday present, music. Stuff. Stuff
that made it a life. Stuff I never had growing up in
Moscow when everything was make-shift and uncertain.
There were memories even now I couldn't trap into
consciousness; I had hated it that much. Even after more
than twenty-five years in New York, I was thrilled by
the routines of city life, my city, my neighborhood, my
life—breakfast at Mike's coffee shop, a bike ride by the
river, sitting at my desk in the sun coming through the
old loft window, ribs at Tennessee Mountain with my
neighbors, Lois and Louise. Pizza with Maxine.

I loved how New York was jammed with people who
told in detail the stories their friends told them and the
stories of their relatives; even distant acquaintances of

casual friends became the stuff of your daily narrative. Everyone gossiped. Everyone relayed news about celebrities as if they were your best friends. Life was dense with people. Having a conversation in New York, the stories over-lapping, everyone interrupting, you had to fight for air time. You were crazy, maybe; you got lonely; you were never alone.

So I got a large pie because it was one of the things I did with Maxine Crabbe on weekends and I didn't want to let go of it and anyhow there was nothing I could do about the case until I heard from Sonny Lippert. I called Maxie from the car again, got through and asked if the twins were around. She said they were away for the weekend with their dad's mother upstate, and she'd been doing laundry all morning and was hanging around, drinking coffee and wasn't even dressed. I said, don't bother.

An hour after I got to Maxine's, she left me in her bed and put the pizza I brought in the microwave.

"You want some?" she called from the kitchen, mouth full. "I really think Grimaldi's is better, you know, honey."

I got up and looked out of the window. The sun was high over the Hudson beyond Shore Drive where Maxie lived. She had grown up nearby in Bay Ridge. It was a peaceful neighborhood, Italian, some Jews, white; it had been Scandinavian once. She had moved back from Staten Island after her husband, Mark, died in the Trade Center.

From her half of the two family house, what they

called a Mother and Daughter out in Brooklyn, she had a spectacular view of the water. I wasn't crazy about how easy the access was to her front door, but she loved it. She had always wanted a view of the Verrazano Bridge she said.

"The Golden Gate," Maxie would say, thickening up her Brooklyn accent. "That's not a bridge. This," she'd say, walking to the window and looking out, "this is a bridge!"

When Mark died on 9/11 she had gone back to her job in forensics, which was how I knew her. She was good at it and it filled up the hours and the girls were in junior high now anyway. She came back to the bedroom, where I was struggling with my jeans.

"You putting on a few pounds, sailor?" She giggled.

Maxine Crabbe was an old friend. We got together once in a while and argued over where you got the best pizza in Brooklyn, Grimaldi's, Totonno's, De Faras on Avenue J. Once in a while we had a pizza orgy and an overnight.

She was thirty-eight and looked younger, a stringbean of a girl, tall, skinny, loose limbed. She wore her hair short and she had freckles. We had known each other before I met Lily. I met Max when she showed up, a kid of twenty-two, at a station house where I was working. She was very sharp.

We had dated on and off, she was practical, funny, smart and uncomplicated, but I was a pain in the ass and couldn't commit and she gave up and married Mark, a handsome fire captain from Staten Island. They had twins, Millie and Maria, identical as babies but different as they grew up; Millie was smooth and blonde, a real little nymphet, and Maria, who hated her sister's obsessions with boys and clothes, wore glasses she didn't need and kept her face in a book even at dinner when Max tried to stop her. But they were both good kids.

Once in a while, in the old days, I went over when they lived on Staten Island. I'd fish with Mark; Maxie would barbecue.

For months after Mark died, Maxine worked long nights at the "Dead House," the makeshift morgue at the Marriott Hotel downtown where they tried to match what remains they could find to DNA samples. It was horrible for her; not because she wasn't used to it, she dealt with dead bodies all the time. She pulled those hours, I knew, because she was waiting for Mark to show up. Something, she thought. Please, God, let them find a piece of him so I can get some rest. They never did.

Like everyone downtown, we got close those months. Lily left New York, Max and me, we went out a few times. Nothing was ever said. We fell into a kind of routine, pizza, a movie, music, a trip to the park with the girls. No big deal. We were friends who fell into bed together once in a while. It filled up the time, but I missed Lily.

"You want a slice?"

"I'm not hungry," I said. "I'll skip it. Is there coffee?" I got dressed, followed her into the kitchen, where she was sampling the pie.

"Grimaldi's is much better," she said. "Artie?"

"Yeah?"

"You believe in God?"

"No."

"I wish I could get rid of believing."

"It's different if you're Catholic, I think."

"But Jews believe."

"I'm not that kind of Jew," I said.

"What kind are you?"

"The kind who doesn't believe in God. Anyway, my father wasn't Jewish at all, but that's not really it. I'm a New York Jew, you know? I'm a Woody Allen Jew, a George Gershwin Jew, a Stan Getz Jew, a Mel Brooks Jew, and Billy Wilder and books by Philip Roth and all the rest, I believe in them, you know? That's all I have. The rest, for me, OK, I don't mean to insult your religion, but for me, it's all bullshit. You want to do dinner, tonight?"

"If you get lucky." She kissed me and looked at her watch. "Christ, it's late. So make it a late dinner, OK? Come back around nine. No pizza, either. I'm cooking. I bought steak for the kids to take up to their grandmother and they left it. New York strip. Salad. Red wine."

"This could go great with steak," I said, and gave her the bottle Johnny gave me.

She looked at it. "Jeez, that's some helluva wine. You forgot to tell me what you were doing in Brooklyn so early in the morning."

"Can we talk about it later?"

"Sure," she said. Maxie was a pro; she knew if I had a case, I'd talk when I was ready. "So you have the keys I gave you, right? If I'm late, just let yourself in."

"Thanks."

"Listen, you can keep those keys, I mean in case you're ever working a case here and you need to crash and you don't want to go all the way back to the city, whatever." She stuttered some when she said it. "I mean no big deal, OK. Just if you want."

I put my arms around her. There was a lot I wanted to say, but I wasn't brave enough. I could work cases in bad places, I could chase bad guys with guns if I had to. I'd seen lousy stuff on the job. This was different. Harder.

"Thanks," was all I said. "That's really nice. Thank you."

6

"Where are you?" It was Sonny Lippert on my cell phone.

"On my way home."

"Stay there," he said. "I might need you later."

"What's going on?" I said but the line went dead.

The bridge was like spun silver behind me. On the hill above was the old fort which had been there since men in wigs and three-cornered hats made a revolution. The traffic was light and the sun blinding. I pulled my sunglasses out of my jacket pocket. It was cold and beautiful. The river was bright with sunlight, navy blue and silver, the way it gets in the winter, and there were chunks of ice jamming it up. The short trip, water always on my left, I felt I was in a boat, I drove without feeling the road under the tires, as if I was driving on water.

I wasn't sure why Sonny Lippert was so agitated, but it was Lippert who helped me get back on the job. Even before 9/11, I had wanted it. I hated the time when I worked as a private investigator. I tried it on my own; I had tried working for Keyes, one of the big security companies. I made more money, I had a fine health plan and an office and regular hours, but there was none of the stuff about being a New York cop that I'd always loved, even when I knew how much bullshit went down.

Keyes was mostly paperwork, bank accounts, corporate stuff; I learned my way around a paper trail, but I was bored. Anyway I could never get rid of the idea that being a private eye was something out of a B movie. Chandler, Ross MacDonald, Elroy, those writers who did it brilliantly in books, but it wasn't like that for me. It was dull and lonely. I never got over missing the guys at work, the station house, the noise and smells, even if the pay was lousy.

"We had fun, didn't we?" a detective I know—I was at the academy with her—said after we both retired. We were sitting over a beer at Fanelli's and regretting it, that we'd left, and remembering the good times, except she had a husband and kids, so it was OK for her. Someone, probably Sonny Lippert whispering in his ear, bent the rules for me so I could go back even though I missed the one-year rule—you could go back on the job up to a year after you quit. I was twice as old as some of the new guys; it was OK.

Lippert took a risk on me. "You'll have to cool it," he'd said. "You'll have to play by the rules. My rules. You'll have to go where I need you, OK? You get it?"

I promised to be good and he got me my job. Nominally, I worked out of headquarters in Manhattan, but in reality I went wherever Sonny went. Ever since I had first worked for him at the Federal Prosecutor's Office at Cadman Plaza over in downtown Brooklyn, I'd been his boy. Most of '01, '02, we worked out of Police Plaza in the city, we worked on terrorism. Things moved on, Lippert formed his unit on crimes against children.

Working on cases connected with children was what made Sonny Lippert nuts. It put him out on a fragile emotional limb, it caused his divorce, it made him febrile. Again I wondered why the bloody clothes had been left where they'd be so easily found? Was that the point? Was it planned? Was it the result of some crack-addled brain, another case of child abuse, another case where someone used a kid as a punching bag, a way to express a hideous rage? It didn't feel Russian; the Russians rarely did anything except for profit; even revenge had pretty much disappeared as a motive. The new age of Russian crime was entirely invested in money, and though you occasionally ran into someone who still cared about the myth, it was mostly the dough. Where was the profit in killing a little girl then burying her bloody clothes? I was still half convinced Lippert had over-reacted. No body. No report. No nothing except the clothes.

I hit the gas harder and slipped my Getz/Gilberto album into the CD slot. People put it down, the album; they said Stan Getz sold out when he got together with João Gilberto and the record sold millions. Snobs those people who loved jazz only if it was Ornette Coleman making weird noises. I listened to the warm music; it was sublime is all.

The music was sweet. Once I would have fantasized about Brazil, going there, hanging out, eating the food, going to Bahia and Rio, meeting the girl from Ipanema. All those years I wanted to travel, to be able to just go. I didn't care anymore. I didn't want to leave New York. I had been, Moscow, London, Paris, Hong Kong, Vienna, Bosnia, you know? Made up for lost time. No more.

I ran my hand along the cream leather seat of the red Caddy I'd bought with a windfall I got a while back. It was in the shop more than out, but I loved it. I had a good sound system put in. Lily had been embarrassed by it, but Maxie loved it; to her it was great, luxurious, easy riding. The kids could fool around in the big back seat.

It was almost new, big and smooth as silk. It was the kind of car—a Cadillac—I had wanted from the time I was a kid in Moscow and I saw one in a picture in an illicit copy of *Life* magazine someone sold me in my school's toilet. The toilet was the center of commerce for Moscow kids in those days.

It was Saturday, but I called Sonny's office and got Rhonda Fisher, his assistant, and she said there was nothing yet, Lippert wasn't back from Coney Island, there were no formal reports in, and I asked if she'd let me have whatever had come, fax, e-mail. I lied and told her Sonny said it was OK. Rhonda said if she could find anything she'd drop it off at my place because she was meeting her sister at a play in the city. I said could she drop it with Mike Rizzi at the coffee shop, and we stayed on the phone exchanging banalities about logistics until I hung up and called Mike and asked him to give Rhonda key lime pie on me. Lemon meringue, if he was out of key lime.

And then there was Ivana Galitzine with the gray eyes and the lithe body. I couldn't shake her image.

"Will you invite me for coffee again?"

7

Put on the TV! Put the TV on!

It was late Saturday afternoon and I was at Mike's coffee shop, listening into my cell phone and yelling out to Mike who was frying bacon for a BLT for me on the griddle.

Turn on the TV, and he reached up to the set he kept on a shelf over the glass case of green melon slices and red Jello; he switched it on in time for us to catch a glimpse of Sonny Lippert and me in Coney Island.

I sat on my stool and stared at the TV and thought about how often I'd heard it, someone calling: Put on the TV. Last time, a few weeks earlier, Mike turned it on and we saw the shuttle fall from the sky. It fell invisibly, leaving only a graceful trail of white smoke. Later that day I saw body parts for sale on eBay.

"How do you think that works? I mean, do people just pick them up off the ground, like a finger or something, and put them up for auction?" I wanted to ask but I kept my mouth shut.

Put on the TV. It had become a regular occurrence,

these early morning phone calls, the news—the attacks, crashes, bombs—passed around the city, relayed, absorbed. 9/11. The snipers in D.C. The shuttle. It always seemed to happen in the morning when I was talking to Mike about the miserable state of New York sports.

I spent a lot of time in Mike Rizzi's coffee shop, which was opposite my building. I ate breakfast there, sometimes lunch. Mike kept the block running. He took packages, he kept an eye on the local kids, he knew the gossip. He was a cheerful optimistic guy. Whenever I left town, the first thing I did when I came home was stop in at Mike's. He'd see me pull up and wave and I'd go in and we'd shoot the breeze—who was moving in on the block, or out, how much the real estate prices were up, which asshole had failed to deliver his pies, if there had been any trouble with the crack-head kid who lived on the corner. Getting back to Mike's gave me a sense I'd survived another round.

Mike was a good-news junkie. He reported small triumphs regularly, his wife's attempts sell the necklaces she made out of seashells, his discovery of a new flavor Krispy Kreme donuts; it didn't matter. His big Italian face would split open and he'd ask me a million questions about my trip and I'd be home.

He picked up the glass coffee pot; I remembered it later, I remembered how the black liquid looked in the half full pot, the way the aromatic stream poured from the lip into the thick cup in front of me, the way the crumbs of the pie I ate littered the plate and made a pattern on it that I examined like tea leaves. I didn't know what the hell I was looking for, some kind of salvation, maybe, something to wake me up, make me stop thinking about Lily leaving.

I'd lost her. I'd done it. Hadn't I? Maxine said to me once, "She loved you, and you just let it go. You didn't really pay attention. You didn't understand she needed taking care of," and I thought, what? What did she mean? Lily was ferociously independent; she hated it when I made a fuss. Didn't she?

I got everything wrong with Lily, I thought now. I got it wrong and I also messed around with other women because I was a jerk and then 9/11 happened and I was at work all day and night and Lily was scared and angry.

"Sometimes I think we got what we deserved, America, I mean," she had said to me, and I blew up at her. She told me she thought we should understand why people hated America so much; she talked and talked about it when all I wanted, me and other cops and firemen, was to hang the bastards who did it to us. Hang them. Fry them. Lock them up forever. There were American flags hanging everywhere in downtown Manhattan; I put one up on my fire escape and it made her nuts; she despised the obsession with the flag. I couldn't listen. I was so angry I couldn't hear anything she was saying. I didn't notice it was her way of dealing with the terror.

She lost friends in the Trade Center, too, friends, a cousin, an ex-boyfriend. I didn't pay much attention. I didn't notice when she started avoiding me. Then she left for good. Got married to someone else, took Beth, and left. I missed Beth, her little girl, the baby I had helped her adopt. I had started believing Beth was mine in a way, and then they left. It was the thing I tried not to say out loud; that Lily was gone for good was a fact, but I denied it. It made me feel short of oxygen. I read somewhere that frogs shut down completely if it's too cold; they turn off all their systems and remain like that, until spring, as if dead. Sometimes I wished I could do it.

This time I would pay attention. I wasn't going to lose Maxine because I was an asshole. I was feeling better. I really was. Sitting there I was celebrating with a huge slice of key lime pie. Tuna without mayo and decaf would have been a better option, I'd already had pie for breakfast but I wanted more pie, and caffeine.

"Cold out, right, Artie?"

"Yeah. Really cold."

"Witch's tit in a brass bra we used to say when we were kids," Mike said. "That's how cold. Maybe I'm going to try skiing this year."

I laughed and he poured more coffee. It was freezing. Coldest winter in twenty years, people said over and over, hating it, loving it, whining. Chunks of ice littered the river. A vicious wind blew all the time, howling, bleating, making you want to stay in bed all day, hibernate like the bears. We complained. New Yorkers loved extremes; it made us feel superior, made us feel we were survivors. People wrapped their babies up in plastic like meat for the freezer, someone said. I thought about the long weekend ahead.

"Artie? You OK?"

I've known Mike Rizzi ever since I moved into the

building across the street, almost a dozen years. He grew up in the neighborhood, over on Mulberry Street. He was Italian but he was nuts about Greece; he figured a guy who inherited a coffee shop in Manhattan along with a lifetime supply of cups with a classical frieze had a debt to Greece. It was his destiny. The picture of Anthony Quinn as Zorba remained on the wall even after Quinn died.

"Quinn's a Mexican," I used to say.

"Greek in spirit," Mikey would say.

"How long have you been down here, Mike?"

"Must be fifteen, sixteen years. Since my old man retired."

He was here when I moved in; this part of Broadway was still raw and cheap and a cop like me could almost afford an apartment. Weird artists squatted in lofts nearby. Sweatshops still occupied most of the buildings then; you could tell by the steam pipes that stuck out of the old walls.

From my window in the building opposite Mike's, I could see his place. Above it there had been a shop where girls, bent over their machines, sewed wedding veils. It was gone now; a design firm had moved in. Pretty girls in black sat by the open window and smoked.

In the afternoons, when business was slow, sometimes I saw Mike studying, Greek history, or the menus from wholesale bakeries; pies were his draw. He liked it known he served the best pies around, which was a magnet for cops and firemen and a few other regulars.

In the early morning in the winter when it was still dark and there was nothing else lit up on the street, I sometimes looked down from my place at the coffee shop below; it looked, illuminated from inside, like a toy diner.

When I was still with Lily, sometimes I went up to Balthazar for breakfast with her and some friends she had there, and we ate the buttery croissants that left flakes on your hands and mouth and oatmeal scones, and we talked books and politics; sometimes I watched another group who were also regulars; they laughed more than we did; sometimes they yelled with laughter and they were older than us; I envied them.

"You OK, man?" Mike said again, watching me. "You have to stop thinking about it, Lily, and the other thing, both." He gestured at the picture on his wall because he saw me looking.

Mike kept the picture of the Trade Center in a place of honor in the middle of the mirrored wall over the juggernaut of cereal boxes and a cake-stand with a pile of Danish pastry. It was a photograph of the buildings before they fell. In the margins, one of Mike's customers had painted angels and over them the names of the friends Mike lost: firemen, cops, people who used to stop by; I looked at it every morning when I ate breakfast. I couldn't stop looking; 9/11 was like an addiction.

September 11. We heard the thunder. We saw the fireballs. Mike's windows cracked, the dust was everywhere. Then people came running. The Dust People, they swamped Mike's place, it was jammed up with people and the dust. We called it dust because we didn't know what else to call it. Eighteen months ago. People felt embarrassed because they were still dreaming bad stuff; they kept it in now, they didn't talk about it, but nothing was the same. Everybody felt it down where I still lived on Walker Street. You couldn't live in downtown Manhattan and stay the same, especially if, like me, you were a cop and knew guys who got incinerated. Cops. Firemen. Emergency workers. The ones who lived through it had asbestos in their lungs. Coughing blood was something you kept to yourself; I was still coughing, but I canceled the doctor's appointments and told myself it was the cigarettes I had to stop, and couldn't.

Downtown that day, I didn't want to think about it anymore, or about the days afterwards we spent digging. I dreamed about it every night. It changed me. People thought: get over it already; you could see it in their faces, so I tried. I didn't want to travel, didn't want to leave my neighborhood, my friends, my apartment. If New York was going to stay standing, I had to put my arms around it.

I was feeling OK, I told myself; I was fine. It was a three-day weekend.

"You doing anything special for the weekend?" Mike said.

"President's Day, right? Which President?" I said.

"Yeah, well they merged them, we used to have Lincoln's Birthday and Washington's Birthday and they were like a week apart, so they made them into one. I thought you took that on your test to be a citizen."

"We're talking twenty-five years since I signed up." I grinned. "More than."

"Yeah? We should have a party. You want me to make you a party, red white and blue cake, all that?"

"I'll think about it, Mike, OK? Maybe that would be nice."

"You want another piece of pie, Artie?" Mike looked at my empty plate. "It was good, right?"

"It was sensational," I said. "Yeah, great."

He slipped a second piece onto my plate and glanced at the sports section of the *Post*, engrossed in the news that Spree had been stopped in his Range Rover for possible speeding, still mumbling about how the Knicks had dismissed Spree the year before and then had to take him back. New York basketball had been in decline for Mike since the Knicks dumped Patrick Ewing. Mikey was a sweet guy, but he held a long hard grudge where sports were concerned.

A noise in the street startled me.

I jumped. Mike looked up. I got the notebook out of my back pocket; instead of writing, I doodled on a page and drank the coffee. I had gotten into the habit of writing stuff down during those weeks when time seemed suspended. Wrote stuff down so I'd know what I was thinking. I was scared. I was scared I was losing my mind like my mother.

War was coming. The economy shot. The shuttle down. Snipers in Washington D.C. Homeland Security, the stupid fucks who didn't know dick about security, just scared everyone. The homeless out on the streets again like you hadn't seen them for ten years. The country on alert. Yellow. Orange. Red. Lily gone. I didn't know how they felt out there in the rest of America; in New York, we blustered and yelled and joked and shopped, but we were scared.

9/11 hovered like a ghost. You looked up, waiting for the next plane, still expecting it, flying too low along West Broadway. I heard about this guy who lived on the 26th floor of a building near Washington Square.

That morning he's shaving and peering in the mirror, working his electric razor along his face, thinking about the day ahead, maybe choosing a tie in his mind, or wondering if he's going to cut the deal he's been working on or get a date with a girl he likes, maybe not thinking at all, and he hears a plane roaring by and he looks out of the window and sees into the plane, into the plane windows, into the faces. He sees their faces.

"Artie?"

"Yeah? Sorry."

"Why don't you get serious about Maxine? She's a nice girl. I like her. Bring her over this weekend. Angie's going to make braciol, OK? I'm calling her now. I'm calling her and saying you're bringing Maxine Sunday, we'll eat and we'll rent a dumb movie and get a little drunk, OK? She's a good girl. She loves you, you know. Come on, say you'll bring her over."

Mike took a UPS package from under the counter.

"This came. I forgot."

"Thanks," I said, and put on my jacket and, on the way across the street, ripped open the package. It was a book on fish for Billy whose birthday was coming up. Twelve already. He'd be twelve.

8

"How the hell do you know it's a girl," I said to Sonny over the phone, the half opened package still in my hand, my front door ajar. It came to me out of the blue: maybe it wasn't a girl.

"Where are you?"

"I just got home."

"Listen to me, Art. It's a girl. Every other case, it's been a girl. The case I told you, the other case, the girl with the green sneakers before, it was the same. The girl on Long Island. This is the same. He goes for girls."

"You're sure?"

"What's the matter with you?" he said and hung up.

I shut the door and put the package on the kitchen counter. Billy would be twelve in a few weeks. Gen had called to say it was a big birthday for him, so I got the book. I also planned on taking him fishing somewhere great, maybe out to Montauk if the weather held. One day I'd take him out to Montana for the real thing. Some day if Gen let me. It was the way I felt about the kid that had made me crazy out in Brooklyn earlier, but it was

OK now, he was upstate, the blood-soaked clothes were not his, I told myself for the fourth time and then I got a beer out of the fridge.

The last of the day's sun was coming through the big loft windows and it lit up the place. When I first bought into the building, the space was pretty raw. It took years to fix it right, I did the floors myself, I scraped down the industrial windows. It was the only place I'd ever owned.

I put Little Richard singing "Tutti Frutti' on the CD player, turned it up loud and ignored the banging on the wall from the next door apartment. The music, the meaningless lyrics, were good and raucous and the beer was cold. I sat on the floor and began looking at the pile of paper Johnny Farone had given me.

Farone's accounts were a mess. I was surprised Genia let him get away with it. Maybe she didn't want to rock the boat. Johnny was her American dreamboat, wasn't he? I dialed Genia's number again; there was no answer. I called her cell phone. Nothing.

For half an hour, I sorted paper. Little Richard irritated me after a while, all that falsetto howling, and I turned it off and put the radio on, listened to Sinatra, then put on Stan Getz's "Spring Is Here". It made me think of Lily.

I matched up the receipts with Johnny's books. I put the disk into my computer. A couple of hours later it was clear to me who was taking from Farone's. Hard to believe, I thought, and went back and checked everything again, called Johnny and asked who had access to his books.

"You found something?" he said into the phone.

"Not yet," I said. "I'm on it, OK?" I added, but I was lying.

77

I was pretty sure it was Genia taking the money from Johnny. Only Gen had access to his checkbooks, his accounts, the cash box. Farone's was a high cash business, like he said, and there was cash missing. Every time I went through it, it came back to Genia.

Maybe she was salting it away for Billy; maybe there was someone in Russia she sent money to; maybe it was for a rainy day or she planned on leaving Farone. But why? He was the best thing that ever happened to her, wasn't he?

And Genia was studying to be an accountant; she'd insisted on doing Farone's books. She was smart; she could fool Farone. I didn't know if she was swiping the truffles and the wine; the cash I was sure about.

I picked up the phone to call her, then put it back. We weren't close. Genia was a distant cousin of my father's who looked me up when she got to New York years ago. I didn't pay much attention. I didn't want to own any part of my past.

After she had Billy, I saw her more often, and she called regularly and invited me to eat with them. Except for my mother who had Alzheimer's and didn't know me, she was the only member of my family I still had any contact with. The others were dead or had disappeared when the Soviet thing broke up and spilled its cracked pieces—those who could get out—in a hundred directions. The imperial crack-up, the Soviet diaspora, gone. Nothing to do with me anymore. I'd left long ago. But Genia called and said it was important, we were all the family we had, and I felt guilty and I went, but always alone. Lily didn't like her.

I looked at Johnny's account book again. I wasn't going to touch this. I'd tell Johnny that I couldn't find out anything, that I couldn't see who was taking his dough. Let them figure it out, I thought, picked up the phone to call Lippert again, got the machine.

I took a shower, I got dressed, then went back to my desk and stared at the photograph of Billy Farone. Lippert made me promise I'd stay by the phone, but I was restless. When the phone rang, I jumped for it. I recognized the voice. It was Ivana Galitzine and she wanted to meet. She said she had thought of something and wondered if we could meet and asked me if I would come out to see her later. Or she would meet me somewhere else, in the city if necessary. I said I'd get to her later, and she gave me the address. It couldn't do any harm to stop by Galitzine's place on my way to Maxie. What harm could it do if I went back to see her?

The long weekend stretched ahead. I'd keep the phone with me, like Sonny wanted. Fill up the time, keep my mind off Lily. Later I'd go over to Maxine's.

It was late Saturday afternoon now, usually a bad time for me. We'd always spent Saturday together, Saturday, Sunday morning, me and Lily. I put some money in my pocket. I'd go get my stuff from the cleaner's, I thought. Get my bike serviced. Buy some flowers to take to Maxie's. A blizzard was predicted for Monday, snow coming up the coast; maybe I'd get out my skis and practice in the park.

Don't do anything, Sonny had said. Just stay with the phone. When the phone rang again, I lurched across the room to answer it.

79

9

"You were expecting maybe someone hot, some hot chicken?"

Tolya Sverdloff bellowed with laughter over the phone. I told him to knock it off and anyway you couldn't say hot chicken. Chick, maybe, though no one said chick anymore, but not chicken, and I could hear his voice turn sulky at the implication that his English wasn't perfect. I was pretty happy to hear his voice, though. As usual, the phone call was followed by the buzzer and a voice that announced he was downstairs with groceries. When Tolya showed up that day, I was glad as hell, tell the truth, to see him.

"Artyom!" he exploded when I opened the door. Tolya was the only person in my life who still called me Artyom, my old Russian nickname. He was the only person I'd told about it. It wasn't a common name and a guy I knew in Moscow said once I stole it from him and never forgave me. Like me, Tolya was born in Moscow but he was a few years younger and we had never met there. He spoke five languages, six if you included Ukrainian.

Tolya's showing up took my mind off everything, especially when he arrived, right off the plane from Miami, with an eighteen-year-old single malt and a bag of food that included fresh crab packed in dry ice. Tolya never simply arrived; he made an appearance. The phone would ring and he'd be there, a rabbit out of a hat, arms full of presents and booze and food. A big rabbit.

I was six one, but I was a shrimp next to Tolya. He was six six, three hundred pounds, give or take. His size and his passion for food were a certainty in a world that had pretty much gone to hell. Terrorism, murder, the break-up of empires, a lousy economy, Tolya loved to eat.

Food was his religion; he believed that good food and booze were essential to a happy life; he believed it like an ethical system, a moral code. Without decent food, he explained to me once in Paris, you couldn't function, your brain was half dead.

"Thank God you're here," he said.

"Why?"

"My mother."

"She's OK?"

"She's here. I mean in America, in Brooklyn. Suddenly she doesn't want to stay in Manhattan, she won't stay at the Four Seasons either anymore, she wants to stay with her people. What fucking people? The Russians, she says. In Brighton Beach. I have to run around and find somewhere she can stay and I have to eat with her tonight, so you'll come, right?"

"Yeah, sure."

"Thank God. So you're hungry?" Tolya asked, eyes full of child-like anticipation.

"I could eat."

"I brought late lunch."

He spread the bags on the kitchen counter. He tossed the ice packs into my freezer and sniffed the crab.

"Still fresh," he said triumphantly.

"They let you carry all this stuff on the plane?"

"Please, Artyom, what's the matter with you, you think I fly commercial?"

We settled at the kitchen counter. We sipped a little whiskey while the wine chilled and Tolya cracked the crab with a hammer and made some mayonnaise fresh and fixed a salad out of the mesclun he also had in his bag. I sliced up a loaf of sourdough and opened the bottle of white Burgundy, then poured it into my best glasses; we ate.

"Nice, huh, Artemy?" he said holding his wine glass up to the light and admiring the lemony color. "Corton-Charlemagne is like drinking paradise."

Anatoly Sverdloff was a civilized guy who could discuss semiotics in French and rock and roll in Chinese, Pushkin in Russian and Conrad in English. His languages, his brains, his charm would have made him a great spy except he had a big mouth, in every sense, and a lot of appetite, and he loved money. Lots of it. Anyhow, as he always said, who would you spy for these days?

In the bad old days he was a DJ in Moscow who broadcast rock records to the fucking miserable Chinese when the poor bastards didn't have anything, no Internet, no music, no fashion. It was after I'd left Russia that he became famous for his sedition; brave and silly, for a while in the last days of the old Soviet Union, he became a cult hero.

Even now he carried around the tattered paper copy of *Nineteen Eighty-Four* that he'd had as a boy, a book he bought, as if it was a drug, from another kid at his school. When the old world fell apart, while I was busy turning myself into an American, he translated himself into a capitalist and made tons of money. His father, Anatoly, Sr., was a famous actor at the Moscow Arts Theater, his mother Lara Sverdlova was an actress; the intellectual's cupcake, they used to called her.

Tolya knew his way around high culture, but he played the part of an international hood: he flaunted it, he wore the silk shirts, the cashmere coats, smoked the Cohibas. "I am not corporate guy," he always said.

"You mean you don't drink the Kool-Aid to get the deal."

"What is this Kool-Aid?" he'd asked and I explained about Jonestown and how Jim Jones, the leader of a sinister cult, made his disciples commit suicide by drinking cyanide-laced Kool-Aid; they did it all together, in unison, they took his orders. Jones just said: drink. They drank. Like good corporate underlings.

Tolya loved it.

When he met other guys in his trade, whatever it was, he hugged them and made as if he was some kind of godfather. I never knew for sure how deep he was involved with these people. When he drank, and he drank plenty, he sometimes spoke English with a low class Russian accent, dropping the articles, making himself sound like a gangster. It suited him, it was an escape from the old life where his parents were part of the intelligentsia and he was the smartest boy in town. He had become his own invention; it was his cover, his escape, the way being a New York cop was for me.

Tolya pulled a CD out of his pocket and gave it to me.

"You heard of these kids?" he said. "I am thinking of putting in money for American tour, you know? Cute," he said. "Dirty."

I looked at the cover. A trio of Russian schoolgirls making out. I put it on, it wasn't bad, and we finished the crab and talked about stuff, his family, Lily, people we knew. All the time I was aware of the cell phone on the counter.

"You expecting a call, Artyom?" he said. "A woman? Someone new?"

I didn't say anything. He finished the wine and poured some of the whiskey into fresh glasses and extracted two big Havanas from a heavy gold case he always carried in his jacket pocket. On it was engraved the outline of a cigar with a big ruby set at one end for the burning tip.

"No, thanks," I said.

"Just for once," he said. "I got them from Fidel. I go see him to talk business, he opens his own humidor and gives them to me. You believe me?"

"Why wouldn't I believe you?"

"Because you have that look, but is true," he said.

"I believe you. So how is Fidel these days? Cracking down on dissidents? Tossing people in the slammer?"

"Old," he said. "He's a crazy old man."

"I used to have a soft spot for him, you know, Tol? My father, when he was in the KGB went to Cuba in the early days of the Revolution, he was a fan, he loved Fidel, Cienfuegos. He idolized Che, he kept pictures of them in his office, him and Che joking around. Che gave him a beret. One of his own. I should have kept it. I could have made a fortune on eBay, right?"

"Commie kitsch is very big, sure, I go to Berlin, the kids are pining for East, they buy old Trabant cars. Shit is what this is," he said then smiled. "I made a killing when I went to auction, my Soviet train set, tablecloth from Kremlin with hammer and sickle embroidered, everything gets big bucks." He started to laugh.

"My mother would take them down, the photographs of Che, and tear them up, but my father kept copies. Long time." I puffed at the cigar. "What a bunch of assholes," I added. "Fucking communism, fucking nothing."

Tolya said, "We'll go on vacation, you and me, I'll show you Cuba. You'll love it, the Malecon at sunset, the music, the women. Oh, Artyom, the women are so beautiful, so sweet, like a dream."

"I'll pass."

"Why, you're worried they'll think we're a couple of queers and lock us up? You worry too much, but it's why I love you, Artyom," he said switching easily from English to the beautiful purring Russian he speaks that makes me feel my soul is being fingered.

I said, "So, any deals? You're still doing business with those creeps in Moscow?"

"Moscow, Kiev, Shanghai, Baku, Havana, Hanoi,

Alaska, I don't give a shit where they come from if they have the money, I feel it's my destiny to do the deals, you know?"

"So you said."

I didn't ask about his deals or how he made his money; he was my friend; we had shared the salt, as the Russians say; it was enough.

"I'm not like you, Artyom. You got rid of the accent, the memories, the past, you came to New York to be an American, and you unloaded it all. I don't want to be an American," he said.

I taunted him. "How come? They won't let you?"

"You want to know?'

"Go on."

"New York, I love, yeah, maybe New Orleans for food and music, Los Angeles for art, OK, fishing in Montana. I love East Hampton for the parties, OK? But the rest? I don't get it," he said and puffed on his cigar. "I don't like the way they make a fetish out of the flag, I don't like the religious bullshit. I look at the TV news, and I think this is the kind of shit I watched at home. This is news by old Pravda. Also, they're not subtle. Americans. They're not subtle, they don't read, they don't go anywhere."

"My father thought like that about America," I said. "The KGB loved him for it."

Tolya laughed. "How's your mother?"

"Lousy," I said. "The same. Nothing ever changes for her."

I was sixteen when we left Moscow for Israel. Two

years later, my father was dead. A bomb blew up the bus he was on. My mother stayed, she had a job, friends. Now she was in the last stages of Alzheimer's at the nursing home in Haifa; she didn't know who the hell I was. I'd had a letter from my friend Hamid the day before. He was a doctor who looked in on her once in a while. There was nothing they could do.

"How come you're not bitter?" I'd polished off a couple of shots of the whiskey and I'd always meant to ask him. "How come?"

"You mean because of those fartofskis in Moscow who locked me once up for a few days when I played rock and roll in public, and humped the bass? Who gives a shit?" he said. "It's old history. So what's going on, you need me to save your ass again, Artyom, what's happening?" He peered over the cigar smoke, then noticed the book about fish on the kitchen counter. He picked it up.

"You're into pictures of fish now?"

"It's for Billy."

"Your cousin's kid? How is he?"

"He's good."

"You like that boy, don't you?"

"Yeah," I said, distracted. I was thinking about the Farones. The first time Tolya had bailed me out was on the case in Brighton Beach when I met Johnny Farone.

I wanted to ask Tolya about Lily because I knew they were in touch, but I felt shy about it. He took care of her when she was attacked and almost died and I loved him for it. They had something between them that I wasn't part of; he took care of her in a way I couldn't because he had access to the best doctors and private planes and because he loved her like a friend, no complications.

"What do you think?" he held out the jacket he wore and stroked the fabric with one hand. "Loro Piano," he said. "I get them made up custom."

"Nice."

"Nice? This is beyond nice. You want me to get you one?"

"OK, beyond nice," I said and touched the fabric. "It's perfection, it's fabulous, it's as if woven by the tiny hands of a thousand virgins. It's terrific."

"I'll get you one."

"Thank you."

"What color?"

"You decide."

"I'll get you two," he said. "I'll get you black and they have a very nice blue. Match your eyes. Women like that. You want gold buttons? Sterling? How come you didn't call me for three weeks, Artie?"

"I've been busy. But I got you something." I went to my desk and picked up the book I'd bought in Brighton Beach.

Tolya's face lit up. "For me?"

"Yeah, I owe you one."

He unwrapped the book, a first edition of a Turgenev novel I knew he loved. He kissed me Russian style, three times on the cheek.

"OK, I accept this apology, for not being in touch," he said. "How come you're so jumpy? What's with the phone? You keep looking at it. This is a woman you're waiting for? Finally you have someone new?"

"No."

He put his hand on my arm.

"Lily's not coming back," he said softly.

"Yeah. You saw her?" I pretended not to care.

"You want me to lie to you?"

I shook my head.

"She's happy," Tolya said. "The husband has no sense of humor. What can I say? He makes a lot of money, he takes care of her like she's a piece of precious glass, he supports her causes."

"Beth?"

"He's very nice with Beth. He has a daughter from his other marriage, a little older, but the girls are friends. I think this is working for all of them."

"And he's not a cop." I poured some more whiskey into my glass and took a puff on the cigar. "Right? So what does he drive?"

"You want me to say he drives a little pussy design car, right?"

"You read my mind."

"Yeah, he does. Don't be sad," he said in Russian. "I have some good news."

"Fine," I said.

"Come on."

"Where?"

"Surprise."

I glanced at the phone.

"Take your cell with you. We're not going far."

I picked up the phone, put on my jacket, waited until Tolya put his on, and both of us smoking the cigars he swore Castro had given him, we left my place, and walked north on Broadway.

On the way, Tolya, like a kid who couldn't wait to open his presents, told me the news. He was leaving Miami. He would keep an apartment in South Beach, but he was moving to the city. He'd bought a place in Soho. He cut west on Spring Street to West Broadway and stopped halfway up the block.

I was glad. Glad he was in New York, glad he'd be close by. I tossed the cigar into the gutter and turned to follow him into the building, clutching my cell phone.

"You get a decent signal in here?"

Tolya looked at me. "Sure. But what's with the obsession, you're hanging onto that phone like it was a lifeline."

"It's just a case I'm working."

The huge vaulted loft was on two floors, his office downstairs, the living space up. A terrace surrounded the top floor; you could see the city in every direction from it, the Soho rooftops and the Chrysler Building. Acres of some rare pale wood covered the floors. The kitchen, all stainless steel and glass, was in and Tolya, like a proud housewife, showed me the Sub-Zero fridge that was stocked with vintage champagne and hummed with power. In the middle of the main space, two architects, a contractor, a designer stood around a makeshift table fingering a sheaf of blueprints and arguing.

In the face of all of it Tolya seemed pretty fucking meek, if you asked me. He listened. He paid attention. He was caught up in the details of the work. He took the half pounder gold lighter out of his pocket and lit a cigarette and when one of the architects—a woman with a sour mouth—waved the smoke away, he put it out. With the toe of one of his green suede Gucci loafers— he got them made up in different colors, a dozen at a time, all with 18 karat gold buckles—he kicked at the newly laid wooden floor. His eyes, set deep in the head that was big as an Easter Island statue, followed the architects. I didn't get it, the way he paid so much heed to these people.

He hustled me into the bedroom, showed me the dressing room he'd had built. Everywhere boxes were piled, tissue paper spilling out, contents scattered around the room like a Christmas morning at Ali Baba's palace.

"I went shopping," he said. "I got carried away."

I glanced at the shoeboxes piled in shaky towers in one corner, and a makeshift coat rack where custom-made suits from Brioni hung in rows.

"I don't fit regular sizes," he said, a little sheepishly. "Come on." He led me back into the main room.

"Fuck off!"

Suddenly, out of nowhere, standing in the middle of the cavernous loft, the architects and designers arguing, bickering, whining like a gang of cats while they considered ways to spend his money, Tolya boiled over.

"Fuck off!" He leaned over the four of them and for a minute I thought he was going to crack their heads together like a quartet of walnuts, but instead he swore at them and ordered them out and there was a sudden hush. In a very chilly voice, in perfect English, Tolya told them, one more time: fuck off. The four picked up their coats and portfolios and scrambled for the door.

I leaned against a trestle table and lit up a cigarette.

"How come you put up with it?" I said.

"I liked the woman," he said. "I wanted her so I gave her the job."

Tolya looked sly. Women were his weakness. Normally he liked them young and gorgeous, strippers, hookers, models, so I didn't get it. The dour architect, dressed in black with a wedge of black hair over her eyes, was a departure for Tolya.

"You're surprised? You thought she was a dog, didn't you, Art?"

I laughed. "For sure not a hot chicken."

"I thought she had class," he said. "She went to Yale. And Oxford. The Sorbonne."

"You're impressed?"

"You think I should stick to hookers, Artyom?" He peered at me as if for the first time. "What's eating you?"

We sat on a pair of chairs in his loft and he poured vodka and we smoked and I told him about the blood-drenched clothes by the beach. Sonny Lippert had told me to keep my mouth shut on the subject but I didn't count Tolya. He kept quiet when it mattered. He had his own secrets and, more important, he was my friend.

I told him about the blood-soaked clothes, told him Lippert said the girl was dead and I wasn't convinced. I unloaded on him and while I talked, he listened, his huge body folding down onto itself as he lit one cigarette after another and knocked back half a bottle of Stoli. I'd never seen so much anguish in him and I didn't understand.

"Tolya?"

He waved me away and turned his back to me and walked across the floor. He faced the wall and leaned against it and I saw him sob; his back heaved with crying. When he turned around, he walked slowly back, sat down, picked up the bottle and drank steadily from it until it was empty.

Watching him I remembered Lippert's warning. Keep it zipped, he'd said. Now I wondered if I should have told Tolya.

I leaned my elbows on my knees and put a hand on his arm.

"What is it, Tol? You know something? You think she's dead?"

"They did this to my daughter once," he said. "I don't mean they killed her, but they kidnapped her, just took her, they stole her from me, and they marked her. I never told you. I never told anyone. I couldn't talk about it. I promised her I would never talk because she was ashamed.

"They took her and held her for one week, Artyom. A whole week they kept her in a closet, she was ten. I sent the money. I offered myself in exchange, but they kept her and when they sent her back, they had cut marks in her face and cut off her finger. They told her they ate little girls and this was why they took the finger, and she believes them and for two years she doesn't eat.

"They marked her. They took my daughter. They took her away in the middle of the night and I was there. You understand? I wake up and I know something is wrong." Tolya's voice cracked. "We have a big

93

apartment, high ceilings, large furniture, something left over from a high apparatchik who had lived in it and lost favor or some shit, you see this, Artyom? Imagine, I'm asleep. I have come in late, so I should be guilty because I have been out with some rock and roll asshole from the West, we still think of it as West, and it's late, and I've been drinking plenty, and my wife is asleep and I think, she'll smell it on me, that I have been places I should not be, vodka, cigars, women, you know the smell of women you cannot wash off?" He got up and sat down again.

"So I go to sleep on the sofa. I remember. Red leather sofa from Poltrona Frau in Germany, you know I'm so into my things, Artyom, first time I have real money, I just shop. Later that night, I get up, the apartment is very large and the kids have their rooms at the other end, so I hear myself walk around like a hippopotamus, and I trample over the floor, and feel it, marble, cold under my feet. I open her door and the bed is empty. She has gone. Just gone. No one there, just the empty room."

"Valentina?"

"Yes," he said.

I knew that the girls, his twins, lived in Florida now with Tolya's second ex-wife. All he ever told me was the good news, their achievements, their successes in high school. He showed their pictures to me once in a while; the pair of them, teenagers with fiery red hair and Tolya's dimples imprinted on their cheeks to remind you they were his.

I said, "What about Masha?"

He said, "She was at a friend's. But Valentina, they kept her. For one week. For one week while I try to

94

make deals with everyone, even God, which is something I hate and despise, the Russian God. But I promise.
They send her back, but it's not her."

"I'm sorry."

"She was not the same kid afterwards," Tolya said.

"Why didn't you tell me?"

"I promised her I would never tell anyone. She's in
high school now. She's an American kid in high school
in Florida. She got early admission for Harvard. It's
better now, but she was never the same. She became an
imitation of her old self, she looks fine, she does well in
school, but she was never the same, the pleasure was all
gone. I don't know who are the monsters who do this
and for what? You want to walk a while?"

He got up slowly, then turned to look at me. "You
know why they do this to children?"

"Why?"

"Sometimes because they are weak and enraged.
Sometimes because it's the best way to get to the parents,
for revenge on the parents, to destroy you. Everywhere
they do this to children. Also," he said and looked at me
hard.

"Also?"

"You believe in evil?"

"I don't know."

"I know. Let's walk."

He turned out the lights and we left the loft. Tolya
locked the door. It was dark now and the wind whipped
in from the river so bitterly cold it hurt my face.

I said, "Listen, even if anyone's missing, we don't
know if there's a dead girl, do we?"

"What else would it be?" he said. "Don't fool yourself."

"How do they know it's a girl?"

He didn't answer.

"You want to stay at my place while they finish your loft?" I said.

He shook his head. "I have the penthouse suite at 60 Mercer," Tolya said. "Let me help you with this case you're on."

"Not yet," I said.

I made excuses. I didn't want him with me. He would attract attention. Later, I would need him but not now, so I lied and told him I was only going home, I was tired, I had paperwork to do, and he just said, OK, he'd be at the hotel. I didn't believe him. I knew he was already figuring who he knew, who could help, who would make a deal to give him information about a little girl whose blood-soaked clothes had been found near the boardwalk. She was like a ghost who had shed her skins. Tolya, carrying his own obsessions, his own hurt, the memories of his daughter, he would scratch at the case until he fixed things.

He said, "You won't forget."

"What?"

"My mother. Dinner, OK? Later? Nine, ten?"

"As soon as I can," I said. "Where?"

"She wants to eat in Brooklyn. What about Farone's place? You'll come?"

"Yes," I said and left him on the corner of Spring Street, a huge figure heading west, head bowed.

Part Two

10

"We know who she is," Sonny said, very flat,

I found him at the gym he used close to his apartment in Battery Park City. He was on the treadmill in worn blue sweatpants, reading, the book propped on the handlebars. He heard me come in and looked up. It was Saturday night. The gym was empty.

"Who? Who is she? Sonny, tell me." I was yelling now, up close to him, as close as I could get to the treadmill.

Sonny said, "I've been going through Dostoyevsky again, you know, man, I'm reading *Notes from the Underground*, and I think, OK, this is it, this is where it begins. I'm sorry, man, I'm rambling. I wish I could sleep."

"Tell me who the girl is."

Most nights if I needed him, I could find Sonny in the gym, tense, coiled, head down, walking the treadmill, reading Dickens or Dostoevsky, Melville, Tolstoy, Conrad. Sonny liked big books. Big in both senses, he told me once; he liked books with big themes, he liked fat books. Weighed them in his hands when he brought a new one into the office. He would take the book out of the bag and balance it on both hands, I saw him do it a few times, palms turned up, the book on them as if his hands were scales.

These books kept him going nights when he couldn't sleep. He had been like this since the Chinatown fire six or seven years back when he had to identify thirty-seven bodies.

"You found her?"

"The parents called her in missing. Her name is May Luca. She went to her grandmother's yesterday morning early, like she was supposed to, there was some miscommunication and they thought she went and only when she didn't come home they figured something was wrong. The grandmother never called because she figured the kid changed her mind. The kid was wearing a blue baseball jacket and green sneaks."

"You weren't going to tell me?" I said. "You weren't planning to let me know you found out who the kid was?"

"Yeah, yeah," Sonny said, distracted.

"So what are you doing here?"

He climbed off the treadmill, picked up a towel from a bench and wiped his face.

"What else am I going to do? Run around Brooklyn? I got a dozen guys on this. Stay home and watch reality TV? I got plenty of reality. What?" he said. "Look, what I said this morning still goes, I want you by the phone, we know who she is, we don't know where she is, OK? We're still nowhere."

"You said you wanted me in clean space. What did you mean?"

"Instinctive."

"You think everyone's corrupt, don't you? You think there's no more good guys."

"Pretty much, yeah, that's right."

"You want to tell me anything about this Luca girl?"

"Come on," he said, disappeared into the locker room, came back ten minutes later, wearing jeans and a sweatshirt and his overcoat. Lippert's hair was wet, plastered to his head like a helmet.

We walked to his apartment, not saying much as we passed the hole in the ground where the Trade Center had been. People said the city had moved on. Outsiders got bored with New York's obsession. People said we were over the worst. It wasn't true.

At night the pit was still floodlit, eerie, secret now with the high fence concealing most of it from traffic. The tourists were gone. The work went on, orderly, professional. The heroics were over; even the thieves who stole from the site were gone, workers plundering the underbelly of the site as if it were a pharaoh's tomb: piles of jeans in the cab of a fire truck; Rolex watches from a shop that had remained almost intact; scrap metal. Now, nothing except barricades and cement blocks were left and cops to keep you from getting close.

There were barricades everywhere in the city. Cops, state troopers, national guardsmen in big camouflage jackets, knitted face masks to keep them warm, AK47s cradled in their arms, were everywhere. On TV pasty-faced bureaucrats urged us to stock up on water and duct

101

tape. Got your duck tape everyone said sarcastically. We were encouraged to root for war in Iraq. We were bombarded with patriotic shit. It made me nuts; like Tolya said, the propaganda was like Moscow in the old days.

War was coming. Terror. Chaos. Some nights it hardly seemed like New York anymore; it seemed like a foreign country, some place in the Balkans, silent, cold, the hole in the ground lit up by the huge sulphurous spotlights, the masked men with automatic weapons.

The government stoked the fear; in New York we laughed about how stupid the FBI was, how idiotic the Homeland Security. They told us to buy duct tape; we went out and got drunk. I knew a girl in the East Village, an artist who turned her tape into an art object and sold it to some dumb tourists for thousands. Someone else made a ball gown from it.

We laughed; we were tense. The whole city was like an armed camp and it got to you eventually. A few days earlier I'd been in the subway on the 6 train, going uptown to the dentist. My car was in the shop. Suddenly, at Union Square, the train emptied out. I was alone. The car I was in shunted forward and back, then stopped. Within a few seconds, there was an announcement: the train ahead of us was late into the station. Nothing to worry about. It got to me. At 23rd Street, I got out and ran up the steps and jogged home in the dark. I was scared.

Lippert's apartment was a one bedroom with a view of the river. It was furnished with a sofa and chair covered in gray tweed and it was as bland as an office except for his books. Sonny had moved in after his divorce. He glanced out at the river and the skyline, then went into the kitchen and found a bottle of Scotch and some glasses.

I sat on a tweed chair. Sonny crouched on the sofa.

"Can we just go over everything, I mean, look, the jogger runs over something this morning, right? What time did you get the call?"

He drank the Scotch. "Around ten," he said.

"The jogger, this Ivana Galitzine, goes out for a run and trips over something that scares her. She looks; it's a kid's clothes drenched in blood. She runs to find a cop, weird, right, I mean she's running down from the beach and she finds these clothes out in plain sight which is already odd, and she's Russian and her first impulse is to call a cop in a neighborhood where everyone's scared of cops?" Sonny drank some more.

"Anyhow, now it turns out the kid who maybe was wearing those clothes lives near Sheepshead Bay. Ivana lives off Brighton 8th Street, a mile away. And what kind of people don't notice their kid's been missing all day? What kind of people don't notice their kid is gone?"

I drank the rest of my Scotch and reached for cigarettes; before I lit up I asked Sonny's permission; these days, you had to ask.

"Poor people," Sonny said. "People who are trying to hold a lot of shit together maybe don't notice their kid is out of the house. They're glad the kid's doing something. People who have three, four kids and two jobs each and not enough money to make it through the week. Those kind of people."

103

"Have another drink," he said and I could see he was lonely.

I looked at my watch. I had promised Tolya I'd be in Brooklyn by nine.

"I have some stuff to do," I said, but I stayed where I was and held out my glass. "Make it a short one."

Lippert picked up a Lucite cube he kept on his glass coffee table. In it was a baseball. He looked at it. "Jackie Robinson hit this homer, you know that, Art? You know who Jackie Robinson even was?"

"I know who Jackie Robinson was." I was restless. I wanted to get going. I wanted to see where the dead girl had lived.

"I was born in Brooklyn," he said suddenly. "Crown Heights," he said. "Did you know that? Did I tell you? My grandfather came from Poland. He was a rabbi. He thought I was an infidel.

"What happened to us, Art? What the fuck happened?" Sonny looked at me. "When I was a kid, we were on the street until dark. We fought each other, we had gangs, we were crazy, but no one worried about us. No creeps kidnapped us. The parents worried about polio. They worried you'd get fucking polio in the summer, but no one worried some freak would snatch you out of your house. Jesus, I wish we had the machine back. It was easy then. It was a lot easier. It was a political machine and it worked. There was this guy called Mead Esposito, you ever hear of him, man?"

I shook my head and said, "There was a guy named Meat? Meat?"

He laughed briefly. "Mead, man. He was called Mead

Esposito and he ran Brooklyn and I wish to God we had him now. Nobody, I mean nobody, did anything in that borough unless he said OK, you know. I mean presidential candidates paid court to him, he could carry Brooklyn for a Democrat. He had a table at a restaurant named Foffe, accent over the e, of course. You went and ate with him and he fixed things."

"Don't go sentimental on me, Sonny, please."

"Yeah, I'm sorry, man." He poured himself more Scotch. "But there was respect. Even kids had respect. Sort of." He laughed.

"What's so funny?"

"When I was a kid in Brooklyn we all wanted to be Jackie Robinson or a member of Murder Inc., you know about that? The crime gangs?"

"Jesus, Sonny."

"Yeah, I was a cut-up. I wish it was like that now. Everything's fucked, you know, nobody cares. People killing kids, taking them, it's like some mirror fucking image of the whole country, of the whole fucking world. We got a nut job for a president who thinks God told him to go to war to avenge his daddy.

My father fought political battles in his sleep. They slept in this little alcove off the living room with yellow wallpaper that peeled when it was damp so I could have the bedroom. My mother snored so loud the whole place shook. When I was little and I had a nightmare, they would bring me into their bed. They had these two single beds and they somehow hooked together. They'd put me in between. He would fight politics all night in his sleep, he would be defending Trotsky or shouting about Sacco and Vanzetti or the Rosenbergs, and I'd be scared shitless, because I thought they would be taken away and fried like Ethel and Julius, you know, the electric chair was a big subject with kids like me, and my mother would be snoring and then I'd fall through a crack between the beds."

I tried not to laugh.

"Laugh," he said. "It's funny. The beds would separate. So I fell through and slept under the beds. In the morning, they'd wake up, and say, 'Leo? What happened to Leo, where's the boy?' "

"They named you for Tolstoy?"

"Leo," he said. "Leo N. Lippert. They compromised between Leon Trotsky and Leo Tolstoy. Everyone called me Sonny. I fucking hated it. I got over it. You get over things. You get over everything. One day you wake up dead and nothing hurts you. Forget it. I'm drunk."

"On a couple of shots?"

"I had a few after work." He reached for the bottle of Johnny Walker and poured himself a fresh glass, picked it up and wandered around the living room, talking.

He had a theory, he said. Told me he felt that somehow the rise in child abuse, in kidnapping, was connected to the fear that was rampant everywhere; you couldn't see it, people went about their business, but the fear expressed itself in outbreaks of violence against children.

We felt helpless so we preyed on the innocent, we did it to them, he said, even our own kids, we made them pawns in divorce cases, we used them, we manipulated them. He looked at me, and for the first time since I'd known him, Sonny looked old. The skin of his neck was slack, his face was sallow. I wondered if he dyed his hair.

"We just do what we feel like, you know?" he said. "We meet someone, we leave, we tell the kids, it will be the same, Mom and Dad will be there for you, we love you like always, but they know it's not true because if it was true, how come we just fucked off?" He sat down and picked up the bottle. Sonny had started drinking hard after he split up with Jennifer, his wife, and he lost his own kids.

I waited.

"I need this case, man, you hear me? It was my fault we never solved the last one, the girl that got her feet cut off. And then 9/11 happened. I let it go. I said to myself, we got 9/11 to deal with. Fucking 9/11, it was an excuse for everything."

"What's her address, the girl, May Luca?"

"I'll get it for you," Sonny said. "Sheepshead Bay, a few blocks from the boats."

"How old?"

"Ten," Sonny said.

Sonny tried to get up and tumbled backwards onto the sofa, his short legs in the air.

"You OK?"

"I've been out there, Art. I've been to the house. There's nothing we can do tonight. I have six guys on this. We took the girl's stuff to the lab," Sonny said.

"Stuff?" I said. "What for?"

"DNA. Get a match. The skin in the sneakers. There's not a lot. Just a little skin, like the girl had a blister or something and someone tore off her sneaks and some skin was left in the bottom. Blood, too. Jesus."

They would have taken her hairbrush, her toothbrush, would have asked the mother for them. Make a match, match the skin inside the sneakers.

The clothes were a tease, someone taunting us. In my bones, I could feel it. I had to see the girl's house. Cases with children, abuse, rape, even murder, it was often inside the family. A look at the house could tell you things about it.

"Who's on this?" I said again.

"Plenty," he said. "I have plenty of people on it. I'm going to wait a day and then I'll make an announcement. I'll go on TV. There's a cell phone. The kid had a cell phone."

"Sonny?"

"Yeah?"

"You said you wanted someone in a clean space. Something you want to tell me about Brooklyn? You had problems with people there?"

"A long time ago. There were some bad cops but they retired. It's just a feeling, it doesn't mean dick. What I meant was I wanted you there, Art, man. I wanted my own. You know?"

I got up. "You're going to be OK?"

He raised his glass in my direction. "Yeah, fine. I'll be fine."

He gave me the Luca address in Brooklyn and I left him staring at the Scotch bottle and let myself out. I got in my car and took the fast route through the flat dark featureless middle of Brooklyn. I'd been drinking, with

Tolya, then Lippert, but I was sober. I opened the window. The freezing air blasted away the last vestiges of booze in my system. It was dark now. I put on the radio; there was snow coming.

Snow was barreling up the east coast in the direction of New York. The air was cold and damp and mixed with the exhaust from cars and produced a thick dense fog that drifted across the windshield as I drove. New York, a night like this, they could have dumped the kid's body anywhere; there were a million places to dump a body—off City Island up in the Bronx or Gravesend in Brooklyn or the Gowanus Canal; a hundred different places. All around the city were the coastal swamps and wetlands where you could hide anything. The archipelago was laced with secret waterways.

I thought about the girl's clothes dumped near Coney Island as if someone wanted them found. He, and you always figured it was a he in these cases, could have stashed her anyplace, out by the airports in the reedy water, or Queens or on Long Island. What did he want? There had been no ransom request, no calls, nothing. Had there? I still didn't know, wouldn't know until I saw the parents and the house. What did I expect to find? I was sure May Luca would be dead by now; they almost always were. I fiddled with the radio, got an oldies station, let the noise of the Supremes singing "Baby Love" drown out some of my worry and watched the red brake lights on the car ahead of me blink through the sticky fog.

11

The yellow ribbons and the lighted candles were what I saw first when I drove up the dark narrow street; there were always yellow ribbons these days at the site of a disaster. COME HOME, MAY, WE LOVE YOU.

The ribbons were tied to trees and fences and outside the Luca house, a small bungalow with aluminum siding, was a shrine, the votives on the pavement shuddering in the wind.

Standing a few yards away, a small crowd had gathered and they muttered and watched and whispered and a few, two elderly women, heads bent, prayed. The shades in the house were drawn, but the door was ajar; a uniformed cop stood outside it. The door was pushed open from inside and a woman with dark hair came out to talk to the cop. Behind her a tall man pulled her back in gently. She put her hands over her face. The door shut.

Still in my car, I watched, then I pulled away. I wanted to see the house in my own time, my own way; the local guys would resent me. They didn't like outsiders. I had worked a couple of cases in Brighton Beach, which was next door to Sheepshead Bay, and they resented it. Resented it because I spoke the language better than they did. Because I had pulled rank through Sonny Lippert. Because I got in the way of them making collars. The Russians didn't like me much, either, sometimes for the same reasons.

It was almost ten. I was late for Tolya's dinner. When I got to Johnny Farone's restaurant there was valet parking, and I climbed out of my car and gave the keys to a kid in a forest green jacket with FARONE'S embroidered in gold on his lapel.

There was a doorman in an overcoat with epaulets and a top hat, also green, who opened the door to Johnny's restaurant.

Coming in from the bleak night, I was knocked back by the sound of voices laughing and the rich spicy meaty smells. I gave my jacket to the coat check girl, and went to the bar, where the far end was jammed with people. On the bar itself was an immense copper vat with a mountain of shaved ice; in it oversized cocktail glasses were chilling upside down.

Nearest to me a man shaped like a barrel with a mahogany tan sat alone with a cigar a foot long inserted into the O that was his mouth. He wore a pair of tinted aviator glasses, had a receding hairline and smelled of flowery cologne; around his neck was a large gold coin on a thick gold chain. I wondered if Johnny hired him as part of the scenery—a Tony Soprano stand-in.

The guy was discussing the fine points of Armagnac; the bottles were lined up on the bar and the bartender uncorked one and poured a sample into a snifter the size of a cabbage and handed it to the man with the cigar.

As I watched the bar scene, a headwaiter in a tux materialized and conducted me to Tolya's table, which was in the middle of the room. There was an empty chair for me and Tolya sat next to his mother. Johnny Farone hovered above her.

Lara Sverdlova, Tolya's ma, had changed so much I wouldn't have recognized her. In Moscow she had been famous for her acting and her looks. The last time I had seen her was at the family dacha in Nikolina Gora the year I met Tolya's cousin, Svetlana. The party on the lawn in the fading summer light had been like a scene from Chekhov.

Her skin was crumpled, the eyes thick with cataracts. Part of her face was stiff and I realized she'd had a stroke. A lot of old Russians, friends' parents, parents of my friends, had strokes after things fell apart. It was the post-communist disease for old people; paralyzed, people who had believed, or learned to believe, could retreat.

Sverdlova wore a two-piece pink tracksuit, black sneakers and thick white socks; at eighty she was skinny and stiff and her voice was shrill and very loud. Only Russians understood mushrooms she was telling Johnny. Only Russians could cook.

Her English was fractured, but she insisted on speaking it. She liked speaking English, but she couldn't get the levels right and her voice rose. She was proud of the English and said she spoke with a British accent that she learned long ago when there were exchanges

112

between the Royal Shakespeare Company in England and the Moscow Arts Theater.

She glanced up at Farone, then back at Tolya; she criticized him for his Russian. He had been infected by slang, she said; he had forgotten his language.

The restaurant was jammed. In the background *The Marriage of Figaro* played softly over the sound system; in the foreground, the voices collided with each other. Russians, Italians, civilians. Some of the women who had made it out of the neighborhood, and came back only to eat, showed off their sables, which they kept over their shoulders. Their men flashed diamond rings and flicked the lapels of their Armanis.

You could pick out the women from Manhattan, the kind who studied Zagat and tried every new restaurant and considered a trip to the Brooklyn coast an anthropological expedition; they wore pale little cashmere sweater sets—it was their idea of casual—one sweater tossed over their shoulders. Their shoes had tiny heels. Prim is what they looked; prim and toned and sexy; you wouldn't mind ripping off those little cashmere sweaters and the rest of it and fooling around with them while they kept those little kittenish shoes on. The husbands wore sports jackets and sweaters underneath; they swirled the liquid in their glasses, muttered about "really big Tuscans" and sniffed knowingly as if they'd been to wine drinking school.

Who was it who told me he'd dated one of the prim women and that she liked it up the ass? I couldn't remember. I knew I should feel embarrassed by my interest. I was a 45-year-old guy and I still wanted to try them all.

I had slipped into the empty chair at Tolya's table, and when his mother finally stopped harassing Johnny Farone, she seemed to suddenly see me.

"Artemy Maximovich!" she yelled. "You look older. You still look good, but older. You think you're still a sexy guy? You do? You think the women still fall down when you pass by? Yes? At least you look better than my Tolya who is fat. You know that," she said to Tolya. "You're a fat man, Anatoly Anatolyavich."

Like a crowd at a tennis match, everyone in the room turned their heads in our direction, then away, then back, drawn by Sverdlova's commentary. Some of them giggled. Johnny scuttled away and returned with a magnum of wine and beckoned the wine waiter, who opened it with plenty of ritual.

Waiters came and went with platters of food: tiny ravioli stuffed with sautéed foie gras; compact mounds of fettuccini with osetra caviar and crème fraiche; salmon wrapped in prosciutto, sea-bass on grilled fennel, scallops in their own foam. Duck with figs, risotto with crab and cilantro had been added to the menu, which still included braciola and osso bucco. Though he watched his mother uneasily, Tolya, unresisting in the face of the food, ate.

"That man needs a haircut," Lara Sverdlova yelled in English, glancing at a Russian I vaguely recognized at the next table. "You put on a few pounds yourself Artemy, right?" she said as I passed her the bread.

Some of the time between bites of food and the wine which she knocked back like Pepsi, Sverdlova switched to Russian. Whenever Tolya shifted his glance away from her, she yelled at him in English, then Russian as if to make sure no one in the room missed a word. The waiter put a discreet finger to his lips. She barely looked up. Someone changed the music on the sound system and turned it up loud so Lara Sverdlova seemed to be yelling in counterpoint to a blast of Verdi.

She gestured at two couples at the table next to ours. "Look at them, those men could be their grandfathers. You think they look in the mirror? You think they figure the girls really want them? Ha!"

By now the whole room was fixed on Lara Sverdlova's performance because that's what it was; she had her audience again. She was on stage and we waited for the curtain.

I looked at Tolya and he looked, for the only time I could remember, embarrassed. I remembered once, when we were out eating somewhere, he told me about his childhood.

"They were very famous, very establishment," he had said. "True believers and great stars, my father was a director, she was a star. She claimed she was only fifteen when she performed with Paul Robeson during a visit to Moscow. There were rumors they had a fling. Once I went in my pop's closet and found a suit of formal evening clothes, tails, the whole thing, which were never worn. No one ever even wore a tux or tails in Moscow, it was an imperialist idea, but for Robeson, they dressed. Even when we got a big apartment, it didn't help. They fought all the time until the day my father died, and then she couldn't manage without him or the system."

In the candlelit room, everyone stared. No one knew what to do while Tolya's mother commented on everyone in the room; like a director with a tracking shot, she moved her camera slowly from one table to another. The Manhattan couples finished in a hurry; they sniffed trouble coming, like rain on a humid day.

Tolya looked helplessly at me, but I had to get away and I got up and practically ran for the bar, where I ordered a glass of red wine, drank it down and asked for another one, then lit a cigarette. The bartender served me, looked away and kept his mouth shut. No smoking laws were for other bars, Johnny always said, laughing.

From the main room I could hear Lara Sverdlova still shouting, and people scraping their chairs back—you could hear the embarrassment in the scrape of the chairs and the suppressed coughs—and shuffling to the door. I could see them through the archway from the bar. I could see them hurrying out of her line of fire.

Rolling his eyes, Johnny Farone emerged from the dining room and climbed on the bar stool next to me. The bartender poured a Jack Daniel's for him.

"Is she nuts or what?" Johnny said nodding in the general direction of Sverdlova. He tossed back his drink. "You like what I did here, the renovations, you like it, Artie?"

Johnny's place was pretty lavish, the mahogany paneling on the walls, a huge painting of a hippo with birds flitting around it on the wall of the bar.

"Walton Ford," he said proudly. "Very in," he said, "I bought two. I had this art guy help me. I didn't want them thinking I was just this Guido from Sheepshead

Bay, you know? I even got the woman who does the flowers for Balthazar," Johnny said and gestured at the enormous bouquets in old terracotta pots.

FARONE'S was embossed in fancy gilt script on the heavy green leather menus, on the matchboxes, printed in gold on the cocktail napkins.

He was a good guy; Johnny was OK. It was just he couldn't get used to his luck. Part of him always believed he belonged in a dingy shop selling secondhand auto parts. That he had hired a nineteen-year-old chef who turned into a celebrity, that he got Genia to marry him, still made him grin with disbelief.

Johnny touched my sleeve. "You have anything for me, the stuff we talked about this morning?"

"Look, Johnny, with the money thing, talk to the guys at the precinct out here, it's probably some local scam, you know?"

"Gen would kill me if I talked to the cops. I can take the loss, but I'd like to know which bastard is soaking me, Art, and I can't go to the cops. You know what it's like."

"I'll talk to her."

"No!"

I didn't have the heart to tell him what I suspected, so I just mumbled about getting something later in the week.

"You didn't forget Billy's birthday next month? We're going to do it big. I'm going to turn the restaurant into a fishing pond or something, you know?"

"I'll be there, sure, I'd like that."

"You look upset, man. Is it about that little Luca girl? I heard. Everyone out here is praying for her."

"You know her?"

"I think I met the mother once." He shrugged. "You figure they'll find her or what?"

"Where's Genia?"

"She's on her way. You'll eat with us?"

"I already ate with Sverdloff."

"But you'll wait for her?"

"I'll wait."

I looked at my watch. There wasn't any point going back to the Luca house for a while; the place would be jammed up with people.

"Oh Christ," I said, and Johnny looked at me and said, "What's wrong?"

I had forgotten about dinner with Maxine. I just forgot. I called her and told her I was running late. She didn't sound happy. It was after eleven.

Johnny glanced at the door. "About the missing money, Gen says if we stir things up, it's bad for business. Maybe I shouldn't have asked you, maybe I should just take the losses, you know, eat it up, it's what they do out here running a cash business. We're doing great, I mean maybe she's right but it's eating my liver, Artie, someone being greedy. I mean I treat them all really good, you know? I got a health care plan." He lowered his voice. "I love her, Artie," he said plaintively and I saw Johnny was a guy afraid of losing his wife.

There was a commotion in the dining room. Tolya and his mother appeared in the archway that led from the main room to the bar, arguing. Tolya got her coat and wrapped it around her and, glancing at me, half carried her out of the front door to the restaurant. I got off the stool where I sat and followed them into the parking lot.

"It's OK," Tolya said to me, bundling his mother into the waiting limo. "Thanks for coming, Artyom. I'll call you." He disappeared into the back seat with his mother and slammed the door.

I went back into the bar and sat next to Johnny and drank some of the wine the bartender set in front of me.

"What are you two talking about?"

Genia's voice came from behind me. It was soft but nervous. She kissed Johnny, then me, three times, Russian style.

"How's Billy?" I said.

"Fine," she said. "Great. He's wonderful. He's with his friend Stevie Gervasi for the weekend. Steve that comes from a nice family, good people, wealthy, educated. They went upstate."

"So he left this morning? Early?" I said.

"Yes, this morning."

She smoothed back her hair and took off her mink jacket.

"Don't you know when he left?"

"I know about my boy, Artemy," she said very softly. "I spend all my time with my boy, I know everything."

12

Genia watched her reflection in the mirror behind the bar.

My cousin's name was Evgenia Borisova Shimkin and she'd been a dowdy woman when I first met her, dowdy and depressed, her shoulders hunched forward, a shopping bag always in her hand; now she was vain. She was Gen Farone, Genny to her women friends.

She looked in the mirror and preened, sleek as a cat as her tongue checked her beautiful white teeth for stray lipstick stains. She had them fixed after she married Johnny. Her hair was short, red and slicked back. She wore black leather pants and a yellow cashmere sweater and high-heeled boots and diamond earrings; like the teeth, Johnny had given her the earrings.

When I was a kid, Russian women all yearned for diamond earrings, even my mother. They were a token of a life these women had not quite given up on even in the drabbest years of the Soviet empire.

My mother's earrings were very small, very dull, with smudgy stones, but they were diamonds given to her by her husband, proof of attention and romance and she wore them even after I got her nicer stones. In the nursing home in Israel, she wore the earrings. She slept in them. She would be buried in them.

Genia put one arm around Johnny's shoulders and whispered into his ear and smiled and glanced at herself again in the mirror behind him.

"So how's Billy?" I said.

"You asked already. Billy's fine," Johnny said. "He's a big boy. He's OK, right, hon? In English, please. Talk English, OK?"

"Please, both of you, I say already, he goes to Stevie Gervasi, this kid in big house on the corner. You said to him, it's fine, you can walk over this morning yourself to Stevie's house. You said." In English Genia had never lost her accent.

She was a lot edgier than her husband. She shied away from any involvement with the cops, even me. In her Russian mind, the police were the enemy; she felt if a case didn't involve her husband or her child or the business, she had no interest in it.

I wasn't crazy about Genia; she was skittish and brittle; with me she was also wary. I was pretty sure she had come to America illegally and she knew I knew, and though she was married to Johnny and a citizen, it never left her. If it wasn't for Billy, I told myself, I wouldn't bother. I wouldn't see Genia. There was nothing that connected us. I couldn't remember my father mentioning her. My mother, even when she had some memory left, couldn't place her. Or maybe I lied to myself and I needed her, this last frail connection to another life.

Out of nowhere I noticed something about her I'd never seen before. She took a cigarette out of the pack, closed it up, folding the foil over the top the way I did. She held the smoke like I did, her finger twisted oddly around it. For a second it seemed odd, both of us with the same eccentric gesture.

I watched Genia greet a customer. She was effusive and charming. Underneath, she was a frightened woman, but who wouldn't be if you grew up the way we did? She'd had it a lot worse than me. Her old man had been a Red Army hero but her grandfather died in a gulag during the purges; for years the whole family were Enemies of the State. Genia's mother, she once told me, had whispered to her about it when she was little. Genia had escaped, first from Russia, then from the brown melancholy of the old house in Brighton Beach. She wasn't going back.

The house in Brighton Beach where she had lived with her old man and her daughter had a sagging couch on the porch and a rusted bicycle in the front yard. Inside, in the dark brown living room, was a stained yellow sofa where I sat and listened to her father's story of his triumphant days in the Red Army. The war medals that hung on his bony chest in rows clanked when he walked or got up to pour me some vodka.

Once Elena, who was a pale girl who refused to learn English, played a melancholy tune on her flute, Ravel, something like that. I ate apple cake and fled.

Elena was the product of an early marriage that had lasted a couple of years, the husband, Genia said, was a

122

drunk. She left him behind in Russia, she told me. Johnny had adopted Ellie.

The old man was dead now. Elena, who turned out to be a musical prodigy, had grown up beautiful. She had a scholarship to Juilliard. And Genia was married to Johnny Farone with an eleven-year-old named Billy who liked fishing; and me.

Johnny got up to greet a guest. Genia said to me in Russian, "Johnny doesn't know the world, you see? Johnny knows about pasta. Veal. He understands mushrooms. He can pick a good Super Tuscan, OK? We have a nice time in Italy in the summer. That's what he knows about, Artemy, he's wonderful with the restaurant, he is in Zagat now, but that's it. You understand me?" She picked up a cashew from a bowl on the bar and ate it and looked at her long, manicured nails. "Johnny's nervous because of the Luca girl," she added. "But it's nothing to do with us."

"What's going on between you and Johnny? He says he sleeps in his office."

"When it's late," she said. "Everything is fine."

"So, nothing. Not my business, right? None of my fucking cop business. So what are you reading, Gen?" I knew she was a passionate reader. I tried to warm her up talking books because Genia was from a generation who read a lot, because they loved books, because there was nothing else to do.

"Bulgakov," she said. "I'm re-reading. Once in a while, I like mysteries, for my English."

"You ever go over to see Dubi Petrovsky?"

"I don't like him."

"How come?"

"He asks too many questions, how do you feel about the USSR, how do you regard America? And he has a big mouth," she said. "Look, please, don't ask Johnny stuff, Artemy," she said. "If you need to know something, something about the neighborhood, something about my son, ask me. Johnny's too easy. He talks too much nonsense. He's too willing. He loves you. He thinks he owes you."

"What for?"

She smiled slightly. "For introducing us, you know? He admires you, too. Johnny gets his ideas about life and cops out of the movies and the TV. He gets his movies mixed up, too, so one day it's the mob, he thinks the people around here are from *The Godfather*, the next day he's in land of Tom Clancy. Johnny is an American. After 9/11, he tells me, Gen, I have to enlist. I say to him, 'What as?'"

"Did he say?"

She shrugged. "The Marines, God help me. He's forty-three years old but he's like a child. He talks too easy," she said. "Especially out here," she added and nodded her head at the room. "He'll get us in trouble."

"What kind of trouble?"

Genia signaled the bartender, who brought her a vodka martini; she drank it in two gulps.

"Why do you ask these things? You know what it's like out here."

"So tell me about this family where Billy is staying over."

She shrugged. "How many times? I told you. Nice

people. Rich and nice. Billy's at school with the kid.
Real private school. Fancy, you know? Not just Catholic
school. I took him out of Catholic school after this
business of priests. Sick dirty men," she said. "Johnny
wanted Catholic school, I said no. Sometimes I begin to
feel like at home, things coming apart, this great
American empire of power is all corrupted, you know,
but I don't say so to Johnny or his family, I just take care
of my boy and wait."

"Wait for what?"

"To know if we have to run again."

I took her hand. "You won't have to run."

"You believe too much," she said.

"Gen? Listen, anything else you can think of about
May Luca, the little girl, anything you heard in the street
or the store or the beauty salon, that kind of thing?"

"She's dead."

"You know that?"

"They're always dead. They always are. They never
find them, not the girls."

No matter how much money and security Johnny
provided, Genia's world remained full of bad things, and
she worked constantly to defend her family. Her terror,
I saw now, was always there, just beneath the surface. I
put my arm around her. "You told the cops?"

"Don't be stupid, Artemy, we don't talk to policemen
here, you know that."

"Hello, Genia," a voice said from behind us.

Suddenly Genia's face lit up, the tension in the tightly
wrapped skin eased and she looked beautiful. We both
turned around. The handsome man who had appeared

plucked her hand off the bar and bent over it as if to kiss it and smiled with just enough irony to make the gesture charming.

"Detective," he said and held out his hand to me.

"Elem Pavelovich, how are you?" Genia said and flushed. "Do you know each other?"

I shook his hand and then stood and watched him and Genia talking together, their heads almost touching.

I knew Elem Zeitsev. His old man, a big time hood, was dead now. The oldest son, Elem was about fifty, good looking, quiet, smart.

He was a lawyer. In the nineties, he got rid of his father's businesses and made his own money and made himself legit. I liked him; I liked him even though he had asked me once if he resembled JFK, or maybe because of it. The vanity was somehow charming.

"Just like JFK's hair," I'd said.

Before he went back to his table, Zeitsev shook my hand again, kissed Genia again, and said, genially, "Tell your husband the duck with the figs is from out of this world."

Genia touched her lips and turned to me.

"It's good for us Elem comes so often. He comes all the way out from the city," she said, as if to make an excuse for talking to Zeitsev.

"What do you mean?"

She said, "Nothing. It's good for business, that's all."

I kissed her cheek. "Is Ellie alright?"

"She's great. You'll come to her next recital?"

"Sure."

"How do you get to Carnegie Hall? Practice,

practice." Johnny guffawed at his own bad joke as he came out of the kitchen with a platter of stuffed clams, but I already had my jacket on. He looked disappointed.

"Johnny, I ate a huge dinner."

"You'll come again soon?" he said. "And you won't forget the thing we talked about?"

I nodded. Genia was watching me.

"What thing?" she said.

"A surprise, hon," Johnny said quickly.

I yawned. I figured I'd go by Maxie's even though I was exhausted.

"You're going home, now?" she asked me eagerly. "You're going back to the city?"

"You mean you want to get rid of me?" I smiled, but I added, "Is that it, Genushka, you mean back to the city where I belong?"

"Yes," she said and walked to the door with me. "Yes. Where you belong."

127

13

They found May Luca's body later that night. Outside her house, the flowers piled up, the shrine grew until it reached halfway down the street. The memorializing escalated as soon as her death appeared on the news. As if the praying helped, as if there was a God who heard. She was ten and she was dead. I sat in my car and watched.

Silently, people tip-toed up to the front gate of the house and placed Cellophane cones of flowers, teddy bears, rosaries, candles, notes; children brought pictures of May they'd drawn with crayons; in one she was an angel in the sky. An elderly woman placed a photograph of the girl and a votive candle on the ground.

It was late Saturday, but somehow people knew and they gathered and the crowd grew. Down the dark block were lines of people, many of them children, all with candles, like a crusade. Reporters hovered around the edge of the crowd. Vans from local TV stations appeared. The place was lit up with their lights. You could hear the buzz of the reporters as they interviewed people on the sidewalk. A police chief with a fancy uniform gave a short speech about the beautiful little girl and the tragedy and how he had committed himself to justice. It was always like this now. Any tragedy, the word got out fast and people moved in with their tributes. I hated it. It reminded me of Russians who gathered at cemeteries and in groups with their pictures of dead relatives and shitty red carnations and the apparatchiks who showed up to get in on the grief.

This morning she'd been alive, now she was dead. I had never seen May alive. She had slipped through our fingers. I'd almost never been on a case that ended so fast, and I hated the fact that part of me was relieved it was over. I had never completely let go of the idea that the clothes by the beach were Billy Farone's even when it didn't make sense. I had been like a man grabbed by some crazy fear and it had made me stupid. Now a little girl was dead.

I went to the Luca place from Farone's. I wanted to see if I could talk to the family, if I could get in. As soon as I got there I knew something bad had happened. I got out of the car and showed one of the uniforms my badge. She was dead, he said.

They found her naked earlier that night, he said. Naked, he said it again and again as if the fact was more offensive than her death. Her little naked ten-year-old body, still a child, he said, still a little girl, dumped on one of the fishing boats over by Gerritsen Beach, the boat rocking in the marina, the wind blowing it around. Just a baby, he said. He added some thoughts about sharing the grief and finding closure; the TV language of mourning had infected even this tough looking cop with the biceps of a body builder. I recognized him from the beach earlier that morning.

Dumped on one of the fishing boats, he said, working up a fury so his steroidal face turned purple. An hour after they found her, they spotted the creep who did it to her. He was cleaning the blood off himself with some rags. Before they could get to him, he ran. The cops fired warning shots, then aimed at him. He fell into the water. No one knew why he did it, but local people recognized him as a crack-head who hung around, a nickel and dime thief. It happened too fast. The murder weapon was a carving knife the creep stole from a deli.

The girl? The cop's voice quivered. She had been grabbed in her own yard; ten hours later, she was dead and so was her killer, and we'd let it all slip away. He stared down at a pink plush teddy bear on the pavement.

"Which boat?"

"What do you mean?"

"The name. What was the name of the boat they found her on?"

"Yeah, *Queen* something, *Queen of Brooklyn*, no, that's not right. Something like that."

"*Queen of the Bay*?"

"Right," he said. "Yeah."

It was the boat I had planned to take Billy on the summer before, the boat we missed. Irrationally, I was glad now that we had missed it.

For a while, I stood outside the house with the crowd of mourners, event freaks, sightseers who had heard about May Luca. With the cars and flashing lights, the area around the Luca house was lit up like the middle of the day.

Sonny Lippert emerged after a while and saw me and gestured aimlessly and opened and closed his hands. as if to hold something he couldn't grasp. His face was riddled with grief.

"Go home, Artie. I don't need you here, she's dead. They got the creep." He was furious. "Three hours ago I was drunk at home and now I'm here trying to explain to a mother why her little girl is dead with a hole in her heart from a knife someone once used to slice pastrami for sandwiches."

I dragged him aside, dogged him until he came to the edge of the street, away from the crowd.

"What happened?"

"He snatched her, he killed her, we shot him, Maybe he wanted us to shoot. I don't know. He was just a fucking crack-head."

"Where's the weapon?"

"We found it on him. It matched the marks on the girl."

"Nobody noticed she was gone?"

He said, "Jesus, we've been through this. The mother said she went to her grandmother alone all the time. It's a safe neighborhood, she said."

"The clothes at the beach?"

"We're waiting," he said. "We're waiting for the match. We described them to the parents. The T-shirt even had part of a label the mother sewed in for May when she went to camp. It's just a technicality now. It's over. Go home, man, get some sleep. Get laid."

I knew he was holding out on me, and I said, "There's something else."

Lippert took a plastic bag out of his pocket, opened it and handed me a crumpled piece of paper towel.

"What?"

He said, "They found a fucking ransom note, OK? The creep who killed her left a note in the backyard. Some crude thing, a piece of paper towel. He wrote it with one of her crayons. Here."

I looked at it. The writing was in crude block letters: GIMME TEN THOUSAND BUX FOR YOUR KID.

"Ten grand," Lippert said. "That was his idea of a big pay-day. It was for nothing, man. Nothing. We could have had her. But the piece of paper blew across the yard and got stuck under a garbage can. No one saw it until she was dead. Like that. Random. Shitty. Nothing. Like this miserable city, you know. We never figure it out in time. We never catch the hijackers. We never get anything right. The fucking feds don't give us a cent for security; all they do is use the Trade Center for propaganda. I was down in D.C. there and they were all talking about 9/11 like it belonged to them. But they cut my budget. I don't even have enough cops to save a little kid like May Luca."

He made a move for his car, followed by a cop, a small woman in uniform. He handed her the plastic bag with the note.

"Just see it gets to the station house before any asshole from the media sees it. I don't want them saying we missed some shit or other, you know?"

The cop nodded and moved off.

I said, "Call me when they get something final on the clothes, will you?"

"Sure," he said. "Whenever. What difference does it make now? I told you, the T-shirt had a label with a letter from the girl's name."

I waited until Sonny Lippert left. I waited until the crowds thinned out. I sat in my car and watched and waited and then I showed my badge to the uniformed cop outside the door and he said, "Let her be, OK? Let the parents alone tonight, will you?"

The cop looked around. "Listen, come early in the morning. Come tomorrow. I'll see if I can get you get in. Except it doesn't matter now what we do, does it?" he said, and I walked away, my feet crunching on the Cellophane wrapping that held a bunch of shriveled pink carnations.

14

I should have gone to Maxie's right away. I should have picked up a pizza, or gone by and eaten the steak or humble pie or whatever the hell she wanted me to eat.

My head was swimming. May Luca was dead, the case was closed. May had been killed by a local crack-head. It was random; it had no meaning. May Luca had been dragged out of her yard and now she was dead. The baseball jacket was hers. The two bit crack-head who killed her had dumped the clothes, half buried, less than a mile away. That was it, I thought.

Genia was right. I didn't belong here. Unless I had business, there was nothing for me except grief along this coastal strip of Brooklyn.

It was after midnight. I got coffee from a deli and drank it black. My adrenalin was pumping. Almost fourteen hours since I'd met Sonny Lippert near the beach. I called Maxie to see if I could persuade her to let me stop by, but there was no answer. She had gone out. Or she was asleep. Or screening her calls and not answering because she was mad at me. Maybe I should have gone by anyhow, maybe I should have just gone and waited for her or used the key she gave me.

I didn't, though. I called Tolya and left a message that I was coming back to the city. I'd hang out with him in some Soho restaurant and drink wine that went for three hundred bucks. I'd get mindless drunk. I'd have stupid fun with the kind of women Tolya always had around him. Maybe I'd sleep better afterwards.

Just one stop, I thought to myself. One more stop before I went back to the city.

It was as if she knew I was coming. Ivana Galitzine was waiting on the porch of the house off Brighton 8th Street, a small, ramshackle house with layers of gray masonry, plastic shingle, fake red brick. The porch was enclosed with glass louvers; some of the slats were missing. Strips of damp wood were nailed over the holes.

The lights were on and I could see her sitting on the porch, looking out. Smoking a cigarette, she was framed in the window, staring, waiting, for someone? For me?

Before I could change my mind, she saw me and bolted out of the house and jogged towards the car. I slammed on the brakes. I reached over and unlocked the door and she got in.

Ivana wore a pair of tight black jeans and a short, thin white sweater. Her midriff was bare. There was a gold stud in her belly button. Her long hair fell over her face. She was a beautiful girl and I was sorry I'd stopped at her house. She was half my age and connected to a case I was working and I knew she had lied that morning. Lied about seeing no one near the scene, lied about how she found the clothing.

"You should have a coat on," I said because I couldn't think of anything else. I got out a pack of cigarettes and offered her one, but she shook her head, and I lit mine.

She looked down at her jeans and the old sweater and picked at a piece of lint that had settled on it.

"It's not so cold, is OK," she said. "I was waiting for you, you know?"

"You knew I'd show up?"

"Sure."

"How's that?" I asked

"You like me," she said. "Don't you?"

"How old are you anyway?"

"Twenty-two, like I told you," she said.

"Yeah, sure."

"OK, I'm nineteen, but so what?"

Petulant and nervous, she was a kid. A kid with a great body who was coming on to me, who wanted something but what?

I said, "How can I help?"

"Take me out someplace. It's my birthday."

"I can't do that," I said. "I'm working. Anyhow it's after midnight."

For a few seconds she was silent and we sat in the warm closed car while the fog crawled up the window outside and the street disappeared. Then, out of the blue, she said, "I want to fuck you."

"No you don't."

"So I go down on you if you want." She licked her lips in a parody of a porn movie.

136

"Forget it."

She sulked and turned away.

"Come on," I said. "Tell me what's bothering you. Tell me what you know about the little girl."

"I don't know nothing."

"Sure you do."

"I don't like cops which scares me, also Chechens, also maybe Putin sends old KGB guys to live in America, gangsters also; everything is bad. Then I find the clothing and I know it belongs to a child, but who? Tell me who is this kid?"

"It's a little girl who lived over by Sheepshead Bay. It's on the TV. She's dead."

"I didn't watch. What's her name?"

"May Luca."

"Not Russian girl."

"What's the difference?"

Ivana looked out of the window as if someone were following her.

"Go on," I said and offered her some Juicy Fruit I found in my jacket pocket.

She peeled the gum wrapper and stuffed the gum in her mouth and started chewing.

"Radiation," she mumbled.

"What?"

"I work at a lab, yes?" she said in Russian. "It's a medical lab, and sometimes I read the material that comes in. I look at pictures in the books. This is radiation. I saw it in the clothes. This girl touched something hot, you understand? I know all about this hot bomb, you know, people think this doesn't exist, but I

137

work in lab I hear people talk about stuff, cesium, plutonium, they are bringing it in suitcases, they bring to lab." She paused. "I see. Yellow Cake is everywhere now, you know, this radioactive shit? Girl who wore clothes touches something hot, I could see it on the clothing. Tell me your address, I send you evidence."

I gave her my card to shut her up. She was crazy from fear. I didn't believe anything she said. She had read too many magazine stories, too many cheap Russian thrillers about hookers and nuclear gangs. I didn't want her running to the cops with her stories, though, so I sat and nodded and listened. I knew she was lying, and she was a dangerous liar.

She sulked for a few minutes and refused to get out of the car, so I leaned over her again and unlocked the door and opened it.

"Get out," I said.

She giggled, and leaned over and kissed me hard, her tongue shoved in my mouth. Then, abruptly, she opened the door and ran away into the house. From inside I could hear people yelling, kids laughing, the sound of something crashing to the floor.

I turned on the engine and pulled away, but afterwards I couldn't get her face out of my mind, the face with the high cheekbones and smooth forehead, the dark hair and light gray eyes. She was less than half my age. She was involved in a case. It was crazy. I was turning into a lonely, aging cop whose girl had dumped him.

On my way out of Brighton Beach, I called Sonny Lippert, woke him up and told him about the jogger and her radiation theories.

"Forget it. She's in la la land, or drunk, or stoned," he said.

"I'm not sure. She's a tease. She's holding back. She knows something she doesn't want to say. She says the clothes at the beach were hot, she works in a lab, she knows radiation when she sees it. I think she probably smokes too much weed and sees too many movies. I don't know what to think."

"So go back. Talk to her. Use your charm, man, isn't that what you do best?"

I said, "She's nineteen."

"It never stopped you before." He hung up without saying goodbye.

It was late. I called Maxie again and she picked up and I said I was sorry. She sounded sad. I said, can I come, but she said no. She said it was OK, but she didn't want to see me.

There wasn't any traffic and I was back in the city in fifteen minutes. I came out of the tunnel and turned towards home. When I was a few blocks away, I felt someone tailing me. I rolled through the cold empty city and I was sure of it. I turned onto Canal Street. I stepped on the gas, lit up a cigarette, glanced in the rear view mirror.

He came up alongside me and I could see Tolya's big face a few feet away. He was yelling, mouthing words. I opened the window a crack.

"Slow down," he said.

I stopped at the corner of Broadway and Canal in front of the post office. He stopped and got out. He was wearing a black mink coat.

I opened the window wider and said, "What the fuck are you doing here?"

"Looking for you," he said, leaning in my window.

"You've been dogging me?"

"Not exactly, anyway you're here, I'm here." He sounded uneasy.

I looked at his vehicle. It was huge, square and yellow.

"What is it?"

"Is my Hummer," he said. "It is my tank. Come on."

"Where are we going?"

"I think to a party," he said.

"What party?"

"Get in."

"You can follow me home. I'll park my car and I'll think about it," I said.

In front of my building, I parked, got out and climbed into Tolya's tank.

The dashboard was crammed with instruments, dials and clocks, and a massive CD system all glowing with blue neon light.

"Jesus."

"You want to smoke, open the window," he said. "Upholstery is kid glove leather."

I gestured at the Hummer. "What's it for?"

He looked sheepish. "This afternoon, got bored, I went shopping."

"They found the girl."

"Tell me," he said.

"She's a kid, ten years old. She lived in Sheepshead Bay, not far from the water. The creep left a ransom note nobody found until it was too late. She's dead. He's

140

dead. It's over. They're waiting for a match on the clothes they found this morning at the beach, but the mother said she had a baseball jacket. It's over."

"But you don't believe it's over." Tolya was serious now. He held out a pack of the Turkish smokes he liked and I took one, and we lit up. We sat in the car.

"I don't believe it. It's too pat. It's too easy." I told him about Ivana.

"You think she knows something?"

"I'm not sure. I don't trust her. Right now I don't even trust Sonny Lippert."

Tolya snorted. "Him I never trusted. He uses you, Artyom. He doesn't give a fuck except for his own promotion."

I didn't answer him, just smoked the black cigarette and leaned against the leather seat.

"What's bugging you about this?" he said.

"Why the blood-soaked clothes were near the beach. If the killer was just a local crack-head who wanted ten grand, why bother leaving the clothes a few miles away from the house. Why take the trouble? You think it was a cry for help?"

"Bullshit," he said.

"I get a call this morning from Sonny Lippert. A jogger finds some bloody clothes out near Coney Island. It's winter. The Russian girl is jogging. She finds the clothes. She calls a cop. She tells me she thought the clothes showed signs of radiation. She tells me she wants me to take care of her. What's she telling me all this shit for?"

"The girl sounds scared," Tolya said. "But what of?

141

And how come this Russki bimbo is running to tell the cops? I don't believe it."

"You know what?"

"What's that?"

"I'm sick of everything," I said. "I want to go home and get some sleep."

"Let's go to a party."

"I have to go home, Tolya. I'm going to pass out. I'm whacked."

He passed me a couple of pills and a bottle of Evian.

"Go on," he said.

"What is it?"

"Just take them."

15

The party was in the penthouse of an empty glass
building that overlooked the frozen river. It was at the
end of Perry Street. Between the building and the
Hudson was only the strip of highway and the bike path
but you could barely see them and water seemed to lap
at the building.

Heavy with chunks of ice, the river looked white.
Beyond it, New Jersey's lights were just visible through
the fog. New Jersey looked romantic, exotic, but, then, I
was drunk. The gin in my martini, ice cold, smelled clean
and it was easy to get through two or three; the pills, the
speed Tolya had given me, woke me up and mixed with
the champagne and martinis and left me flying.

I went out onto the balcony and I could see the building reflected in its mate opposite. The apartments in both
buildings were glass, floor to ceiling, and the two
reflected each other like a see-through cubist sculpture.
In one apartment I could see paintings propped up
against a glass wall. In another furniture covered in
ghostly dustsheets. A roll of paper, architectural drawings,

maybe, fluttered on a trestle table made of shiny metal.

The apartments were still uninhabited. Architects and designers were at work, though, and you could see odd pieces of furniture and pictures and mirrors.

We had entered on Perry Street in the West Village, where security was tight. Men with bulging jackets talked into their collars and listened through earpieces. Limos were parked three deep.

The penthouse where I stood drinking heaved with a mass of people; celebrities swirled around, exquisite creatures, in the glass cage. Puff Daddy was on his way out when we arrived, and I wondered if I should call him Mr. Daddy. I thought I saw Nicole Kidman in the crowd talking to Denzel Washington. Her hair was red. Her silky dress was green. He wore jeans and a T-shirt. Martha Stewart made her way through the throng, the heaving mass of celebrity. People looked unsure how to address Stewart. Most expressed sympathy over her business problems, the pending indictment; a few shied away as if she stank like meat turned rotten.

Everywhere I heard chatter about the buildings, about Richard Meier's architecture, that it was awesome or dull, people dissecting the meaning of ceiling to floor glass and ways in which the structure expressed itself. I listened and laughed to myself and drank some more and wondered if Nicole would have dinner with me. Her red hair reminded me of Lily's. Over a sound system Charlie Parker played "Autumn in New York".

The booze took the edge off the drugs and both combined to make me mellow and alert at the same time. I thought of Parker and what he said once about New

York somewhere. I couldn't remember his words, I tried, but I was too far gone. Something about how when he got to New York the first time, he rode uptown and downtown and loved it because you looked one way and saw rich people and the other a couple making love and behind you was a guy living in a cardboard box. Something like that.

Bird was right. I sipped the drink. I had come to this glamorous glass box from Brooklyn, from the blood-soaked clothes by the beach in Coney Island and a woman mourning her kid, yellow ribbons, reporters on TV, a grieving cop. It was only ten miles away, along the same coast.

Everything happened in New York at the same time. Love, murder, birth, kids playing in the street, people shopping, begging. Millions of people packed onto the island and the outlying territories.

New York was so big, so tribal, though, that stuff happening out in coastal Brooklyn seemed to be on a different planet from the party in Manhattan. The only things that connected May Luca's world in Brooklyn with this glass box in Manhattan were the candles, the candles everywhere, reflected in all the glass here, the votive candles on the cold Brooklyn street. One tribe barely cared about another or knew about it or understood its rituals; except for a few manufactured celebs and sightings of them as retailed by the *Post*, there was nothing that connected us all except the weather and the water. I looked out at the river. I could never get enough.

Sverdloff introduced me to the two women who owned the place, but I forgot their names. One was a famous food writer, the other was an astronomer who appeared on television. Both had dumped their husbands for each other. The astronomer's little girl lived with them and she swirled, a twelve-year-old straight out of *Lolita*, into view with a platter of tiny food. I snatched a tiny pastry sailboat filled with caviar off her tray. She moved away. There was also a boy, about fourteen, who played a gleaming black Steinway for a while. I didn't ask who the father was.

They had not moved into the glass house yet, one of them said. They were still in Tribeca, they said. Couldn't wait to get out. It was over; Tribeca was over, they said, and laughed at how astute they'd been in selling out.

The women held hands and kissed each other on the mouth a lot, kissed with open mouths, as if marking out territory like animals. They wore things—you couldn't exactly call them clothes—that seemed to be made of some rare species of Japanese moth. Floaty, drifty, pleated, subtly colored.

I stood on the sidelines and gaped at the famous faces.

"Incredible, right?"

I turned around. It was a woman I knew who wrote crime novels—her name was Janie; we went and sat on a couple of chairs in a corner and drank more martinis and talked about murder.

I liked Janie; she was sharp and funny, but she was taken. After a while, a guy with a young face and white hair showed up to take her home.

"Long way from Brighton Beach," another voice said, a man's, a light almost gentle voice, and before I turned I saw Elem Zeitsev reflected in a pane of glass.

I turned around and we shook hands. He wore black jeans and a black turtleneck, a tweedy jacket that was soft and expensive but unpretentious, and loafers, no socks.

I shook his hand. "You know these people?"

"I bought a place here," he said. "Some day it will be ready. Designers! Architects! They say getting your place done in Manhattan is like going through Elisabeth Kübler-Ross' Seven Stages of Dying," he added, laughing in the silvery, knowing, Manhattan tones.

"Like a goldfish bowl," I said. I'd had a lot to drink.

"That's what they all say."

"I should have been more original."

"It's OK," he said. "I love looking at the river. I love the way the structure of the building expresses itself," he added. "But I guess you've heard that too." Zeitsev turned to the right and I followed his gaze.

"Wow," he whistled softly.

A few feet away from us, a black model, six two, six three, was wrapped like a coat around Tolya. A few minutes later, his architect, the dour woman I'd met at his loft, came through the door, her face grim as if she was clutching razor blades.

The uncompromising wedge of black hair fell over her face. She wore a strict black dress and bright red lipstick. She glanced at Tolya, saw the model, and turned in the other direction. He looked miserable.

Zeitsev said softly, "I thought you'd be working on the Luca case. Poor kid," he added. "Bastards."

"The girl's dead, we found the creep who did it, I'm sure you know all of it. There's not much of a case to work," I said. "You enjoyed your dinner at Farone's place?"

147

"Sure."

"You're friendly with the Farones?"

"I go there to eat when I have business in Brooklyn. It's good, it's convenient, people from the city think it's exotic, you know? Brooklyn has Peter Luger and Farone's. I wish I'd bought into Williamsburg; if I'd had any brains I would have bought real estate there and in DUMBO. I remember when these were areas you wouldn't even walk around at night. You must have done pretty well yourself over near Broadway," he added in an approving voice.

"It did OK."

He smiled, making friends. "That's pretty modest."

I said, "You put money into the Farone place?"

"What? No. Why? I never put money into restaurants. Once in a blue moon it works out, otherwise you might as well eat the cash. You know what they say, never buy anything that eats while you sleep. Genia is your cousin, of course, so you keep on eye on them, isn't that right?"

"My father's cousin. Distant."

"But Billy, you're friends with Billy."

"Yes. We go fishing."

"I've met Billy," he said. "Smart kid." He lit up when he talked about Billy. "I like kids. Mine are almost grown up. I wish I still had a little one."

A girl passed with a tray of martinis and I pulled one off and drank half of it.

Zeitsev turned towards the window again and so did I. Side by side we looked out through the glass, our reflections visible. We were about the same height. Both of us in black sweaters. His hair grayer than mine. His face almost grave.

Speaking to my image in the glass, he said, "I know you don't trust me, I know you think I'm my father's son. I can't fix things like he did, I gave that up, but if you need anything, if you need help in Brooklyn, if your cousin needs something, or the boy, you can come to me."

"You're the boss?" I said.

"I'm just a guy, and I'm a little drunk. No, really drunk."

"Well, I'm just a cop, and also drunk."

"Yeah, well, we all have our problems," he said, smiling. "Call if you want to."

He laughed and took a miniature foie gras sandwich off a table near him and ate it. A woman in red and pearls the size of small eggs plucked at his sleeve. I recognized Zeitsev's wife. He followed her into the crowd towards the door.

It was four in the morning when I found a taxi on Greenwich Street. It was quiet as a tomb outside, everything shut up, the warehouses, the apartment buildings, even the bars. Sunday morning. Even Bleecker Street, when we passed, was quiet on the freezing night; in the hours before daylight, it was peaceful, silent.

I'd get a few hours' sleep before I went back to Brooklyn and tried to talk to May Luca's mother. It was just a wild shot. Just to make sure something hadn't been overlooked. Then it would be over. The case was already closed. I was coming down from the drugs and the booze and all I wanted was sleep.

16

"Hello, Mr. Artie," the voice said as I slammed the cab door and walked to my building.

The block was silent, Mike's was shut, no one out. I was very drunk and very tired. You're getting old, man, I thought to myself.

She was there, leaning against the wall, waiting for me.

"I'll drive you home," I said feeling bone weary. "Come on."

Ivana Galitzine wore a long black coat tied at the waist and high-heeled boots. Her hair was piled on top of her head and covered by a red corduroy cap and she was smoking. She held her cigarette case daintily between her thumb and forefinger. It was all she carried, no purse, nothing except the cigarettes.

"You'll freeze to death," I said.

"Can I come upstairs?"

"No."

"Why not?"

"I have a cold."

"Fuck you."

"Listen, if you don't want a ride, then go home yourself. I'm going to bed," I said and got out my keys and opened the door. She followed me inside.

"Is cold," she said.

I took my time. I unlocked the mailbox. I took out the mail and sorted it. Slowly, I read it, standing in the cramped overheated vestibule. In the small hot space, I could smell her. She followed me into the elevator. I was too tired, or too strung out, to stop her. By the time we were at my place, I was furious. I turned on the lights.

"What do you want?"

"I told you."

"Listen, cut it out. You're a kid."

"Then give me a drink," she said, pulling off her coat.

"I'll give you a drink and then I'll call a car service and send you home, OK?"

"Maybe, maybe not." She was playing a role she'd seen in some movie, but what made her sexy wasn't the act; it was the way she looked and dressed. It was crude but it worked; she knew it. She removed her coat slowly. Underneath she wore a mini skirt and tight low cut sweater. She flopped on my couch, legs apart. She wore stockings, but no underpants.

She reached down. "You like my thong?" she said.

I ignored her. She got up and came over to the counter and perched on a stool and leaned forward so I could almost see the nipples. I told myself this was a case I was working and the girl was nineteen.

I got an open bottle of white wine out of the fridge, but she said, "Vodka, please. Then I could give you some boom boom," she said. "Isn't this what all men want?"

"Where'd you hear that?"

I found some vodka in the freezer and poured a shot into a water glass and gave it to her and watched her knock it back. I put the bottle on the counter. She poured herself another drink.

I tossed some cigarettes on the counter. Under the bravado, she was scared. I wondered if she knew something after all.

"Why don't you tell me what's bugging you?" I said. "You're scared, right? So tell me how I can help you." I was on automatic pilot I was so tired.

"Why you don't want to fuck me?"

"Stop it. Just stop, OK? I'm on a job, you're a kid and if you keep this up, I'll just walk away. So talk to me."

She reached for the vodka bottle. "I was only offering," she said. "You like American girls who are more coy? You like it better if I use metaphors. Boom boom? Shagging. This is what they say in Austin Powers movies. Shag me. This is what they say in England?"

"Tell me how you found the girl's clothing near the boardwalk."

"I'm hungry."

I got out some bread and ham and cheese and made her a sandwich.

She said, "Give me mustard."

I got out the jar. She spread the mustard and then ate hungrily.

"Don't they feed you where you live?"

Her mouth full, she nodded her head. "This is better," she mumbled.

For a few minutes I drank some wine and watched her. When she had finished, she drank a glass of vodka without stopping, and took one of my cigarettes. I made coffee.

"Better?"

She smiled. "Thank you. Is really cold outside."

"So tell me, is it your birthday?"

She jumped off the stool and made for the couch again, where she threw herself onto it, put her feet up and looked at me.

"I can sit here, it's OK?"

I sat down in the chair next to her. "Just tell me."

Ivana pulled her legs under her like a schoolgirl and sat forward.

"Yes," she said. "This is true. You know, all my life I think if I can just get to the United States, it will be OK. I'll be safe, you know? And then I come here and everything is not safe, planes fall from sky, people are scared, people are buying plastic bags to keep out radiation, duct tape, for what? Everyone is worried, television is propaganda just like when I'm little kid at home, you understand?"

I nodded.

"I can maybe have some more vodka, please?" She went to the kitchen and brought back the bottle and drank from it steadily.

"So I come and I think, OK, I will be American. I study English, which I already learn in school, I read newspapers, I try to hang out with American people, but

153

I am bored," she said. "Here nobody reads books. Nobody cares for nothing. You know what I study to be at home?"

"What's that?"

"I am going to be famous scientist. Doctor, maybe." She shook her head. "Never mind. So I'll tell you about what I know about this little girl, this May Luca, if you want."

"Go on."

"They make money off these children."

"Who does?"

"Men. They take them, they sell them, you understand me?"

"This isn't Thailand."

"You think men in Brooklyn doesn't like little girls? Listen, one time I'm hearing there's a group, men who want little girls, little boys also, and they pay good."

"How did you hear it?"

"I have friend," she said.

"Who's the friend?"

"Friend of my aunt. Name is Evgenia Borisova who is married to Mr. Farone with the restaurant."

I poured myself a drink.

"Yes, she is your cousin, right?" Ivana winked and reached for the vodka bottle. "Right? She talks to my aunt about you all the time, Artemy this, Artemy that. I ask myself who is this wonderful Artemy."

I was surprised. Most of the time Genia seemed eager to get rid of me.

"So what's her name, this aunt of yours?"

To hide my unease, I got up and went to the kitchen,

where I took a fresh bottle of white out of the fridge, got the corkscrew from the drawer, pulled the cork, and poured the cold wine into a glass. I stayed there and drank half a glass in one gulp while Ivana lolled on my couch.

"Name is Marina Jones."

"Jones?"

"For convenience she is Jones, OK?"

On the floor not far from where Ivana inhabited my couch was the stack of receipts from Johnny Farone's. Hurriedly, I swept them up and carried them to my desk and stuffed them into a drawer. I looked idly at the bookshelf. The books seemed out of order. It looked as if someone had moved my books, but I was drunk and exhausted and I figured I was starting to hallucinate.

I said, "What else?"

"Can I stay here tonight, Mr. Artie?" she asked. "It's cold and I don't like taking the train when is still dark out."

"I'll call you a car."

"Please," she said. "We can talk more."

"I don't blackmail easy," I said. "What else do you know?"

"I know your cousin Genia is having big affair."

"So?"

"You don't want to know who with?"

I shrugged. "It doesn't make any difference to me."

"Elem Zeitsev," she said, triumphantly.

"How do you know?"

"I forgot maybe to tell you I worked as coat check girl for a while at Farone's. Did I forget to tell you? Ivana is a bad girl. Maybe you want to punish her?"

I picked up the phone and called a radio car and they put me on hold.

"I'll be good," she said and reached down and pulled up her sweater from the bottom up, rolled it slowly, then yanked it off so I could see her breasts. With one hand, she rubbed her left nipple until it was hard.

So I hung up the phone, and somehow she was in my bed and we were both naked and I had my hands on her.

I thought: what am I doing with this kid in my bed, and she was awake suddenly and wrapped around me. I thought to myself: grow up.

For a few minutes I feigned sleep. All my life I'd been a sucker for women and I was trying to grow up, but I was lousy at it. I didn't mess with kids, though. I didn't like them. It wasn't that I was judgmental; I just didn't get it. Young girls seemed dull, unformed and needy; once you'd slept with them, and they weren't much fun in the sack, either, what else was there?

Ivana was dirty. She had her hands on my cock, then her mouth, and I was dumb with booze and drugs and sex.

Later, half asleep, my mind drifted. I thought about Lily. Sometimes I still believed she was coming back.

The yearning took over, the welling up of wanting her. I missed Lily horribly. Sometimes, when I'd had too much to drink, I could feel myself think, oh, Lily, please come back. When I called Beth in London, if Lily picked up the phone, I kept it light. I kept it friendly. I didn't want her to cut me off and she could be brutal if you transgressed. But at night when I was alone, watching TV or listening to music, sometimes I thought I heard the door.

It opened. Lily would be leaning against the doorframe like she always did. Tall, lanky, pushing the thick red hair back from her face, tying it up in a pony tail with one of the rubber bands she kept in her pockets. I imagined her standing there, smiling at me. It never happened.

Now her face, her voice floated into my dreams and got mixed up with Maxine and my cousin Genia and this girl next to me, what was her name? Ivana.

Startled, I woke up.

"Mr. Artie?" Ivana said.

"Christ, what do you call me that stupid name for?"

"I think is funny, you know? Respectful for older guy."

The clock was near the bed. It was 8.30.

"Get up," I said. "Come on. Now."

"Why should I go?"

"I'm going to take you home is why. Or to work. Don't you have to go to work?"

"Is Sunday."

Sullen now, she climbed out of bed. She had a fantastic body, long, lithe, big shoulders, and the sort of breasts you wanted to put your face in.

I got up. I felt her watching me. I grabbed the jeans that were crumpled on the floor and put them on and went into the kitchen and made coffee.

"Let's go." I handed her a mug of coffee.

She was furious. I'd made a bad mistake sleeping with her.

I pulled on a sweater and shoes and grabbed my jacket and waited by the door while she got dressed. It was after

157

nine by the time we got downstairs and out onto the street. It was Sunday but I saw Mike through the coffee shop window, scrubbing down the counter, taking inventory. He looked up and saw me with the girl and waved.

"Stop acting like a four-year-old and get in the car," I said to Ivana.

"I want to go upstairs."

"Get in the car."

"I forget something. My cigarette case." She grinned at me suddenly and added, "It doesn't matter. I make you present."

Suddenly, Ivana edged away from me and without saying anything, pulled her coat tight around her and started running. Faster and faster, not looking back, she ran down the block and disappeared around the corner. I watched her go and for a minute I wondered if she'd make trouble. She was a fantasist. She made up stuff about radioactive clothes. But she was a kid looking for something, security, fun, mischief, and I thought: to hell with her.

I went upstairs and crawled into bed. I had to sleep. I didn't care about anything except sleep. Have to go to Brooklyn, have to see May Luca's mother, call Sonny Lippert, call Maxine, pay bills, car needs servicing, murder, blood-soaked clothes . . . Perched on the edge of sleep, before I fell over, I suddenly remembered feeling someone had been in my loft. I couldn't hang onto what it was that made me think it, and I was so tired I had to grab the edges of the mattress to try to stay awake. It was no good. I was too tired to care and I slept hard.

The phone woke me. It was light out. I looked at my watch. It was one o'clock and my head hurt like hell.

"You're still asleep?"

"What's going on?"

"It's May Luca, man," Lippert said and I sat up and fumbled on the table by the bed for some cigarettes and couldn't find any.

"The case is closed, right? The kid was snatched from the backyard by a creep, and he killed her. Like we thought. End of story. You asked about the clothes. You asked about the baseball jacket. It was the girl's. May had a baseball jacket."

"No, man, it's not." Sonny's voice went quiet. "The first results on the clothes from near the beach, they came back from the lab. You're interested?"

"I'm listening," I said, but I was out of bed, stumbling across the room, looking for cigarettes.

"Go on," I said to Sonny Lippert.

"The preliminary reports are in," he said.

My heart was hitting against my chest.

"I heard you," I said.

"There's no match with May Luca's blood. The clothes didn't belong to her."

"But the blood type was the same."

"Yeah, some of it. But it was O positive, like a million other people. It was the DNA we needed."

"I thought you told me her ma said she had a blue baseball jacket, she was a tomboy, she loved the game."

Sonny said, "What type of blue? Did any of us ask? Jesus, man, we fucked up, you know. The jacket we found was a dark blue Yankees jacket. May's jacket was

159

from the Brooklyn Cyclones, the Mets farm team, out by Coney Island. You know where I mean. It was blue but it wasn't from the Yankees. The father came in this morning and looked at it. It wasn't hers. None of the stuff was hers. We just assumed. We fucking assumed too much. We had a creep, we had a body, we had a weapon, we tied them together, so we assumed."

By now I had clothes on and my car keys in my hand, and a fresh battery for my cell phone, which had gone dead. As I made for the front door I saw a pink plastic cigarette case on the kitchen counter. It was Ivana's and I grabbed it, and yanked the pack out, desperate for a smoke.

A small gold cross on a thin chain fell out. I turned it over and over. I read the initials. I had seen it before. I had seen it on Billy Farone.

"I make you a present," Ivana had said. She had left the cross for me; it wasn't an accident.

Part Three

17

On a very quiet day, you could almost hear the ocean from the Farones' house in Manhattan Beach. You could walk to the beach easily. Once, I'd gone with Billy, who showed me how to surf cast.

It was maybe ten minutes from Brighton Beach, but it was quiet and expensive and the houses were big and the streets had English names: Coleridge, Dover, Exeter, Hastings, Kensington, Norfolk.

The Farone place was large and beige and there was a light in the downstairs window. I parked out front and, the gold cross in my hand, ran up the walk and leaned on the bell until Genia opened the door. I held out the cross.

"Is this Billy's? Is it his, Genia? Listen to me, don't look in the other direction, OK? Where's Johnny? Does he stay at his restaurant every night? Do you two fucking care about your kid? When were either of you going to call and tell me Billy's missing?"

She took the gold cross from my hand and held it close to her face and, suddenly, slumped onto a chair in the hall.

"My God," she said. "Where did you get this? What do you mean missing?"

"Where's Billy?" I said.

"I told you, he went upstate yesterday morning, with Stevie and his father, the kid across the street. They promised to get him home early today, in time for church, they promised, but it gets later and later, Artemy, and I think, OK, it's a few hours, so what, and then I call and no answer and no one home at the Gervasis'." Genia talked mostly in Russian, switching on and off to English, hysteria rising in both.

I said, "You didn't think to call me."

"I try. Your cell phone is not working."

"You could call at home."

"I'm scared." Her face was pinched, but she was dry-eyed. "I wanted to call you," she said. "I've been waiting. I went out to look for my boy but he's not there. They're not there. The people, Stevie's parents weren't at home. I am hoping you come. Johnny said you were asking about Billy, and then you asked me about him and his friend, Stevie, the kid down the street. So you knew something? You knew and you didn't tell me?" She stopped for breath and to light a cigarette.

"I didn't want you to worry."

"You think I'm a bad mother, you think I don't pay attention my son is missing?" she whispered in Russian, looking up from a little white silk chair in the hall of her house. She crouched low, as if to protect herself from a blow. Genia looked crumpled and tiny.

"He was supposed to call last night," she said. "He didn't call. I tried him, he has a cell phone, nothing.

Nothing from Stevie's parents, and I was petrified. I sat here alone in this house and convinced myself he was fine, he was with Stevie, but I couldn't move."

She held the cross in one hand and gestured at the living room of the big house with the other. She peered at the inscription; it was a date. Billy's first communion, she said. From Tiffany's. She went to the city, she went to Tiffany's and bought it and had the date engraved. Genia put out the cigarette and looked at her hands as if they were distinct objects, separate from herself.

"What about Johnny?"

"What about him? He says leave the boy, he's a boy, Gen, he has to be tough, OK. Nothing is wrong with him. Give him some rope, he says and I think what for? To hang himself?"

"Come on, let's go sit in the living room," I said and Genia, looking at the gold cross again, began to cry.

We sat on the white sofa. Suddenly, Genia's sleek, made-up face seemed to crack. Tears fell down her face in a way I'd never seen tears. They fell steadily without any break, streams of them, coming down her cheeks. I held her hand and waited for her to stop and looked towards the living room.

Everything in the house was white, white silk chairs, white carpet, a white velvet sectional in the sunken living room, which was white. As soon as Johnny had the money, he'd bought it for her.

Johnny got her the brand new big house she had wanted all her life. The façade was red brick. The entryway—she called it the portico—had slender white columns and between them a light shaped like a lantern and big as a wrecking ball. The driveway was lined with cement planters and little topiary bushes and there were two Chinese dragons made of stone that flanked the two-car garage. It had all seemed a paradise to her when she moved in.

Most of all it was the smell she loved; everything in the house, the house itself, was brand new: the carpets, the furniture, the appliances, the ruched taffeta curtains in all the windows, the pale mauve Formica panels that hid the closets in her bedroom, the matching silk spread and curtains, the granite in the kitchen, the marble in the bathrooms.

In another room was a wall-size plasma screen and a cream leather sofa: Genia's own home entertainment center. In all her life she had never expected to live in a big house with a living room like the one where she sat now, her feet planted on the thick carpet. A house with a sunken living room, the floor covered in pale carpet. Wall to wall, she had said.

The first time she told me about the carpet was one of the few times I'd seen her really smile. She didn't smile much in the old days; she was afraid to show her lousy teeth. The teeth had been fixed. She had the house.

To her, the best part, she had said, was the smell. It smelled new. She had gone up and down the stairs, in and out of the rooms, sniffing it. Sometimes she bent over to be closer to the smell, putting her nose against the fresh shining surfaces. In the dining room was lots of black teak, an enormous table with silk orchids on it and a breakfront with glass doors; inside was Genia's collection of fancy china, all of it black and gold. From France, she had said; it was French.

To me the house smelled like plastic. Or vomit. The faint smell that lingered after someone had puked. It smelled unwrapped and unlived in, but it wasn't my house, so it didn't matter; it was Genia's fantasy, a place she entered every day of her life as if through the pearly gates. She had told me all this once when she first moved in and invited me over for tea.

Instead of tea, she had opened a magnum of Dom Pérignon some well wisher had presented to her. We drank it all and smoked cigarettes, and sat on the white sofa together and reminisced like a pair of old Russians. Just that once, tipsy from the bubbles and laughing at old bad Russian jokes about bad sausage and corrupt politicians, I had felt close to her, as if we were brother and sister and had grown up together.

Again I noticed how she held her pack of cigarettes; like me, I thought again.

I put my arm around her now and said, "Scared of me? Scared, who of?"

"Cops. Give me a cigarette, please."

"You have one in your hand."

She stubbed it out in a crystal ashtray on the coffee table and I gave her another one and lit it and she smoked it silently all the way down to the filter, then dropped it in a thin porcelain coffee cup next to the ashtray, where it sizzled and died.

"Where did they go, Billy and the friend?"

"Upstate. He's with Stevie Gervasi, his friend, like I said. It's only Sunday. He only left yesterday morning;

the father was taking them upstate. To learn skiing. I think. Or maybe skate. Hockey skating on a lake."

"What's the name of the town, Gen?"

"Indian name. Not far. Maybe an hour, they said. Mahopac, something like this?"

"If he was only a few hours late, how come you're so scared?"

"I told you. I called. There was no one home. I wanted to speak to Billy. I called at the place they go, Stevie's people, I called to Billy's cell phone. I called the mother. I don't know. Now you bring his cross so I know something is bad."

I said, "Johnny's still at the restaurant?"

She nodded.

"He slept there last night?"

"Yes. Weekends, it gets late, sometimes he sleeps in his office."

"Yeah, sure, but two nights in a row? Gen?"

"It's OK. I don't want him driving when he's drunk." She glanced out of the window. "It's almost snowing."

"He could call a cab. You could pick him up. It's not far."

"It works for us, OK? It's OK. You understand. He likes it. He stays late with the guys, he plays cards with the bussers. He enjoys this." She looked at me. "We don't know if anything is wrong. Do we? Artie? I mean until the Gervasis get home." She was frantic.

I found some Kleenex in my pocket and gave it to her. "Wipe your face, Genuska," I said in Russian and put my arm around her.

She leaned against me and wiped the tears and snot

168

and mascara off and balled up the tissue in her hand.

I said, "What was Billy wearing when he left the house this morning?"

She looked up.

"You saw him leave, right?" I said. "You saw him go, didn't you? You wouldn't let your kid go without seeing him, isn't that right, Genia? What was he wearing?"

She nodded. "Around 6.30 yesterday morning. It was foggy, so I watched him. He went across the street. He went to the Gervasi house. It was OK."

I thought about Ivana. She had stumbled over the clothes around ten. Four hours after Billy left home.

Genia played with the sharp little ends of her short red hair. It was a mess, the ends wet with sweat, as if she'd been running her hands through it for hours.

"What did he have on?"

Genia didn't hear me, or didn't want to. "He said I want to do this myself. He said I'm almost twelve. I want to go to Stevie's alone. I can do it myself. My grandpa always let me, he said."

"Your father? The old man?"

"Billy liked him. They were OK together before he died. Except for once. Once I found Billy screaming, just sitting, screaming. I said, what did he say to you, the old man? And he said, about the war, like always."

"Go on."

"When Billy gets an idea, he's very intense. He talks really good, Artemy, he was talking when he was two years old, he talks with big words in English I don't understand. It's very hard to say no. He gets upset, and I want this, for him to be independent. Isn't that right?

Artemy? It's right, isn't it? So I said, OK. OK. It was all set. The day before I talk to Stevie's mother, very nice, very wealthy and decent woman, and nice to me, you know, and everything is arranged."

"You went over there already?"

"Of course, you think I'm an idiot? Billy was supposed to be home this morning, As soon as I see he is late, I call and when there is no answer I go over. The house is dark." She looked at her square gold watch. From Cartier, she told me once. From Cartier.

"But you saw him go."

"Yes. Johnny said, I want him home for church Sunday, but what for? Johnny never comes home for church. I go to that church with Billy for their sake, I become Catholic, I did all that, to be an American. Then I discover these priests they do dirty things with little boys." She laughed bitterly. "This will kill Johnny. He loves the kid, or pretends he does."

"What does that mean?"

"Johnny's a hugger, you know? He gives you big sloppy kiss, he thinks this shows his love. He's like a child himself."

Straightening her spine, Genia leaned forward again as if she couldn't support her own weight. She combed her hand through her hair over and over, then looked up as if to study my expression.

I got out my cell phone. "I'm going to call this in, Gen. I can't do anything until you say he's missing officially."

"Please, wait. A little while longer, OK, Artemy? It's only Sunday. It's only a few hours. Wait a few hours. It's not even dark."

She picked up the gold cross and worked the chain through her fingers like rosary beads.

"He was wearing it when he left?" I said.

She nodded.

"What else was he wearing? Take me through it."

"I didn't want him growing up frightened like me. I know he's a funny child, strange sometimes, but Johnny says, let him grow up, and this way Johnny is sometimes right. He takes the bus to school. I let him walk to Stevie's. He goes to his grandmother on the bus. I let him bike to the restaurant when weather is good, you see? Even the old general let him go around the block alone."

"How come you call your father the general like that?"

She shrugged.

I said, "Tell me about Billy's clothes."

But she was on another track again. She led me into the kitchen, where she made coffee and I sat in the breakfast nook. She talked. You couldn't stop her. She talked without stopping so I had to pay attention. She held me in the endless talk like a bug in a web.

"Yes. So Friday night I said, he could go. I said you can walk to Stevie's by yourself Saturday morning. Tomorrow morning. Saturday. Then the two of them would be together all day with Stevie's family in the country. Then he'd stay over. I pretended not to see him. I didn't let him know I was awake. It was early in the morning. A little before 6.30. So I heard him get up. I heard him go downstairs and let himself out and I watch him all the way across the street and over two houses. I can see him all the way to the front of the Gervasi house because the streetlights are still on and also people on block have lights outside their houses." Genia paused. "So it was OK. I went back to sleep. He's very independent. He's not an emotional kid. He's very sure, you see, very determined. He's . . ."

"What is he?" I asked.

"Nothing."

"He's what, you were going to say? He's . . . Tell me!"

"Do you want some coffee, Artemy? I have cake. Cheesecake. Good cheesecake from Junior's."

Sometimes I thought, when I was in a better mood, that the biggest danger of being a cop was the cake. People who talked to you—and plenty did—wanted you on their side. They made coffee. They put out cake. I loved cake. You could gain a ton of weight on a long case. You could also get so wired from drinking coffee to keep them talking, you almost freaked out.

She said, "I can't remember."

"Remember what?"

"If Stevie's mother said what time they'd be back. I can't remember now. I'm confused." Her face was pallid, a whitish green and slick with a faint sheen of sweat. "What do you want to know?"

Again, I said, "What was Billy wearing when he left?"

"I told him, dress warm. I put his clothes out."

"He does what you say?"

"He's very smart," she said. "He's a good boy. Very neat, you know."

"So what was he wearing?"

"I put them out for him. Jeans, OK. Sweatpants. T-shirt. A heavy sweater. The baseball jacket you got him, he likes the jacket, Yankees jacket, you remember? He doesn't care about baseball but he wears the jacket. I wanted him to wear his winter coat, but I knew he wouldn't so I put out a heavy sweater. I made him wear sweatpants under his jeans."

"Why wouldn't he wear the coat?"

"Because," she said. "I'm telling you, he always wears his baseball jacket, the one with the tear in the sleeve. He wouldn't let me fix it. He said he got the tear when you took him to the stadium. It had to be that way."

"Shoes?"

"Sneakers," she said.

"What color?"

"Green."

"Socks?"

"No socks. I put them out. He doesn't like socks."

"What do you mean?" I tried not to show what I was feeling.

"He doesn't like them. He gets obsessed with stupid stuff. Sometimes he starts yelling about nothing and I just say, OK."

"Did he have anything with him? Was he carrying anything?"

She nodded. "Sports bag he takes to school."

"But no socks."

"No socks. They make him itch."

"You're sure he didn't change his mind?"

"He does not change his mind. What is it about his clothes, Artemy?"

I hesitated. "Let's go over to Billy's friend and see if anyone's home yet. Come on."

She said, "I have to fix myself. I can't go like this."

"Then go fix yourself, Gen. Go on."

I waited in the living room while she went upstairs. I heard the water running. At first I wanted to run after her. She was febrile, fragile, weirded out; I thought Genia might hurt herself.

Did Johnny always spend the weekends at his restaurant? Was he asleep, drunk, knocked out? I got up and looked out of the kitchen window at the yard in back. Ice clung to the bare trees; the barbecue set, the furniture, the tool shed were shrouded in black plastic.

Upstairs I heard Genia moving from room to room. I waited for her at the bottom of the stairs. After a while she came down in a skirt and sweater and her pearls; Genia resembled an Upper East Side mother. She fidgeted with the sweater as if it were a costume.

"You look nice," I said, holding my cell phone.

She was panicky. "Who are you calling?"

"My boss. We need to get on this. You need to say he's missing."

"No! Not yet." She gripped the sleeve of my jacket. "Not yet. Let's go, OK? I'm ready."

I zipped my jacket. She went to the hall closet and pushed aside the furs and took out a camel's hair coat and put it on.

I looked at her fur coat on a hanger and said, "It's cold out."

"I don't want to look like Russian, like immigrant," she said. "I don't want to look that way, you understand?"

The streets were empty. Genia's silver Land Rover—Johnny bought it for her fortieth birthday—was parked outside her house.

"Which house?" I said.

"On the corner," she said, pointing to a white colonial with an ocean view. I turned to look back. You could see the corner of the Farone place from the white house.

There was an SUV in the drive. We walked up to the front door and Genia rang the bell. We waited.

The door opened. A woman in her late thirties stood in the doorway. She wore jeans and a loose plaid shirt. She had shoulder length hair, dirty blonde, a pencil behind her ear, and a placid expression.

"Hi," she said. "I was just going to call you back. I spent the night over at my sister's place. I just got back. Genny, I got your message. What's the matter?"

"Is Billy here?" I said. "Is Billy at your house?"

She said, "No, of course not. I thought the boys canceled their date. Come in," she said, but Genia shook her head.

"Stevie said sometimes your Billy just doesn't show up. I mean the kids are like that. But Stevie said Billy did call this time. He called before six yesterday morning. He said he wasn't coming. He had something else. He had to go out with his father. Stevie was pretty upset, but his father said, listen, never mind, honey, we'll go have a nice time."

"Where's Stevie?" Genia said.

"He's still out with his dad. They went to the country like they planned. They planned to come home this morning so Billy could go to church like his father wanted, but when Billy didn't show, they said they'd stay late. I'm sorry, Genny, I am, we thought Billy had something else on."

"Can you call?"

She shook her head. "They're skiing. They'll be on the slopes all day. The cell doesn't work there. I'll try but it never works. I think they'll be back tonight, you know, but sometimes they stay over. I'll try the cabin again tonight. What is it?"

Genia nodded, thanked her, turned to go.

"What's the matter?" the woman called as we went down the front drive, along the irregular paving stones set into the path, Genia looking down as if to count them one at a time.

"Thank you," I said. "Thanks. Call us when your family gets back."

Behind us, she closed the door and I realized I didn't know her first name.

Not crying, Genia walked with her shoulders held stiff and her arms hanging rigid by her sides. I put my arm around her, but she shook free.

"No cops, Artemy. Promise me. Not yet. Nothing good comes from this going to police. You'll find him. You're a detective, you're good, you do it. For me. Please?"

"You're sure the sneakers were green? Were they All Star high tops?"

She looked at me. "He wears them every day. What is this about sneakers?"

"Does Billy wander away, Genia? Does Billy do that?"

176

"Sometimes," she said. "Maybe. Sometimes he goes to Johnny's mother."

"You're close with Mrs. Farone, with Johnny's old lady?"

"You met her?"

"Yeah I met her."

"Then you know. I can't stand her. I brought up Billy Catholic, it's still not good enough for her. She's a peasant, Artemy, she's a red-neck peasant villager, you know this type? Italian. Crude people. No books, no nothing in that house, just statues of Jesus Christ. Ugly pictures of saints, and the old lady dressed like a disco queen."

"You called her?"

"I called her. She didn't see Billy, she said. She hasn't seen him in at least two weeks, she was furious."

"What about the husband, Billy's grandfather?"

"Bastard," she said. "I called Johnny's sister. The old man is in Florida. He's in Florida. They say he needs rest."

"When did he go?"

"January."

"I want to see Billy's room," I said.

She led me up the stairs that were covered in the same pale carpeting as the living room. The first door on the right opened to the boy's room. I had only been inside a few times. Billy always waited for me outside when I picked him up.

"You've been cleaning? I don't remember his room this neat."

She shook her head. "Lately he changes. He wants

everything perfect," she said, looking at the walls that were papered with pictures of fish, fishing rods, boats, nets. "He did it himself," she added. "He put those pictures up, one at a time, until there was no space left. I was very proud of that. He is smart, good boy, right, Artie? You know, he can name all kinds of fish, he tells me. He can make what do you call them, flies to go for fishing with."

"Tell me who his friends were."

Genia sat down on the edge of the bed and fingered the bedspread. "I don't know, Artemy He didn't say so much about friends. I went to school and I ask, does he have some friends and they don't know. We take and put him in private school. I say to Johnny this boy needs extra help, for what do they call this, socializing. But Johnny says forget about it. He's perfect. He's OK."

I looked at the shelf of books over the desk that held his computer. Schoolbooks were neatly filed next to encyclopedias and there were more fishing books. There were volumes of boys' adventure stories that looked untouched. Three paperbacks by Joseph Conrad were next to the adventure stories. I pulled one out.

"He reads this stuff?" I said to Genia.

"Someone tells him these are stories of the sea and he gets them on Amazon. The teacher says he reads 11th grade level, even higher, like sixteen-year-old kid. I let him. If he reads so good, this is great, right, Artemy?"

"He still plays Little League ball?"

"He quit. He didn't like baseball. He wanted to be with his fish tank. He designs feeding system for fish. In garage, you want me to show you?"

We went back downstairs and while I tried to persuade her to let me call Lippert, she smoked, one cigarette lit from the butt of the one before, and begged me not to.

Finally I asked the question I had been dreading.

"What kind of shirt did he wear yesterday, under his sweater?"

"T-shirt," Genia said.

"What kind of T-shirt, what color?"

"Oh, Artemy, this is one of Billy's crazy things. He has this red T-shirt he always is wearing, always, too small for him, like from when he is a little boy, but he wears it like some prize, something, how do you say?" Again she switched back to Russian. "Something sacred," she said. 'Something holy."

It wasn't a holy shirt, it was a shroud. I told Genia about the clothes near the beach.

"You have to look at them, Gen. I have to take you."

"Where?"

"To police headquarters, where they have the clothes in a lab. Lippert will meet us. He'll be nice, I promise, and I'll go with you, but you have to look."

"This Lippert? He's the one you worked for before?"

"Yes."

"I don't like him," she said. "He reminds me of a KGB official that came to our school once, to tell us about security, I remember. He looked like that. No one said he was KGB, but we knew. We knew because he has this suit that is Western and no one has Western clothes."

179

"That was a long time ago. This is America. Brooklyn."

"Nothing changes," she said. "Except we become less safe, more frightened, terrorist, disease, war coming. I read they pick up immigrants now, they can arrest you for anything."

"That's illegal immigrants, Gen. Or maybe Arabs, you know? It's not us. You're married to an American. You're a citizen."

"How long?" she said. "How long since you found these clothes?" She was stalling, watching the door, listening for the phone, still waiting for Billy.

"Yesterday morning," I said.

"You waited so long?"

"I wasn't sure. I asked Johnny if Billy was OK, he said sure. Then the little girl, May Luca, you know, she turned up dead and we got the thug that killed her. We assumed the clothes were hers."

"You assumed?" she said.

"I didn't want to upset you."

"If I tell you this thing, you can't tell Johnny."

"Go on."

"Christmas time, Johnny's mother, you know, this old lady, very devout, Italian and Polack woman, forty-seven years she is married, she throws out the husband."

"Why?"

She leaned close to me and her voice was ragged.

"You can never say this, that you hear this from me," she said over and over. "I don't want it has any connection to me."

I was silent.

"Swear."

"Yes."

"On your father's grave."

"Sure, if you want."

"Johnny loves the old man, and he makes cuddly granddad for the kid, but I know something and maybe the mother figured it out. It was one thing that makes me wonder about marrying Johnny, but I want to marry him, so I deny it even to myself. I knew the old man, you see, before I married Johnny. He was Italian, but he was friendly with my father. He had also been in World War II."

"Like your old man."

"They talk about Red Army," she said. "They talk about the war and how they liberate Europe, Russians, Americans. They got out their medals. Bullshit stuff. When my Elena was little, I once found old man Farone with his hands under her dress and I tell to him, get out of this house. My father didn't believe it. I said if he comes here again, I call the welfare and have him removed. So the old men they meet on the boardwalk and play chess together. He was a dirty bastard and I hated him. He was a pig."

"So Johnny's mother threw him out and Billy never saw him after that?"

"I don't let him. Johnny gets furious. After forty-seven years, Christmas Eve, she throws him away."

"What was his job, the husband, when he was younger?" I said, not sure why it mattered.

Genia looked up.

"He was policeman," she said. "Except for Johnny, whole family was cops."

"Gen?"

"What?"

"Could the old man have something to do with Billy disappearing?"

"Just find Billy."

"Let's call Johnny and I'll sit with you until he gets here."

"I think Billy will come home this evening," she said. "I'm sure of this." She looked at her watch. "It's only four o'clock. I am sure he will be back for supper. I'm sure. Everything will be OK. Will you give me until tomorrow morning, Artemy? Artemy, no police, please. I beg you. Please."

Genia let go of my hand and slipped to her knees. She kneeled on the thick pale carpet and I didn't know if she was praying or begging. She whispered, "I know this is right. I know you feel like father for Billy, right, and he tells me once he wishes you were his real father."

"Get up," I said.

I felt myself dragged back into a world of secrecy, unofficial deals, meaningless talk where everybody lied or told half-truths. You learned, where I grew up, to hide things even from yourself. Most of all from yourself. Genia's face was twisted with fear, fear of the cops, of Johnny, Zeitsev, her own past. Maybe me. I wanted to get out. I felt like I was suffocating. I looked at the door.

"Billy loves you most in the world, Artemy, OK, so promise me we do this right way for him, OK? Just until tomorrow. I don't want his picture in papers or TV, I don't want. Please."

"I'll be back in the morning. You call me. You call me regularly, you promise me?"

She took my hand and I thought she might kiss it.

"We'll find Billy ourselves, won't we?" Genia asked.

Billy loves you most in the world. Genia's words stayed with me and as I left the house, I felt heavy with it. I didn't know what to do. I didn't know if I should keep my promise to her or if I should call Lippert and get the word out. I was terrified for Billy, but I had promised Genia.

Trapped, the door still open, my hand on the knob, I turned around. I was going to tell her I couldn't wait. That I had to report in. Lippert would kill me; he would fire me. Worse, Billy might die.

But Genia was right: Billy's picture would be on TV, in the papers; once it was official that he was missing, his image would be everywhere. It might scare the guy who took him. Billy might die.

I wasn't sure if Lippert's guys would find Billy either; they could descend on a case like dinosaurs, they could come down heavy, trample the territory, destroy the evidence. Caught. I felt paralyzed.

My hand was on the door, but the door was still open, and now I heard Genia on the phone. Who did she call as soon as I was gone?

A few minutes later when I was in my car, my own phone rang and I searched my pockets frantically for it. It was in my hand.

18

Fire power, fire balls, people falling, limbs, flesh impaled on railings, and the noise, the rumble, thunder, the short burst, and then the bright hot airplane fuel and the snap and shutter of cameras everywhere, and he's alone, covered in dust, a glass of orange juice still in his hand, a piece of bagel in his mouth. The taste of dough, the sesame seeds, orange juice, blood. Dust in his nose, eyes, throat, coughing blood.

Elem Zeitsev told me, when I got to his place, that Genia's call had grabbed him out of the nightmare. She called him, he called me. He knew we were related. He was worried about her. Worried sick about the boy, about Billy.

Her call, he said again, awakened him from the repeating dream and now he sat on the edge of the sofa in his apartment, in Brighton Beach, holding a bottle of vodka questioningly in my direction. I shook my head. He put down the vodka and picked up his coffee cup and stared out of the window at the ocean.

When he'd heard Genia's voice on the phone, he got

up off the sofa where he'd been sleeping with the Sunday papers on his chest, and went into the bathroom.

He had looked at himself in the mirror. He was almost fifty-one now and haggard; nothing had been the same since September 11, when he found himself on the 79th floor of Tower One. He had gone up to the Trade Center to have breakfast with his broker, who was a friend, and drop off a present for his broker's kid, who was Zeitsev's goddaughter.

Eighteen already, he says. Do you remember when the kids were born? So he goes up in the elevator, holding the blue Tiffany bag, eager to chew the fat about the market. Grab some breakfast. Discuss plans for a vacation together, all of them, both families. Colorado, they were thinking, maybe Napa Valley.

He wore a Hermes tie that morning; it was yellow, he remembered, he remembered choosing it when he woke up that morning in his place in Tribeca. Yellow with pink watermelon slices. An old tie. A tie he loved. A tie that Genia had given him.

A few hours later, the tie is stiff with dust, stiff as paste. He has thrown water over himself to stop the sense he is burning up and it mixes with the dust and makes paste.

The beautiful morning. Everything bright, clean, fresh. He waves his driver away and walks. He rides the elevator. He meets Peter, his friend, whose secretary brings orange juice and bagels.

And then the world blows up, so he fights his way through the fire and dust and starts walking and on the way he loses Peter. He can't find him. He disappears into the maelstrom. One building is down.

Zeitsev walks down seventy-nine flights half carrying a woman in bare feet, her feet so cut up by glass there's blood all over him, and when they get out, she clings to him, they're covered with dust, he drags her up Broadway to a coffee shop that's jammed with dust people. Inside people are crammed together, hiding behind the counter, groping for the phone. Then the eerie silence settles. Then the other building collapses into itself.

"You're OK," he said to his image as he brushed his hair carefully and then glanced out of the bathroom window. Snow coming, he thought.

He surveyed the beach, almost empty now; he let his eyes roam across the boardwalk, the cafés and restaurants. He should have been happy; most of what he saw had belonged to his father, and he'd sold it and made himself legitimate. He rarely used the apartment; he had the place in the city and, when he wanted the beach, there was the house in East Hampton on the south side of the highway, near Georgica Pond. He had run into Steven Spielberg once and the guy actually said hi.

Zeitsev hated Brighton Beach, but he kept the apartment for business, and because he needed a place close to Genia. If she needed him, he was there. He never admitted it was about the boy. About Billy. He wanted to be close.

Genia Farone had called him. He took the call because he liked Genia and there had been stuff between them and she was Billy's mother. Genia's older kid, Ellie, had been at school, at St Anne's, with Justine, his own daughter. When Ellie turned out to be a talented musician, Zeitsev put up the money for Juilliard. Nobody knew.

He looked out of the window at the ocean and thought about his father. He had detested the life with his father. His father had been a killer; he killed for profit; he enjoyed the killing.

I don't want this, Elem Zeitsev remembered thinking very early on. And he got out, didn't he? He took not just English lessons but elocution to lose his accent, he went to Columbia Law School, he clerked for a federal judge, he moved to Manhattan.

A businessman now, legit, his daughter at Princeton, he was on the board of the Tribeca Film Festival. He donated money to liberal causes. At first he gave to liberals because they were more credulous than the right and didn't ask as many questions, and afterwards, after he went legit, because he liked what they believed and also they had better parties; you met Bobby de Niro and Bono and former President Bill Clinton at their parties, and the women were smarter and better dressed.

He looked in the mirror. He was still crazy about Genia, he couldn't help it. He didn't know why, it was some animal attraction. There were younger, better looking women, there were smarter girls, there were the models and movie stars he met in Manhattan, and he was a good-looking guy even now.

The bathroom door opened and Elem Zeitsev saw his wife's reflection in the mirror. He followed her into the living room, where he sat down, and picked up the *Times*.

Her pearls preceded her; she always wore them, the

huge pearls the color of thick cream. He'd bought them for her once upon a time when they were in love and their Justine was born.

"What did she want?"

"Who, Katya, darling?"

"I prefer if you would use Katherine," she said. "You know who. Genia Farone."

"She needed some help."

She sat on the couch. "What kind of help, I thought you gave her plenty of help."

"I told you it was over with Genia a long time ago. It was nothing. One time." He lied to Katya but it was easier than enduring the tantrums.

He looked at his watch. "You're late, aren't you?"

She went into the office, even on Sundays. It was her refuge. Katya was obsessed with animals and she had carved out a legal practice for herself representing people who sued on behalf of their pets.

Straightening the jacket of her Prada suit, she adjusted the pearls, brushed down her skirt, picked up her bag and shrugged, then turned and left the room. The always unasked question remained. It hung between them. If she never asked whether Billy was Zeitsev's, it would never quite be true.

He stuck with Katya because she had helped him. She had given up breeding her stupid dogs, which had been her obsession, and gone to law school and then to work in the Estates Department of Story, Middleberg, Cole and McGowan on Madison Avenue. Katya bought the right clothes at Bergdorf's and got her hair cut by John Barratt at his salon, where she made friends with the

English babes she met there. She could work a room. She could charm. Zeitsev stuck it out with her.

He looked at his own shoes, which he ordered twice a year from London, and then out at the ocean. I have to get out of here, he thought; I have to get rid of this apartment. I don't know why I keep it, he said to himself, or what drags me back to this shithole of a neighborhood. He knew it was because of Genia.

Divorce him, Gen, he had said over and over. For years he asked her, but she couldn't. Johnny didn't deserve it, she said.

Christ, I hate this fucking apartment, Zeitsev thought.

He hated the brand new condos that backed onto Brighton Beach and faced the ocean. There was a gate at the front. The buildings had no patina; they were the kind of buildings men who had worked for his father coveted, expensive buildings, expensive apartments with acres of marble in the bathrooms and slick granite surfaces in the kitchen.

I didn't understand why Elem Zeitsev called me. He knew we were related, me and Genia, he said. He needed a favor. A few minutes later I was sitting in the living room of his apartment overlooking the ocean, listening while he talked about his nightmares. It was surreal. I barely knew Zeitsev. He wore jeans and a sweatshirt and looked haggard. His wife was out. We were alone in the room.

Zeitsev was raised by his father to be his heir. The father, Pavel, who was a kind of monster and who ran Brighton Beach for a while, owned land all over Brooklyn that he sold off when he needed cash. He was thought to have masterminded some of the gas scams that made a lot of Russians rich; the Medicare rip-offs were his invention, too, along with some of the most brutal forms of killing. He was never indicted. I met him once.

Years earlier, I'd visited the Zeitsevs in the old man's house near the ocean. In his presence, the rest of the family had behaved like serfs. He sat in an armchair with an orange cat between his hands. He watched the animal as if he might be thinking about strangling it.

Then when I came closer—he had summoned me to his side—he let the cat slip to the floor and got up to show me his books. He kept them in glass-fronted cases. The first editions were beautifully bound in green leather with gold writing on the spines; his passions were Emily Dickinson's poems and Emerson.

The old man made out he was some kind of literary scholar and a connoisseur; when *Boris Godunov* was on at the Met, he took a box. But he was a murderous thug. When he died, though, thousands of people turned out. It was like Stalin's funeral.

Elem Zeitsev talked now, untangling his life for me, a binge of self-revelation; I remembered that Genia was sleeping with him. Ivana had told me.

I said, "You want to tell me why Genia called you when she realized Billy was missing?"

He nodded. "I'm a friend."

"She's one of your charities?"

His tone stiffened. "Genia doesn't need charity."

"So, just to get it out of the way, where were you yesterday morning?"

He smiled slightly. "Are you asking me as a cop or her cousin?"

"What's the difference?"

"I didn't kidnap Billy. I was in the city. I ate breakfast at Balthazar. I left my apartment at seven, you can ask the doorman, if you want, if you don't want to ask my wife. I went for a run with a neighbor. I'll give you his name and number. I was at Balthazar by eight. They all know me there. I stayed until after nine. I had another cup of coffee on the way home. I went shopping with Katya at Jeffrey's in the Meat District. More?"

"No," I said.

"I hate it here." He looked out of the window. "It's everything about my family I hate. The way you hate Russia," he added.

I was startled.

Zeitsev said, "You wonder how I know that about you? It shows. You come out here and you hate it and it shows. You're uncomfortable. You feel as if it's yanking you back. Don't you? Am I right? We're a lot alike."

I got up.

"I'll come with you," he said.

"No, thanks."

"I have people looking for Billy."

"I'm not surprised."

"You're going to make it official. Aren't you?" Zeitsev's voice was weary.

"And if I do, what? You'll shoot me? You'll get some creep to interfere?"

He shook his head. "You don't understand, do you? I know you think I'm like my father," he said. "I'm not.

I would call the police, but I think out here the police are the problem. You know these cases that were never solved, the girl whose feet they cut? The other girl out on Long Island?" His voice went cold with anger. "You remember this? You heard about it, the way they destroyed the child's body, killed her, then cut her up?"

"Yes."

"I care about Billy. I care very much about the boy, more than you understand. That's as much as I feel like telling you now," he said. "You want to do business with me on this at all? Because I'll be staying with it one way or the other."

I said, "Probably not."

"Then it was a mistake to call you. I'm sorry." He stood up and walked to the door and opened it.

Without knowing why, I said, "You grew up in Moscow, didn't you?"

He nodded. "You can't hear it?"

"No. I just wondered."

"You neither," he said. "I took lessons to lose the accent I wanted so bad to get rid of all of it, you know, I wanted to dump the past. I couldn't until the old man died, but God how much I wanted that."

I wanted to say: "Is he yours? Is Billy your son?" I didn't, though; I knew he'd clam up. Instead I just said, "What do you want?"

"Give me until tomorrow," he said. "Please."

"Is that what Genia asked you?"

"Yes, but it's not the same reason. She's scared of the cops."

"But you're not."

Zeitsev said, "Not in the same way."

"What way?"

"Like I said, I'm scared of the way they fuck up. Look at how they let May Luca die. It was a simple case," he said. "I'm scared of the way they have a sense of entitlement, some of them, like a separate government, not accountable, at least out here." He gestured to the window and the coast beyond it. "This place is changing," Zeitsev added. "There are people who want to cash out before it becomes a complete little theme park, a tourist attraction, you know, see the old time Russkis, eat the pirogi and the borscht, see the hookers and criminals. The Russians move out, they move over to Mill Basin or Manhattan Beach and then there are people who don't like them, us, moving into their neighborhoods. To them, we're like blacks." He grinned. "You could call us black Russians."

"Which people?"

"I think you know."

I thought of Belle Harbor and Gerritsen Beach and the small tight insular communities a few miles away where a lot of cops lived.

Zeitsev said, "Have you seen the clothes from the beach?"

I nodded.

"I saw them, too. I know they were Billy's," he said. "I know it was the jacket you gave him."

"You knew?"

"He told me about the jacket. He was very proud of it. He loves you. He told me he wished you were his dad."

I said, "When did you know?"

"When Genia called me. She called earlier. She called again after she saw you."

Genia had called him first, she called Zeitsev before I got to her. How did she know? What made her think Billy was missing?

"How the hell did you see the clothes? They're in a forensics lab. No one gets in."

Zeitsev shrugged. "I have friends."

From my car I called Sonny Lippert to tell him what had happened; there was no answer. I tried his office, then his apartment. I tried his ex-wife. If the story broke, if it got out that the blood-soaked clothes did not belong to May Luca, all hell would break loose. There would be accusations of police incompetence. Worse, there would be the fear. It would spread. Mostly, though, I needed help finding Billy.

I was ready to betray Genia; so what, I thought, trying to reassure myself. So what? The kid was missing. I had to find him. I didn't know what the Farones' agenda was; Genia was terrified; Johnny was drunk; Zeitsev was unreliable. If I had to lie to Genia, tell her I was working the case myself, I'd lie. Where's Lippert, I thought. Where was he? I called again. Then, driving away from Brighton Beach, I thought: maybe someone close to Billy wants him dead.

19

Mrs. Farone opened the door before I rang the bell. She had been watching out of the window, or she knew I was coming. I followed her into the living room. I sat down on a chair without her inviting me.

"Where's Billy?" I said.

"You were already here. We already talked."

"Yesterday I dropped off something Johnny sent you. Now I'm here to ask about Billy."

"Another cop. It's always cops. Billy is OK," she said. "My Johnny said he went skiing with his friend."

"What do you mean, another cop? Someone was here today already?"

"I'm talking about my husband. Bastard," she said, spitting it out.

I said, "Yeah, I heard."

She was defensive. "Who from? Who did you hear from?"

"What's the difference?"

"I never knew nothing about him. You hear me? Just ask what you got to ask," she said. "Then go."

"Billy didn't go upstate. He's gone. He's disappeared." I watched carefully when I said it. Her face remained expressionless.

I moved closer to her and looked in her eyes and they were dead and flat and cold as fish.

"You're not interested?"

She said, "Sure I'm interested. Sure. I know this boy, he likes to go for a walk or on his bike by himself. I'm his grandmother, I know him. I know he's OK. He just went for a bike ride. OK? You hear me?" Her voice rose, shrill, panicky, irritated.

"Where does Billy play? Who are his friends?"

She hesitated. She turned to look out of the window as if there was something that required her attention.

"Listen to me, lady, Billy is missing. Tell me whatever you know or a lot more cops will be stopping by."

"I don't know nothing."

I leaned so close I could smell the sweet stink of the vanilla perfume.

"How is he with you?" I said. "Is he ever violent or passive, shy? He likes burgers, he plays ball, he visits friends, what? Just tell me something that could help me find him," I was enraged now. "Or don't you want me to find him? You know he's gone but you like it better this way, it's less trouble, is that it?"

She swore under her breath. I knew that as soon as I left, she'd call Johnny. I wanted her to call. He'd go crazy when he heard about Billy from her and she'd get under his skin and maybe Johnny would blow up and I'd learn something. I planted the land-mine in her and I'd wait for him to step on it.

Mrs. Farone was silent. Then suddenly, out of the blue, she looked at me hard.

"Billy is a very handsome little boy. You understand? Sexy almost. He don't know what it means, but he knows enough. People turn around to look at him in the street. He don't see it. Men. Women. Or maybe he knows and keeps it secret. He has secrets. Most of the time, he can't tell what other people are feeling or thinking, or anything. Most kids, they got instinctive information on people, you know? But Billy, he can't see, he don't pay no attention to other people. He likes playing alone, so he don't understand what's in their minds."

"No friends?"

She hesitated.

I leaned forward. "You want to be an accessory? You want to stand up and say, I didn't tell the truth and Billy died?"

"OK, there's one girl. Sometimes she comes to play with him. Sometimes he goes there. They're in Catholic school together, then my son's wife takes Billy out of Catholic school."

"What girl?"

"Because of her I have to throw out my husband. Because he touches this girl. I find them and I tell him to go."

"What girl? What was her name?" I said.

"You don't harass me, you hear, or you can get out."

"Then tell me."

Suddenly she looked frightened. She glanced at the front door as if someone might appear.

"If you don't tell me, I can arrange for you to come

with me and someone else can talk to you," I said. "Someone who's not family," I said.

"He was a nice man, my husband." She tossed her head in the direction of a photograph on her mantel. "He was OK until this girl comes. Old days, he took Billy fishing. All the time. There's a shack near Breezy Point, out by the water, you know where I mean. I think he took Billy once or twice," she said. "Yeah, he did."

"Write it down for me." I shoved a piece of paper under her nose. "Just do it."

"Why should I?"

"Where's your husband?"

"Yeah, Florida," she said. "With Johnny's sister."

"What was he?" I said. "What was his work?"

"He was a cop," she said. "Whole fucking lousy family is cops. Here, Russia. Poland. Italy. The army. All cops."

"Write down the address," I said. "The place near Breezy Point."

She grabbed the piece of paper and a pen. She scribbled it hurriedly. She wanted me out. She got up and held the door open.

"Thanks for your time," I said, and she barely nodded. "Now you can tell me the name of the little girl Billy played with."

"I think you already knew, right? Her name was May Luca, and now she's dead."

It was May's red T-shirt near the beach after all; it was May's but it was Billy who had left home wearing it that morning. Had she given it to him? Was her death connected to Billy's disappearance? Billy's sacred shirt, something that obsessed him, belonged to May Luca.

20

A state trooper pulled me over as soon as I got to the
Marine Bay Bridge. In the rear view mirror, I could see
Manhattan behind me, the skyline pale gray, like a ghost
disappearing as it turned dark.

Just routine, the trooper said. Routine. The country
on Orange Alert, he said. Going up to Red. New York
already on Red all the time. He was a garrulous fat man
and when I showed him my badge, he made a joke about
Osama. We didn't believe anything, so we told jokes.

On the other side of the bridge was a spit of land, the
Rockaways at one end, Breezy Point at the other, a thin
finger of land between Jamaica Bay and the Atlantic.
Normally dozens of planes circled and swooped in the
mysterious patterns of arrival and departure, but the
weather was closing in and only a single plane circled,
looking for a gap in the low ceiling of cloud that hung
down almost to the water.

Nearby were New York's salt marshes and wetlands
and swamplands; in Pumpkin Channel a body would
sink without trace. There were deep woods, too; a

terrorist with a shoulder-to-air missile could reach a plane as it took off. The woods were easy to get to and in the winter, when it was deserted and snow fell, no one would see you.

It was over Rockaway Beach that a plane went down in October 2001, a month after 9/11. Officials said the American Airlines jet broke up because of a mechanical defect. A lot of cops and firemen I knew believed it was terrorists. Officials hid the truth and called it accidental because the city couldn't stand another attack. People had no reserves left. I can't do this again, Maxine said to me. I don't have anything left.

Glancing at the scrap of paper where Mrs. Farone had written an address, I turned right and drove slowly. I was looking for the fishing shack. Her husband had brought Billy fishing out here. Maybe he had taken May Luca, too. I tried to use my phone, call Lippert, call Maxine; there was no signal.

Along the road were rows of small ramshackle bungalows, a bar, a church. I didn't know how this place was connected to the kidnapper, or if the old man was involved, but it was something. It was better than driving around Brooklyn blind; it was better than waiting; I tried to reach Lippert again, got through to his machine, left a message, or thought I did; the machine cut me off suddenly and again the signal died.

On my left was nothing except marshlands. On the right were more fishing shacks, most shuttered for the winter, dark and unheated. No one came here in the winter, and the gas station at the corner was closed.

The fog moved in, heavy now, seeming to carry

sheets of snow in its folds. I switched stations on the radio to get a clear signal. LaGuardia was closed, so was Newark and only a few flights were coming in at JFK. In the headlights, I could see the shafts of snow.

Along the narrow roads where I drove up and back again were more bungalows, windows boarded up, hibernating, eyeless. At the end of one street was a small house with a green fence. The number was rubbed off the door, but the house matched Mrs. Farone's description. The windows were dark. The geraniums in a plastic pot were dead. I parked and went up the front walk.

The snow coming down hard froze the skin on my face. I banged on the front door, stopped, and banged some more. I yelled out. I peered in windows.

I went around to the back, where a couple of metal garbage cans rolled on their sides. The wind tossed them together and the discordant banging seemed so loud I half expected to hear someone coming to find out what the noise was, a car, a siren, a gun. A third can was still upright, its lid weighted down with small rocks. I yanked off the lid. Inside was a black plastic bag with some trash in it.

A noise distracted me and I to the back door of the shack. It was padlocked and bolted. I got hold of my gun and wrapped my hand around the butt, thinking I'd break a window.

I didn't have a warrant. I wasn't a local detective. If I got it wrong and screwed up, the guys out here would come down hard on me. There would be resentment. They'd make finding Billy harder. They'd want me off the case.

I was still waiting for Lippert's call back. Maybe It was irrelevant now. Maybe he was punishing me. My eyelids sank over my eyes. I was exhausted. I was edgy. Genia would be furious that I had called Lippert.

Except for the pale heavy sky and the slanty sheets of snow coming down, I could barely see anything. I crashed into one of the garbage cans and tripped and fell against a pile of fishing gear half shrouded in garbage bags. I stumbled to my feet.

Take it easy, I thought, and wanted a cigarette. If I made too much noise and they were nearby, the creep who took Billy would kill him. It would be my fault.

I grabbed at the padlock on the door and tried to force it open. It wouldn't give and I went back towards the car to get some tools. Better to break the lock than a window.

From the car, I looked back at the house that, in the storm, was only a smudge. Suddenly I saw a light flash on and off in the house next door. There was the blue glow of a TV set for a second, then it went off. I wasn't sure what I saw. The snow got in my eyes. The wind coming off the water whined.

For a minute or two I sat in the car. Did the light go on again? Was it a signal? Had I drifted off to sleep? I thought: I'm lost. I was lost and there was a child somewhere out there and someone going to kill him. Or already had. Not just any kid. It was Billy and I saw him as a small helpless figure wandering through a vast open expanse of snow and fog.

Bolt cutters in my hand, I went back to the house. Something bugged me now, some half remembered story I couldn't pull into shape enough to make sense of it. In spite of the cold, I began to sweat. In my pocket I found Ivana's crumpled pack of cigarettes and put one in my mouth. I was afraid to light a match but the tobacco smelled good.

I edged my way towards the house. I believed that Billy was inside because I had to. Or he was inside one of the other shacks. I didn't know how I knew; I believed it. I thought about Mrs. Farone, her telling me about the shack in Breezy Point and about her husband who liked little girls. Maybe he liked boys. Maybe he liked Billy. It happened. Most of the creeps who abused children were inside a family; they had been abused, and they did it to their kids and their grandchildren and it never ended.

Then another light, this one from across the street. I hurried over. Something had stopped me from breaking the padlock on the house with the green fence. I had to check this other house, maybe other shacks and cottages, squat and ghostly in the storm. My feet slipping out from under me, I moved forward slowly. The fog in front of me was substantial, hard to penetrate, everything seemed to slump under its weight. Then the light I had seen disappeared.

In the distance I heard a fire engine. Snow fell in my collar and down my neck. It settled, wet and creepy, a ring of damp, a noose.

I went house to house. I peered through windows. I went around into backyards that were covered in snow. The shacks were empty. No one came here in the dead of winter. There were no footsteps in the snow, no tracks.

Back at the house behind the low green fence, my hand wrapped around the bolt cutters, ready to break the lock.

The bolt cutters raised, I stopped. There was something, a noise, a scuttling, like mice running for cover. It came from inside. Again, I scanned the yard. I noticed the upright garbage can and leaned over to pull up the plastic bag that contained trash, boxes, newspaper, empty cans. Maybe there was something in the garbage can. My head was inside it when I heard a noise behind me. I wasn't fast enough.

I heard him at the same time I felt the cold damp steel of the knife against my neck.

A fleshy arm big as a log tightened around my shoulders. I could smell him. I could smell his sweat and his boozy breath and I could feel the scratchy wool of his sleeve.

"What the fuck do you want?" I said.

There was no answer.

The arm that held me was big as a ham and the knife was sharp and I felt a thin trickle of warm blood running down my face. I felt for my gun and somehow got hold of the grip.

"Who are you?" I said and gagged on his sleeve, but there was no answer and when I half-turned around I saw his face was covered with a balaclava, slits for the eyes, a hole for the mouth and the stinking breath coming out. My head hurt.

Somehow, I got him onto the ground. There was more blood, his, mine, and I was punching his face as hard as I could, I could feel my knuckles break and bleed.

Somewhere in the near distance I heard something thump along the pavement, along the ice, his head, I thought it was the sound of a head but my ears were stuffed. The noise was like a ghetto-blaster, like a plane when your ears are stuffed and all you hear is your heart. Like sonic boom over Howard Beach. Boom. My head. A plane. Concorde. Blood in my mouth. Hot. Salty. Viscous.

His eyes, slits through the hood, peered up at me. I showed him the gun. The eyes widened. He was scared.

"Who the fuck are you?" I said in Russian and put the gun next to his head.

He mumbled something. I caught the accent. He was a red-neck. He was a Russian peasant, probably an illegal, and he was scared.

"Who?"

"Zeitsev," he said.

I didn't believe him. Everyone knew Zeitsev's name. It was too easy. I hit him again.

A noise from the house distracted me for a split second, the creep stumbled to his feet and began to run. I fired off a round and missed. He ran like an athlete; he was faster than me. He disappeared. I stumbled towards my car. I couldn't see anything except the snow. I had lost him.

There was blood on the steering wheel. I put my hand to my head and it came away bloody. There were deep scratches. I felt hot and sick, and when I looked at my watch, I saw it was eleven at night. My body ached like hell, I was bent over the wheel like an arthritic pretzel, but I saw in the rear view that the wounds on my face were superficial. I sneezed. I was getting a fucking cold.

It pissed me off, getting a cold. OK, I said to myself trying to light a cigarette while my hands shook, OK, you want to cut me up, you want my head on a plate, OK, fine. But not in the middle of some godforsaken part of godforsaken Breezy Point in the middle of a storm. I hated the prick who did it, I hated how I felt. My throat hurt. I was shivering. My nose dripped.

On the seat beside me was a plastic bag and I tossed it on the back seat. Somehow I had carried it from the garbage can in back of the shack. I needed a Band-Aid and an aspirin and I wasn't sure I could make it back to the city.

21

"You were bleeding and you stopped for donuts?"

"Yeah," I said and closed my eyes. "I wasn't sure you'd want to see me so I got an offering. I couldn't find a pizza place."

"You're an idiot," Maxine said. "Get in the shower."

After I took a hot shower, and Maxie smeared some antiseptic on my face and put on Band-Aids and gave me a couple of Advil, she made me a steak sandwich, poured out some wine and brought it all into the living room, where I sat wrapped in a blanket. She set the tray on the coffee table.

"Listen, I'm sorry to come so late. I'm sorry I never showed last night, too. I'm just generally sorry."

"Who else would take you in?" She smiled. "I was up anyway. Honest. I was watching TV."

I bit into the sandwich. "I'll just eat this and then I'll go."

"Don't be an asshole."

"I have to go back."

"You're not going anywhere tonight. You look like

shit." She put her hand on my forehead. "You have a lousy fever."

I drank and the wine tasted wonderful.

"Where are the girls?"

"I let them stay on with Mark's mother upstate for a few days," she said. "I was a little freaked after they found that girl dead out by Sheepshead Bay." Maxie settled on the couch next to me. She was wearing jeans and an old red plaid flannel shirt that must have belonged to Mark. "What's going on, Artie? What do you need?"

"You," I said.

Maxie sampled a donut.

"These are good," she said. "Krispy Kreme, right? Listen I was thinking that you might be onto something with Totonno's pizza."

"Yeah?"

"Yeah, Totonno's is great, it's more like artisan pizza, really light, I mean you can eat a whole pie by yourself, it doesn't amount to more than two slices it's so light, but I'm still a Grimaldi's girl." She held up the donut that was covered with pink frosting and colored sprinkles and bit into it and the frosting left a pink sugar mustache on her upper lip. Maxine looked about twelve.

She tried to distract me, cheer me up, keep me focused on eating and resting. The pizza talk was code. With me and Max, it was the way we ran the relationship. We invested way too much in the relative merits of pizza and we both knew it, but it made us laugh. It made things easy. For me. Maybe it was only easy for me.

She kicked off her loafers and pulled her long legs under her.

"Can I ask you something, Artie? You feel up to it, I mean you don't want to just go to sleep?"

"I want to sit here with you. Talk to me."

But first she got back up and went to the stereo and put on *The Steamer*, an old Stan Getz album I bought her. Maxie was a rock chick; she liked Melissa Etheridge, she liked girl bands; she liked, though she never actually admitted it, Britney and Madonna and Jewel. For me, though, she listened to Stan and I liked her for it.

She sat down, leaned against me, listened for a few minutes and said, "It's nice. The music. I'm getting into it."

"I'm really glad. But what? You said could you ask me something."

"Did you like Mark?"

"Why?" I drank my wine down and poured some more then held up a pack of cigarettes.

She shook her head. "I think I really quit this time. I promised the girls. You go ahead. So, did you?"

"What?"

"Like him. I mean tell me the truth."

"I liked him OK. I think I was jealous, you know? You'd found this big handsome guy and you got married and had the girls. You had it figured out."

"You met Lily."

"That was after you married Mark," I said. "A lot later."

"Come on, Artie. You didn't want to settle down, not back then and not with me. Probably not with me at all. But, listen, I mean about Mark."

"He was OK. He did a good job. I thought he was

209

kind of obsessive if you're asking. You went fishing with him, the gear had to be in perfect order. You played some pick-up ball, he counted points. The rest of us sat around and guzzled beer, he went to the gym. It was like he was keeping stuff in or something."

"You think he was smart?"

"How do you mean? What is this anyway, what's going on with you?"

Restless, Maxie got up again and changed the music and sat down again. The shirt she wore was too big on her, the neckline gaped. I could see her breasts.

She shrugged and said, "I feel guilty."

"Because he died?"

"Because I'm tired of feeling guilty. Because I want to sort of get on with my life. Because I like sleeping with you, and I keep feeling like I have to go on being a widow, like I have to be in mourning, not for me but for other people. It's eighteen months." She hesitated. "Maybe I'm shallow, maybe I'm unfeeling, I don't fucking know, but I don't want to go to any more public events, any more memorials, any more anniversaries. I don't want to be some kind of pawn for politicians. I know other women who feel the same way. OK, I loved Mark, but the last few years were crummy and maybe we would have split up except I have enough Catholic guilt not to." Maxie was speeding.

"I'm sorry." I put my arms around her.

"You know what my mother said to me when I was twenty-three, she said, honey, you are twenty-three years old, this was a long time ago, she was a cleaning lady, you know, she never got an education so she cleaned people's houses, she said, when you are twenty-seven you should find a nice Asian guy and you marry him and you have some kids, even if the marriage don't last, that's what she said. But you get an Asian boy because they are smart and the genes, you know, they rub off." She laughed. "Mark wasn't really smart. He was a good guy, though. You want me to get another bottle of wine out?"

I shook my head, finished the food and sat back.

"So you want to talk about the case, or not, it's OK, either way."

"I think I know who the clothes from the beach belong to."

Maxie sat up. "Who is she?"

"It's not a girl. I think it's my cousin's kid."

"Billy? That kid you take fishing with the mother who married the restaurant guy? Shit, Artie. You're kidding. He got snatched? Why didn't you tell me?"

"Yeah. I was only sure today, sure enough anyhow."

"You think it has something to do with you?"

"What makes you ask that?"

"I don't know, but you talk about that boy a lot, I mean I know he matters a lot, and I know you worked some cases out by Brighton Beach back when and the creeps there probably have it in for you, they can be very personal when it comes to someone they don't like. Remind me how old Billy is?"

"Almost twelve," I said. "Twelve in a few weeks, but smart. Maybe he'll be OK, he's really smart, he could maybe think his way out of trouble."

Maxine took my hand. "I'm sorry, I'm really sorry."

My head hurt, my tongue was furry with fever and wine. I felt like crying. I put my head down on Maxie's shoulder.

"Artie? Listen, I have to tell you something and I can't, officially, because I was asked to keep my mouth shut. I saw the clothes from the beach."

I stared at her.

"A friend of mine in my old forensics lab was working on the ID. She asked my opinion."

"You didn't mention it yesterday."

"She told me to keep it to myself, she shouldn't have asked me, maybe, or they told her not to and you didn't ask me to get involved officially. And anyhow, it only happened yesterday afternoon." Maxie was rambling.

"It's OK," I said. "It's OK. What do you think?"

"Unofficially?"

I nodded.

"I think that the kid who wore those clothes was a sacrifice. The way the cut marks looked, the way the T-shirt was cut off with a razor, I'm sure it was a razor blade. There was so much blood," Maxie said. "There something ritualistic and horrible about the way they took the clothes and hid them, a clue, a sign, so we'd know the next thing we found would be the feet or the hands. You remember that case a while back? I saw the body on that case. The clothes here look similar."

For a few minutes we sat together on the couch, holding hands, silent. Then Maxine leaned over and said, "Do you want to sleep with me?" She reached up and kissed me lightly.

For a minute I was distracted. Genia's face, her old woman's face, pale and bleak, floated in front of my eyes.

Maxie said irritably, "Never mind."

"I want to."

"I don't need a mercy fuck, OK?"

I kissed her back. "That never crossed my mind."

By the time we got to her bedroom, most of our clothes were on the floor and we were laughing.

Later, half asleep, the snow sliding down her bedroom window, listening to Maxie breathe, I stared at the ceiling and felt, for the first time in years, content. Contentment's not something I was on regular terms with. It was good. Funny how it could come over you in the middle of all the shit.

Lying in the tangled sheets and blankets, Maxie exhaled and made warm mewing noises. It was like sleeping with a comfortable cat. I dozed off.

I couldn't tell if it was five minutes or a couple of hours, but I woke up suddenly, aware of another noise. Something different, something that had disturbed the balance, a noise coming from the other room.

It was dark in the apartment. I glanced at the window; outside it was completely white. There was nothing except snow.

Again from the living room came a noise, the faint creak of floorboards; the boards were laid over concrete and not nailed down and in certain places they creaked when you walked on them.

Maxie was fast asleep, unreachable, impervious. I didn't

wake her. My clothes, my gun, were in the other room. I lay still, listening. Someone was in the apartment.

Silently, I rolled to the side of the bed and then off it. In the dark, I fumbled for the flashlight on the bedside table. My hand wrapped around it.

My fingers felt the heavy metal tube. From the girls' room now I heard footsteps. Someone moving from room to room, coming in our direction.

Naked, with the flashlight in my hand and a blanket stuffed under my arm, I moved slowly towards the door.

Did he follow me from Breezy Point? Was someone on my tail? Did they want me bad enough to come for me miles away at Maxine's apartment? It was a couple of miles so they had come by car.

The way Maxie's building was set up always worried me. It was two stories high with two apartments, one upstairs, one down. You reached the upper floor—Maxie's—by an outside staircase to the street. On the other side of the building was a stretch of grass, a few trees, then Shore Drive and the river. You could come across the grass easy if you wanted to. You could get around to the front of the building and up those outside stairs without much trouble.

Throw a blanket, they told us. You suspect a terrorist on a plane, they had said, throw things. Water bottles. Fruit. Throw blankets. It was crazy, me, naked, with a flashlight and a blanket; I caught a glimpse of myself in the bedroom mirror. I wanted to laugh out loud. I was feverish. My head was burning.

Artemy often makes inappropriate jokes in class, the music teacher told my mother when I was thirteen. She was a pretty woman and I had asked if her G-string was tight enough. I had read about this G-string item in a Mickey Spillane novel I found in a black market bookshop near the Arbat in Moscow.

The floor creaked harder. The footsteps belonged to someone heavy. I positioned myself flat against the wall at the entrance to the living room and waited in the dark. Then I saw him.

The dark figure was tall and bulky, as big as Tolya Sverdloff. I saw him emerge from the children's room and move towards me. My eyes adjusted to the dark and I saw now that the front door was ajar. He seemed to see me at the same time I saw him and he lunged, but I was faster. I threw the blanket over him and he fought it for a moment and I tried to shove him onto the floor, but he was huge; it was like pushing a mountain.

From the street somewhere came the sudden sound of a siren, and it distracted me for a split second. The monster in my arms was as agile as he was big; graceful as a dancer even under the blanket, he slipped from my grasp, got to the front door and ran. I found my jeans, pulled them on, got my gun from the coffee table, and went after him, but he was fast. By the time I got down the stairs from Maxie's place to the path outside, he was halfway down across the snow-covered grass. He reached the highway. He skidded across the road in spite of the on-coming traffic and disappeared and I couldn't tell if he'd been run over or if he made it to the walkway along the river. The snow blotted out everything.

I ran. The snow under my bare feet. I reached the highway but he was gone. By the time I got back,

Maxine was already in the living room, phone in her hands, clutching a terry bathrobe around her.

"You're shaking," she said.

"It's alright," I said.

"I'm glad you were here," she said. "They came for the girls, didn't they?"

I thought about the creep who stuffed me into the garbage can out by Breezy Point and wondered again if I'd been followed.

"I'm not sure. I think it was me. But you want to call Mark's mother? Talk to the girls?"

She shook her head. "It's four in the morning. They'd be more scared by the phone ringing than anything else," she said, but already she was dialing the number.

A conversation with Maxie's mother-in-law followed, though I could only hear Max's end. The kids were OK. The mother-in-law was nervous.

Maxie said, "They're fine up there. They're OK. What can happen to them in Accord, New York? Right? What's your guess about this?"

"Right, sure. The kids will be fine. But I don't know if the kidnapping is just some goofball, you know, someone who only goes for family members, or a wing-nut or a serial, I don't know. I don't think anyone knows." I took her hand. "Let's make some coffee and you tell me if there's been anyone hanging around the girls, though, lately. OK? If anyone said anything to you or to them or anyone you know."

I got dressed and we went into the kitchen and sat at the table and Maxie opened the cabinet and took out a jar of coffee. "I'll make coffee," she said. "Or you want

Scotch? I might have a drink. But the girls are OK, right? I mean there's no creeps up there?"

Maxine was insistent and I heard a kind of denial. No more bad stuff, she was thinking. She had had her share. I knew that it didn't work like that.

"Yes," I said.

She poured the drinks and we stood in the kitchen and downed the Scotch.

"I have to get back to the city."

"Why?" she said.

I didn't answer.

"You want him to follow you, don't you? You want to see if whoever this creep is, if he goes after you. Listen, get some help, OK? Please. Let me call someone."

" I don't know who the thug was who bust in here or if it had anything to do with the stuff out by the beach, but I have to go. You get to bed. I'll wait until you fall asleep," I said.

"Honey, I'm a big girl. I have a gun locked up in the nightstand. The girls are upstate. I'm fine. I'll probably do laundry."

"Why?"

"Keeps me calm," Maxine smiled. "Passes the time."

"I think you're terrific." I put on the rest of my clothes and picked up my jacket.

"Because of the laundry?"

I kissed her.

"Because you're lovely, you're a really fabulous woman."

"It's mutual," she said and I could see she wanted to

say something else but she only smiled, kissed me on the cheek, put an ancient Martha Reeves album on the CD player, went into the bathroom and began sorting out laundry from the hamper.

22

Out of my window, a kid slid down the street on an orange plastic tray and, while I watched, he tumbled off the tray into high soft white drifts. After a while, he gave up; he trudged home, the tray on his head, lifting his feet high, trying to follow in the footsteps of a dog-walker who had made tracks ahead of him.

The blizzard, the holiday, everything was shut. When I got home from Maxie's around five that morning, hoping the creep who broke into her place would follow me, the snow was already knee deep. I had stayed in my car outside my front door, watching the street. No one came. I stumbled upstairs and into bed, put my gun on the floor along with my cell phone and slept.

When I woke up a few hours later, the snow was coming down two, three inches an hour. My head hurt. My body ached.

I rolled over and sat up and swung my legs over the edge of the bed. The floor was freezing and I ran for the kitchen, grabbed a bottle of water and some Advil, put coffee on and ran back to the bed. I felt lousy. My head was on fire. My feet were frozen. I stopped myself from falling back to sleep. I could have slept standing up. I could have slept around the clock, but somewhere in the oceans of white coming out of the sky was Billy Farone.

I had promised Genia I'd work the case myself for a day, but I didn't want Billy dying because his mother was terrified of cops, so I had left Lippert messages every hour. I didn't know if he had picked them up and I called Rhonda, his assistant, at home.

He'd flown up to Boston, Rhonda said, chasing some information about a kiddie porn ring that involved dirty cops and was connected to a case Lippert was involved with in the Bronx. He got the last shuttle up before the airports shut down. Rhonda promised to find him, give him my message.

I reached out for the radio and switched it on and listened to the news reports of the biggest blizzard in a decade. I loved the snow in the city. Lily had loved it. She would lie in bed and look out and yawn and yearn for more snow, for the kind of storm that paralyzed the city and where people skied to work on Fifth Avenue and stayed late in neighborhood bars and sometimes fell in love. I should have paid more attention to Lily.

Where women were concerned, I was usually a jerk. I knew I should settle down with Maxine. She was fun and smart and pretty. We had nice times in bed and out. I loved her girls; we could have a life. What difference did it make if I wasn't exactly besotted with her? So what if Lily had made me feel better than I was, smarter, more connected to the world; Lily was gone for good.

From the kitchen the smell of coffee reached me and

I forced myself out of bed and went and poured some in a mug. I sat at the counter and drank it and tried to eat the eggs I fried and couldn't. My jaw hurt. I stared at a cereal box. Everything, the words on the box, the pieces of Billy's case, seemed distant and disconnected. The fragments of the puzzle drifted free in my head like mental garbage and I tried to put them together and knew something was missing.

I spilled some of the coffee and hopped around for a while like a scalded cat, and then went and took a hot shower and wrapped myself in a robe and went back for more coffee.

Suddenly I noticed the red light blinking on the answering machine and I played the messages. One was from the nursing home in Haifa. I called back, and got the nurse who said my mother had been calling for me by name; for years she hadn't known who I was or my name, but now she had said it out loud: Artyom, she had called. Artemy!

Once, years earlier, I had picked up the phone and heard her voice, my mother, speaking Russian, calling to me: get me out of here, Artyom, get me out, your father has locked me up, I'm locked up, help me! The message on my answering machine had lasted twenty minutes, her repeating herself over and over.

Now I got through to her floor at the nursing home. She was asleep, the attendant said, and muttered something in Hebrew I didn't understand. Call back, she said after that. Call tomorrow.

On the shelf above the desk I kept a row of dictionaries: Russian, French, Hebrew, Arabic, most of

221

them shabby now, left over from school or jobs I'd done a decade earlier. Two decades. I reached up for the Hebrew dictionary and then I saw it. The dictionaries had been moved. The Arabic dictionary was on its side. Someone had taken it down from the shelf, then put it back hastily. I put it on the desk and flipped through the pages, but there was nothing. I stared out of the window, unnerved.

Someone had been here, in my place, the only place I had ever owned. When I moved into the loft it had pipes hanging from the ceiling, stained linoleum on the concrete floor, a century of crud on the radiators and window sills crusted black from the filth that settles everywhere in New York. One of the windows was broken and a dead pigeon lay on the floor underneath it, surrounded by broken glass. The bird had shattered the glass when it flew through it and killed itself. The loft had taken me years to fix, but it was mine—at least the part that didn't belong to the bank.

Someone had been here and for a minute I hesitated, desperate to look for more evidence. But I had to go. Maxine had called earlier. She was coming into the city, to catch up on her paperwork at the office. She wanted to meet for coffee. I promised her, so I got dressed. I grabbed my gun and went out to meet Max, and put a wedge of paper in the front door so anyone who broke in would disturb it.

The snow was deep and soft and I tumbled into a pile of the stuff, got up, walked stiff legged to a coffee shop near Police Plaza. Max was waiting.

I said, "How'd you get into the city?"

"I caught a ride with a guy I know. A cop. It took hours," she said. "I did what you wanted, honey." She ignored the no smoking rule and pulled out a pack of Kools. The place was empty. It was a holiday, and with the snow piling up, the city was silent and lovely.

"You want one?"

"It's like smoking candy." I smiled and got one of my own. "I thought you quit."

"That was yesterday. Artie, I raised an issue on the clothes that will take them another twenty-four hours at least. You've got a day, OK, is that what you wanted? By then I'll know who else has been to see the kid's clothes. I'll get you the list, if you want. I know you saw them at the beach, but in case you want another look."

"Thank you. I didn't ask, but thank you."

"Yeah, you did. You just didn't say the words. Listen, I can't do this often, Artie, you can't pull me into your private stuff too often, OK? I did it this time because I know how you feel about that kid, Billy."

"I didn't mean to pull you in."

"But you do. You just do. You know how I am. As soon as you tell me you need something on a job, you know I'll try and help."

"I promise I'll try not to," I said. "You want me to see if I can do anything about who broke into your house?" I asked.

"No. I talked to a guy I know at my station house in Bay Ridge. He's a cousin of Mark's. He came and looked at everything and he helped me get the locks changed because you can imagine trying to get someone in this weather at the crack of dawn. I'm sure it was just some local creep. They weren't exactly prime time crooks looking for my diamonds."

"What about the kids?"

"I'll go get them tonight if this storm breaks, if I can even get a bus that's going upstate. Thank God today's a holiday. It's only assholes like you and me at work. But the kids have school tomorrow. I can't leave them up at Mark's mom forever; also I don't want to owe her, you know?"

"How come?"

"Like I said, I can't play the grieving widow anymore, and that's what she needs." She crushed her smoke out in a saucer on the table and got up.

"Say hi to the girls."

"Sure." Maxie was uneasy, she fumbled for her jacket, looked away from me.

"What's the matter?"

"Nothing," she said and waved and started towards the door, then stopped suddenly, came back and sat opposite me. She took a deep breath.

"You OK?"

"Not really," she said.

Maxine took out her cigarettes. She took one out of the pack but didn't light it. She looked out of the window and then pulled a paper napkin from the metal dispenser and folded it into a triangle. She kept her eyes on her hands.

"What? Tell me." I reached for her hand, but she pulled back, sat up straight and looked at me.

"Artie, honey, I can't waste any more of my life. OK,

224

so, it's like this: I'm in love with you. I was in love with you before Mark, but I knew it was no use, and I wanted kids and stuff and I loved him in a way, so I married him. But I'm still in love with you. You went with Lily, so I knew that was it and anyhow I was married." She fumbled with her cigarette, tearing the paper, pulling out the shreds of tobacco. "Look, I know this is a lousy time, everything coming down on you, your godson missing or whatever out by Brighton Beach, Billy is like your own, I understand. I think you kind of replaced Lily's little girl with him. Is that enough? More?"

"Go on."

"I want to give you the space to do this case, you know, but there's always stuff coming down in our jobs, so I can't go on waiting to talk to you between jobs and other women, and I don't want to talk about pizza all the time, I know it's code, it's shtick between us, it's a way we do things, but it's not enough for me. So, well, listen, I'm in love with you." She stopped and her eyes filled up and then she said, "So that's it."

Maxine tossed the broken cigarette on the table. "I want a life. I don't care about getting married again but I want a life with a guy in it who's home most of the time and who doesn't fuck around with other women. My girls are also crazy about you."

"Likewise," I said, feeling incredibly warm about Maxie. It surprised me. I didn't feel trapped. I didn't feel put upon. I felt warm.

"I love them," I said. "I love you."

"You do?"

"You know I do."

"I don't mean it like that," she said. "I don't mean it like friends who have pizza and sometimes a fuck, OK, I don't want a fuck buddy, but someone who would be there when I look shitty and have a cold or to go on vacation with and for Christmas."

"Yes," I said.

"What do you mean?"

"I mean do you want to get married?"

"In general?"

"In general, to me, whatever."

"Is this a proposal?"

"Sort of. Yeah. I don't know."

"Well, you let me know, OK, because this is just the kind of shit I was talking about. I need to know, Artie, honey, I have to get on." She got up. "I have to run now," she said. "I really have to go."

"So you want to do pizza next weekend?"

"You're not listening."

"I meant it as a joke."

She leaned over and kissed me on the cheek. "I don't think so, Artie. The pizza, I mean. But thanks."

"Can I come to the girls' birthday party anyway?"

"Sure you can, honey. Of course," she said and having sat down again, unfolded her long legs and got up and went back out of the door. I saw her through the glass as she walked, back to me. She gave a jaunty wave but without looking back.

I watched her go, loping along the street, and thought what a jerk I was not to run after her. It was as if I was glued to the chair in the coffee shop, my face pressed against the window, watching her go, unable to follow, wanting to follow. No, what I wanted was to want it. To want the thing that would make me like everyone else, a wife, kids, and I couldn't go, couldn't follow her, I just sat and smoked and looked through the window.

For a while longer I sat in the coffee shop and then I called Rhonda again, who said Lippert was making his way back from Boston by train.

"Sit tight," Rhonda said. "He'll call you in a few minutes."

When Lippert called, I tried to tell him about Billy Farone, I tried to say, it's my cousin's kid, it's Billy, but he shut me up and said never the fuck mind about Brooklyn. We're done with it, he yelled, May Luca is dead, the killer is dead, the locals can wrap it up. The line crackled.

I tried to break into his stream of talk but the signal went dead. I called him back. He said I was too involved, too emotionally screwed up about the Russian thing in Brighton Beach and he didn't want me working out there. If I had a problem out there, I should call the locals. I knew he didn't hear me. I knew he didn't understand.

Forget it, he said, and anyhow, a little girl had disappeared from a fancy loft building over in Tribeca. He said, get the hell over there, he said. Use your nice manners, man, OK, just make nice with them because with this one media shit is going to rain down on us for real. The girl that disappeared from Tribeca belonged to a couple of lezzies, he said, you know, man, I mean one of them had the kid with somebody's sperm, turkey baster stuff, you know the deal and they're both rich and

227

pretty famous and connected. Fashion. Architecture. Astronomy. Who knows? Who cares? Some kind of downtown shit and they're already calling in lawyers, squads of fat-ass lawyers, Jonnie Cochran style, Bruce Cutler, he said contemptuously. A phalanx of lawyers, he added, enjoying the word.

Listen, man, Lippert said, it's one thing some girl in Brooklyn gets murdered, it makes the police page in the *Post*. This one is rich and white, you know what I'm saying, also it's Tribeca so these people were downtown when the towers fell, so, like heroic. Right? I got the networks, the papers, every fucking media asshole is on me, and I want you there. It's probably a circus. He told me the street and the building.

"Get the fuck over there. OK? I need you. I need you to sweet-talk these babes, as much as anything. You know that world, right? You're the social babes' favorite detective, right?"

By now, I was yelling into the phone. Listen to me, Sonny, I yelled. LISTEN! But the signal was gone and I couldn't get him back.

23

The walls of the apartment on North Moore Street were red and lined with original movie posters from pre-war Germany; Dietrich, Billy Wilder, Von Stroheim gazed down at me while I negotiated with the security guard to let me in. Billy Wilder had an impish face; a magician's face; it said this guy can do amazing tricks. I seemed to remember that he had been a gigolo in Berlin in the 1920s. Except for Woody Allen's pictures, or maybe even counting Woody, *Some Like It Hot* was my favorite movie.

Grudgingly, the guard passed me on to another guy, who led me through the enormous loft to a collection of couches and chairs which contained three women, also perfectly arranged, like sculptures waiting for the viewing public.

One answered a phone that rang constantly; she spoke softly; she avoided touching the receiver with her fingernails, which, glistening with polish, were almost black. Another sat perfectly still; eyes shut, she wove her fingers together, apparently on hold until the next task.

The third woman, seated in front of a long low green glass table on short steel legs, snipped and plucked cards off the bouquets of flowers that were lined up in front of her. She read them, then added each card to a growing stack on the table and, a short fat gold fountain pen gripped between her thumb and her middle finger, made notes on a yellow legal pad.

When I introduced myself, she pushed her glasses up onto her head.

"Are you Olivia Blixen?" I said.

"Olivia is resting," she said. "She can't see anyone."

Dull snowy light flooded the apartment; there were skylights in the eighteen-foot ceilings, and the light and snow showed through them.

"What about Marianne Vallaeys?"

She corrected my pronunciation and said, "I'll see."

There was no invitation to sit, so I stood and looked at the flowers: tight bundles of pale roses, mauve, pink, yellow, in small round jars; translucent orchids potted in moss and lime green crackle vases; cream colored tulips, two feet long, that bent over the pots they were in, their fleshy heads touching the glass table. But who sent flowers to people whose kid had disappeared? Was there floral protocol for a kidnapping?

"Detective?"

I turned around.

"I'm Marianne Vallaeys." She held out her hand. The fingers were very long, the nails short and pale, the grip firm. She wore gray slacks and a gray cashmere sweater; I felt the softness of it as a sleeve grazed my hand.

She was small and self-contained and she gestured to

230

a chocolate colored leather chair. I sat. She sat on the edge of its twin and leaned forward.

I shaded my eyes against the light and looked at her and I remembered. She was one of the women from the glass apartment on Perry Street. She had worn one of the floaty Japanese dresses and spent the evening kissing the other Jap dress a lot, marking territory.

"We've met," I said. "Saturday night. The party on Perry Street. Your party, I think."

"I don't remember. So many people."

"You're the mother?"

"I am one of Tatiana's mothers. Olivia is the other. If you mean which of us literally gave birth to Tati, it was Olivia."

"So she's the real mother. Who's the father?"

"It's not important," she said.

I said, "It would help me."

"Her father is a film director in Denmark. Copenhagen," she said. "He's a friend of ours. He came over, we brought him over, and he fathered Tatiana, but he's not involved in her upbringing."

I nodded towards the three other women. "So who are they?"

"Sally is our secretary," she said gesturing at the woman with the phone. "Dana looks after the house." She indicated the woman with the flowers. "I don't mean she's a maid, we have people who do the cleaning, of course, Dana takes care of the household, she organizes other staff, she orders food, that sort of thing."

The woman with the locked fingers had risen from her chair and was pacing up and down. Her head was bowed as if in prayer and she wore black jeans and a black sweater; a necklace made out of huge chunks of raw coral bobbed on her chest as she paced.

"She's my ex. Andrea Mariano. She's also the mother of my other child. My son, Sacha."

"I'm confused."

"Before I was with Olivia, I was with Andrea. We have a son. Andrea and I are civilized about it, we have shared custody. Sacha spends three and a half days with each of us. Obviously his other mother, my ex, would want to be here with us." She held her hands out, palms up, then clasped them together. "I can't imagine how this could happen. I researched everything, the building, our security people, the neighbors. I was very careful. I realized this kind of thing happened to people like us, and I took every precaution and now I think, what for? I think I'm cursed. I think I've missed something."

Her involvement with herself made her impenetrable. She barely mentioned the missing girl. Everything was turned back on her. She was her own most interesting subject.

"Where is your son?"

"Sacha is at school," she said. "It was too horrible for him to stay home. It's alright. He has a bodyguard who waits for him outside the school."

"How old is he?"

"Fourteen."

"Do you want to take me through what happened?"

"I've told the police the whole story, we have private investigators on it, we don't know what else to do."

The girl, Tatiana, had been going to a friend's for

supper the night before. The friend lived in the building. It was arranged with her mother.

She would go by herself, Tati insisted. She was almost eleven and it was only four floors down, and she begged. The women, Vallaeys, Blixen, said no, absolutely not, but Tati cried and stamped her foot and said it was unfair, that she felt as if she lived in a prison. If she had a father, she'd said, he would understand. The kid pulled out all the stops. She worked on the women. And they let her go.

They watched her leave the apartment and get into the elevator. It was only four floors, after all. I'll be back after supper, Tati called. I'll be back. Come home by eight. Call us. We'll come get you, they said, but she made her lip tremble again and they said, OK, OK. They watched her get into the elevator, watched the door shut. The girl never came back.

It only took a couple of hours for them to discover the kid was gone. When Tatiana failed to return at eight, Blixen called the kid's friend. It turned out that Tatiana had called her friend to say she wasn't coming. No one worried. They assumed that Tati had changed her mind. The story was eerily like Billy Farone's.

"We called all her friends," Vallaeys said. "We called everyone and then we called your people. You're the third detective we've seen. In a way we've been expecting this, we've lived in a kind of horror of something happening to one of the children, it's why we have private security."

"Expecting?"

"Olivia, my partner, is very famous in her own circles; people know how much money she has; we knew our

233

child was vulnerable. Christ, I wish we'd stayed in Sweden."

"Excuse me?"

"I was born in Uppsala. In Sweden. It is in Sweden."

"I know where it is."

"I'd like you to go now," she said abruptly. "This is not helping me. We have many people on this. Mr. Lippert promised he would come himself."

"I'll be glad to tell him."

I was pissed off. I had to get out of the hothouse. The smell of the flowers was making me gag. I gave her my card.

"If you think of anything, any way I can help, just call," I said, not meaning it. Our conversation had lasted less than five minutes and that was plenty.

"Thank you," she said. She was very cool.

All day the image of those banked flowers floated into my head, a funeral for a child who had only been missing for a few hours. Flowers for sympathy, corporate communication. The bouquets cost hundreds and were fabulous and reminded me of times I used to hang around with some of Lily's friends. She knew people like that who lived in startling apartments with big-ticket art. I had liked it a lot when she took me to their parties; I was a sucker for it all. I loved the glamor. I loved the smell. It almost fucked me up completely, especially the year I worked a case on Sutton Place.

Even before I left the building, I knew I had to get back to Brooklyn. I had to make Lippert understand or if I couldn't, I was going back anyhow, back to

Brooklyn, to find Billy. Half the detectives in New York would work the Tribeca case, if there was a case. I tried not to think about May Luca. I tried not to remember her body the way it was, tossed, naked, like a piece of meat, out on a boat in the marina.

As I left the building in Tribeca and walked down the street, I realized it was a block away from the place where JFK, Jr., had lived. I remembered now, I remembered when he died and the flowers piled up in mountains. People came and stood all day and night after he died.

Tribeca was jammed with expensive lofts and fancy furniture stores and antique shops, but it was still forlorn. After 9/11 it remained in the "Zone" for months; there was no traffic at all, only the cloud of dust hanging in the perfect autumn sky. At night, in the light from the stadium spots, you could see it, too, but hazy, eerie, surreal. Kids played baseball in the street watched by National Guardsmen, young soldiers from a different America. People wandered, half dazed by what had happened, half intoxicated by the sublime weather.

I dug a couple of Advil out of my pocket and swallowed them dry, and then I heard the sound of hooves. A horse emerged from the stable out back of the First Precinct; another followed and the two mounted cops clip-clopped daintily into the snow-covered streets.

You could imagine New York as it had once been down here, the cobbles, the horses, the sound of horseshoes, the horseshit steaming up from the snow. For a second, a minute, I watched the horses step high down Hudson Street.

24

All that mattered now was getting my car started. I had made it home from Tribeca on foot. I cleaned the snow off my car and then decided to give it an hour before I set off to Brooklyn, hoping the main roads would be plowed. The roads across the city were in lousy shape.

I turned to look across the street. Mike's was shut up. The block, my backyard, my village, looked unfamiliar, abandoned, desolate. I went back upstairs, killing time.

In my front door, the wedge of paper had remained in place. Everything was the way I'd left it an hour earlier. Through the walls of the building I could hear kids yelling and laughing and blasting music; someone was using a vacuum cleaner. I thought about Lily for the hundredth time. I was lonely as hell.

The only solid thing I knew about Billy's case was that he had been friends with May Luca and that his grandfather had messed with her. And he had worn her red T-shirt the morning he left home, the shirt that was found near the boardwalk in Brooklyn, soaked in blood, slashed with a razor. Nothing else, just Ivana's desperation, Genia's fear, Johnny's helplessness.

I'd listened to their stories and their lies, I let myself be dragged in without telling anyone and now I was on my own, without the support of the office, or Lippert who was distracted by the Tribeca case. When he focused, he'd be pissed off I hadn't told him about Billy as soon as I suspected.

Genia was hiding something about Billy, something about the kid that wasn't right, something no one mentioned. Over and over, like a mantra, they said how bright he was, how good at school, at fishing, at reading grown-up books. OK, unlike his father, he wasn't a hugger and he kept to himself and what he loved, fishing most of all, obsessed him. They worried, but I thought: so what?

I tried to think back to the times I'd been with him; times we went fishing. Billy was always so passionate, it thrilled me. He liked to touch the fish, he liked the feel of their flesh. Liked to put them in his net and then, tenderly, put his fingers through the string. His face would break into a smile, he would fling his arms out with joy.

Once we cooked some of the fish at a campsite out on the island. Once we made sashimi and he ate the raw fish. The Billy I knew was not the same boy his parents worried about.

Genia had made me promise I'd give it a day before I told Lippert about Billy. I had promised. And then I told him or at least I left him a message telling him. Better to betray the promise I made to Genia than find myself adrift in this community of lies. It was time to declare

Billy a missing child; time to let the air in before we all choked to death.

In the old days, my father, who spent most of his career in the KGB, said you did what you had to, you told your people, it wasn't a lie, or a betrayal if you were an agent; it was your business, your game, and it was an honorable game. My mother would say, "bullshit," or the Russian equivalent. She never swore. Peasants, anti-Semites with thick necks and crude accents, these people used filthy language, she said. They were illiterate; they didn't know better.

Before I went out, I tried my mother in Haifa again and a nurse put her on the phone. I waited for her to say my name. The nurse had said she'd been calling for me.

She didn't know who I was, though, and she was incoherent and talked in disjointed sentences, sometimes in Russian, sometimes in Yiddish, which she had spoken as a child and which I didn't understand. Frustrated she started to cry. Someone took the phone away from her, and I sat, smoking and feeling my eyes fill up.

I called my old friend Hamid in Haifa at his office and got the answering machine with his gentle worried musical voice.

Hamid looked in on my mother every month or so. A Palestinian whose family had lived in Israel for generations, he was the only friend I made at Hebrew University I still kept in touch with. He went on to medical school, I came to New York.

We had met in a café in Tel Aviv and we both liked the same music—he was a die-hard Chet Baker fan, and he loved Stan Getz; we both felt like outsiders, though he was born in Israel. He was also the handsomest man I ever knew, and girls flocked around him, but he was shy and eventually he married Sarah—I introduced them—whose parents never forgave me.

I picked up the phone and called their house and she answered, sounding harassed. They were all fine, she said, but I didn't believe her.

All the time I was calling, I was looking at the Arabic dictionary I'd taken down earlier when I realized someone had been in my apartment. I yanked open the desk drawers and pulled out a pile of paper, letters, bills, a manila folder where I kept important documents. Hamid's letters were in it.

Hamid wrote letters. He liked writing and had taught himself calligraphy; he wrote with a pen his grandfather gave him when he graduated med school, his prize possession and he used it for letters and at work but also to draw the perfect cartoons of people he knew and places he saw; his stuff made me laugh out loud.

Hamid's letters came once a month with news of my mother and clippings and the cartoons, always with an American stamp on the light blue airmail envelopes. He got a friend who traveled to the US a lot to mail them here; Hamid said it was faster. I should have paid attention. It wasn't about speed. It was about Hamid being frightened

"The mail here is terrible, Artie," he said when we talked, but I should have known things were lousy for him in Israel and he was scared. Scared to send e-mails, scared to mail letters, he was cautious on the phone. I had asked, the last time I saw him, if he wanted me to get them out, or try, or see if I could work something, and he shook his head. He couldn't leave home. He said it was OK and I let myself believe him.

"Maybe I'll send the kids over for summer camp if I can," he said. "Maybe I'll try." He never mentioned it again.

I was a lazy-ass letter writer so I always called back instead of writing and Hamid always gave me the same news: my mother's condition was unchanged, she had no memory, nothing; she didn't know me or him or anyone else. Mostly she sat in a chair and hummed.

Opening the folder, I got out Hamid's letters and looked at the one on top. On the corner of the blue airmail paper was a faint mark. I found a loupe Lily had sometimes used to look at the photographs she took, and stared at the blue paper through it, which embarrassed me: I felt like a cartoon Sherlock Holmes. Through the magnifying glass, I could see a faint stain, like grease.

Increasingly frantic, I looked through the letters; some were missing, others were out of order. Whoever had been here was interested in Hamid and Hamid was an Arab and it had been the Arabic dictionary where they looked first.

I called Hamid's cell phone and left a message and went back to the letters. Then I got up and got a beer and lit a cigarette, and stared at the books on the shelf over my desk, pulling them out one at a time, seeing that they'd all been taken out and put back.

There were some books in Russian I inherited from my aunt. Novels from a reading group Lily made me go to that I hated. People expressed so many pompous and received ideas I figured they must spend half their lives reading the *New York Review of Books* in the can; I preferred Lily's fashion magazines. I liked the pictures of the girls. The ragged Tony Hillerman paperbacks were there.

I loved Hillerman's stuff, I loved the desert, the Indians, the clans and tribes, the rituals. Lily and I went to New Mexico on vacation once. It was as far away from New York as you could get. Sometimes I fantasized about moving. I could live out there on the clean empty desert. I loved it, wild, empty, the Navajo DJs on the radio. Sometimes when I thought about running away, I thought about New Mexico, but I knew I couldn't survive anywhere except New York. It was home. But someone had been in my stuff and it made me livid.

Of all the languages I could do, English, Russian, Hebrew, the Arabic came hardest. Mine was nothing special, it was kitchen Arabic I'd picked up in Israel.

My head was throbbing; someone had read my letters and I didn't know why and I was furious; it filled me with fury that someone had been here and it never occurred to me until much later that it was the kind of thing I'd done on the job, gone into people's apartments, ransacked their stuff. That was my job; I'd do it again if it would help me find Billy Farone.

But what the hell did they want with my dictionaries? With Hamid's letters? Who were they?

Ever since the Patriot Act—they called it the Patriot Act, though it really meant anyone could smash down your door—was enacted, I had been subconsciously frightened. Like other cops I said it was a fucking good

241

idea, help us catch the bastards, but with me it was bravado. Great, I said. Less hassle with warrants, the judges, the lawyer stuff that kept bad guys out of jail. Anything that helps nail them, the fucks who killed my friends. Let's go for it, I said. I was a hard-ass, of course I was; I could shoot the shit with the other cops about the perps and creeps and how we should fry them.

This was different. This scared me, this patriotic fervor, people beaten up for wearing peace T-shirts, the crazy Iraq thing looming. My loft had been ransacked once. Long time ago when I was working the Chinatown immigrant case. It was obvious back then who did it, they were thugs. They turned my place upside down, the couch upended, papers spilled over the floor, the refrigerator door left open. I had been away and when I came back, the food was rotten. I could still remember the stink of spoiled food, the milk curdled, the lemons green with rot.

This was different. This was covert. They, whoever they were, ghosts, spooks, had been careful. I was more scared in some ways than in London or Bosnia or Vienna. This was my place. My city. My neighborhood, the fringes of Tribeca, Chinatown, lower Broadway; I'd lived here longer than I'd lived anywhere else in my life and I loved it.

I loved it especially when summer came and you could sit on the roof and see the East River smoking in the haze. Or in the fall when the leaves turned gold and were crunchy underfoot or when snow fell. Every romantic version of New York, I was a sucker for it.

Someone had attacked me out at Breezy Point, had

followed me to Maxine's. Someone had invaded my apartment and I was betting they were the same person or worked for the same person and it made me feel vulnerable.

As I worked methodically around the apartment looking for more evidence, suddenly it came to me: I'd been an idiot to offer help after 9/11; I had been crazy to mention I spoke some Arabic. After September 11, when all the agencies were desperate for translators, I told them and someone wondered how I learned and the gossip about me took hold and turned into curiosity and questions were asked. I knew how it worked.

I hated the spy world, the self-aggrandizing legends, the myths, the crappy men in crappy clothes that didn't fit. I'd grown up on it—KGB, the Israelis. Or for that matter, the Brits, the CIA—there wasn't much difference. I knew its feel, the shifting shape of a world where nothing was clear and the rules changed all the time. It had destroyed my father and mother; it had wrecked our lives. My parents left Moscow because of the stifling sense someone was always watching.

But New York. For twenty years, more, I did and said what I wanted, I could be myself or somebody else. Now that had changed. I was a suspect. Someone had been here, if they took me in, who would go get Billy?

Panicked, I grabbed my jacket and phone and my gun and ran out to the car. I had to take a chance. Had to risk the car stalling; there wasn't any other way. Out there in Brooklyn, Billy was waiting for me.

I never made it. Before I hit the tunnel, something inside the engine of my car whined and shuddered. The car spun on the icy street, the wheels sank in a drift of snow. I was stuck. It took three hours for a tow truck to get through. It took three more hours to get it into a shop near the Westside highway that was still open, and when I did, it turned out the guy who could fix it was stuck somewhere in the Bronx. I chain smoked, waiting. Eventually he showed up, opened the hood, messed around inside, and charged me seven hundred bucks.

While I waited, something tried to press up through my memory, something out of the past, some image, some event, something that made me feel my father looking over my shoulder. I couldn't tell if I'd dozed off in the chair in the garage and dreamed it or if it was real, the memory of my pop, looking at me. I couldn't fish it out.

Part Four

25

A reporter for Fox TV who lived out in Brooklyn near the beach got wind of Billy's disappearance Tuesday morning and broke the story. Genia blamed me for it. She called up and yelled at me in Russian and said I had betrayed her and that I was my father's son and I had killed her boy by putting it all on the TV; he would be dead because of it, she screamed. I didn't, I said; it wasn't me who put it on TV, but she wasn't listening.

Johnny Farone called a few minutes later and begged me to come out to Brooklyn. Please, Artie, man, he said. Find my boy for me. He was still holed up at the restaurant, snowed in, he said, taking care of business. A couple of his workers couldn't get home; they had bedded down in the bar. He couldn't leave them.

Please, Art; please. I'm begging you, he said. In his voice I could hear the panic that would make everything worse. Johnny was not a subtle guy. The men who worked for him would know by now that his boy was gone. Reporters would call him and he'd talk to them and blub on the air.

Already there were pictures of Billy on TV and in them he looked angelic, and these images of innocence and its betrayal would set off a kind of communal hysteria, especially combined with the kidnapping of the girl in Tribeca.

Already, as I flipped through the channels on my set, the box was filling up with images of the two children. God knew how the TV station got Billy's pictures, unless it was Johnny who gave them out. Or his mother, or the school, or the church. Good intentions really did pave the road to hell and probably to kids dying, which was the same thing.

There was always someone who could be seduced by a reporter with a beseeching voice and tears in her eyes—we only want to find Billy, we only want to help—into handing over pictures, usually for free. It didn't help. It gave the monsters who did this stuff more reason to kill.

A Florida station tracked down old man Farone, Billy's grandfather; on camera he wept and called for people to return his Billy safe.

On Tuesday, because I knew all hell would break loose, now the long weekend was over and the snow had stopped, I went to see a guy I hated. I'd lost most of Monday getting my car fixed, and I was in a hurry. It was a guy I saved up for special occasions.

Somehow Britz—his name was Samson Britz—got information no one else could, but he was a creep. As soon as I called him I was sorry; stepping into a room with him was like stepping into a sewer. He held court in a bar not far from the fish market. You could smell it.

Britz had been a cop. I was pretty sure he specialized in fake green cards and other immigrant necessities. He was originally from Odessa and he lived out in Brighton Beach. He spent his days, though, in the bar on the fringes of Chinatown not far from the East River. From the window of the bar, he could see the Manhattan Bridge and Brooklyn on the other side.

He was short and dapper and one of his ears had been cut off and sewn back in the wrong place. He said, with a chilly laugh, it was because he always had his ear to the ground, and then someone stepped on it. Stepped on it literally, he said, held him down and trampled his ear because he heard too much. Next time it will be your tongue. If you don't shut up, it will be your tongue. Monkey no hear, no see. He had reported this to me years earlier and then cackled.

Britz liked an audience, he liked his own performance. Now he offered me a thick loose joint like the Jamaican guys smoke. I didn't want it because it had been in his mouth and was damp from his saliva. I said I was allergic to marijuana.

The bar was long and dark and shabby, and gold tinsel left over from Christmas dangled halfway down the dirty front window which was plastered with beer ads. A quartet of elderly Chinese guys sat at a round table in the front, playing cards and drinking Tsing Tsao. In back sat Britz; he sat there most of the day, drinking Diet Coke.

When I arrived, he was waiting for me at his table, impeccably dressed as always in a suit and tie, as always with well-shined shoes. His hair was clean and freshly cut; he looked like a little elderly boy. He was probably about fifty; hard to tell.

He got up and shook my hand, gestured to the chair next to him and asked what I needed. He pretended he would always do you a favor gratis; he kept track. Britz was always adding up how much he had done for you, how you had repaid him, you could see him calculating, and he was ice cold about it; he was an accountant of small favors.

Currently I was in the black and he owed me. Still you had to put out a little for him, so we sat and I drank coffee and we looked at the catalogue from Sotheby's he had on the table in front of him.

He said he planned on collecting art some day. He had connections with some members of the Ukuza, the Jap mafia, he said, who came to New York once in a while to shop. They said, buy art. There's no record of ownership, no fixed prices; art was whatever the market said it was. Britz told me about guys in Nippoland—it was what Britz called Japan—who kept Renoirs hidden for years, or decades, until the prices soared. You could fix the market and no one came at you with knives. The auction houses were very sedate, he giggled.

Renoirs were good business, Britz added, turning over the slick pages of the fat catalogue. He pointed out the prettily colored paintings he liked best. I didn't like Renoir, I thought the stuff was like pictures on a Christmas card, but I hadn't come for the art.

OK, he said, so, what you need? I asked him what he knew about people in Brooklyn who molested children, who might live out by the water, who might snatch a kid. I asked him if he knew any cops by the Brooklyn Coast who might be involved.

"They put you on this shit, detective? They dump you in Brooklyn, you don't got no promotion or nothing? Listen, I don't like what they do to kids, you know. I don't go near that stuff, maybe except someone needs a vacation in Thailand, that kind of thing, maybe a woman, maybe someone likes them young. I don't know if I can help on this one." He leaned back and looked at me, wondering what I would offer, even though he knew it was his turn to put out.

"Just get me something, Sam, OK? Who likes little kids, boys, out by the water, that kind of thing. Is there a ring? Are they buying and selling? Kiddie porn? Babies involved? Call me, OK." It wasn't a question.

I let him ramble a while more.

OK, he said, he would look into it and see what he could find, and then he wanted to shake my hand again. I hated it. His hand was very small and very dry, and crippled with arthritis and it was like shaking with a dead man where rigor had already set in.

All hell did break loose that day. School was out, kids were restless, they made their parents nuts trying to keep after them. Children who left home for an hour without telling someone became instant victims. The city ran wild with rumors. At Billy's school out in Brooklyn, when I checked, a worried teacher whispered to me that there had been problems in his class, other kids didn't like him, and I said, what kind of problems, what kids, but she just shook her head and I couldn't get any more.

When the third child disappeared, the city went berserk and some people thought it was terrorism. May Luca dead. Billy Farone disappeared. The girl from Tribeca. As soon as the news about the kid in Tribeca broke, the media was at the story like a starving tribe on a group of aid workers bringing food.

A reporter on NY1 unearthed the old cases that Lippert had told me about. The cases had never been solved, not the murder of the girl whose feet were chopped off or the kid left on a Long Island beach. Pictures surfaced on obscure web sites, pictures showing the bloody stumps where the girl's feet should have been. Again there were reports of body parts for sale on auction sites. The twenty-first century's big trade wasn't in drugs, it was in human beings, for sex, or illegals or slave workers, or organs for transplant; now body parts. Cheaper than drugs.

The ambient fear in the city, the leftover terror that had lingered since 9/11, the lousy economy, the cold weather, the constant pummeling by the government— red alerts, duct tape—the coming war, people went nuts. I went nuts.

On TV, people talked biological weapons; they talked nukes. I had worked on a case involving a suitcase nuke once. I knew what even minute amounts of nuclear material could do: a few spoonfuls of cesium and you could make downtown Manhattan uninhabitable for years. It was the first thing I thought on 9/11.

Running down to the towers, I thought: nukes. As soon as I saw people streaming uptown covered in dust,

I imagined them with their skins flayed, trailing their own skins, like coats, in the dust.

When I left Britz, Chinatown was almost empty. Where the sidewalks were normally jammed with people shopping for fish and vegetables and money and deals, it was empty and not just because of the snow. SARS had scared everyone off the streets. The virus that began in China—another country that messed its people up with the commie legacy of secrets—had infested whole buildings in Hong Kong. Lousy plumbing in one building meant shit dripped through the pipes and the virus with it. Without knowing they had it—or maybe they did know—people flew with it on planes and it broke out in Canada.

Toronto was shut down. New York would be next, people were convinced; people thought SARS and remembered AIDS. SARS would come through Chinatown. People stayed away. The neighborhood was empty as if grief stricken. The plague year, someone had said to me the week before. On the street near my car, in white masks, a pair of women hurried past me.

People canceled their travel plans. They avoided Asia for the virus and France for the politics and the Middle East for war and Israel for the suicide bombings. Instead, they stayed home, watched the fearful news on the tube and made their kids stay in and the kids played video games and had nightmares. I couldn't remember so much fear except when I was a kid in Moscow and I woke up nights, screaming, sure the Americans were going to bomb us, nuke us, turn us into dust.

I stopped at a newsstand and grabbed the papers.

Billy's face was on the front of the *Daily News*. I drove away and stopped at a red light. An old man skidded across the street in front of me and fell, then crumpled over. Somehow, he got himself upright.

Still feverish, even inside my car I was shivering. While I waited for the old man to cross, I reached in the back of the car for a sweater. My hand touched the plastic garbage bag from Breezy Point. I pulled over to the curb, got the bag onto the seat next to me and opened it. There wasn't much in it—some paper towel balled up, an empty Marlboro carton, the stub of a candle, a pizza box. A cardboard box that stank of pizza sauce from a place near Sheepshead Bay. I wrote down the address and wondered how it had ended up in a garbage can behind a fishing shack in Breezy Point. I was clutching at straws.

26

Waiting for me in Lippert's outer office, wearing tight jeans that showed the curve of her hips and a short furry red sweater, was Rhonda Fisher. She looked good. I'd never seen Rhonda in anything except the shapeless suits she wore to work most days.

In a sense, in Sonny's office, only Rhonda mattered; she was the backbone, she ran things, she knew where the bodies were buried; they were in her filing cabinet and in her computer files and in the back of her tidy brain. Every case Sonny had worked for twenty-five years, every place he had been, every request for help, Rhonda had filed or shredded or coded. She also knew where and when he had fucked up and if he was on the take.

Not money. Lippert would never deal for money. Power. He wanted the kind of power that put you on the inside and that got you what you needed when you wanted to solve a case or work a problem. He wanted to be a hero; he longed for a profile like Bratten or one of the other super-cops, and I was never sure how bad he wanted it or what he'd do to get it.

Early on when I first went to work for Sonny, I got to know Rhonda. I found out her birthday. I sent flowers. I remembered Secretary's Day. I took her to dinner at Windows on the World once when it was there, at the top of the World Trade Center.

After a glass of wine, Rhonda sometimes, when she was in the mood, told me things Sonny wouldn't; she told me about his ambition, about some of the people he stepped on, on his way up. It took me years to figure out that Rhonda only talked if she thought it served his purposes. It was Lippert who wanted me to know how tough he was and she was the conduit.

For years after Sonny's divorce, I waited for Rhonda to leave her husband and marry him; she never did.

Rhonda kissed me on the cheek and gestured towards Sonny's office.

"Thanks for coming so fast," she said.

"That's OK." I'd been driving through Chinatown on my way from the meeting with Samson Britz when Rhonda called.

"He's making an appeal, he wants you there."

"What?"

"TV." She looked at me. "Go on in."

I went into Lippert's office. A two-man video crew was setting up. Lippert was behind his desk. He saw me, he got up and before he could open his mouth, I said, "What am I doing here, Sonny?"

"I'm making something for TV, man. I'm making a request. I want you with me."

I looked down at my jeans and jacket.

"Not on the TV, man. Just keep me company, OK?"

"On the kid in Tribeca?"

"No. The Farone boy."

"Don't."

"Why the fuck not?"

"Leave it alone. The publicity won't help," I said. "Why don't you get one of your guys to check out the grandfather in Florida?"

"I did that. He's been down there since January, like they keep saying on the box."

"I wish you would have talked to me, you know?"

He said, "It's not about you."

"Yeah, well it's always about you. You're doing this because you don't want people saying Lippert's only on the case when it comes to rich kids, you want them saying, oh, yeah, Lippert, man of the fucking people, he's on it big time and not just the rich kid in Tribeca, he's on it with the Brooklyn thing, he cares, man, he's really in there caring and sharing. Right?" I was scared of how the TV appeal would push Billy's kidnapper.

I pushed him into the outer office.

"Listen to me," I said.

His back was against the wall so he listened.

"Billy Farone is my cousin's kid. I tried to tell you on the phone when you were on the train from fucking Boston." I'd never told Lippert about Billy and me. It was something I kept pretty much for myself.

I could see that Lippert, already furious at a God who let kids disappear and die, wanted to take it out on me the way I laid my own anger on him. But maybe because it was Billy, all he said was, "What do you know about the kid?"

"I know he liked to fish. Was obsessed with it. I took him fishing. His father owns Farone's in Sheepshead Bay. The restaurant? Billy was supposed to go to a friend's early Saturday, a kid across the street, he never showed up. The mother said he called to say he wasn't coming. No one thought about it until Sunday morning when Billy was late getting home."

"Go on."

"Billy sometimes played with May Luca. He wore her T-shirt?" I said.

"Jesus."

"I know there was some trouble at Billy's school, in his class, kids threatening, I couldn't get anything out of the teacher. I also know Billy's grandmother, Farone's mother, told me the old man, her husband, sometimes took Billy fishing. There was a shack out at Breezy Point."

"You went?"

"Sure I went."

"By yourself?"

"Yeah."

"You're a fucking idiot, man, you know that?" Lippert said and looked over my shoulder as one of the video crew appeared and waved at him. "I have to do this now."

"There's one other thing."

"What's that?"

"The grandfather, old man Farone, he was a retired cop, and the wife threw him out because he liked little girls. Mrs. Farone once found him feeling up May, or that's what she told me."

258

Lippert tried to sidestep me, but I didn't let him. I held onto his arm.

"Listen to me. Let me work this, please. I'm saying please, Sonny. If you put a bunch of guys on it, they'll trample all over it and Billy will die for sure. Do your TV thing, if you have to, but rein them in. Please."

I knew it was my saying please that convinced him.

He said, "I'll buy you twenty-four hours if I can, OK? I'll put you in charge. I can't stop the local guys, it's already out there, but I'll rein them in, like you say."

"What about this appeal?"

Lippert told the guy with the video camera he could go.

"I'll call the station later," he said. "Tell them it was my decision. Say I'm sorry."

The video guy nodded and said, "I hope you get the bastard. I have two little girls," he added. "If it was me, I'd string him up."

I said, "Where do you live?"

"Greenpoint," he said. "Over in Brooklyn."

Afterwards, Lippert seemed calmer and he got out the bottle of Scotch he kept in his bottom drawer and some glasses and poured a couple of drinks. I was itching to get back to Brooklyn, but I needed him on my side.

He said, "You're not going to let go of the Farone case, are you?"

"Don't ask, don't tell."

"You're close to the boy?"

"Yeah."

"I'll take you off Tribeca if you want."

"Thank you."

"You're welcome," he said. "I don't know how the girl in Tribeca disappeared with all the security they've got. I'm not sure she didn't walk out. Wouldn't you, with those women? They must have called me fifty times. They call the chief, they call the mayor."

I said, "You can't just say that, because they're rich freaks their kid would walk out."

"Yeah I can." Sonny was in a rage now. "You don't know what people are doing to kids, anyhow. I mean you know there's people out there that watches kiddie porn on the Net, there's people that watches images of child abuse. This stuff has exploded. We live in a country where everyone's praying and calling on Jesus and pedophiles are just getting cagier. Dear Jesus, please redeem me I just abused my nine-month-old baby. Sure I can say it. To you. I can say anything to you, right, man? You're my guy, isn't that right?"

Suddenly everything boiled over in me. I didn't need a lecture.

"Fuck you," I said.

"Back at you, man."

"You ever find yourself tempted, Sonny?"

"What the fuck does that mean?"

"I'm asking. You must have been tempted. You must have known plenty of cops and prosecutors, a dinner at Rao's, a bottle of Chivas at Christmas, a little bag of money or coke, you know the way they do it in those nice little Gucci leather briefcases?"

"Fuck you, man, you are so full of shit," he said avoiding the subject. "What's with you? You been listening to the lower orders, you been gossiping with the workers? You been sleeping with the help?"

I knew he meant Maxine. I didn't take the bait.

"So your only addiction is old novels, right, Sonny? Anyone ever offer you a first edition Dickens? *Moby Dick*? Come on, Sonny, what would it take?"

I baited him. I let off steam and it felt good. I went for him some more, sick of Lippert's volatility, sick of his patronizing me, sick of him.

"What about something for your kids, a place at the 92nd Street Y nursery school when they were little? A job at a good firm for the one that's in law school now? What would you sell out for, Sonny?"

"Get the fuck out of here."

"I'm going." I walked to the door and opened it and didn't look back.

"Artie?" Lippert's voice was mournful.

"Yeah?"

He looked up from his drink, forlorn now.

"Who does this shit to kids?" he said.

But I had stopped paying attention. We didn't say goodbye. There was too much hostility in the room. We both knew it.

I was leaving Lippert's building, a cigarette already in my mouth but still unlit because you couldn't smoke anywhere in the city anymore when I slipped on the ice. The snow was frozen into hedges along the sidewalk and there was black ice under the snow and I fell. I tried to get up. I wanted to check out the pizza box from the garbage can in Breezy Point. It probably wasn't much but it was something, and anyhow I had to see Genia. I scrambled up onto my feet and dived into my car.

The fact that someone had been in my apartment—I'd meant to raise it with Lippert—nagged at me constantly, raised itself even when I focused on Genia and Brooklyn and the pizza place. I tried to push it away. I drove like a maniac, not the shore route I took to Maxine's, but through the middle of Brooklyn, down Atlantic Avenue. A lone Arab woman in a headscarf hurried into Sahadi's, the food store. In Flatbush, I nearly collided with a man ambling across the street. No one else was out until I reached Ocean Parkway.

Even in the snow and cold, the Hassidic men, black coats flapping, walked to the synagogues and schools, ringlets catching in the wind, holding onto their large black hats. They resembled a flock of birds, a group of visitors from another century; they seemed foreign, alien, different. Further along, waiting for a red light, I saw a swastika scribbled on the wall of a local school.

For the first time, I felt it was me they wanted, the xenophobes, the patriots, the people who looked anxiously at their neighbors and put up more flags. An Egyptian guy I knew—a US citizen—played some Moroccan music in his apartment one night not long after 9/11; the next morning the super approached his wife and told her it was terrorist music and to shut it off.

Did people look at me? Did they see through the façade, the veneer, the all American, all New York cop? Could they see the Russian, the immigrant, the man whose father was a KGB hero, a KGB creep?

I had adored my father. He was handsome and very

262

tall and blue-eyed and he brought home special treats for me in his pockets—little chocolaty candies from Hungary wrapped in waxy paper; medals, too, and badges, sometimes with the baby Lenin's face on them. Maybe it was political conditioning, the candy to be associated with Lenin, but I didn't care, not then. My father helped me with homework and told me tales of his adventures in the Red Army.

He had been to Berlin and Vienna and he had taken photographs that I still have, black and whites of himself and other officers on the great wrecked boulevards of post-war Europe. Once, he had even been to Paris.

I think my mother married him because of it and secretly hoped one day he would take her and she made him tell her about it over and over until, at home, we could all recite the names of Paris streets, cafés and bookshops, parks, fountains, museums, shops.

He liked games, my dad; he taught me chess and he played practical jokes. But, then, games were his business. Games that involved sneaking around and foreign travel. My father laughed and joked with me and he brought me candy and he never really felt like an adult.

It wasn't until later that I understood what he did; that his games included secrets and duplicity and death. When I was fourteen, because of my mother who was rebellious and made a fuss about refuseniks and became one herself, the KGB dumped my father and then I understood.

I began to hate everything around me, the rote lessons at school, the dreary way people dressed, the obsessive little faces of the Young Pioneers as glazed and zealous as their Nazi counterparts in another era.

Still, secretly, part of me believed my father was different, that he had been a hero. It was confusing, but I was a kid and so long as he took me fishing to the river on Sundays, it was OK. I remember thinking, when we went fishing, when we left before light Sundays with our gear, when we sat by the water and he told me stories: this is how it will be when I have sons.

I never had the sons. I was always afraid that if I got married and had a child, I'd lose my escape route. A family would weigh me down and I would drown. All my life I had wanted to escape; now I was a middle-aged adolescent, unmarried, no kids, still frightened. The men I knew seemed grown up, New Age men who attended the births of their children and took turns caring for them.

Finally, on my way through Brooklyn, sliding on ice, I got it. Road to Damascus, blinding revelation, call it whatever you want. I was terrified for Billy because he was the closest thing I had to a child. I'd thought it before, I had known it somehow, but now I saw it clearly: my relationship with Billy validated me as a human being.

Driving, watching the old Jews move through the landscape like a black and white photograph, I thought about my father and Billy, and then I made myself stop thinking and concentrate. Keep moving, I said half aloud. Keep going.

27

The guy behind the counter at the Pie Palace was a short fat man with a powdery complexion. He pulled the pie I ordered out of the oven and brought it over with a cold beer. The thin crust was blistered and black, the sauce and mozzarella were homemade and the discs of pepperoni were spicy. I ate a couple of slices and finished the beer and paid the check.

He took the money and said. "You're a cop?"

"What makes you think that?"

"After the Luca girl got killed, a lot of people started coming around." He wiped his hand on his apron, put it out and said, "Fred Capestro." He leaned against the edge of my table. "I'm interested in crime stuff. I watch all the shows. Re-runs. Nothing ever as good as *Hill Street Blues*, right? Maybe early *Law and Order*. I read a lot of stuff. Everyone around here thinks I'm a wacko, but it pays off. I once figured out who was doing drug deals in the toilet out back. OK, it was only weed, but what the hell."

I nodded. "Good for you. Go on."

"I just know what I know."

"So what do you think you do know?"

"You think I'm too old to do this professional? Tell me seriously."

"How old are you?"

"Thirty-five."

"You could still have a shot," I said to encourage him.

"You want another beer?"

I shook my head.

"Soda?"

"Soda would be great."

"Diet Coke? Regular? Seven-Up?"

"Coke," I said. "Thanks."

"Bottle OK? Ice? You want some lemon? I probably also got some Pepsis."

"Coke is good."

"Can or bottle?"

"Bottle's fine."

He got up and took a pair of Cokes out of the fridge and came back and put them on the table. "I like them in bottles like the old days," he said.

"Listen, you know a kid named Billy Farone?"

"Shit, yes. I been trying to get in touch with somebody about Billy all day. I been stuck in Jersey at the airport until this morning. I saw something on Fox about Billy and I tried, shit, man, I tried, but the local precinct, the phone is busy all the time and they told us only use 911 for emergencies and I didn't know if this counts."

"You know Billy Farone?"

"Yeah, man, sure."

I said, "Go on."

"Billy's my pal," he said. "I take care of Billy when his mother has school, you know? We look at fishing books together. My old man worked the party boats by Sheepshead Bay."

"His mother knows about this, that Billy comes here a lot?"

"No. He told me, don't tell my mom, she don't like me hanging around here. He's a smart kid. He rides his bike over, and he could make it in ten, fifteen minutes. In between rush hours, I used to be happy when he showed up."

"Used?"

He shrugged. "One day he shows up with a guy that I never saw, a big goofball, sort of a retard, you know, what do you call them, mongoose?"

"Mongoloid?"

"Yeah? You alright? You went like white suddenly, it's not my pie, is it?"

"I'm OK. You ever see him again?"

"Yeah, they spent a lot of time together, they were here, maybe, four, five, six times." He was an enthusiastic witness.

"How did it seem, the two of them?"

"What do you mean?"

"I mean like friends, what?"

"They ate pizza and laughed and then I'd see them through the window going down the street, I think the goofball was taking him over to see the boats. I think they were planning a trip. I got that feeling."

"You didn't say anything to his mother?" I asked.

"No. Why would I? I told you, she don't know Billy and me are friends, right? Then I see the thing on TV so I'm worried. I remember he don't come by on Saturday which he always comes on. Or Sunday. Monday I'm stuck at the goddamn airport all day and night waiting for my niece to get in from D.C. This morning I see the thing on Fox, so I get worried."

I said softly, "Tell me about the goofball."

"He would come in and when he would see Billy, he'd buy a slice for him and two for himself and slap them together you know, doggie style like John Travolta in *Saturday Night Fever*, and shove them in his mouth in two bites, three tops. I noticed that, like he was starving or something. Like he was always hungry."

"You're sure?" I said.

"Sure I'm sure."

"So Billy was friendly with the guy? When did he start coming?"

"The mongoose?"

"Yeah."

"About a month ago. First it was once in a while, you know, and then more times, and it was like he was an uncle or something. Like family, you know? Billy's mom is Russian and they got these extending families and I didn't want to get involved."

I said, "Was he Russian, the mongoose guy?"

"I don't think so. I'm not sure, he didn't talk like no one else, but that was his retard thing, I think."

The creep, the mongoose, had been coming here for a month; over a month. He befriended Billy and no one knew. Who would notice? The pizza place was ten, fifteen minutes from the Farones' house, but Genia never knew; unaware of the creep who made her son into a friend, she nagged him about wearing socks and made sure he brushed his teeth.

It hit me: Billy went willingly. My God, I thought; Billy just went. The goofball offered him something, pizza, maybe. Billy was independent, he rode his bike everywhere. He had come here. He had eaten pizza with the goofball and with Fred Capestro, and now I sat, frozen in my seat, and something pressed on the back of my brain, something from the past.

As calm as I could I said, "Can you tell me what he looked like? The goofball?"

"Sure. Young. Like early twenties, big. Goofy. He smiled a lot. Brown hair, I guess. He usually wore jeans, those big hanging down jeans with the crotch near his knees, you know? A big T-shirt and he had a winter jacket with a hood. Red. The jacket."

"Anything else?"

"Not really. Can I come with you, I mean, can I help you look for Billy?"

"I need you here in case anyone comes by or you think of anything. Your job is to be here." I said. "I'll give you my cell number. OK?"

"Sure."

"Could you keep this to yourself for a while? That's important."

"OK," Fred Capestro said. "I'll write down my cell number for you. You can call me. You want me to call you if I see the goofball? Or Billy?"

"Yes."

He looked pleased and I finished my Coke and started to leave, but he ran after me, yelling, "Hey. Mister, I mean detective."

I turned around.

"Yeah?"

"Listen, there was one other thing."

"Go on."

"The mongoose, you know? He had this old little tape recorder. A crummy one, you know, but he was obsessed like it was his best thing, and sometimes I saw him talk into it. It was just one of those crap ones you see guys use to make notes on or dictate shit into, but if he saw you watching him, he always jammed it into a pocket. I asked him about it once, and he said it was a book he was writing, and I laughed and I thought he was going to hit me."

The Farones' street was planted thick with video surveillance cameras and as soon as I pulled up at the house I saw what an idiot I'd been not to notice. There was a camera mounted over the Farone door.

I got out my phone and called Genia, who didn't answer. She had never mentioned surveillance. Maybe there was stuff she didn't want me to see, but what? Banging on the front door, my phone in my hand, I rang the bell, listened to the chimes and waited. No one answered.

Across the street at the house where Billy's friend lived was another camera. I went up the walk and leaned on the bell.

"Yes?" It was Mrs. Gervasi, the blonde I'd met with

Genia. I showed her my ID, introduced myself, talked my way into her kitchen and a cup of coffee.

I couldn't understand how the local cops had overlooked the video cameras, but Billy's disappearance had only been public a few hours. And people just overlooked the obvious. Most crimes went unsolved because we fucked up, like me not noticing the videos.

Mrs. Gervasi said she had seen the news about Billy. Her husband and son returned Sunday night, she said, and she called Genia right away. Gen sounded nervous. I asked about security on the block. Plenty, she said. We have plenty.

"Look, we're nice people in a nice area," she said. "For years we got along. I grew up here. We had Italians, we had Jews. We were OK. The kids had the ocean. We went over to Lundy's for seafood. It was nice. The Russians stayed over in Brighton Beach."

"Then they moved in," I said.

"I'm sure some of them are very nice. Genny Farone isn't even like a Russian girl, not exactly, so I was fine when her Billy wants to play with my Stevie and I thought the kid was lonely. I felt for him."

"Can I have some more of that coffee?" I said. "It's really good."

"Milk?"

"Yeah, please."

"I have cream."

"Milk, thanks."

"Sugar or Sweet n Low?"

"Just the milk."

"I have Splenda."

"That's OK," I said.

"Sure," she said and made some more coffee and I drank it.

"Tell me what you know about Billy."

"Is this official?" She was nervous.

"Genia's my cousin. I'm Billy's godfather."

"I see," she said. "I understand. He was such a handsome boy. I mean is, of course, really like a little movie star and Genny dresses him up so nice, and everybody thought it was great when they moved onto the block. They take good care of the house and the yard. Johnny always offers us nice wine on the house when we go to eat at his restaurant."

"Billy?"

"I thought he was quiet at first. He would come over and sit in a corner and watch TV, but he didn't talk much. Then Marty, that's my husband, took the boys out on one of the party boats that parks over at Sheepshead Bay, you know, and he said to me later, Margie, he loved it, was really good to see, and after that Billy never stopped coming over, he was always here, always asking about another fishing trip." She was thoughtful. "I don't know why, but I got the feeling he changed his mind about going upstate with my husband and Stevie Saturday because he realized they were going skiing and not fishing. I can't say why. He didn't actually say."

I asked her if I could take a look at her surveillance camera, maybe borrow the tape, and she said, sure, it was almost finished, this tape, Marty could put in a new one later when he got home. I was surprised when she agreed so easily.

"To tell you the truth, I actually forgot about it. I never liked having the damn thing, but Marty says with the people around here, I don't mean here exactly, we have nice neighbors, but nearby, it was a good idea. He set it up. I don't even know how to use it,' she said and led me upstairs and showed me where the camera was set up.

The house was big and quiet and beige, tasteful and bland. She hovered behind me while I took the tape out of the camera and thanked her. She stood where she was. I didn't know what she wanted.

"Thank you," I said. "I'll write out a receipt."

"It's alright." She looked out the window. "It's snowing again," she said.

For a minute I thought she might change her mind; she might take the tape away from me and call her husband. I wasn't sure about anything, and then she skipped away down the carpeted stairs and into the kitchen.

I wrote out a receipt for the tape on a piece of paper I found in my pocket and thanked her again. She offered more coffee and it was then I smelled the sourish odor of white wine on her breath. I could see she wanted company and I said I was in a hurry.

I was desperate to watch the tape. I was betting Billy would be on it. If I was right and he went of his own free will, there might be a picture of the goofball who kidnapped him. Maybe the goofball just pulled up and Billy got in his car.

As I left the Gervasi house, my phone rang. It was Samson Britz. His sing-song voice was triumphant.

"I have something for you."

"What?"

"Go back to the beach again, to Coney Island, by the boardwalk. Take another look and think about it."

"That's it?"

"That's just the appetizer," he said. "You asked me if there was anything I could get on people who's supposed to like little girls, right? So I heard about this cop named Farone. John Farone, Sr. The son owns a restaurant out by Sheepshead Bay."

"Go on."

"They tried to get John, Sr., on a charge of messing with some kid?"

"What else?"

"They got him off, he retired," Britz said. "I knew him. He was OK. They said it was little girls. I didn't believe it. I think his wife wanted to fuck with his head and she set it up. You ever meet the old lady? She was a monster. He was OK, Farone. He had this crazy partner, though, used to key the cars of people he didn't like is what I remember about him." Britz laughed.

"He what?" I said.

"He'd see a big fancy car, it was holding up the traffic or something, waiting for someone to come out of a store, and this guy, he'd stand nearby and wait for it to pull away and scratch it the whole length with his keys. He was famous for it. Stanley the 'Keyster' Shank. They called him the 'Keyster.' He was a stupid fuck, but he made some good cases. I never believed it about the kids, though. Farone doing stuff with kids, I mean. But you asked. That good for you?" Britz sounded smug.

"Yeah."

"You're not going to thank me?"

I hung up and thought about calling old man Farone, but I had to see the video tape. It would take me hours to get back to the city. In the end I found a cheap video equipment store on Brighton Beach Avenue, where I rented a camera. I got back in my car, drove a mile or so, pulled into an empty municipal parking lot near Coney Island and shoved the tape into the camera.

On the video, as soon as I turned it on, you could hear the general background buzz of the city, but the Farones' street, which was in view, was silent. Taken from the second floor of the Gervasi house, the pictures showed the Farone place across the street. The picture was lousy but I could make out the house, the street, some lawn, the corner of another front yard. Somewhere in the background an ambulance shrieked, got louder, went away. I got out my cell phone and called a guy I knew who did security. He told me a surveillance tape that recorded for more than a few hours used some kind of time-lapse system. It recorded for a few frames, stopped, then restarted, but after just a fraction of a second. He talked me through it.

I rewound the tape, then fast forwarded, looked at the date and time code until I got to Saturday morning. I hit play, and then as I slowed the tape, a figure emerged from the Farones' door. It was Billy. He was wearing the Yankees jacket, jeans, High Top sneakers. In his hand was his sports bag and his fishing rod.

He disappeared from view briefly, then reappeared as he started across the street. When he was almost at the

275

Gervasi front walk, he turned away suddenly and moved out of sight again. For a second I thought he was avoiding the camera. Then he was back. A banged up old Honda chugged into view.

At first it seemed to follow Billy along the empty street, stalking him, going very slow to keep pace with the boy. I rewound the tape and watched a couple of days' worth of pictures from a street where nothing ever seemed to happen. The Farones went out, they came home, so did the Gervasis. Kids went to school. The school bus came by. So did the garbage truck.

Then the Honda again. I checked the date. A week before Billy had disappeared, the car pulled into shot and parked in front of the Farone house. A tall, heavy young man got out of the driver's seat and seemed to look around, though the black and white pictures were blurry.

The Farones' door opened and this time Billy appeared with an adult behind him. I assumed it was Genia until I wound the tape back again. It wasn't Gen; it was someone older. A woman but old. Sweat pouring down my neck now, I knew who it was. Johnny's mother whose skin smelled of vanilla. She kissed the kid, then, as if she'd heard a voice, turned and went back inside the house. The door behind her shut. Billy was alone on the street. Canvas bag in hand, as if he might be going to the school bus, he ran for the Honda and got in and the car pulled away.

I thought: the creep was waiting for him.

For half an hour, I rolled the tape backwards and forwards, and over the course of a week, the Honda appeared three times. Someone—the goofball—had staked out the place and was waiting for Billy. None of it was accidental. Long before he left home Saturday morning, Billy was a victim.

About to turn the camera off, I noticed a different car just barely in frame. A woman got out. It looked like Genia. The car looked like a BMW. Elem Zeitsev had a BMW.

I sat for a few minutes more, smoked, looked at the video. It occurred to me that if I could get the picture enlarged, I might get a read-out of the license plate on the Honda. I'd have to get to the city, but first I wanted to look at the place where Billy's clothes had been found.

The snow was coming down heavy now, the sky was white, the water invisible. I couldn't see out of the window. I stopped the car, got out and scrubbed at the windshield of the car with my bare hands. I'd left my gloves at home.

Frozen, I crawled inside again, put the heat on, switched the radio to a news station. The airports were closing down again; the city was socked in, the roads had turned, as the temperature fell, to ice. The heater made me sleepy. I had to see where Billy's clothes had been, had to see one more time. I had to get back to the city. Had to get to Maxine's, at least. Get a read-out on the license number. Get a read-out. I turned the radio up loud. I wanted to sleep.

Along Neptune Avenue, everything was closed, even the auto repair shops. They called it the "odometer turn-back capital of the world." You wanted to sell your car secondhand, you could get thousands of miles off it and you paid by the thousand. A guy once offered me a freebie on a "turn back" as he called it.

Trying to stay awake, I focused on the stores I passed. The pigeon feed shop was shut. Did the birds die of starvation in the winter or freeze to death or did people take them in? In New York, especially in Brooklyn, everyone kept pigeons since way back. Irish. Italians. They kept pigeons for sport and probably for company in wire cages on the roofs of the tenements.

I was only ten, maybe twelve miles from home, but Brooklyn was like Siberia. There were almost no cars on the road, no snow plows. All I could see was the white piling up, the flakes caught in my headlights. Streaming tubes of lit-up snow and nothing else.

One more time, I climbed out of my car. I had to know what Ivana had seen Saturday morning and how she'd really found Billy's bloody clothes.

28

A figure in a red fox coat emerged from the white landscape like a character in a set for a Russian play. It was the woman I'd seen on Saturday morning. I had seen the red coat, the wind tearing at it, the big black poodles at the end of the leash, the dogs pulling her, or seeming to. Then she disappeared behind the snow curtain and I was alone on the boardwalk.

I climbed down the stairs and looked under the boardwalk as best I could because I was sure Ivana had found the clothes here. No one would have left the blood-soaked garments where she claimed she'd tripped over them. She must have moved the clothes. She had moved them. Maybe she knew where they'd be and it was intentional, her finding them.

Did someone want the clothes found and the cops informed? Was Ivana the messenger? Did someone set her up? Was this what Samson Britz meant when he said: take another look.

Under the boardwalk was where people went to drink and shoot up and fuck, to toss their garbage and maybe hide stuff. Once, whole families had lived here. In the forties and fifties, black families had lived whole lives under the boardwalk. They cooked on makeshift barbecues; they slept; they did their laundry.

I jogged half a block, skidding on ice, and passed a small wood shack with a sign over the door: Iceberg Winter Bathers of C.I. Since the beginning of the twentieth century people had been swimming off Coney Island in the winter. Same time my grandfather started fighting revolution. My father, who was in his forties when he had me—strange having a first child so late in those days, though I never asked—was born in Russia in 1913. He met them all: Lenin; Trotsky; later, Stalin. They shook his hand or patted his head; as a child he had been anointed. I looked at the ramshackle club house. The Polar Bears, they called the winter swimmers. Ivana Galitzine said she sometimes swam on cold days. She had been a swimmer all her life.

I drove away from the boardwalk and the ocean, thinking at least I knew who had snatched Billy. The camera was next to me; on the tape I had the goofball who took Billy Farone from his house. I dialed Maxine. I hated doing it, but she could help me with the license number. She had friends who could run IDs fast. There was no answer and I drove faster, then I skidded.

The car spun on the ice, banged the curb and stopped dead. I turned the key and stepped on the gas and nothing happened. I turned the key again, frantically. I climbed out and looked under the hood.

All the time I was thinking: where was Billy? Where

did the goofball take him? Was he freezing to death in Brooklyn? Was he dead? I knew he was dead. Nine times out of ten they were dead or so abused they were better off dead. I had to ID the retard in the video, we had to find out who he was and why he had staked out the Farone house.

Gradually, the heat in the car died. I was frozen. I knew the bastard who allegedly fixed my car the day before had messed up the job. I looked out of the window; no one was out; no cars passed. For five minutes, huddled into my jacket, smoking, I sat and waited and tried not to panic.

Billy's disappearance was not random, it wasn't accidental. Again I wondered about the big man who broke into Maxine's apartment. It wasn't Tolya, I told myself. It was crazy. All he had in common with the creep was his size. I was on the edge and grabbing at anything.

I loved Tolya. I wanted to trust him. He had saved my ass and had rescued Lily; he was my friend. And Billy. I had to find him. Find him, find him, find him, it went around like a broken CD, like a digital movie where scenes break up in jagged patterns.

I couldn't make a pattern. I couldn't assemble the pieces into a picture. All I could do was sit helplessly in my car, the radio dead, the heat off, my cell phone not working because of the blizzard. I needed help. I stuffed the video tape in my pocket, turned up my jacket collar, got out of the car, found an old blanket in the trunk and wrapped it around me. I locked the car. Hands in my pockets, I started walking. I felt like a bum. I pulled the blanket tight, and bent my head and stayed in the middle of the road.

In my loafers, which were soaked, snow turning to water inside them, I stumbled forward. Suddenly like an oasis on the desert, I saw a light. A grocery store was in front of me, shuttered and silent but with a light in back. I banged on the metal gate hard. I rattled it.

A small Korean woman peered through the window. I gesticulated. She looked at me fearfully; I showed her my badge. She retreated to the back of the shop. I shouted, but my words drifted away and snow filled my mouth. I was shaking.

Suddenly, the woman reappeared with a set of keys, unlocked the door, unlocked the gate, and raised it far enough so, if I crouched low, I could get through.

What you want, she yelled at me, her face contorted with anger or fear, I couldn't tell, couldn't read her. But she offered me a cup of the tea she was drinking and I figured maybe the fear was cultural. I was a big white cop, she was a squashed Asian woman. All I really wanted was her phone.

She led me into the dark cluttered back room where there were boxes of groceries, and a hot plate and a table and chair.

I figured she was stuck, like me, in the storm. I found a ten-dollar bill and put it on the table, and gestured at the chipped black phone and started calling. The woman listened intently, though I wasn't sure how much she understood, but her eyes never left me. I called everyone I could think of: Lippert, Maxie, Tolya. I needed help bad. No one answered. Only answering machines or dead cell phones.

For ten minutes I sat in silence with the Korean woman and drank tea, both of us like stranded hikers in some alpine hut. She broke out a package of Oreos and ate one, licking the white cream off first. I took one and ate it the same way, and then ate another one. Her face relaxed and I saw she wasn't old at all. Not more than forty. Tiny and wrinkled but pretty.

Once she had been a very pretty girl. She drank more tea, nibbled a second Oreo and then ate a Milky Way. I grinned and took a candy bar and ate it. I went back to the phone. I think she figured I really was a guy in trouble, and not just a son of a bitch cop who was going to break her ass for some minor infringement.

"Where the hell are you?" Lippert mumbled when I finally got hold of him.

I told him. He said there was no one he could send, nothing he could do, everybody was up to their asses in snow. I slammed down the phone, and dialed Tolya again. I left a message with the address of the grocery store and told him to get himself over because I didn't know who else to call and I couldn't walk back to Manhattan. An hour later, Tolya rolled up to the door in his yellow tank.

I pulled some money out of my pocket and offered it to the Korean woman and she bowed her head delicately and refused, but I left it anyway on the candy counter at the front of the store. She unlocked the door and the gates, and I handed her my card. Said if she ever needed anything, she could call me and didn't know if she understood, but she bowed again and waited until we left, then and pulled the gates shut closed the door. By the time we pulled away, she was locked back into the store, all the lights off except the dim bulb in the back.

"Thank Christ you got my message," I said to Tolya who was bundled up in his black mink coat. He wore a towering Russian hat, curly gray fur that looked like a sheep stuck on his head.

The Hummer, Tolya's tank, was warm and smelled of the rich soft leather, and the CD player poured Tchaikovsky into the enclosed space.

"I'm homesick when it's like this, the snow, the cold, I'm a Russian," he said, chuckling. "I have some extra shoes in the back. There's a bottle of Scotch, too, and I brought some sandwiches," he added as he pulled away from the store and roared through the streets. "Where's your car?"

I told him the location and he got out his phone and called a tow truck.

"OK?" he said.

"Yeah," I said and it wasn't until the truck drove away, my car in tow, I forgot the camera was still in it. It would cost me, but I had the tape, which was all that mattered.

I reached into the back of Tolya's vehicle and found a pair of his shoes; grass green suede Guccis with gold buckles, they were three sizes too big. I put them on and looked at my feet. I looked like a kid in his father's shoes, but they were dry. I found the Scotch and drank from the bottle. The sandwiches were made out of black bread, sweet butter and caviar the color of very dark gray metal.

When I bit into one of the sandwiches, the caviar was rich on my tongue, the big eggs burst, the flavor was almost sweet. I ate a couple more bites, then stuffed another sandwich in my mouth.

"I've been looking for you and you've been avoiding me," Tolya said.

"Looking for me before I left you a message?"

"Since yesterday, but you screen my calls and you don't answer the messages, Artyom. Isn't that so?"

"I'm sorry," I said. "What's the deal?"

"Some creep comes to talk to me about you, and I get worried that this case with Evgenia's boy is a signal for you. Someone wants you out here in Brooklyn, someone wants to keep an eye on you, someone wants to hurt you. And."

"And?"

"Someone uses Billy as bait for you," he said.

I lit up and smoked without saying anything.

"Artyom?"

"What kind of creep?" I said.

"Where are we going?" Tolya asked. "Where do you need to go?"

Without thinking, I said, "Where were you Sunday night?"

"What?"

"I'm curious, you were with the blonde, the brunette, the architect, you were with your mother, where?"

He glanced in my direction, his face expressionless. An effusive man, Tolya: he laughed, he got angry, his

285

enormous face was a kaleidoscope of his emotional state, and the changes played out over the features. Now his face was chilly and immobile.

He said, "This is a policeman that's asking me, or is friend? This is interrogation? Third degree. What it is, detective?"

If I told him about the guy who broke into Maxine's, if I said I was suspicious, if I spelled it out, it would be the end of the friendship. Instead, I put out my cigarette in the ashtray and fumbled for the bottle of Scotch.

"You think I'm connected out here, is that it?" Tolya's voice was very cold. "You think I work with these putrid thugs out here near the beach, this is what you think? You imply this with me, right? You think all Russians are criminal assholes? You're a fucking racist, you know that?" He lapsed into Russian. "You tell me why you ask, I tell you where I've been."

So, finally, I told him. I told him about Maxine's apartment and the shadowy figure I thought looked like him. He looked back at me, pitying but disdainful. Tolya was silent.

I apologized. He didn't tell me where he'd been Sunday night, though, but I didn't ask again. I told him about the tape. I told him I needed a video camera because mine was in the abandoned car and a computer and a fax machine and that I had to get to the city. I had to get to the lab where there was a guy Maxine knew who could read the license off the video tape and ID the car's owner from it.

"I'll go by subway, if you don't want to drive with me," I said. "You can drop me at the train."

"I have what we need," Tolya said. "I have editing stuff, I have video equipment. I have everything. One of my girls, my younger daughter, she wants to be in films so she says, Pa, get me this stuff. She never uses it, but I keep anyway. We can send pictures with my stuff."

I gestured at the vehicle. "You think we can make it back to the city? The roads are solid ice."

"We're not going to the city," he said.

"Please, Tolya, I have to get there. Please."

"I put the stuff in an apartment out here. I told you my mother was crazy, she wants to stay with Russians, with what she calls family, you remember?"

"Yeah, sure."

"I bought her an apartment in Brighton Beach. I couldn't stand the relatives, I couldn't stand the cousins' house, which stank of borscht and nail polish remover."

"You bought an apartment?"

"I bought it. It was cheap, Artyom, it was fine. I can always sell. It was cheaper than putting her in the Four Seasons, which she didn't like anyway."

"She's there, at this apartment?"

"Yes. She said she wanted to go home. There aren't any flights. She won't bother us."

I thought of Lara Sverdlova in her pink sweatsuit.

I said, "You have a fax machine, a computer?"

He looked at me with comic disdain. "You think I'm some poor Russian schmuck that communicates by homing pigeon?"

He stepped on the gas and the vehicle shoved through the snow like a giant dust-buster. We moved about a mile an hour.

"You're in trouble," he said.

"I know. Just watch the road."

"You don't like my driving? I don't mean trouble with the missing boy."

He took the Scotch and drank and passed it back. I swallowed a mouthful.

Tolya said, "Sunday night I was with the architect, the woman with short hair you met."

"You like her."

"Crazy for her, I'm nuts about her, I don't even get it," he said. "She's harsh, she's skinny, she has no tits, she has no ass, she wears only this black, she criticizes my taste."

"So what's she for?"

"She's funny. You know what, Artyom? The hookers, my usual type woman, is never ever funny. Also not usually smart. This one is smart. She makes me laugh. She reads books. She knows philosophy. We discuss mathematics."

I glanced at him. For a split second his face was flushed with excitement.

"That's nice, Tolya. I'm happy. What did you mean, trouble? Someone came to see you about me. Right? What kind of someone?"

Sometimes, once in a while, nerve endings seemed alive like electric wires had singed my skin. Waiting for Tolya's answer, I felt my whole system was sending signals.

"What kind of someone?" I said again.

"Someone I know who was maybe connected with the government. I had this visit."

"Pull over, will you?" I said. "I want to talk before we get to your mother's place."

"My place."

"OK, your place, her place, just please pull over. Which government?" I said. "Mine? Yours?"

"What's the difference? But yours, since you ask. American."

29

We were in Brighton Beach, parked alongside the curb,
and Tolya said, "Anything out of order with you,
Artyom? Anybody been snooping?"

The heat was on high and the windows shut tight; I
was shivering.

"How come you're asking?"

"Do you want to play games, or do you want to know
what happened? I can play games, if you like, Artyom,"
he said.

"OK."

"You want to hear?"

"Sure."

"Then relax for a minute. You're making me
nervous."

I sucked down the cigarette smoke like a life-saving
drug and waited until Tolya gulped another mouthful of
Scotch. He took off his left shoe and rubbed his foot.
Outside, a small boy wearing green earmuffs peered in
the window of the vehicle. He widened his eyes, made

them bulge, stuck out his tongue. Tolya grinned, shooed him away.

"Did you do anything in 9/11, were you involved in the arrests, these detentions, were in contact with any Arab types?"

"Why?" I said.

"Just tell me."

"I helped with the digging. I worked as a volunteer at the site. The rest of it, I worked inside the department. A lot of what we did was basic stuff, identification, escorting VIPs, attending funerals. I didn't have much to do with the arrests, it wasn't my area."

"What about Sonny Lippert?"

"I know you hate him, but so what?" I said.

"Nothing."

"Tell me who visited you. It was about me?"

"Yes." Tolya hesitated.

"Go on."

"I'm at my hotel, in my suite, nice girl is with me, we are passing the time."

"The architect?" I interrupted, but he shut me up.

"I get a call on my phone. It is friend from the old days. Someone who moves around, does a little this a little that. Someone your father might have trained, you know, Artyom? The type, I mean, not literally, from the old days."

"You said that, so he was KGB."

"He's in business now."

"Like you."

"Like me." Tolya shifted his weight in the driver's seat, turning towards me, watching me.

"And?"

"He asks would I see a pal of his, an American he knew."

"From where?"

"He doesn't say at first. I guess FBI, CIA, free-lance, British. I don't really know, but I owe him, so I say sure he can send the friend. I say I'll meet him in the hotel bar, but he shows up and comes to my room."

"Where's the girlfriend?"

"I send her away shopping."

"Go on," I said, reaching for the Scotch and seeing, on my right out the window, the little boy in green earmuffs, peering through my window this time, clown-like. I opened the window.

"Get lost," I said.

"The guy, the agent, whatever, he's interested in me, I think at first, business stuff, cementing international relations, as they used to say, someone after my ass. Then I see he wants to talk about you."

Nausea rose up through my throat; I could taste bile.

I said, "He knew we were connected?"

"This is not hard to figure out," Tolya said. "You want another drink?"

"Tell me about this guy."

"It's alright, Artyom, you're not your father's son. You're just a cop, you're not a spook. They can't touch you. Take it easy."

"I was willing," I said. "I was almost willing if they wanted me, after 9/11, I would have done anything, become a spook even, whatever the fuck they are, if anyone wanted me, even though I hate it, and also

American spies so-called are cretins. But we were all so crazy in New York, I would have done anything. Jesus, I know people who joined the Marines. I would have joined the Marines." I shifted my weight and stared out the window again. "Except I'm too old."

Tolya pressed the electric button on his left and his seat slid backward. He hauled one leg over the other and relaxed against the back of the leather seat. The cold sun that had come out caught in the stubble on his chin and made it glitter.

"He was a small man," Tolya said. "Small and messy and thin, you know, and he comes into my suite at the hotel and he looks around and sees the shopping bag and it's as if I'm some kind of queen or something." Tolya clasped his foot. "You know, Artyom, I am looking at this guy and the bad suit and I think, he can be FBI only, but he doesn't show me his badge at first, it's like cat and mouse, and I don't ask, so I think maybe CIA. I can't tell. One or the other. Then I think: this suit definitely is from FBI, gray, cheap, you can get this suit for two hundred dollars. White shirt. Crummy tie. Suit is rumpled like he sleeps in it, and the coat is not regular coat but kind of ski jacket. A student's coat. He sits down when I sat please sit down, but he keeps on the blue jacket."

"Tolya, please, enough with the fashion."

"It's important."

"Why?"

"Let me finish, OK?"

"He sits and I understand he keeps on the jacket because he's carrying a gun and doesn't want me to know, though this seems quite idiotic, don't you think, he could have worn in the waist of his pants, but he is skinny and his pants kept slipping down, I notice this, he has to haul them up all the time. So I ask him do you want a drink and he looks at me like I ask if he wants to shoot up. The type you would see around US Embassy in Moscow in old days.

"When he hauls up his pants, his ankles show, the pants are too short, the socks are white and are too short and the shoes are cheap, light brown and scuffed, maybe he is forty or fifty, but always old; from birth this guy is old. You know these people that never have an age? Anyway, finally he says, 'You are friends with Detective Arthur Cohen?'"

It struck us both as funny at the same time, the agent calling me Arthur, and we both, Tolya and me, laughed.

I suddenly wondered if Sonny Lippert knew about the man in the too-short pants from the FBI. Would I be unwelcome on the job when he found out?

"Artyom?"

"What?"

"Then the guy takes off his coat. I say, what's your name please, and he says Agent John Smith. I think he is telling truth, no one makes up John Smith, so he shows me some identification, and he takes off the blue ski jacket and accepts a cup of coffee, which he stirs very slowly," he said. "Americans stir coffee slowly, also they put so many things in it, first coffee, then cream and sugar and stirring for minutes very very slowly. He is sizing me up while he stirs the coffee. The white shirt is clean, but wrinkled, and he loosens his tie, one of those striped ties, some cheesy synthetic."

"I don't care about his tie." I was feeling restless.

"He plays with it, and suddenly, when he finishes his coffee, John Smith puts the cup down on the coffee table, and looks up and I realize it is all an act, the suit, the tie, the coffee. He is giving the impression he is this stupid FBI dummy, this cliché agent, because then I will tell him anything. He is good."

Mr. Sverdloff, he says. I gather you've bought a loft style apartment on West Broadway?

Yes.

The building has some code violations, there have been some problems in the building, John Smith says.

Are you threatening me? replies Tolya, sipping the Bloody Mary he's ordered from room service. Are you, in fact leaning on me about this?

Smith shakes his head. We just want to help you get past this. We're not sure if Detective Cohen should be working on certain cases when we're uncertain about his background, you see, and I just mentioned the possible violations in the building that you've bought in case we can help in any way.

I said to Tolya, "You bought the whole fucking building?"

"It was a bargain."

To Smith, sitting in his hotel room, he says: And you think this will pressure me? For what?

We'd like to know whatever you know about Detective Cohen.

I know he's a good cop, Tolya says. I know he loves this country, I don't know what you want to know, so how can I help you know it?

Yes, we know about his service record, we can access that, I mean anything else, about his background, for instance.

He left the fucking Soviet Union when he was sixteen.

But after, said Smith. After that.

He spent a couple of years in Israel. He went to university there, he went in the army, he came here. I don't know what the fuck you want because there's nothing. He's the cleanest son of a bitch I know.

Does he know any people of the Arab race?

What?

Arabs. Does he have friends who are Arabian?

How the fuck would I know, Tolya says, angry now. I don't keep tabs on his friends. What's this about?

Smith is completely calm and casual and only mentions the Patriot Act once, hinting that he has the power to pick up anyone. Anyone he says again, if there's a suspicion. 9/11 changed things, he says.

Tolya tells him to get out: GET OUT!

I thought about John Smith, if it was his name, the agent who had visited Tolya. Who had broken into my place. I wished it had been gangsters with guns, thieves, killers.

I thought about my old friend, Roy Pettus, the only FBI guy I ever liked or trusted, but he had a heart attack and retired to Chugwater, Wyoming, years ago where he came from and where he was now bored and sad. I called him once in a while; he hated the way things went after 9/11, the random stop and search, the arrests, the detentions. It didn't work, Pettus said; it made things worse.

"Did he threaten you? This John Smith?"

Tolya laughed. "You think I feel threatened? I have green card, right, I am legal. You are citizen, Artyom. Fuck them."

But the fury I felt made me hot. I understood about the dictionaries, the letters from Hamid. Whoever had been in my place wasn't connected to the kidnappings. They were looking for me, for my past, for evidence I was a bad American. It was because I was foreign. I sat in the vehicle, half listening to Tolya, and was terrified. I had done jobs in countries where I didn't speak the language. I'd been threatened with knives. Lily had been attacked. I had never been scared the way I was now. I felt foreign.

Inside the apartment Tolya had bought for his mother, we shed our coats. Lara Sverdlova was in the bedroom asleep and snoring and you could hear her through the bedroom door.

"Can we do this?" I said holding out the tape. "I want to take some stills off this and send them to someone, can you do it?"

He nodded. "To send the whole tape or just the pictures we make?"

"The whole tape if you can, but also some stills. I want to make some stills off it. I'll show you. I want the people in it, anyone who's in it. OK? Can you do it? You know how? You know I'm lousy with technology," I said.

"What is it?" he asked.

I was silent.

"You either trust me or fuck off, Artyom, because I'm really tired of your suspicions. You know who I am, you know what I do."

"I don't know."

"I do business," he said. "I make deals. I buy and sell, property, money, gold, whatever, I make money. I buy my mother an apartment in Brooklyn, OK? Is that OK with you? If there's real estate to buy I buy it if I can. I deal like everyone else in business."

"Who do you make deals with out here?"

"What do you care? I'm your friend."

I said, "Are you? Is that why you let a creep from the FBI into the room?"

"This is insulting," Tolya said. "I hate this. We already went through this before, in London. You remember London? You know I'm your friend. You can't get over it because I'm still Russian, can you, you despise me when I speak English and drop articles. You don't want to be connected with foreigners, Russkis especially, you're afraid it will drag you back."

"So why do you do it?"

"What?"

"Talk like a gangster?"

"Sometimes because I forget," he said. "My English is not like yours exactly. Sometimes because it makes me laugh inside, I hear myself talking like hood, like biznesssman, from this I keep myself going."

He was already at the far end of the living room where he had assembled a mountain of machines: two big screens, editing equipment, computers, a DVD player.

Tolya shoved the tape into a video camera he picked

up off the pile of equipment and plugged the camera into his computer. The images rolled up onto the screen. Again from the other room came the sound of Lara Sverdlova snoring. Tolya shut the door.

"You have money, you have houses, now you've found a woman you like, something who's for real, why not stop all the dealing?" I said.

"I can't stop. You don't mean stop, anyway, you mean why don't I go corporate. Like your friend, Zeitsev, right? I am what I am, that's why Zeitsev gives me a pain in the ass, with his fake American façade, it's like a cheap veneer, like the hair, like the poses. Did he ever say to you people tell him he resembles JFK?"

I nodded.

"He's just the son of a Russian monster who decided life was more fun legit, but what kind of legit is that?" Tolya snorted. "He deals with insurance companies, he gives money to political parties, he supports people who sell cigarettes to children in the Third World, he probably parties with assholes who give Dick Cheney money for his campaigns when Cheney goes way back with companies like Enron that sucks the lifeblood out of regular people, you think this is better? You think this is legit life? Fuck that, man. Zeitsev fucks with stuff just like everyone else."

"Zeitsev is a Democrat."

"For God's sake, Artyom, what's the bloody difference?"

"I'm not Zeitsev's publicist, OK? You sound like an old Commie."

"Yeah, well maybe I'm a new Commie. I'm a realist."

He fumbled in his pocket for the cigar case and lit a Cohiba.

The aromatic smoke filled the room that was furnished with only a leather sofa and two chairs, a coffee table and the computer gear. On the balcony outside, a small mountain of snow trembled until it seemed it would topple.

Tolya was messing with the machinery and talking at the same time.

"You know something, Artyom," he said in Russian now. "I consider you like a brother. You almost married my cousin Svetlana, who loved you very much. I took care of your Lily, and Beth, and I still take care of her, too, when Lily lets me."

"She's not my Lily anymore."

Tolya ignored me and said in English now, "You know what, I rescue your ass many times. But you don't trust me. I don't know if you like me. Maybe because I'm not American, maybe because I don't love your country so much, or I make you feel less American. I don't know." He sounded mournful. He gestured to the screen. "Is this what you want?"

On the screen were the pictures I had already seen, the goofball, the Honda, Billy getting into it.

"I want you to send them to this e-mail address I'm going to get you," I said, and picked up the phone.

I called Maxine's friend, Mel, a geek she knew who worked weekends and nights and could pull up license plate idents. He was brilliant with drivers' licenses; he could match numbers and pictures.

Mel said he could do it but he needed an OK from

Maxine, needed to know that it was fine with her; so I called her. I didn't want to call her but I didn't have much choice. It was after working hours and I needed the information fast.

I could hear from her voice that she was happy to hear from me. I could hear she thought I was calling because I'd made a decision about us.

"I need help," I said. "I'm sorry."

I told her I had to get Mel to put some images through the system for an ID, and her voice was disappointed. She said she'd call him and hung up and I felt lousy about it.

I turned to Tolya, who was crouched over the computer. I watched him while I called Mel back; he said Maxine had called; he said I could put through the pictures, the picture of the guy, the picture of the license plate. I passed the phone to Tolya and Mel told him how to send the material.

I sneezed.

"Jesus, I've never heard anyone sneeze so loud," Tolya said. "Go make coffee while I finish sending this stuff."

My throat was raw. I sneezed again. I went into Tolya's kitchen and made coffee and poured brandy out of a two-liter bottle and knocked it back, as much as I could without puking it up. I hated brandy, but it warmed me up. I took Tolya a mug of coffee, black and bitter, and I drank one down myself.

In the living room, while Tolya drank his coffee, I looked over his shoulder at the printer which spat out the pictures: first Billy Farone, then the goofball. In another I could see Genia very clearly. For black and white surveillance pictures, they were pretty good. I stared at the goofball's face and waited for Mel to call.

Goofy was twenty-five, twenty-six, and big, but not fat or heavily muscled; just big and loose and large. He wore a puffy down-filled jacket and fat boy jeans that hung below his crotch and flapped around his ankles. He had dark hair and there was something vacant about his face. I remembered what Fred Capestro, the guy in the pizza store, said: he was a mongoose. He was a retard. The face was benign, almost sweet, but vacant.

Without any warning, the bedroom door burst open and Lara Sverdlova exploded into the living room, still in the pink sweatsuit, her gray hair springing up from her head as if she'd been electrocuted. Ignoring us, she went into the kitchen, where I heard the refrigerator bang open and shut, pots and pans rattled and, without a word, she emerged holding a plate of food and went back into the bedroom.

The rackety noise of the fax started up, the sound that was like cicadas in the bush at night in the countryside. Tolya reached for the pages as they fell off the fax into a basket. One at a time, he handed them to me.

The way things sometimes did, it floated into my head while I held the faxes that the only person who for sure knew I spoke Arabic was Sonny Lippert; he had known from the beginning.

"What's the matter?" It was Tolya and he was staring at me. "You look like you saw demons."

The fax in my hand distracted me. In it, Mel had scribbled the identification of the guy, the mongoose, the creep, in the video surveillance picture. He had matched him to the license plate and a driver's license. I knew for sure it was his Honda, the car Billy got into, the car that took him away.

30

His name was Herschel Shank. Heshey was what people called him, except when they called him Mickey because, in spite of his size, he was timid as a mouse. Sometimes, they actually called him Goofy.

All this and more was scribbled by hand in the margin of a piece of paper in the file on Shank. Because Shank had been in and out of state institutions, misdiagnosed variously as schizophrenic or bi-polar before someone figured out he was mildly retarded. He was twenty-five. Apparently, for years, no one had wanted him at home.

After he was diagnosed as harmless, his brother took him in and he was released permanently from the institutional treadmill. A job was found for Heshey and for years he stayed at it, working as an assistant janitor at a school in Sheepshead Bay. Like all school employees, he had been fingerprinted.

So much information, so easy to get. I had fucked up just because I didn't notice the surveillance cameras and no one else did either. There was a trail of material on Shank: he had a social security number, a current driver's license with an address on it, and a brother who was a retired cop. Name was Stanley Shank.

Shank was a name I already knew. Samson Britz had told me he was partners with old man Farone, Johnny's father. Shank who they called the "Keyster" because he liked scratching cars with a key. Farone, Sr., was older, probably Shank's mentor, his rabbi.

I looked at the paper in my hand. Shank lived in Gerritsen Beach, a few blocks from Mrs. Farone. It wasn't far from the marina where they found May Luca's body.

"I need your car," I said to Tolya.

"I'm going with you."

"What about your mother?"

Tolya glanced at the bedroom where his mother had resumed sleeping.

"She'll be fine," he said. "You don't trust me, do you? You want my fucking vehicle but you don't want me with you, is that it?"

He took the keys out of his pocket and tossed them to me. He opened a closet and pulled out a ski jacket, a hat and gloves and threw them in my direction. From a shelf he got boots for me and dumped them on the floor then put on his own coat that resembled a big black animal.

"Leave the mink, please," I said.

"Why? You think I look like some fat transvestite fuck? I'm not coming with you anyhow, you remember, you asked me not to."

I said, "I'm sorry. I am. Come with me." I put on the jacket.

"I'll think about it," he said and opened the door.

We went into the hallway and took the elevator down and I said, "Tolya?"

"What?"

"So, I have this thing going."

"What thing?"

"You're going to think this is crazy."

"I know you're crazy."

"There's this woman I like. I'm getting married."

He was silent.

"Tolya?"

"Who is she?"

"She's a really nice girl. She's a good friend. I like her, we have a good time."

"I'm listening," he said, but I could see he had shut down.

"What?"

"You won't be happy."

"Why the fuck not? I want a life. I'm sick of everything, I just want to stop."

We walked out of the building without saying anything and when we got to the street, he hurried away.

I wanted to call out. In that second I realized I'd been insanely stupid about Tolya. He was my friend; in the Russian way, he was completely loyal. It had hurt him bad that I seemed not to trust him. I hesitated. But I had to get to Shank, and I climbed into the yellow Hummer and turned the key. I hated driving it; people turned to stare; I felt like a monkey in a cage

Stanley Shank opened the door and let me in grudgingly. He wasn't surprised I had come, though.

From another room I could hear the TV and the sound of voices.

Shank was fat. He had soft heavy shoulders and a round head set between them like a bowling ball between mashed potatoes. His hair was thinning and his pants had slipped so the enormous belly rested precariously on his belt. I got the picture out of my pocket and held it up.

"Is this your brother, Herschel?"

"Half brother," he said. "My father remarried. She was younger. The woman."

"He lives here?" Shank looked past me at the yellow Hummer. "That yours?" he asked.

"Let's talk about your brother."

"He uses the address. Sometimes he stays. There's a room for him over the garage. I'm a Christian," he said as if it explained why he kept his crazy brother at all, as if the deal with the room over the garage made him a good man. "Jesus," he mumbled and I couldn't tell if he meant it as the source of his religion or as an expletive about his brother.

"The car is registered to this address," I said. "How did he get a car?"

"I gave him an old car so he could go to work. It was a piece of crap but I got it tuned up. It was OK to get him to his job. He works at a copy shop off Brighton Beach Avenue."

"You're a cop, right?"

"Was. I was on the job. I retired."

I said, "You didn't think about it when your brother didn't show up for a few days?"

"No. Like I told you he moves around. He's twenty-five years old. Something the matter with him?"

"I think you already know."

"Listen, I don't fucking know what you mean. All I know is that I heard from Samson Britz and Britz said I owed him and I told him, OK, I knew Farone, sure, he was my partner. Now tell me what's wrong with Heshey?"

"And you like doing him a favor, Britz, I mean."

"Don't we all," he said. "I'll tell you something, detective, I'll tell you why we're standing in the hallway here and I don't ask you into the parlor for a cup of coffee with the family, OK? You want to know?"

"Sure." I waited.

"Britz asked me to say hello to you if you came by," Shank said. "But I don't like you, though, or your Russians, and I hate that prick Lippert you work for. I can't stand him. He doesn't understand anything. He's a fucking liberal, man, and he's a snob, and I don't trust him, I don't like him, I don't think he's in any of this except for the glory. Maybe money."

I didn't answer.

"Listen, I get it. I can talk some Russian. The army sent me to language school and I came back and I went on the job, it was the seventies, and they threw me into it, no one else spoke any Russki and the thugs out here bit my head off. I got beat up and one of my kids got hurt. I don't like them. Or you," he added.

"What about your brother? What about him and the little boy? We have pictures. We have pictures of your brother and that boy in the Honda. Your car. The boy is John Farone's grandson, John, Sr., your ex-partner, maybe more than your partner. Isn't that right? Wasn't Farone your first boss, your rabbi?"

"Yeah, he was. I was a kid, twenty years old, he took care of me when we partnered," he said.

"You knew the kid that disappeared is his grandson?"

Shank stayed standing but he put one hand against the doorframe as if he needed support.

"I heard that, sure I did. I called him in Florida to say I was sorry. You don't think word doesn't get out? You've been messing around with forensics, with the people downtown, you been calling and making waves with old man Farone's wife that tossed him out on some stupid trumped up thing about little girls, just like they tried to lay on me.

"You think I wouldn't know? I don't believe it is what. Heshey is a retard, my father married an idiot after my mother died, a Russian, a Jew. She calls the kid Herschel. Then when he turned out to be a moron, she dumps both of them. OK, so Hesh was slow in school, but he was harmless."

"Then where is he?" I said.

"My father's dead." His face was closed, expressionless.

"I mean Heshey."

"I don't know. He took the car. He said he was going away for a few days. Before the storm. He said he had to be like a grown-up and he wanted to go away by himself."

I said, "And you thought maybe he'd never come back, right? Maybe he would go forever and you wouldn't have to bother with Heshey anymore?"

309

"Get out," he said. "Get the fuck out."

I was halfway out of the front door. Then I turned around and said to Shank, "So where did Heshey say he was going?"

"Fishing," he said and slammed the door in my face.

It wasn't until I was halfway to Farone's restaurant that I realized I'd met Stanley Shank before.

It took me a couple of minutes to play his face back through my memory, and at first I put him somewhere by the coast, somewhere with water, until I remembered: Stanley Shank was the owner of the party boat when Billy and me went night fishing; he was the guy who took our money when we made it by a couple seconds onto his boat that was called *Just a Fluke*.

31

A couple of bussers sat in Farone's empty restaurant, playing cards, drinking coffee, gabbing in Spanish. Stranded by the storm, they had stayed over at Farone's. Most of them, the bus-boys, were Dominican and lived in Washington Heights up near the Bronx. There were no customers.

On a stool Johnny Farone sat, alone, a glass half full of red wine in front of him, his elbows on the bar, his head in his hands.

He looked up and saw me; his eyes were bloodshot.

I climbed up on the stool next to him. To shake him out of his torpor I said, very softly, "Genia took your money, Johnny. It's Genia that's been ripping you off. Did you know and not tell me? What else is there that she's keeping to herself that's going to kill your little boy? If he's still alive. If Billy's alive."

"I thought it was her," he said. " I wanted you to find someone else, I prayed for it, man, that it would turn out to be a crooked accountant or a slime ball maître d'. Anything. I couldn't stand it, the idea, I give her everything. I told her she could have what she wanted, but she needs the secrets. You understand that, Art? She has to have secrets from me. You get it? I don't get it. That's why I don't go home, that's why I sleep in the fucking office here. She told me: don't call the cops. So she calls you. Now she's mad at you, she says, Artie betrayed us. He's like his old man that was a spook. I don't know what she means. I listened to her, and I did what she said and now I figure now my boy is dead because of it." Tears streamed down Johnny's face.

I took a photograph out from my pocket and placed it on the bar and said, "You ever see this guy?"

Johnny looked at the picture of Heshey Shank.

"Is this him?"

"I think so."

"I never saw him," Johnny said. "Oh shit, man, I never saw him and he took my boy. But why?"

"Talk to me, Johnny. What is it you didn't tell me about Billy?"

He picked up his wine.

"She made me promise, Genia made me."

"I love Billy," I said. "You know that, right? You have to help me."

He said, "Genia thinks Billy isn't right. She wants to take him to doctors and stuff, she thinks he's sick in the head. You don't know what I'm talking about, do you? I tell her it's just a phase, let him grow up. I say let him spend some time with my mother, the older people are patient, don't make him play with kids he doesn't like, but Gen thinks she puts an evil eye on him. She says

312

when he was little he spent time with her old man, that general, you know, that's dead now, and he scared Billy. Then my ma tells me Billy's not even mine. I'm fucked up, Artie. I don't know what's what anymore."

Johnny turned his head in my direction and his face was uncomprehending.

"You believe it, that Billy isn't yours?" I asked, as gently as I could.

"I don't know what the hell I believe anymore. I'm just scared. I'm scared shitless, they took Billy, they killed the Luca girl, they snatched the kid in the city. Maybe it's them terrorists. I don't know."

I was dry as dust from talking and a sore throat and I reached over the bar for a bottle of water and drank some. Next to me, Johnny stared straight ahead and in the mirror his face and mine were reflected behind the bottles.

"Johnny, tell me what's wrong with Billy, tell me, OK? I'm on your side." I said it softly in an even voice, then added, "I don't want to have to go to Gen, I don't want to, she's already hysterical, she can't focus."

"I wish the weather would fucking clear up," he said. "I think of Billy out there alone and no shoes, maybe, they took off his shoes and cut off his shirt with a razor, I heard the reports, and he's out there with some creep and it makes me crazy and I don't know what to do. Maybe he froze to death."

"I'll help you, I will, but you have to give me something to go on." I put my hand on his arm.

"You knew all along it was Gen taking the money?"

"It looked that way."

"Yeah, I know," he said. "But why? I give her

everything she wants. I say, whatever, you can have it, but why would she want cash?"

"I don't know. Let's talk about Billy."

He said, "You heard Gen was with Zeitsev, right?"

"I heard. Is it true?"

"Yeah, it's probably true. But what could I do?" Johnny mumbled. "Everyone was nuts, 9/11, that shit, everyone running around crazy, everyone fucking everyone and crying all the time, and people with the fucking yellow ribbons and memorial services and we knew loads of those guys, cops, firemen from over by Rockaway. So I thought it would pass. It didn't pass, you know? It just seemed like things got better, but they didn't." He paused and wiped his eyes. "I love him, Artie, man, Billy is still my kid."

"Tell me about him," I said again.

"I think it was my old man that ruined him. You know about my old man, the way he felt up little girls, you heard? I'm not saying he did anything to Billy, but Billy was crazy for him, he just seemed like a really cuddly grandpa. We didn't know dick about his other pastimes until maybe it was too late. And the Luca girl. Billy was friends with her. She was the only kid in the neighborhood that played with him. Sweet girl, OK? He wore her red T-shirt. The one they cut off him. And the old man touched her, and my ma went crazy.

"May's mother went nuts too, of course, and said Billy could never see May again, she said Billy probably inherited his granddad's, you know, tendencies, which is bullshit, Artie. Bullshit. He's a little boy. He sat in his

314

room for weeks afterwards and if I tried to explain he would just sit and rock and shriek her name."

"Go on," I said.

"We didn't know until last Christmas, that's when the girl's mother told him never come in this house again and then told us why. She's dead. Billy's gone. Then Gen told me my old man done it to her girl, too, to Ellie. I mean he didn't fuck them or nothing, you know, but he liked to feel them up. Or maybe he did worse. I don't know. I can't think about it. He's my father, Artie, " Johnny said, and wiped his eyes. I didn't want him to stop. Go on, I thought, keep going.

"My ma threw him out. My pop was furious, he needed the kid, he said, he'd come here and cry. Billy felt deserted. He loved his grandfather. He's not like other kids. He's very smart, creepy smart, he can talk like grown-ups, he talks like people in books, he can remember things, he can remember like a hundred kinds of fish from a book, he can remember the colors of fishing flies, gaffer hooks, knives, he can make fancy flies. He sold some to people. We used to go by the Aquarium over by Coney and he'd stay for hours and hours and hours looking in the tanks. Sometimes I see him at home staring at the fish tank for hours. He makes up ways to feed them, it's really fucking weird, he says you have to release the fish food in a certain way. You tell him, listen, it's time to go to school and he screams. I said to Gen this kid need some discipline, but she says, no he needs a doctor. She wants to take him to a different city for a doctor. She doesn't want people knowing. She thinks they put people who need help in a nut house. I say,

Gen, honey, it's not Russia, it's not the old days, she won't let me help." Johnny stopped suddenly. "My God, Artie, I don't know what to do," he said.

"Do you think Genia's glad Billy's gone?" I said, getting out some cigarettes and offering them to Johnny, who shook his head. "I know this is tough but she wouldn't let me call the cops and I had to and then she got mad and I had to ask myself, does she even want Billy back?"

He shuddered. "I don't want to think about that," he said. "I can't think about it. What should I do? Tell me. I'll do what you say, Artie, I'll do whatever, even if Gen doesn't want it. Anything. I'll ask Zeitsev for help, if I have to. You think Billy is his kid?" he said suddenly. "I don't care if he is, I just want him back."

"You never saw this guy, Heshey Shank?"

"I knew a cop named Shank," he said. "Stan Shank, right? Sure. He partnered with my dad. My old man loved him. He loved him more than me."

"Heshey, the guy we think took Johnny, is Shank's half brother."

"Oh Christ," Johnny said.

I said, "I have to see Genia. Stay here, OK. Just sit tight. In case anyone comes. Is she alone?"

"I think she has a girlfriend with her."

"What girlfriend."

"A friend from Russia. Marina something, I think."

"Try to remember her last name."

"G, something with a G."

I thought of Ivana, the jogger from the beach. Her aunt was friends with Genia.

"Is it Galitzine?" I said to Johnny.

"Yeah, her. Artie, man, listen I'm useless, but I want my boy back. Tell me, anything, I went to the bank." He pulled a wad of money out of his back pocket. "Take it. In case. I don't care how much. I'll sell the restaurant. I know you'll find him, you were like another dad for him. I was never jealous, I mean I was a little bit but I saw how good you were for him. OK? You'll find him?"

"I'll try, Johnny," I said, and he hugged me, then turned to talk to one of his guys who approached the bar.

The guy, a tall man with a solemn face, held out a piece of paper.

"They put this under the door in back," he said with a heavy accent. "Just now. I seen it slide under."

Wordlessly, Farone looked at the sheet of paper and passed it to me.

On the single sheet of cheap copy paper was the face of a clock drawn in perfect detail. The hands showed midnight; next to the twelve was a drawing of a bomb exploding.

"You think it's a warning, you think they're going to kill Billy by midnight. Tonight?"

I took the piece of paper and ran.

"Where's your friend?" I said to Genia as soon as she opened the door of her house. "Where the fuck is she?"

"Hospital," Genia said holding the door open. I went inside but I kept my jacket on.

"What's wrong with her?"

"Her niece," she said. "Ivana."

"What?"

"She cuts her wrists."

317

I was sick of it, sick of Genia, sick of everybody, sick of the fear.

"You wanted it, didn't you? You wanted Billy to disappear? It was too much of a problem for you? Isn't that it?" I was holding her arm tight, but she yanked it free.

"You're crazy, you know that, Artemy? You're crazy. You think I wanted my boy to disappear. Talk to my husband if you're looking for problems with Billy. I wanted that boy, he was wonderful but Johnny was always saying he had to grow up, he needs discipline, I want him to see doctor, Johnny and that mother say, take him to church. I think, sure take him to American church where priests touch little boys."

I didn't know what to do. I couldn't leave Genia alone, she was falling apart silently.

"Where's Ellie?"

"She's in the city. She's at Juilliard. I don't want her involved," Genia said. "She has her life. Leave her be."

"I don't want you alone," I said.

"Why, you don't trust me?"

"Yeah," I said. "That's right. I don't trust you. Just call someone, will you?"

"Sure. Sure, I call."

"Promise me, OK?" I said and looked at her and put my arms around her. She held onto me and I realized I really cared about her. More than I thought. More than I understood.

"Promise?'

"Yes, Artemy, yes," she said and I knew as soon as I left she'd call Elem Zeitsev.

32

On Tuesday night, the kid from Tribeca showed up, but the dread had already settled over the city and people were disturbed and a little crazy. Tatiana, the girl with two mothers, had gone to the airport to fly to Denmark to find her father. She had seen *Sleepless in Seattle*.

In it she sees a little boy who books an air ticket on-line and flies across the country alone, Seattle to New York, and he's just a dorky eight-year-old, so why not me, Tatiana asks herself. She's eleven. She lives in New York and she has her mothers' credit card and she knows the limo service number by heart, and she goes. Just like that. Sick of being a baby. Sick of being attended by nannies and bodyguards. Anyhow, anyway, she knows her way around airports. She's been in all the first class lounges.

Only the storm grounded her. That and because she curled up in the first class lounge and made a fuss when the woman who ran the lounge told her she could not sit in the first class lounge and would have to move to business class. Tatiana burst into tears and then threw a tantrum. She was her mothers' daughter.

I heard it on the car radio on my way from Genia's house. In the dark, I drove two miles an hour through narrow streets that were frozen hard as a skating rink.

On the radio, every ten minutes the news cycled around; more details of the Tatiana trip emerged. She had planned it. She promised her mothers she was going to supper at her friend's in the apartment building, and she whined and cried and got her way and when she got in the elevator she simply went downstairs, waited until the doorman was preoccupied and skipped across the street where her limo was waiting. She said she wanted to meet her father; she was going to Copenhagen, Denmark.

Maxine made me sleep on the couch. When I left Genia, I didn't know where to go. My own car wouldn't be ready until the morning and there wasn't any point going back to the city and I was scared, scared someone would be in my apartment, scared I might be arrested before I could find Billy.

My mind raced; I didn't know where to go; it was way past midnight; if the drawing with the bomb meant anything, Billy was dead. I kept going. Paranoia took over, and in Tolya's yellow Hummer I felt too visible; I was a sitting duck.

As I drove away from Sheepshead Bay, all I could think about was sleep. All I could think about was Maxie's cozy apartment, her daughters, even the smell of the place. It smelled of girls. It smelled of talcum powder and almond shampoo and Maxie's make-up. I got to her place and I wanted to climb into her big bed and roll around with her and sleep for hours in the warm sheets. But she met me at the door with only a professional welcome.

She put her finger to her lips. The girls were fast asleep in their bunk beds in their pajamas with ducks on them. Max was bundled up in a bathrobe. She got out pillows and blankets and tossed them on the couch, and told me I could stay and retreated to her own room. I went in after her. I said I just needed time, I had to finish the case, before I could think straight about her and me, and she laughed without any humor and went into the bathroom and closed the door.

In the living room, I fell asleep with scrap of paper with the clock on it Johnny had given me clutched in my hand. Bad dreams washed over me.

I woke up a few hours later and, staring at the ceiling, I tried to stay awake and put things together, but I couldn't. I slept so hard that when I dreamed, I was in Moscow, I was a kid and it was winter and I woke up to the sound of the snow plows. "Capitalists" we called them because they worked hard and steady, unlike anything else, rackety rackety rackety; in Moscow you could hear them everywhere, early in the morning. I woke up, for the second time, in Brooklyn.

Rubbing my eyes, I went into the kitchen but Maxine and the girls were gone. A note on the table had my name on it and when I unfolded it, it was in Maxie's handwriting, asking me to lock up and put my keys under the door. She wanted her keys back.

I felt like a bum, crashing on her couch, waking up after she left. I hadn't shaved. And something kept pushing up at me, something in my head wanted to explode and I couldn't catch hold of it.

I took a shower and used a razor I found in the medicine chest. From the fridge I got a quart of orange juice and drank it in huge gulps most of the way down. I felt parched and my throat was ragged and I was sneezing and feverish. I got dressed and went downstairs, where Maxie's neighbor, a young guy with a cleft palate, was shoveling snow.

Like military machines, the snow plows were out in ranks. The sun shone, the snow on the streets was clean, the sky was a blue bowl. Across the highway, the Verrazano Bridge glittered.

I called the tow service, got the name of the shop where my car was, took Tolya's vehicle back to Brighton Beach and parked it outside his building and went and got my own Caddy. The video camera was still on the front seat. Then I went to see if Ivana Galitzine was out of the hospital.

There was black bread on the kitchen table and a bowl of soft butter and the rancid smell from the butter assaulted you as soon as you got through the door. Ivana stood looking at a cigarette that burned on the edge of the sink that was piled with filthy dishes; what looked like meat stew was smeared on them.

I said, "You lied, didn't you? No one around here just goes to a cop, right? You knew where the clothes would be. You wanted the cops to know. You didn't stumble on them, isn't that right? Because if you did, you would have left them and moved on, wouldn't you? You knew where to find them. It was a set-up. Isn't that right?"

She turned around, her eyes were ringed with greasy make-up from the night before. Wearing a pink bathrobe with tufts of dog hair clinging to it, she picked up the cigarette from the sink where it left a burn mark and inhaled. Her wrists were wrapped with bandages.

"I don't know," she said. "I thought there might be reward. I think maybe I get on TV."

"There's a little boy," I said. "He's going to die. He might be dead already."

She held her hands up as if she thought I was going to hit her.

"Tell me," I said.

"Not here."

"Why not?"

"They're listening through the walls," she said and I knew she had been doing bad drugs.

"What are you on?"

She shrugged.

I said, "Then get dressed."

She sat down on a chair.

"Get dressed."

My back hurt from sleeping on Maxine's lumpy couch and my throat was still raw. I coughed and took out a pack of cigarettes anyway and lit one with a lighter Tolya had given me. I'd found it at home in a drawer, a sterling silver Dunhill. I held it in my hand and rolled it between my fingers like rosary beads.

She was staring out of the window and I went to where she stood and caressed her arm lightly.

"Please, Ivana," I said. "Please get dressed and come

323

out for some breakfast and talk to me. I need your help."

Speaking Russian to her in that coercive way, again I remembered my father. I'd never seen him at work, of course; interrogations were conducted somewhere dark and mysterious and we never talked about it at home. But I got a whiff of how good he was when he wanted me to do better at school. I could hear him even now, his voice, soft, beautifully cultured, persuasive, his face attentive; his adhesive blue eyes never left yours.

"Ivana?"

She looked up.

"Come upstairs with me," she said pleading, childish.

I followed her up the stairs with the frayed rotting tan carpet.

Her room was just big enough for a bed and a dresser. Clothes were heaped in teetering piles on the bed, and on the dresser were some photographs.

"Get dressed," I said and turned my back to her.

"OK," she said. "You can turn around."

She was naked. She was a very sexy girl, sexy in a dirty, corrosive way; this time her come-on stuck to me like napalm and I could barely turn away; wanting her was an animal reaction. I was tired, I hadn't eaten and I could barely think.

Cunningly, she watched me; she gave me the creeps and a hard-on at the same time. She ran her hands over her body; she looked in my eyes; she stuck a finger inside herself.

Finally I grabbed her wrist and said, "Stop it."

"Why? I hear this is how people gets ahead in America," Ivana said. "Russian girls, especially. You become whore, you make money, you arrived in promised land, right? Is right? So I do. You see? I learn fast. Already I had three, four customers."

I hesitated and she took it as assent, but I shoved her away hard and she half fell on the bed and cowered there. Then, briskly, as if she'd made some kind of decision, she picked up some clothes from a pile and went out of the room.

I followed her. Business-like, she got dressed. In jeans, a man's shirt, a sweater and jacket and winter boots, she waited passively and then followed me to the car. At a deli nearby, I got hot coffee and bagels and made her eat while I drove. The food and coffee calmed her down some.

"Where are we going?" She stared out of the window as I drove towards Coney Island and parked up near the spot where Billy's clothes had been found.

I think she knew all along where we were going, but when I slammed on the brakes, for a second she shrank back against the seat, and said, "Not here."

"Come on," I said.

"Give me cigarette," she said.

"You knew him, didn't you? You knew Billy Farone. Your aunt is friends with Genia, you said so, she sat with Genia yesterday, didn't she, she kept her company. She knew Genia had an affair with Zeitsev, so they were close, your aunt and her. Is it him? Is Zeitsev involved with all this?" I waved towards the waste ground where there was snow now, some yellow police tape sticking up out of it. "What about Genia? Or your aunt? Did you make up all the bullshit about radiation?"

In the front seat of my car, she drank her coffee and watched me.

"I can tell you about boy, this Billy, OK? My aunt that is friends with Evgenia Borisova, like you say, tells me everything. He's not good, this kid. Something wrong with him."

"What's wrong with him?"

"You know, for all my life I want to be American," she said. "I get here, nobody wants me. OK, so I go looking for something. Maybe something under boardwalk, some way to make myself important, so I find this clothes."

"Don't lie." In Russian, I could frighten her. I hated myself for what I knew sounded like abuse.

I reached across her and opened the door on her side.

"Get out."

Again I could see a kind of resolve take over her features and she got out of the car, still clutching a piece of raisin bagel, a smear of cream cheese on her unformed mouth. In the hard cold daylight, she looked like a kid. Out on the ocean, the sun glinted off the blue water.

"Show me," I said.

"Not here," she said. "Under."

Under the boardwalk steps in the dirt and frozen snow, we half walked, half crawled. Here, she said. Here is where the blood–soaked clothes were. I blinked. It was hard to see, strings of sunlight came through the cracks in the boards overhead and blinded me.

We backed out. She asked for cigarettes. I gave her one and lit it.

"So how did it work?" I said. "The business with the

326

clothes? The business with Billy?"

"I can't," she said.

"Yeah you can. Sure you can."

Suddenly, she said, "OK, I know Billy Farone. I baby-sit him one or two times."

"And?"

"Sick kid," she said. "Weird sick little boy. I try to make better. He has evil eye put upon him, so I try to fix for him."

"You knew where he went, what he liked, so you helped the kidnapper, is that it? You were going to get some money, is that right?" I asked her all this softly, and she pulled away from me and started up the steps towards the boardwalk. I followed her.

"I want to walk on beach." She climbed the steps and I followed.

"Tell me what happened."

"I prefer to be dead."

"There's nothing to be scared of."

But she was scared of ghosts, she said. She believed in God and gangsters and her star sign and in the lines in her palm. For all I knew she believed that hair grew on billiard balls.

"Come on," I said. "We'll take a walk on the beach, like you want, OK?"

Shivering she walked beside me on the beach, turning her face up to the wintry sun. She talked in Russian. She told me that every week when she ran, on her Saturday run down the beach, she looked under the boardwalk. She was convinced that she would find something, jewelry, money, a winning lottery ticket. She had been to a psychic, a Russian fortune-teller who told her it would be her lucky month. For luck, she was to look everywhere, and she believed it.

On Saturday mornings when she ran, she looked on the beach and under the boardwalk for her piece of luck. This was how she found the bloody clothes. She saw them and she thought: if I go to a cop there will be a reward. I'll be rich. I'll go on TV. People will like me in America.

What made her think there was money? That if she found something precious under the boardwalk, she'd get rich? Ivana said that an old man told her, a man who said he knew because he had been a cop.

"What old man?" I said. " Was his name Farone? Was the old man's daughter-in-law your friend Genia Farone? Was he named Shank? Ivana? Tell me his name." I held onto her arm.

She didn't remember. She didn't answer me. She broke away and started running. Tall and agile, she ran fast in spite of the wind. She ran into the wind, towards the water.

Stop, I yelled at her, but the wind seemed to push my words back at me and Ivana kept running, down the beach, her feet seeming to skim the sand, her arms pumping, and I followed her but she was too fast and my feet stuck in the snow and sand like in a bad dream.

A tall, graceful figure in jeans and a red jacket and pink sneakers, she ran as if she'd been released from everything in her life that she hated and was suddenly free. I could see the flash of her pink sneakers, All Stars, like Billy's, only pink. As she went, she shed the jacket,

I could see it, bright red, on the sand. She kicked off her pink sneakers and pulled off her jeans and now she sprinted towards the ocean and for a second I thought crazily: she's going for a swim.

"Stop!"

Stop, I yelled, it's too cold, you can't swim in this weather, I said.

By the time I got to the edge of the water where the surf came up and made foam on the hard packed sand, she was already in up to her waist. She plunged forward into the water and started swimming. Even in the ice cold water, she swam, gliding through the waves, with long strong strokes.

The surf was around my ankles; it poured into my boots; it was freezing. I felt my feet go numb. I kept swimming.

Ivana pulled away from me. She swam towards the horizon. She was swimming fast, and the crazy thought came into my head again: she likes swimming in the winter; she joined the Polar Bears; she was a swim champ in her Moscow school.

The water was up to my waist and I was yelling, half English, half Russian, and somewhere in the back of my mind I was thinking: I have to get to Florida. I have to get to old man Farone. Maybe Billy was down there, maybe that's where he was.

Still shouting for Ivana, the salt water filled my mouth and nose. I choked. My feet slipped. I started falling backwards, but I kept yelling. It didn't matter. By then, Ivana's head had stopped bobbing above the waves.

Part Five

34

I opened my eyes and realized I had no sensation in my feet. From somewhere I could hear a dog barking. It was next door. I was in my own bed. Sonny Lippert was looking down at me. For a few seconds while I struggled to get awake I thought I was still in a bad dream. I pushed against it as if I'd been caught in a plastic cocoon and couldn't get out. I couldn't breathe. I sat up suddenly.

"What happened?" I said.

"You're at home," he said. "You're OK. A couple of guys running on the beach pulled you out of the water, man, and you were out, you swallowed a gallon of water, they had to get you warm, you understand. You were two minutes away from hypothermia. They took you to the hospital."

I sat up. "What day is it?"

"It's Saturday."

"Shit." I'd lost three days. "Billy?"

"No news."

"Ivana?"

"Dead. Drowned."

"How did I get home from the hospital?"

"That Maxine Crabbe brought you home. She sat with you. You were frozen. You almost could have lost a hand. Also you had a fever and you were delirious."

Again I said, "What about Billy?"

"Nada," Sonny said. "No body, no kid, no nothing. I'm sorry, man. I am." Sonny sat on the edge of a chair next to the bed.

"You said you wanted me in a clean space, Sonny, you were thinking there were dirty cops involved? Someone like John Farone, Sr., Johnny's father? What about him? What about Stanley Shank?"

"I don't know. Farone, we had the house in Florida checked. He's there OK. He can't move. He's a sick old man, lousy lungs, attached to an oxygen tank he schleps everywhere. Billy's not with him. Farone and Shank, they were partners, you knew that, right? The old guy, the younger guy, they were tight, they liked to control their territory, even after they retired."

"Shank said he hated the Russians."

"It's an act," Sonny said. "It was perfect. They could do business because everyone thought they hated each other. And there were rumors, since the Howard Beach beatings. You remember? You remember the black kids that got beat up bad? Shank was always a suspect. Farone protected him. Shank's a creep."

"It's mutual. He hates your guts. He wants you out of Brooklyn. And me."

"You're one of them now, man? You're passing messages. You're so desperate about the kid that you're willing to be their messenger boy?" Lippert buttoned his coat.

"How come you always want to break my ass, Sonny?"

"I just came by to see you were alive and also to tell you that the girl drowned herself, OK? You tried to save her, you stupid bastard. You almost died." He looked at me. "I need you. I don't like it that you almost died, you got it?"

By now I knew the case wasn't only about Billy Farone; it was about the way business was done on the coast of Brooklyn. It was about fear. And money. If you made people afraid, you could own them.

Old man Farone, Stanley Shank, maybe others, they were retired cops who wanted the place for themselves. I didn't know yet if they were dealing meds, sex, kids, probably all of them. But they worked in tandem with some of the Russian creeps, overt, covert, it didn't matter so long as they made the dough. With some of it, Stanley Shank bought a party boat and named it *Just a Fluke*.

"Maybe it wasn't me they wanted out of the way. Is that what you're thinking?" Lippert could always read me. "Maybe it was you. Maybe they knew you were the kid's godfather, maybe they wanted to draw you in. Someone who knew you. Knew how you think. Buy you, own you, in return for Billy. Someone who knew you'd do anything for the kid."

I said, "You're saying someone set up Heshey Shank to snatch Billy Farone because they knew I'd get involved? Because they knew Genia's my cousin and I'd end up working the case one way or another, and I'd trip up and they'd be rid of me?"

"Hey, why not? They want you, they got you, they want me, they get me through you, either way, man, they win. I mean you're my boy, aren't you?" Lippert said.

"Get out."

"So, the girl, Ivana. You fucked her, man?"

I knew Lippert was upset I almost died and his way of dealing was dumping on me, but I felt lousy and I just said, "Get out of my place."

There were a million places Heshey Shank could have hidden Billy. His brother Stanley had a boat. He knew his way around the waterways out by the coast of Brooklyn. I knew, deep down, he had already unloaded the body. I knew that Billy was at the bottom of the marina, under the ice; until the ice broke up, no one would find him.

After Sonny finished breaking my balls, after he left, somehow I got up and took a shower and got dressed. I put on three pairs of socks. My legs trembled but I fixed some coffee, drank it, got downstairs, car keys in my hand. I had lost time. I had to get back to Brooklyn. I needed Zeitsev's help.

As I fumbled with the car door, Maxine appeared. Wrapped in a pink down coat, knitted hat pulled low, scarf twisted around her neck, her feet in old-fashioned red galoshes, she looked about twelve. In her arms was a bag stuffed with groceries.

"Where the hell are you going?" she said.

"I have to find Billy," I said. "Listen, thanks. Thank you for being with me." I kissed her and took the groceries. "I'll take them upstairs. How come you bothered with me? If I was you I would have let me suffer."

"It's mysterious to me, honey." She followed me into the building. "I have something for you" she said.

"About Billy?"

"Yes."

In my apartment, I put the groceries away and started for the door.

"I'll come with you," she said.

"I can't ask you to do that," I said.

"Why not? We're friends aren't we? You're in trouble aren't you? Who the hell else can you ask?" She grinned. "Come on, let's get the fuck on the road. I'll tell you while we drive."

I looked at Maxie with her long loose limbs like a rag doll's and her pretty, humorous face. She was warm as toast. She could keep quiet. She could keep things to herself if you were troubled.

With Lily it was different. I had been obsessed with her, but Lily always told you what was on her mind and sometimes it was like a slap with an open hand. But she was never coy, never unsure. When she almost died, later when she went away, I felt like someone cut off my oxygen. She loved the music I loved, she was a real grown-up, she called me on the stuff where I was stupid, I loved being in bed with her.

With Max it was different. She felt like a younger sister. She was crazy about me and had been for years.

She was completely transparent, and suddenly I thought: I could make a life with her. I loved her twins. I was getting sick of being alone and getting older and looking at myself in men like Sonny Lippert who spent nights at the gym. I was stupid. I still don't know why Lily left me, not really. She didn't say. She just said she was going. She couldn't stand New York anymore, she said.

"Artie? Honey? Come on."

I put my arm around Maxie's shoulder and for a second, while we stood in the street, she leaned on me, just listed in my direction. I liked her a lot. I kissed her. I knew it was a big deal, her helping me, after she'd said she was in love with me and I'd responded like a jerk. The generosity of her coming by made me love her. Maybe I was in love with her, after all. Maxie Crabbe would take care of me. She was still young, she was only thirty-eight; maybe we could even have a kid.

"You know what?" I said

"What?"

"Let's get married."

"You're serious?"

"Yeah. I am serious. I really am. Is that OK?"

"You thought about it?"

"I thought a lot."

She smiled and kissed me. "Get in the car."

We got in and I turned the engine on. My mind was racing, the clock in my head ticking, the heater coming on in the car, the news radio blasting out details of another alleged kidnapping, this one on the Upper West Side. I forced myself to pay attention to Maxine. It was how I'd lost Lily, obsessed with work, not paying attention. I wasn't going to do it again. I couldn't afford it.

"Maxie, listen . . ."

"They pulled you out of the ocean half dead, you're feeling desperate about Billy, so let's wait until the case is over, OK? I don't want you saying anything you have to go back on later, OK? Just think about it. If we're OK with each other when this case is done, and then if you still want to, so maybe I'll meet you at City Hall." She was breathless. "Give me a smoke."

I handed her the cigarettes and said, "I thought you'd want a church."

"I did the church thing with Mark. I had the white dress. I had six bridesmaids in peach charmeuse. I had all of it. Once was enough. Anyway you don't believe in God."

"I told you once, if you want a church, I'm good with that. I will wear a tux and a ruffled shirt and the girls can throw rose petals."

She smiled. "Gosh, for being in the middle of a case you're very eloquent. I mean, wow, Artie. That's really nice. I like that."

I glanced at my phone; there was a message from Tolya.

"You know my friend from Moscow, Tolya Sverdloff, right?"

She looked uncomfortable.

"What's the matter?"

"He's friends with Lily Hanes, isn't he?"

"So?"

She tried to smile. "I don't really live up to Lily, I

mean, she was a very smart woman, educated, gorgeous, high flying," she mumbled. "You know."

"Don't be ridiculous. You live up to anyone. More than." I leaned over and kissed her.

But she was right. I'd introduced her to Tolya once and he was cagey; he was polite, he shook hands, he smiled, he exuded charm, but he did it on automatic pilot, and she knew it.

"You want to hear what I have? I'm very good on blood."

"I know you are." Forcing myself to concentrate on her, I said, "Are you alright?"

"I'm good." Waiting for me to drive off, she pulled some notes out of her purse. "Look, I came over because I found something out. I had to sneak it, but I got there." Softly, Maxie added, "It's not his blood."

"What?"

"On the clothes. It's not Billy Farone's blood."

"How could they make that kind of mistake?"

"The blood on the clothes. Some of it was Billy Farone's, according to the blood type his mother gave, but most of it wasn't. Once they knew he was missing, and his mother ID'd the clothes, they assumed it was his. No one paid attention. Everyone was too busy. It was like 9/11, you know? People doing the minimum."

"Anything on the blood?"

"Some of it was an animal's," she said. "The blood."

"What?"

"That's why I had to come," she said. "Slow down. You'll kill us."

"I'm sorry." I was thinking about Billy.

"I don't understand, but maybe you will. I just want it all to end. I hate it. I have two girls I'm afraid to let go out of the house. I walk them to school. Another woman brings them home. I can't leave them for a minute."

"Listen, Maxie, look. I want you to go home and get the girls and go back up to Mark's mother, or stay home with them. I don't think this is random, this thing with Billy. Even if he's dead, and I think he is probably dead, I think I'm involved, and I don't understand how, not yet." I forced myself to say it. Billy was dead. Billy dead. "I'll drop you."

"How are you involved?" she said.

"I'm not sure, but go home and be with your girls. Please. I'll drop you at the subway."

"You can always call on the cell," she said. "I'm always there for you."

"I love you for it, I really do," I said. "What kind of animal?"

"Probably a cat."

Saturday evening, candles reflected in the windows, music floated out over the high-ceilinged room in the apartment on Riverside Drive. It was a piece for flute and piano. On little gold folding chairs, attentive listeners, parents, friends, teachers, were focused on the students who played on a small stage at the end of the room in front of the bow windows that looked over the Hudson.

The room, the shelves full of books, the polished floor and worn but silky Persian rugs, the music, it was a world apart, as far from Brooklyn as you could get, and the cold and death. It could have been the Moscow I grew up in, the cultured audience, everything in a surreal suspension of other-worldliness, the gorgeous music as its soundtrack.

It was Genia's daughter, Ellie, who played the flute. She was tall and slim and wore a clinging red dress. Her neck was long, her arms were slightly muscular and bare and she held the flute to her mouth as if it were part of her body. The audience was rapt. At the piano, a boy in a white shirt and a black bow-tie was bent low, watching his own fingers fly across the keys.

I stood near a window and glanced at the Hudson white with ice. If it cracked, if the waterways around the city thawed, the bodies would bob up from under the ice. Billy Farone's body, bloated, the flesh raw, the face distorted, destroyed, would surface somewhere in Brooklyn, somewhere in the marshlands or off the beach. Elem Zeitsev was at the back of the room. I'd called on his cell phone after I dropped Maxine. I'd been on my way to Brooklyn when it occurred to me to call Zeitsev. He told me about the recital. He'd meet me, he said.

Genia wasn't at the recital. She was at home waiting for Billy. But Zeitsev was here, leaning against the wall at the back, wearing an old corduroy jacket. From the time I'd opened my eyes that morning in my own bed, Lippert staring at me, I had worked every lead I could. I was at the recital because when I called Zeitsev, he told me he was coming, and I figured maybe he could help after all. He still had connections. The local cops out by the coast worried me more than he did, more even than the thugs who had worked for Zeitsev's father.

At the back of the room Zeitsev leaned against the wall and watched. I saw there was a patch on the elbow of his jacket. He could have been the parent of any kid in the room. Zeitsev always knew his part; he always, in a subtle way, dressed for it. In one hand he held a bouquet of pink roses wrapped in white tissue with a white silk bow. I edged towards him.

On a large table near Zeitsev were plates with

Pepperidge Farm cookies—Mint Milanos, someone whispered to me—and gallon jugs of white wine and large plastic bottles of Sprite and Diet Coke. Plastic glasses were stacked nearby.

I leaned over and whispered to Zeitsev, "I need to talk."

No, he said. We would wait for Ellie's performance to end and give her flowers. Her mother couldn't come, so we would wait. He looked gray, his skin, hair; his face was folded with weariness and slack with fatigue.

"Do you like this Poulenc?" he said nodding towards the musicians, then added, "I'm not really crazy about the flute."

I shrugged and under my breath, I said, "I need you to tell me what you know about Billy Farone."

"Yes," he said. "I've done everything I could think of. All week. You must know that. I've been everywhere. I've used everyone."

"Now," I said. "Tell me."

"Wait," he said.

I said, "I can't wait."

Around us people in baggy cords and floral skirts and sweaters and glasses heard us and looked annoyed.

"Alright," Zeitsev said, "let's go."

In the kitchen a woman in a brown dress was preparing gray dip and, when Zeitsev approached, she set down the can of Campbell's cream of mushroom and took the flowers and the note for Ellie.

"At least she'll know I was here," Zeitsev said. "I'll come back afterwards and take her out to dinner."

We went downstairs and stood in the art deco lobby.

I said, "Tell me. Now."

Already he was walking through the lobby, through the front door and down the block until we reached a bar.

"Come on," he said. "I need a drink."

We sat together and ordered Scotch. The place was half empty. A row of men sat at the bar and watched basketball on the overhead TV.

"You're not close, you and Genia," Zeitsev said. "This is about Billy as far as you're concerned, isn't it?"

"How do you know?"

"I know because Billy told me. He woke up one night sweating and calling for you and I said what did you dream and he said, I dreamed Artie was dead and I was crying." Zeitsev hesitated.

"You were sleeping at Genia's?"

"Johnny was out of town," Zeitsev said, then added, "You've heard that Billy's my child."

"Yes."

"I don't know if it's true," he said. "I think it's true," he added. "I hope it's true."

"Why?"

"I feel it," he said. "Look, there are too many people involved." He drank down his drink and ordered another one and, waiting, stared at his hands. "Farone's idiot mother who throws out her husband because he used to put his hands up the little girls' skirts, including Elena."

"Genia told me."

"Farone believes Genia had an affair with me," he said.

345

I picked up my own drink and said, "Johnny's not going to kill his kid over it," I said.

"That crazy girl Ivana Galitzine listened to her aunt retail stuff that Genia told her, and that they both told some psychic they visited. I hear she's dead. She walked into the ocean, I hear," Zeitsev said.

"Yes."

"I hear you tried to save her."

"You get around," I said. "Tell me about Billy."

"He's not completely like other children." Zeitsev took his fresh drink from the bartender and drank half of it. "He's a strange kid, very smart, obsessive, but wonderful in his own way, and with help he could be fine. I keep telling Genia, but she says Johnny won't take him to a doctor, and she's scared to let me help and meanwhile Billy's become a pawn. He's trapped in their fearfulness. Her Russian madness, his macho sense that no boy of his should need a shrink. I tried to talk to Billy but he won't talk to me. He talks to you, though. Genia told me."

I said, "We go fishing. We talk about fishing. Does it have a name, what's wrong with Billy?"

"Maybe you don't see it because you have some bond with him, and you're patient and there's the fishing," Zeitzev said. "I think he's autistic. Or some form of autism, they have this thing, Asperger's syndrome, there's a lot of it, boys mostly and the kids can seem almost normal, but they're not. They have all kinds of problems. They're very very smart, at least some are, but they see everything in pictures instead of in a linear, verbal way. There's often too much noise in their heads,

346

too many colors. They turn away from emotion. Many of them are obsessive." He paused and looked at me.

"Most of all they don't really get other people. Billy can't take it in, how other people feel, do you see? He can't connect. It's like this whole fucking country, you know, we're so obsessed with ourselves, we're like little children, we can't judge what anyone else wants or thinks, it's like that, and now everyone's terrified and my kid's in danger," he said. "Or dead."

"Please, no metaphors."

"I'm sorry."

"Go on."

"I watched him the few times when I was over at Genia's. He could never judge other people's feelings or sense that he could upset them. Once, Genia found him submerged in the bathtub with his eyes open. Johnny was at the restaurant, she called, hysterical, and I drove over. Billy almost drowned. I realized he was trying to get a fish-eye view," he said. "I begged her to take him to a doctor, there are good doctors, there are special schools, but Johnny didn't want it and she was scared of him and his mother and someone finding out she had come here illegally. I said, look that's all over. You're married to an American. You're American. You have an American child. She didn't care."

I said, "So Billy might take a ride with some creep who offered him a fishing trip. He might go willingly. You wouldn't have to grab him."

"Yes."

"And he wouldn't be able to judge that the creep, that this Heshey Shank, would hurt him."

"That's what I've been thinking," Zeitsev said. "I've been desperate because I knew this and I've been everywhere I could think of and called in a hundred favors, and nothing." Zeitsev's voice shook.

"You have any idea where he is?"

He shook his head.

"You're not in business out in Brooklyn anymore?" I asked. "I don't care right now. You understand that, right? I just need to know."

"When my father died, before he died, when he was shot by some other thug in the street, he called me. He summoned me, you know, as if he was a czar, and I had to sit by the bed, we all sat, it was like an audience. You remember how it was in his house? You came to eat once, didn't you?"

I nodded.

"He had this idea of himself as a ruler, a man of power and taste, and every other bullshit Russian idea." Zeitsev ordered another Scotch.

"Yes."

"I hated it. I hated it all my life. I swore when he died, I'd separate myself from all of it. It took a while, I closed everything down, all of it, the gas scams, the Medicare deals, the drugs. OK, I still have a few minority interests mostly because if I gave them up it would get noticed and I'd probably go to jail, but mostly it's over." The drink came over, and he drank it fast. "You know who helped me? You want to know? Your friend Anatoly Sverdloff. Tolya understood. He helped me sell, he didn't ask for money, he just understood and helped me. He's a good guy. I'm indebted to him." Zeitsev emptied his glass and, aimlessly, put it to his eye and looked through it.

"You're kidding."

"I know Sverdloff doesn't like me, but that's the thing about him. He'll help you anyhow, in his way.

"So now my father is buried, thank Christ, and it's over. I'm telling you so you'll trust me about Billy. OK? It's all over, it's been over for almost ten years. They hate me there for it, people think I told the feds everything I knew. A few think I'm still some kind of power broker. Ironic, right? Either way, I'm probably dead." He laughed bitterly. "The truth is they hate me and it's mutual. But I wish to God I could get some help this time. No more. The guys I could once count on, I begged for help, I offered anything, and they said, fuck you."

"You really don't have any idea where Billy is, do you?"

Suddenly, as Zeitsev ordered his fourth Scotch, he started to cry.

"No," he said. "I don't. I don't know anything."

36

Tolya was my next stop. It dawned on me as I drove away from Riverside Drive that I had to tell him I'd been an asshole. The last time I'd seen him he had turned the corner out in Brighton Beach and vanished, and when I returned the yellow Hummer, I didn't thank him.

On my way to Brooklyn, I went to his building in Soho. He was out. The hotel on Thompson Street said they hadn't seen him that day. I got to Brighton Beach, to the building where his mother lived, just in time to see the ambulance cart him away.

At Coney Island Hospital, his mother sat in the hallway, half cracked now, unable to speak English, talking Russian in fractured sentences. I held her hand, which was waxy and covered in brown spots. Lara Sverdlova had been in the apartment when Tolya stumbled in, a hole in his side, blood pouring out. Somehow she called the doorman, who called an ambulance, and the Hassidic medics, who were passing, got Tolya out of the apartment and to the hospital.

Now he lay on the hospital bed like a beached whale,

tubes stuck in his nose and arms, an oxygen mask over his mouth. He seemed dead. He didn't move while I looked at him or when I leaned over and talked into his ear. I wanted to cry.

All around us the ER was jammed with patients; the noise, people screaming, doctors running, nurses yelling out orders, rattled me. Worst of all was that Tolya didn't hear anything. He didn't move. To me, Tolya seemed to have disappeared, leaving behind only his immense body like a prehistoric carapace. Someone had removed his shoes and his feet hung over the edge of the bed. On the greasy linoleum floor, his black suede Guccis were stranded like abandoned boats.

An intern, coat smeared with blood, saw me and pulled me to one side.

"You're family?"

I showed him my badge.

"Then you might want this," he said and held out a flat object that had been hastily wrapped in brown paper.

It was a fishing knife with a long sharp blade. It was covered in blood.

"He had it inside his jacket when we brought him in," the doctor said. "You're the first cop that's showed up."

I gave him a card.

"You call me, you understand?" I said. "Any change. OK? Any change in his condition, you let me know right away."

"Yeah, OK, you're pretty upset for a cop."

"He's my brother," I said. It was how I felt.

★

351

It was Sunday and it rained like crazy that night; buckets of rain poured down and hit the still frozen streets, the snow left from the blizzard the week before. The temperature dropped, ice covered the streets and cars spun and hit each other like bumper cars, the whole city like a deadly arcade game.

On 125th Street there was a nineteen-car pile-up. It rained so much the roads flooded. On the FDR, people abandoned their cars and waded, knee deep in some places, to the off-ramps and the exits.

Around midnight, still sitting in the emergency room, watching the traffic reports on a soundless TV, I got a call from Samson Britz. Glee in his voice because I would owe him, he told me that Stan Shank's wife had called him. A big Russian came to the house, she said, and accused Stan of involvement with the Billy Farone case. Shank told the Russian to go fuck himself and then he went for him.

"There were weapons involved?" I asked

"Stan's fishing knife," Britz said. "You're in the red now, man, you know? You owe me now. So call me."

Without me knowing, Tolya had been working the case. Because he knew how I felt about Billy. Because it reminded him of his own child and how she had been kidnapped. All the time I'd been suspicious of him, he was crashing through minefields, unworried about himself. Now he lay, silent, motionless, beached on the hospital bed that was too narrow and too short for him.

I got on the phone and arranged a transfer to a decent hospital for as soon as he could be moved. Then I called

Mike Rizzi. I needed wheels no one would recognize. I woke him up and asked if I could trade cars with him for a day. Yeah, he said, happy to ride the Caddy, could it wait until morning when he'd be back at the coffee shop? No, I said.

An hour later, in the pouring rain, he met me near the entrance to Greenwood Cemetery; I didn't want to go to his house, which was close by, so we met and he tossed me the keys to his battered old van. I gave him mine.

"You OK, man?" he said before he drove away. "You sure you don't want to come home for some soup or something?"

I said, "No," and asked about the kids and said to keep them safe. He drove away and I climbed into his van and pushed aside battered pie boxes. Driving the van, I felt invisible.

I drove back towards the coast. Worked through everything I knew while I drove. Drove slowly up and down every back alley I could think of peering at nothing, helpless. Where was Billy?

The streets were empty. People were home; their kids were home. The city seemed deserted. Overhead I heard planes, passenger planes, fighter jets, I didn't know. I tried to keep Maxie in my head while I drove; it kept me sane. I loved her, didn't I? It was right to marry her and settle down, the right thing, the good deal; it's what a grown-up would do. I was tired.

Billy Farone would have been easy prey for a sicko like Heshey Shank. I'd seen it in the video. Billy went willingly. Smiling, buying him pizza, Shank had befriended Billy. And someone told Ivana where to look for the clothes that were drenched in blood, some of it from a cat's blood. Someone told the FBI I had letters from an Arab friend. It wasn't because of the crackpot homeland defense act; it was because someone wanted me out of the way.

Heshey Shank was not a smart guy. Vicious maybe. Retarded. He could have butchered Billy. He could have killed a cat and put the blood on the clothes. Used the cat's blood as a blind. Kill a cat, or half a dozen, it wouldn't matter to someone like Shank; it wasn't rational. Not unless someone really had whispered in Ivana's ear: find your luck under the boardwalk, make yourself rich, or famous. Tell the cops.

Did Heshey's brother Stan play a role? What about old man Farone? I'd tried to get to him in Florida but a woman at the house where he was staying slammed the phone down over and over and I didn't have the resources or the time to get a plane and I didn't believe he would hurt his own grandkid.

Again I wondered: did someone want me in a trap? Was I the bait for Lippert? The big catch?

How far could Shank have gone without someone, a gas station guy, a toll taker, a crazy reporter, seeing them, seeing the big goofball, the kid, their pictures on every TV station?

On a hunch I went back to the pizza place; it was shut for the night, but there was a light on in the back and I banged on the metal gates. Fred Capestro peered through the window then let me in. He looked wary. It took about two minutes to break him down.

"Last night. I had a feeling he was here," Capestro said.

"Who?"

"Billy."

"How did you get the feeling?" I asked.

"I don't know. I was in the back, there was no one around, so I was just changing my clothes and maybe the door wasn't locked, and I heard someone. I heard someone in the place, I thought I heard a voice, so I came out of the toilet and he was gone." Capestro was out of breath.

"Was Billy alone? What about the mongoose?"

"I didn't see nothing. It just somehow smelled like Billy."

"How does that smell?" I asked.

"Fish," he said.

"But you could have been imagining. Right? Fred, you could have imagined it."

"There was a pie on the counter and when I came out it was gone, so someone came in. I made that pie to deliver to a guy who likes his pie with Swiss instead of mozzarella and Billy's the only other person I ever met who gets Swiss on a pizza."

"You called the cops?"

"I tried, but they were jammed up, and what could I say? A ghost came and stole a pizza?" He shrugged. "I'm sorry. I'm real sorry, man, I am, but it was dark, and I couldn't tell. And it's not such a good idea to run to the cops out here, they get pissed off, they got plenty of trouble, and you run to them with bullshit, they don't come when you got real problems."

I left Capestro. I figured he dreamed it; he liked Billy and wanted him alive so he believed the kid stole a pizza with Swiss cheese, or did he? Had Billy been back in the neighborhood?

So I went to Genia's. Through the windows, behind the silk drapes, I could see the lights, though it was already two in the morning. I rang the bell. She opened the door and behind her I saw Johnny and his mother. I gestured to her to come outside.

"It's cold," she said.

"What's going on in there?" I said.

"I don't know what the two of them want from me, Johnny, his mother. It's not my fault."

I half dragged her out of the door.

"I'm cold, Artemy. Please."

I took off my jacket and put it around her shoulders and we stood in the portico of her house, her clutching her keys. I reached around her and closed the door.

I said, "I don't care if you die of cold. You knew your boy was sick. Didn't you? You knew and you didn't tell me?"

Genia's eyes were wild. Frantic, she switched between Russian and English, speaking as if she'd lost her ability to speak either language right.

"Special," she said in the hectic whisper. "Billy is special."

"But not sick?"

"Is special," she said. "Special boy, that is all. Different. I talk to people, this is different, not crazy, normal is bullshit. What it means, normal?"

"Zeitsev says he talked to you about a doctor for Billy."

"I was scared. Even after I said OK, I mean OK for doctor, there's Johnny and the mother. They say, Billy is fine." Her eyes on the ground, she barely looked at me.

I took hold of Genia's arm and said, "He was here. Wasn't he? Yesterday? Last night? Was he here? Listen to me, I'm going to find Billy whatever it takes. You hear me? I'll arrest anyone I have to. I'll feed it to the TV people that his own mother wanted him lost. Whatever."

"He was here," she said. 'I think. I was out for ten minutes. Johnny was at his mother's." She spat the words. "I went to get cigarettes. I go in my car. I go fast. I never left before in three days, Artemy. I came back, something is different, something in the how do you say, molecules.

"I hear from my friend her niece Ivana killed herself, she is dead, because she knew Billy, my friend says. Because she lives in wrong place. Because she wants to become American and be rich and safe. I don't know anything that's going on, I have to get out just for cigarettes, I come back, and the door is not locked. I always lock this door. I couldn't remember, maybe I did not lock it, but I'm not sure. Also, there is a smell."

"What kind of smell?'

"Fish," she said. "Fish. Like somebody who works in fish market, or goes fishing, something you can't get rid of even if you wash with lemons. Always I made Billy wash with lemons so he doesn't stink, he likes touching fish, gutting, cleaning, with knife, smell never goes away." She was weeping now.

"His room?"

She nodded.

"Something was missing?"

"Yes."

"What?"

"Fishing nets."

"You think the creep that kidnapped him brought him back for nets?"

"I don't know."

"There's something else."

"Fishing knife was gone from Billy's room same time he disappears. Always I told Johnny you don't give a little boy a big knife, but he says, he's little man now, and he wants this and this is OK."

I said, "Did anyone around here lose a cat recently?"

"Billy's friend, Stevie. His cat goes away. Nobody knows where. Artemy?"

"What?"

Suddenly, she pushed me towards the wall of the house, still inside the portico but away from the door. We were sheltered from the wind that was blowing dense fog from the ocean so thick you could see it move.

Softly, she said in Russian, "You remember when I first called you, years and years back, when I was living with my father on Brighton 6th Street, remember, when Elena was little?"

"Sure."

"You didn't think about it, this woman, this Russian who gives you a call from out of nowhere, you never heard of me, did you? You were just polite. I said I was some relative of your father, a cousin, something like this?"

I didn't want to hear, so I said, "I have to go."

She grabbed my wrists and held on.

"You never wonder why I call?" Genia said. "You didn't say to yourself, how can this Russian find me of all the Cohens in the phone book, how does she know my name is Cohen and not Ostalsky, how come she picks me? You are never surprised? You never thought, how does this Evgenia Borisova find me? Your father was already dead, your mother was already sick, you didn't ask yourself how did this Russian woman make contact?"

"I was working on a case in Brighton Beach," I said. "I dropped by after you called, it seemed useful to have someone there."

"That's cruel, Artemy. Also untrue. You felt something. Even before Billy was born, and after, afterwards, you kept coming back for Billy, isn't that right?" She wouldn't let go.

I nodded and bent over a cigarette, trying to get it lit. The wind blew out the match.

"You felt something about us, you and me, so I am going to tell you what it is," she said. "You never noticed how come you and me we always take the cigarettes out of the pack the same way, we hold it same way, we always sit on the couch together the same way?"

Genia lit a cigarette. Again I noticed the way she took the smoke out of the pack. The fog seemed to drape itself over my face and it was wet and cold.

"This old man where I lived before on Brighton 6th, the general, the man you know as my father?"

"Yes?"

"He was not my father," she said. "He was not anything to me, just old man who takes me in, lets me work as maid. I came illegal to this country, you knew that, right? But he takes me in and he lets me send for Ellie, whose father I married and get divorced from even before she is born in Moscow. The old general, I live with him as kind of maid but he adopts Ellie, gets me a green card, is not bad man. But not my father. My father was someone else. I decide never to tell you, or tell anyone, but now I am telling you, Artemy." She took off my jacket and gave it back to me because I was shivering. I put it on.

"Who was your father?"

She raised her head and looked at me.

"We have the same father," Genia said. "Your father was also mine."

"Listen to me, Artemy, your father, our father, he has an illegitimate child a few years before you are born, which is me. He has girlfriend, I don't know, one night stand or big love affair, I don't know. But he is married so this is lousy for his career.

"My mother is young lady who cannot take care of me, they say, so I go to orphanage. Later I hear that the woman, my mother which I never meet, is sent away. I think he makes this happen. He has a family, he is a top young guy in KGB. Where does she go away to, my mother, where does she disappear to, my mom?"

"How did you find out about him?"

"People talk," she said. "Later, when I am almost grown, people at orphanage, people who knew my mom, they talk. You think because it was Soviet Union, people don't gossip?" She laughed. "So I find him, I ask him once. I go to see him. I find him on the street in Moscow nearby his office and I ask, and he says I don't know anything. I'm sorry, he says, it wasn't anything to do with me. He is very nice, very handsome." Genia paused. "He gives me some chocolate sweets. But I learn nothing."

"You're not saying he had her killed, your mother?"

Genia said, "Oh, Artemy, you remember these days, it was like bad spy novel. It wasn't always so simple, so crude. Things happened. People got sent to different cities. Children went to orphanage or were adopted. Me, I had both. For a while I had nice family to live with, but poor and like peasants, no culture, no books. Then back to orphanage. It was OK, I don't go to some gulag, probably not even my mother went. People like my mom just evaporated into a different life."

"Do you know where Billy is?"

"I heard Johnny's mother mention Breezy Point," Genia said. "She doesn't know I heard. I was going to call you as soon as I got rid of her. I think you should go there, Artemy. Just go, OK?" Abruptly, Genia kissed me on the cheek three times, Russian style, and retreated towards her big house, then turned to watch me.

It was after three in the morning when I drove away and in the rear-view mirror I could just see Genia through the foggy night. Lit up from the light on her porch, she stood and rocked, arms locked around her body, like an old Russian woman trying to sell her shoes on the street and knowing no one would buy them.

I held onto the idea that Billy was alive. The fog closed in. Barely able to see my own headlights, I drove towards Breezy Point. I knew I should have smashed down the door on the fishing shack, but I should have done a lot of things.

Looking in the rear view, seeing my own face, I knew what Genia had told me was true. From my pocket, I got out a picture of Billy and put it on the dashboard; in it I saw my father's ghost. It was the kind of resemblance you might not see if you didn't look for it, if you didn't know the truth, but once you knew, it was obvious: my father was Billy's grandfather. The same piercing perfect blue eyes; the sweet smile; the blond hair. I looked in the mirror again. I had my mother's dark hair and my eyes were a different blue, but I could see the resemblance between the three of us. Had I known? Had I known this all along?

I thought about my father, about the day he came home and told us he was no longer needed, and I heard my parents fighting. He said he was sad, losing his job. My mother called the KGB monsters and slammed the door. Eventually we all left Moscow and went to Israel and she hated it. She thought it was provincial, but my father liked it.

Mossad guys came to the apartment in Tel Aviv and sat with him and he advised them. He had been a top intelligence strategist, and they liked him and played chess with him. He wasn't even Jewish but he was OK with Israel. He died because he got on the wrong bus one day and it was bombed. My mother was left behind in a country she hated.

I drove back to Marine Park and over the bridge where, for the second time, a state trooper stopped me and joked about Red Alert, then warned me about the fog. A ship had run aground off Jersey. Most of the roads on Long Island were shut because of the fog. Take it easy, he said, and I said I would, but as soon as I was over the bridge, I picked up speed.

Billy was out there. Heshey Shank knew about the fishing shack and he had taken Billy to it, I was sure now; I tried to believe Billy was still alive. I smoked and talked to myself and drove as fast as I could on the roads that were solid ice. I hit the accelerator hard and Mike's van rattled and pie boxes flew off the seat. I didn't care. I inhaled nicotine as deep as I could and watched Jamaica Bay, where fog lapped the wetlands, and it came to me, this thing in my own past. I felt both terrified and relieved. I felt like an Alzheimer's patient on the verge of release from the jail cell, the lock-up of my own memory.

37

It was like paradise, the first time he went fishing. It wasn't a word he was supposed to know: paradise. It wasn't a word people used in public, not forbidden, but not nice. He didn't know what it meant but he read about it in books and he read that people said the word in churches, though he had only been in a church once when it was raining and he got caught and sheltered in an old run-down church where a few elderly women kneeled and moaned and prayed.

For him paradise was a place where there was a river. Paradise, he imagined, felt like this, blissful, cool, a breeze off the water. Normally he was a city kid. The countryside was usually boring, a place where people talked about mushrooms and the Russian soul. He was a city kid. He liked Moscow's winding streets and the ramshackle old houses and shops where you could get certain records and books that no one else had. He liked the food markets. He was drawn to places in the huge gray city where there was color, especially in the winter.

This part of the countryside, this place by the river, was different—the fishing, the sitting in the sun, the being with his father. It was only a little river, a crook in a river, the place where it turned in a different direction.

The water was cold and clear and the two of them sat on the edge and dangled their lines and ate ice cream. He was ten. He could remember every detail, the silver birch trees, tall and thin, the leaves like coins rustling when the breeze blew, the hot sun, the damp of the bank under his thighs, mossy damp, cool and solid. His bare feet were in the water; his toes dug in the cold squishy mud.

For years and years afterwards, he could remember the days by the river, the exact way the river looked, the stones in it, the feel of the mud, taste of the sour vanilla ice cream, the tall man beside him. The ice cream came in a paper cone. Birds chirped in the trees or the hedges, though he didn't think of it as chirping. Humming. They hummed and twittered.

He had a canvas satchel on the ground next to him. It was the bag he used for school, but it contained thick slabs of good white bread and real sausage made with meat and yellow cheese and hard-boiled eggs. It also held fishing line and a can of grubs he'd dug up in a friend's backyard. There were books in it, too: Oliver Twist by Charles Dickens because his father approved of Charles Dickens; an American western novel by Zane Gray that he'd read so many times the pages were falling out. His father pretended not to notice when he read silly books. He glanced over at his father who was leaning against a tree, his pants rolled up over his calves, his shoes and socks on the ground next to him, his bare feet just touching the water. The fishing line looped lazily from the pole he held lightly in one hand. The smoke from his cigarette curled up into the tree above him. Once in a while, he turned his head slightly and opened his eyes and smiled at his son next to him on the river bank.

He could remember all of it, even the texture and color of the *fish that he caught, a short fat silvery fish that flopped on the grassy bank where they sat, but, as the years passed, he couldn't quite picture the man beside him, his still young handsome father. It was his father, he was sure of it, but he could never get the picture back.*

The storm came up out of nowhere. The humidity rose. The heat simmered up like a bathhouse filling with steam. The sky turned dark as if a fuse had suddenly blown and all the lights went out. Then the lightning cut across the sky and the trees rattled their leaves and rain smashed down on them. The man grabbed him by the hand, and he tried to grab the fish and his satchel and both of them dropped out of his hand.

Then he looked and saw it wasn't the narrow familiar river, but huge, too wide to cross without a boat. Rostov, his father called it. A big city called Rostov on the Don River. An important port, his father said, a crossroads, a canal to the Volga, a place of important shipping and rail transport, of science and culture. When he was a boy, he had worked on the big rivers, he had been on a life journey, he had been part of a great revolution, he said, still a romantic, sentimental man.

In the port—his father was allowed in ports because of his job—they walked by the big freighters. The wind blew off the river, the cargo nets swayed in the sky above them. They were heavy nets made of thick rope. Bulging with giant crates like shopping in immense string bags, one of the nets was lowered into the hold of a ship. And when it was lifted out, it was empty. The empty net swung faster, and he remembered trying to run backwards, his father holding his hand. He felt the net was coming to pick him up, trap him, entangle him so he could never escape. Maybe someone would force his head in between the thick ropes. He had heard how it happened.

Somewhere, he heard about a boy or man whose head was forced into the openings of a net. The squares that made up the nets were big and the rope was strong, big and strong enough for a man to get his head stuck in. He had heard that somewhere, and he didn't know by whom or where, these nets were used as restraints. As punishment for people who committed crimes. He heard that if you got your head stuck or if someone forced it into the square of rope, you strangled to death. It took a long time. It took days for a boy or man to strangle to death.

In spite of the cold, I was sweating. Thinking about Billy, about the fishing trip the summer before on Shank's boat, had triggered it. The trip when the fish spilled out of our bucket on the dock in a storm and Billy caught them in his net. I had mixed them up, the trip with Billy, the fishing with my father and the stories about the punishment nets.

I had always remembered the fishing trips to the little river bend. To Nikolina Gora outside Moscow, where my father had a friend with a dacha, a famous, official writer. But I had never until now remembered the trip to Rostov. We went in a plane. It was a big deal. Before we went, everyone talked about the river at Rostov, the wonderful quality of the water, the fish that swam in it. It was a big deal because people didn't travel much and I had never been on a plane, but I had pushed it out of my mind. I had forgotten Rostov. Now I remembered the port and the cargo ships and the heavy nets and the kid in Moscow who told me about the KGB's use of nets for punishment.

When I asked my mother, she told me to keep quiet

about it, but I didn't. I asked my Uncle Gennadi, who was my father's best friend and who was in the KGB with him, and I asked my father. Did you? I asked. Did you do that?

By their silences and grim looks I knew not to ask again, but I also knew it was one of them, or both, who had been involved in the use of nets. Or they knew. At least they knew.

38

When I realized I'd fallen asleep at the wheel, I began to panic. I was desperate, I'd been up all night, it was almost morning, I didn't know how long I could go on.

The road was slick and bumpy, the van seemed out of control as raw brush along the shoulder scratched at my door. The Golden Nets Beach Club was at the end of a long narrow road off the highway, past Breezy Point where the shacks were.

It was remembering the nets, Billy's net, the fishing with my father that made me recall a place I'd been with Maxine years earlier, when the twins were still little. It wasn't much to go on, but I was crazy enough to try.

At the entrance to the beach club was a concrete hut; in the summer you paid a fee or showed your season pass or asked about the availability of cabanas. It was streaked with salt, dirt and snow, and it was empty, shut up for the winter.

I drove through and parked at the back of the main building, a white wood structure that looked as if it dated from the 1930s. Signs, dripping with snow and fog, announced summer hours and pool openings, mahjong tournaments and a yoga class.

I put my gun in my waistband, took a flashlight from the glove compartment, got out, locked the van and walked around to the front of the club on foot and went up the stairs to the main deck.

The light from my flash illuminated part of the huge deck where there were three swimming pools, all empty. Near the entrance was a café with large glass windows and when I peered through one of them I could see a few tattered nets that had been painted gold and hung on the walls for decoration.

On the far side of the deck was a railing and then the beach and the ocean, but I couldn't see the water and I could barely see the sand. Surrounding the deck were the cabanas, a long row of little wooden huts with the doors locked. In the summer, the doors open, there would be deck chairs in front of the cabanas. People in bathing suits would run in and out, laughing, eating, talking. There was also an upper level, with more cabanas and smaller lockers, that you reached by a long wooden staircase.

Vaguely, as if in a long-forgotten dream, I remembered the scene: the little kids running and screaming in and out of the baby pools; older kids showing off on the diving board; the brightly colored deck chairs, green and white, and the oiled bodies of women in bikinis; the older men, their bellies hanging over their shorts, playing checkers or cards at rickety card tables. A jumble of color, yellow sun, blue pools, the azure ocean, it was like a child's drawing of paradise.

Except for my flash, it was pitch dark. As I made my way along the ground level, I heard something, the constant banging of a door to one of the cabanas; somewhere in the fog, a door was hanging loose on its hinges, banging constantly; I couldn't see it until it was in front of me. I yanked it open and turned the flashlight on the interior.

Inside was a big old fashioned humpback refrigerator, the enamel chipped; a microwave sat on a card table next to a small TV. There were three canvas chairs. Behind a plastic curtain with seashells on it was a shower. There was also a large wooden locker painted green. It was locked.

With a pocket knife I pried the lock open and pulled back the lid. Inside were pots and pans, an electric kettle and faded beach towels. Nothing else. I went back out. I closed the door and twisted the wire that held it shut. From somewhere there seemed to be a faint sound, but it was only the water, I told myself, only the wind. I climbed the stairs to the second level.

Near where I stood was a long row of lockers for people who didn't have cabanas and used them to change and stash their clothes while they swam. The other side of the narrow platform where I stood, away from the lockers, was a high wire fence with barbed wire on top. Through it, when I turned the flashlight to my right, I could see the parking lot. The way the light fell, the long alley of lockers ahead of me on one side and the high wire wall on the other, it looked like a jail, a row of cells, a lock-up.

To keep myself calm, I lit a cigarette and tossed the

match away and thought, for a second because I was half out of my mind with fatigue, that I hadn't put it out. The old wooden club would go up in flames in a second. I waited. Nothing happened, but again I heard the faint noise. This time I knew it wasn't the wind or water; a tiny creaking noise, not far away from where I stood, reached me. I held my breath. From where I was I could barely see a foot ahead.

Slowly I felt my way down the row of lockers, the rough wood icy and wet under my hand. I reached the last door in the row and it was ajar and I wanted to turn and run as ghosts seemed to rise up out of the fog, but I pulled it open. I turned the flashlight on the interior.

From the ceiling hung a fixture for a single bulb. The bulb had been removed. By a piece of heavy rope hung a cat. The noise I'd heard came from the faint creak of the wooden ceiling as the dead cat swung in the wind that blew through the cracks between the wood slats of the locker.

Scruffy, orange and white. I unhooked it. It was frozen stiff. The wire coat hanger it was hanging from came off in my hand. I put the dead cat on the floor.

I went on, turned the corner, looking in locker after locker. At the end of the row, closest to the beach and the ocean, were four big cabanas, like cottages, overlooking the sweep of the Atlantic Ocean. All of them were padlocked and bolted. Again, as with the cat, I thought I heard a faint sound.

One at a time, I leaned up against the doors, my ear against the wood planks, trying not to breathe. At the last one, I thought I heard something. My gun was in my hand. I tried the door handle; the door wouldn't give and the walls were solid. There was a window, though and I used the butt of my gun to chip away enough glass to loosen the frame, then pulled out part of the pane and reached through it and unlocked the window.

The dread I felt had a palpable shape, it took a solid form, it filled the space with horror and I almost backed away and turned and ran, but there was nowhere to go.

Billy? Billy?

I was talking to myself. Shoving open the broken window, I climbed through and stepped down into the wire mesh of the window screens that were piled on the floor for the winter. The metal mesh caught at my ankle and I pulled my foot out and I heard the wire rip. I turned my flashlight on the room. There was a table, three plastic chairs, a TV on a stand; outdoor furniture was neatly stacked.

At the far side of the room was a door and from behind it came the sound I had heard except it was louder now. I stumbled against the table in the semi-darkness.

Billy?

Someone was in the bathroom. Billy, I thought. Billy. I yanked the door open.

39

The first thing I saw when I turned the beam of my flashlight on the room was a tangled mess of gold colored fishing nets like those I'd seen in the beach club café. Trapped in them like a large animal was Heshey Shank. He was a big man and his body sprawled across the bathroom floor, his feet under the rusty sink, his head near a toilet with a broken seat. Above him from a white plastic rod hung a shower curtain with clowns on it that was smeared with blood.

The nets were heavy; they were draped over him and twisted around his limbs, head and arms. I crouched beside him. Blood was everywhere. He was naked from the waist up. A faint animal noise came out of his mouth.

I pushed my hand through the nets, my fingers caught in the knotted strings, and tried to find a pulse in his neck. The flesh was still warm, though a sheen of cold clammy wetness clung to it. The flesh was cut, I could feel it, and when I put the flashlight on Shank, I saw small chunks had been cut out of his cheek, one of his arms, his shoulder.

Again I felt for a pulse, but there was none and even while I tried, desperate, frantic, to untangle him, the noise stopped. Shank was dead. It was as if he had waited for me before he gave up, or maybe not, maybe he had been dead for hours. I couldn't tell.

On the floor next to Shank was a newspaper, partly soaked in blood, dated three days earlier.

Had Shank been trapped here for three days? Had he wrestled with the thick rope that made up the nets? Did he bleed to death? Did anyone know or hear him call? I got out my cell and started to dial Lippert's number, then shut the phone, got to my feet and walked softly into the other room then out to the corridor and called out, "Billy?"

I turned off the flashlight and said again, softly at first, then louder, "Billy?"

My voice echoed into the darkness, down the row of cabanas, and I thought, out of the blue because I was half crazed, that cabana was the wrong word for this, it was a word that called up sunlight and Latino music and girls in bikinis and drinks with fruit in them and paper parasols on top.

"Billy?"

Pushing myself forward, my feet heavy, I wanted to lie down on the old salt soaked boards of the beach club and drift off. I kept going, down the row, one, two, three doors from the place where Shank lay dead.

There was no noise, no cars, no planes, nothing, just my footsteps and then, suddenly, a tiny noise, creaking, scuttling, near me, next to me, behind the door in front of me.

I yelled out, "Hey, Billy, it's me, it's Artie."

"I'm in here," a voice said. "The door is open."

His voice was normal. The invitation was spoken like an adult would speak it, domesticated, pleasant. The door is open, come on in.

What I felt, first, was hysterical relief: Billy was alive. It was over. The days of looking for him and not finding him, the feeling I'd failed, that one more time I'd used people—Maxine most of all—to get what I needed and then screwed up, that I had looked at the wrong picture or looked at it the wrong way and that I'd find Billy dead at the end of it, it was all over. The tension went; for a second I thought I'd have to sit down. I wasn't much of a crybaby—you'd be surprised how many guys are weepers—but my eyes stung from tears in them. I put my gun away and leaned against the doorjamb with relief. Billy was OK; or, at least, he was alive.

Come on in, Artie, he called again, and I opened the door.

His back was to me. A faint smudge of morning light was coming up outside the window and I set the flashlight, still on, on a table and I could see Billy's fine blond hair was matted and his blue sweater was smeared with blood. On a red plastic chair he sat staring at the TV which was on a shelf that also held a vase of plastic flowers. The electricity was off; the screen was blank. Billy didn't turn around when I came through the door, just sat looking at the set.

"Do you know who hurt Heshey Shank?" I said to the back of Billy's head. "Billy, look at me."

He turned halfway in his chair. I moved towards him and held out my arms and he got up and hugged me. I tried to hold onto him, but he slumped back onto the chair.

"I did it," he said. "I had to." Billy saw me reach for my phone. "Please don't call anyone yet, Artie, please. I just want you."

I put the phone away.

"Did he hurt you?" I sat on the chair next to his. "Did Heshey make you get in his car? Are you hurt anywhere?"

"You mean like the priests, you mean like that, like they put on TV all the time, the priests that stick their hands down the kids' pants? Like that?"

"Like that. Or anything else."

"I would have killed him if he did that," he said. "Right away."

Abruptly he shifted his weight again and looked straight at me; his face seemed formed now, like a little adult. Already you could see how he'd look as a man. The blue eyes were set wide apart in the pale face, like my father's.

It was true: Billy was my nephew; my father had been his grandfather. I noticed the blood on his faded jeans. He wore black sneakers; no socks.

"I'll take you home," I said.

"No."

"Then let me take you somewhere else. It's freezing here. You could come back with me to the city, if you want."

In a dented metal locker, I found some cotton

blankets. I wrapped one around Billy and put another over my own shoulders. My cigarettes were in my pocket and I got them out and lit one.

"Can I have one?" Billy said.

"You're too young."

He smiled wide and said, "Come on, Artie, please please please please, give me one. I'll love you forever, I won't tell. Come on, I smoke my mom's when she's out all the time."

I gave him a cigarette and lit it for him and he sat huddled under the blanket, a twelve-year-old man, self-possessed, smoking the cigarette, talking in bursts.

From outside there was only silence, and the cold that seeped in through the broken window and the faint smell of salt, and garbage. There was something else. It was spicy salsa. The blanket had been used for a picnic; in the folds I could feel the crumbs. Chips, I thought; tortilla chips.

"I wanted to fish," Billy said. "I liked it when you took me, but you didn't come all the time. My father didn't take me a lot. I had to see the sheepshead. You remember? They said the sheepshead fish came back to Brooklyn and I never saw one and I had to."

"The fishing really mattered, didn't it?"

He said, "It took my mind off things."

"You met Heshey at the pizza place?"

Billy took a drag on his cigarette and made a face and said, "Yeah. He was always there and he would buy me as many slices as I want and then he would talk blah blah blah about how he's scared, and how he knew the Trade

378

Center was like going to fall before it happened and no one believed him, and he's scared things are coming down from the sky. Creep," Billy said. "He liked me. He just wanted company because he was this retard and I'm like, this is boring, but he has a car. Heshey says his brother knows my grandpa and his brother says it's OK for us to hang out. I didn't believe him first, but he has the car."

"What about friends your own age?"

"They're boring. I try to make friends, I say, let's go on an adventure, a journey, and they say, let's look up some girl's skirt."

"You liked May Luca."

"Fuck you." He tossed the cigarette butt on the floor and crushed it under his heel. "She's dead, OK?"

"You're sorry?"

He looked up. "Sure I'm sorry. Course I am. Jesus fucking Christ, Artie, course I'm sorry. I loved May. I know, OK, we're like little kids, but I loved her and she was nice to me. She gave me her shirt for a present. May didn't buy into this thing I supposedly got, some disease, I hear my mom on the phone talking about it. I know she steals money from my dad for the doctors and she gives it to me, too, to buy me things."

He dug into his jeans and pulled out some matches and a fishing fly; with them, a wad of cash spilled from the pocket.

"Genia gave you the money?"

"She stole it from my father and she gave me some and I took the rest from her purse."

"You were short of cash?"

379

He laughed. "Always, yeah. Aren't you? I'm not crazy. I'm not sick. They like it better if they think I have something with a name."

"Can I ask you something, Billy?"

"You can ask me anything."

In Russian I said, "Do you speak other languages?"

"Of course," he replied in Russian. "Russian, Italian, even some shitty Spanish I picked up at school."

Like me, he was a mynah bird, a mimic. It ran in the family. He was a little spy, a secret boy. He could join the family business; he had all the talents, the looks, the charm, the softness of speech, the persuasive blue eyes.

"Anyone know about the languages?"

"You must be kidding. Course not. It's my weapon. You know why I learned?"

"Why?"

"I wanted to be like you." He held out his hand and took mine and talked for about an hour, sometimes fluently, sometimes in disjoined sentences.

It started when Heshey Shank invited him to go out fishing and Billy told his grandpa in Florida; they talked almost every day, Billy loved the old man and he was miserable when they sent him away. For what? Billy said. Because he liked little girls? Billy didn't believe it.

"All I wanted was an adventure," Billy said suddenly. "Like in books. My own adventure, a trip, you know?" With his stubby boy's fingers he extracted another cigarette from my pack and lit it.

The trip was set for Saturday. Billy worked it fine. He got Stevie Gervasi across from his own house to invite him for an overnight to the country. He told his mom

380

he was old enough to cross the street alone and she had to let him, he told her, don't baby me, he said. She promised to stay in her room even if she was awake that morning he left.

Early, he called Stevie on his cell—all the kids had their own phones—and said it was off, he wasn't coming, and he watched from the window as Stevie and his dad drove away. Then Billy picked up his bag, jogged down the stairs and left the house. He had to go or he'd miss the timing. He couldn't find his nets, but he had his fishing knife, so it was OK. When Heshey came by in the crappy Honda, Billy was ready.

There was a bonus, he said. A block away he saw Stevie's horrible cat, and he told Heshey to pull over, then raced out of the car, grabbed the cat and slung it in the back seat.

Billy used his fishing knife on the cat and the blood got on his clothes and in the car he changed. He made Heshey drive to Coney Island so he could stuff the blood-soaked clothes under the boardwalk. Later he would string up the cat at the beach club. He also carried extra blood in a jar in his bag. He got it from a butcher store near the pizza joint.

"You put them there so someone would find them?"

Billy shrugged. "Maybe, maybe not. I once heard this girl that babysat—I didn't need a babysitter, but my mom said you can't stay alone, blah blah blah—I heard her on the phone saying you could find treasure there, and I thought if someone found the clothes it would be more fun."

"And you put cuts in May's T-shirt, that right? There

was a lot of blood for one cat. You cut yourself to confuse everyone, that right? It was a game? Billy?"

Billy didn't answer.

After he hid the clothes, he told Heshey to drive to Breezy Point, where his grandpa Farone had a shack. Then they would go fishing. It started to snow. There was a TV in the shack and after a while, Billy realized people were searching for him. It was fun, he said. It was fun watching, like being at your own funeral and listening to what people said about you.

I said, "I was there. I was at the shack."

"I know. I saw your car. But we were in a different shack by then. I told Heshey he had to do what I wanted or people would say he kidnapped me."

"I would have fixed things," I said.

"I know. But I had to go on this trip. See the sheepshead, stuff like that."

Billy got bored, he said. In the shack in Breezy Point, he found some Tylenol PM in the medicine cabinet, and he knew what it was; he had seen it on TV. He crushed it with a spoon and put it in Heshey's chilli.

"I put tons of it. Heshey was a fat guy."

"And the clock, the drawing? You did it?"

"You liked it?"

"How did you get to the beach club if Heshey was drugged?"

Billy smiled. "I drove. Pretty cool, right? Like you taught me," he said.

"Billy?"

"Yeah, Artie?"

"You think your grandma knew about you going to

the shack, you think she knew?"

"Maybe. She knew a lot of stuff. She's a witch, you know? I mean a real one?"

"There aren't any witches, honey."

"I don't know, OK?" He smiled sleepily. "Artie, I'm tired. I want to sleep a while."

I didn't let him sleep. I made him talk. I made Billy tell me how he got Shank to the beach club and half dragged him into the cabana. He told me how Heshey fell asleep and how he got the nets and covered him, and left him. Billy talked and I didn't know how much was true, if he had gone home to the Farones or to the pizza place, but I knew he had cut Heshey Shank.

"Did you?"

Billy looked up at me with those see-through blue eyes and said, "I wanted to see how it felt."

"How did it feel?"

"Like cutting a fish," he said. "I got scared, so I locked him in and came in here and went to sleep for a while."

"He was bleeding? He suffocated in the nets?"

"Whatever," Billy said. "But everything is shit, isn't it? I listen to grown-ups and the TV, and they say how bad everything is and no one answers my questions and I wanted to have an adventure before I died. You ever feel like that?"

But there was something else. I thought about the way Heshey's flesh looked, the small chunks carved out of it. I sat on the floor with Billy and we talked for what seemed like hours until the sky outside was light and most of the fog was gone.

"You remember my ma's pop?" Billy asked and for a

moment I thought he meant my father. He couldn't know, of course. He couldn't.

I said, "You mean the general?"

Billy nodded. He had liked the general. He had liked his stories. When Billy was little, he told me, they went fishing. The old man was the first guy who took Billy fishing and they sat by the water and the general told him stories about the war in Leningrad, where he lived.

"He told me they ate wallpaper paste," Billy said, suddenly. "Other stuff."

"What other stuff?" I said.

Billy didn't answer, and I didn't ask. I didn't want to know what I already knew. The general told stories about Leningrad and the siege and how people foraged for food among the dead. Ate the dead. I knew why Billy had taken chunks out of Heshey Shank.

Out of the blue, Billy got up off the floor and went to the window. I watched him and knew that he left Shank trapped in the nets and bleeding, left him there for days until he bled to death.

Billy said, "The fog is going away, I can see the ocean. Artie?"

Heavy with fatigue, he moved slowly across the few feet between us. I was still sitting on the floor and Billy knelt down next to me and put his arms around me. I could feel his weight and the soft skin.

Against my chest, Billy nodded his head. Then he said, "I love you."

After a while, curled up against me, Billy fell asleep. A faintly puzzled look was on his face as if he slept perplexed by the fact that what he had done was wrong. He didn't really understand what he did or why; it occurred to me that in that way he was like America.

Carefully, I laid him on the floor, still in his blanket, got up and went outside. I could barely breathe. I managed to get out my cell phone and call Sonny Lippert, and then I went back and sat beside Billy again and waited until Lippert and some of his guys arrived.

"Don't use any sirens," I'd said to Lippert and he put out the word.

When I heard Lippert's footsteps on the wooden walkway outside the cabana, I got up and opened the door and showed Lippert where Heshey Shank lay, dead, on the bare floor of the cabana.

"Go home" was all Lippert said to me.

We looked at each other briefly and didn't speak because we both knew this was something you couldn't say, not yet, we both knew it, and I felt his hand on my arm for a moment.

After some of Lippert's guys showed up, I went to the Farones' and told them Billy was in custody. And I left them. I'd had it for now. There was nothing else I could do. Zeitsev would fix up a lawyer and maybe Billy would get help if he needed help.

Maybe he was just a rotten kid; you could be a kid and be evil. Maybe he was a shattered little boy, crushed by all the grown-ups who surrounded him. I couldn't tell, and if he was sick, it didn't have a name. I couldn't shake the memory of the warm body against me and him saying, "I love you."

No one gave a rat's ass about Heshey Shank; he was

just a retard, a pervert who got what he deserved. A cop found Heshey's tape recorder shoved in his pants pocket. He had recorded what happened while he could; it took him three days, like I figured, to die. The tape disappeared somewhere into Brooklyn.

Billy became a kind of hero. Billy, the kid, they called him. BILLY THE KID. That was how the media played it. Zeitsev had all the right lawyers, and within a day or two people were saying what a smart, brave kid he was, a child soldier. His photograph appeared in the papers; every time I saw his face, I saw my own father.

There was much more. There were things that went back thirty-five years, connections I still had to untangle: Genia was my half sister and my father was Billy's grandpa. Heshey Shank had been set up by his brother to get rid of Billy Farone. Was it because old Mrs. Farone asked him? Because she was jealous of the husband she had kicked out but whom Billy adored? Because she knew the kid was Zeitsev's and not her son's? Was it a way to draw me into a trap? In the end, the two crazy innocents, Heshey and Ivana, died from it.

I went back to the city and returned Mike's van and got something to eat. All I wanted was food and sleep. I had been so obsessed with the danger Billy was in, I never figured it for him as the killer. He had made everyone afraid in a city that was already scared to death, it was an easy place to raise the terror. Now he was a hero. At Mike's, I glanced up at the TV on the shelf over the cake-stand and saw Billy's face.

Afterwards

Afterwards, I went home and slept. For the next couple of weeks all I did was sleep and spend time, in between sleeping, with Tolya. He was at St Vincent's where I got him transferred because I knew people there, and they were good and I trusted them.

Maxine and I saw each other and, knowing we were almost a married couple, made plans. We behaved like a couple. We held hands. We inspected furniture we couldn't afford in fancy Soho stores; we lay on an Italian leather bed in Flou and giggled. We looked at converting my loft to make rooms for her girls. I liked it. I liked the sense of security. It was almost spring.

On the first warm glorious day, hot sun, blue sky, my bike propped up just outside, I was at the counter of Mike's coffee shop. Someone came in the door and I looked up from the BLT I had in one hand.

Tolya didn't say anything. He climbed on the stool next to me, ordered bacon and eggs and ate silently while I finished my sandwich.

"How are you?" I said.

"I lost twenty pounds," he said. "I must buy new clothes. We'll shop."

"I'd love to shop with you. I need a new suit. You'll be my best man?"

"You want to talk about the other thing?" he asked finally. "About Billy?"

Genia had taken Billy away to a school out of state.

"No," I said. "Not now."

I didn't want to think about anything except Maxie. I was going through with it. I wanted to marry her. It would change everything.

I took some cash out of my pocket and started to put it on the counter. Tolya pushed my hand away.

"Please."

"Yeah, OK," I said. "Where do you want to shop?"

"You're really going to marry her? The girl who lives in Brooklyn?"

"Yes."

"Artyom, it's not for you, you know, this nice ordinary girl, this marriage, that's stuff for regular, boring people."

"I want to be regular and boring."

He buttered the last piece of toast on his plate, and ate it, then drank another cup of coffee while Mike went in the back and talked on the phone.

"Why not?"

"I got a call last night," he said finally.

My stomach turned over. I pulled a cigarette out of the pack.

"What kind of call?" I said to Tolya again.

He turned to look at me and said, "Lily's in New York."

"Good for her," I said. "Say hi, for me."

"Don't you want to see her?"

"No," I lied. "No." I wanted to see her more than anything I could think of; I wanted it, but I said, "No."

We sat for a few minutes not talking. I drank another cup of coffee, the thick smooth rim between my lips. Then Tolya's phone rang. He listened for a few seconds and turned to me.

"It's Lily," he said. "She wants to see you." He held out the phone. "She misses you."